# TOLD YOU SO

## A SARATOGA FALLS LOVE STORY

**LINDSEY POGUE**

**SCARLET ST. JAMES**

**ROAR PRESS LLC**

**Told You So**
A Saratoga Falls Love Story

By Lindsey Pogue writing as Scarlet St. James

Editing by Lauren McNerney
Cover Design by Covers by Combs

Written and Published by Lindsey Pogue
101 W. American Canyon Road, Ste. 508-262
American Canyon, CA 94503
Printed in the USA

ISBN: 978-1723009914

*For Nick. Thank you for inspiring such a beloved character. And for Ginny and the gang. This book wouldn't have happened without our summer adventures and shenanigans. Anna Marie, you'll always be my bubbles girl.*

# PROLOGUE

## BETHANY

### NEW YEAR'S EVE

THE NIGHT IS DARK, the road covered in snow, and my heart thumps in time with the blinker as Nick turns onto Main Street.

"Are you all right?" His voice is tentative and breaks the charged silence that hangs in the warm air blasting from the heater —it's thick and almost smothering in my panic, but I can't stop shaking. I don't think it's because of the cold, though.

"Not really," I rasp. "It's twelve degrees outside and my baby brother is out there." *Alone.*

My mind races with unease, but my vision is still a little hazy from too much sparkling wine. I press my eyelids closed and take a deep breath. When I blink them open, I force the night surrounding us into focus. "This is all my fault."

I peer out at the passing streetlights and each of my panicked breaths steam up the passenger side window. I knew I shouldn't have gone out partying tonight—I knew something like this would happen. "I shouldn't have left him."

"*Left* him?" Nick grinds out. "Left him where? Jesus, Bethany.

1

I know you like to party, but you *left* him—*alone?*" His voice is sharp and drips with judgement, more than I can stomach right now.

"No." I laugh bitterly. "I didn't leave him alone. You have no idea what you're talking about, Nick." I glare at him, staring into his wide, hazel eyes.

"I know enough," he says caustically, a strand of brown hair falling into his face.

"Excuse me?" I have no idea what Nick *thinks* he knows about me, but he's clueless if it's that I would ever put my brother in danger. "What the hell is that supposed to mean? You know *nothing* about me, no matter what you might think." I shake my head, scoffing at my idiocy. "I confide in you when I'm like, twelve, and you think you have me and my life all figured out?" The words form and roll off my tongue too easily, and I've had too many drinks tonight to stop them. "You're clueless, Nick, no matter what you and your perfect, preppy group of friends think. So just mind your own business."

"Hey, I might be clueless, but I could've left you freaking out in the parking lot at Lick's." His anger is sobering, and he's right. I have no idea what I would be doing right now if he hadn't offered to help me.

Balling my purse strap in my hands, I force myself to calm down. The constant tug and pull between Nick and me is not some-thing I can deal with right now. Unable to meet his eyes, I peer out the window, willing Jesse's form to come into view.

"I told you I would help you, and I will," Nick says, breaking the wounded silence. He rests his hand on mine. "I'm just—I'm really confused right now." His eyes shift back to the road. "You have an AWOL brother, and I have no clue what happened," he says more calmly, and his fingers squeeze mine reassuringly.

His touch makes me feel like I'm sixteen again. His hand is big and warm, and I can't tear my gaze away from the way it wraps around mine. The last time he held my hand we were only kids, and even if I'm not as innocent, Nick still affects me the same way. Only, this time he smells of Old Spice and his voice is more commanding. Even now, after all these years and what's transpired between us, I feel emboldened and want to confide in him again.

"Thank you for helping me," I say and pull my hand away from his.

He looks at me askance. "You're welcome, but you're not very forthcoming with information, you know? You never have been." It's a light-hearted gibe that I appreciate in the tension, and I choke out a sad, pathetic laugh. All I remember from the day we first met are my tears and Nick's infectious smile. It was comforting and pulled me in. It's stuck with me ever since.

"I guess very little changes, despite the years," I think aloud. "It's exhausting, you know. Keeping it all in."

"So, tell me what happened," he urges.

"I don't know what happened after I left, but I needed to get out of the house tonight. I should've stayed, I knew I should have, but I just . . . you don't know what it's like. It's never enough, nothing is *ever* enough." My voice is foreign to me, desperate like I haven't heard it in a while, and I do everything I can to reel my frayed emotions back in and spare us both the humiliation of my impending breakdown. In spite of the alcohol in my blood and the fear clouding my mind, I have to keep it together long enough to find Jesse and get him home.

Running my fingers through my loose curls, I take a deep breath. Sweat still lingers on my skin from dancing in a drunken throng of handsy party-goers. "If I would've slept in just a little bit longer this morning," I say under my breath, "none of this would've happened." I would've missed my dad's homecoming, as well as his disappointment, and I would've stayed home tonight with Jesse.

"He was supposed to be at home with my parents. I knew something was wrong when I had a missed call from my mom. My dad said something—he upset Jesse somehow. I know how it goes, even if I wasn't there." Shaking my head, I wonder if nothing will ever change. "I'd just stepped outside to listen to my mom's message, when you walked out." I eye the snow-covered sidewalks as we drive down Main Street. "I didn't expect Jesse to have run away. Not in the middle of the night." Not in the snow with nowhere to go.

"Are you sure he ran away?" Nick asks tentatively. "Maybe he went to a friend's house." The incredulity in his voice is both painstakingly sweet and maddeningly naïve. It's just another reminder of how different Nick and I are.

"Jesse doesn't have friends," I explain. "Not really. He's obsessed with movies, science, and he likes building things. He knows more pop culture trivia than anyone I know." The awe in my voice seems to surprise him. "But, sometimes Jesse gets triggered and spirals, and he goes off on his own. It's how he's been acting out lately, and it's scary as hell because an autistic eleven-year-old on his own, relatively high-functioning or not, is like a mouse running across a highway, everything is fast and scary, and . . ." My voice breaks off, and I glance at Nick. He's frowning, staring out the windshield.

"He's done this twice now, but he's always gone to the ice cream shop down the street from my house. It's familiar and safe. At this time of night—I have no idea where he would've gone."

"Why isn't your mom helping you look for him?" Nick almost spits out the words.

"She is," I breathe. "I think. But she won't find him. She doesn't know him like I do." It's a sad, pathetic truth, but it's the truth all the same. I brace my elbow on the door and watch the flurries of snow pass by the window.

"I feel like the police should be involved in this, Bethany. It's freezing out, and if you don't know where to look for him—"

"Let's just check the park, and then I'll call them, okay? Just—not yet." I'm still living the aftermath of the last time I acted preemptively, and I'm not ready to get the authorities involved just yet. "Turn here," I say, pointing to Beecham Street.

"You think he might be at the park?"

I stare out at the passing shadows, searching for any sign of my brother, trudging along or sitting on the curb, or even fallen down in the snow. "Jesse liked organizing Mac's shop the other day when we were in there dropping off the Range Rover," I say, more frantic as it hits me that, if he's not here, he might actually be lost or in danger. "For a few days after, every time we got in the car, he asked if we were going to see Mac. He's got it in his head that he likes the shop or her. Maybe he'll show up there. Or—he likes to read all the info boards at the park . . . It's all I can think of." I breathe out my last bit of hope.

Nick's hands tighten audibly around the leather-bound steering wheel before he lets out a despondent sigh. "If he's not here, Bethany, we're calling the police. We can't search the whole town in the dark by ourselves. Especially if he's cold and scared."

I nod because Nick's right, even if it's the last thing I want to do. Glancing at the clock approaching midnight, I wipe the silent tears from my cheeks. "I know."

I scour the shadows of Cal's Auto, where I half expect Jesse to be standing, staring in the window at the Christmas tree's blinking lights he seemed so taken with the other day. But he's not there.

I grip my cell phone in my hand, prepared to make the call, when Nick brings the Explorer to a stop.

"Is that him?" He leans closer to the window.

Heart racing with hopefulness, I peer through the windshield into the park. Moonlight illuminates the seesaw and roundabout settled in the snow. Everything is a glistening blue against utter darkness, and at first nothing appears out of place.

Then, I see a shadowed outline on one of the swings.

Throwing my seatbelt off, I fling open the door. "Jesse!" I shout out his name, praying it's him as I climb out of the car and hurry over as quickly as I can, even if my high heels make it seem-

5

ingly impossible over the frozen pavement and snow. Frigid air bites at my legs and face, and snow crumbles into my shoes, but I welcome it as my brother's outline becomes clearer. "Jesse!"

He's staring down at his feet when I reach him, wrapped in a down jacket and in his beanie and boots. "Oh my God, what the hell were you thinking!" I want to smack the crap out of him, but I pull him into my arms instead. "Running off like that—I've been so worried! Mom and Dad had no idea where you were."

"I wanted ice cream," Jesse mutters against my chest. His breath is warm on my neck, and I grip him tighter. "I went to the ice cream store but they were closed."

I nearly laugh with hysteria. "That's because it's midnight, J. I know you wanted to get out of the house, but you could've called me," I tell him, breathing in the scent of his hair—his clothes—anything to reassure my senses that he's here and real and that he's okay. I catch my breath and temper the tears in my eyes. "Don't ever do that again. Like, *ever*. Okay? You're going to give me a heart attack and then who will you design your theme park with?"

He tries to pull away from me, but I grip him tighter. "Hey," I bite out. "I know you're not a hugger, but you don't get to pull away from me, not after what you just put me through. Consider it punishment."

When I finally let go long enough to look at him, a small smile pulls at the corner of his mouth. "I just wanted ice cream," he repeats.

"I know, J." I allow myself a heavy sigh in relief, then shiver. "Come on." I turn toward the car. "Nick's waiting."

Jesse's eyes shift toward the Explorer, or maybe at Nick standing beside it. "Was he with you?" he asks as I lead him along.

"No, I ran into him when I was going to look for you. Nick's the one that spotted you out here all alone. I was about to call the police."

Jesse crunches through the snow behind me as I slog my way back to the Explorer, utterly shaking with relief and cold.

"Hey, kid," Nick says as we reach the car. "I'm glad you're not frozen to the swing." He opens the back-passenger door in offering.

Jesse barely tilts his head, but I can tell he's concentrating on Nick the best he can as he starts to climb in. I take my brother's hand. "J," I say briskly. I try to keep my composure, but the adrenaline and panic all come crashing back down over me. "Wait for a sec."

He looks around at the dark night and up at the street lamps and the flurries floating in the air—anywhere but at me.

"Jesse," I say calmly—earnestly, "you can *never* do that again. I need you to promise me." The sudden pitch in my voice is like a crack in a glass mirror, and I hate the way it fractures, but I can't help it. I squeeze his hand, knowing a squeeze back means he understands. I know he can sense my distress, he can even feel it, and after a brief moment, he finally squeezes my hand back.

"Thank you—I love you." I kiss his forehead and nod for him to climb into the car.

"The heat's on," Nick tells him, and Jesse situates himself inside without another word.

Closing the door, I turn to Nick, tears of gratitude filling my eyes. "Thank you," I say, and white puffs of breath surround us.

Nick looks at me, concerned . . . and curious. "Yeah, of course. I'm just glad you found him."

With the panic in the air dissipating, the charged current of attraction I've always had for him enlivens the space between us again. He can feel it. It's in the tension of his shoulders. *I* can feel it, humming through my body with anticipation and unease. I can't seem to look away from him, and thankfully, it's too dark for him to notice my reddening cheeks under his gaze.

Sometimes he's the boy who sat with me all those years ago as I cried, thinking my entire world was coming to an end. Sometimes he's the jock who broke my heart, even if he doesn't realize it. So much passes between us in a single exhale, a lifetime of unspoken questions and drowning attraction. It's an inescapable pull and the promise of ecstasy, as well as heartbreak.

"You're cold," Nick says, and he clears his throat. "Let's get you in the car." His voice is low and his actions swift as he opens the passenger door for me.

"Thanks," I whisper and climb inside. I think about the past ten years and how many times I've both despised Nick and wished he was mine. Now, here we are. Two people who are more than acquaintances, but have never been friends. *And he's the one who found my brother.*

Rubbing the warmth back into my legs and arms, I turn around to find Jesse's eyes on me from the backseat. It happens so rarely, I can always feel his gaze. Watching. Wondering. Processing.

He looks away when my eyes meet his dark blue ones, but I know the way his mind works—everything is a puzzle that needs to be solved, a chronology of memories that lead to a single moment. Everything is a question he wants to ask or that he works to solve himself. I just don't know what he's processing now or what he's deciding.

"Let's get you home, J," I say, turning back to the front. I shut my eyes against the heat pumping in from the vents, and chills trickle over my skin as warmth envelops me.

Nick climbs into the driver seat and quickly shuts the door. "So, where to?" He pulls his seatbelt over his shoulder and runs the windshield wipers to brush off the bits of fallen snow.

"Home," I breathe out, as Jesse speaks over me, "Denny's."

I turn around to look at him. "Excuse me?"

Jesse looks at the clock. "I still want an ice cream."

"A hot fudge sundae does sound primo right about now," Nick muses and looks at me, expectant. "Besides, it's New Year's."

"I think we've earned it. Don't you?"

Spending more time with Nick feels significant, and I'm not sure that it's a good idea.

Then, Nick smiles at me.

With two sets of eyes staring back at me, waiting, I can't possibly say no. "Yeah, okay. Sure."

## NICK

"What's your favorite," Jesse asks between spoonfuls of hot fudge. It's all over his lips and he's got a little on his cheek, but Bethany just sits there, smiling at him, laughing and happy. She's relieved, I think. "The Last Crusade, Temple of Doom, Raiders of the Lost Ark, or Crystal Skull?"

"You know all of the Indiana Jones movies?" I ask, surprised. "Aren't those a bit before your time?"

Jesse's brow furrows as he stares into his ice cream dish. He shrugs. "I like all movies."

"*All* movies?" I clarify. I wonder what this kid watches with his free time, other than Jurassic Park.

He shrugs again, more of an inability to sit still than out of indifference, I think. "A lot of movies."

"Jesse's a movie buff," Bethany explains.

"I'm starting to get that. Well, in that case, Crusade, hands down."

Bethany frowns down at her phone as it buzzes on the table. I get the impression she's texting her parents, but I haven't asked.

"That one's all right." Jesse's brow is still furrowed, like he's deep in thought as he watches the fudge dripping off his spoon.

"Just *all right?* The Last Crusade is epic. The Holy Grail—Sean Connery . . . It's a classic."

"You *are* a smidge older than him," Bethany teases, finally peering up from her phone as she drops it into her purse. "What's considered *classic* is sort of relative, right?"

I shake my head. "I'm disappointed in you. Classic is *classic,* there's a difference between what's currently 'cool' and what's 'classic.'"

Jesse doesn't bother looking up at us. I'm beginning to pick up on a pattern with him, so I don't take it personally that he doesn't really look at me. At least he's not tapping on the table anymore, which makes me feel better, like maybe he's warming up to me a bit more.

"Cool verses classic, huh?" Bethany says with amusement. "You seem very certain of this."

I shrug. "Of course I am." I drop my spoon in my dish and sit back in the booth. "Queen, the best band of all time, is classic; and The Goonies movie is another classic, one I think even you would like, Jesse, since you're so keen on adventure." It's a harmless dig, but true given his midnight outing and penchant for taking off once in a while. "And of course, Indiana Jones and the Last Crusade is a motion picture classic to everyone."

"Maybe to people born in the 90s," Jesse clarifies and he finally looks up at me.

Eyes wide, I gape at him, then at Bethany. "A sense of humor? I didn't see that one coming."

"Sometimes," she says. She smiles and runs her fingers through his brown hair.

Though Jesse doesn't seem to take much notice to her attention, I get the feeling she's the one person in the world he probably cares most about. There's something calming in the way they are together, putting Jesse more at ease. I've only been drip-fed information about her parents over the years, but they seem like cold-hearted ass-hats. And, after tonight, learning how careless they've been with Jesse, I doubt his relationship with them is half as easy as his relationship with his sister.

He stares thoughtfully at his sundae. "They were inducted into the Rock and Roll Hall of Fame," he says, catching me off guard.

"Who was, Queen?" I ask, and lean my elbows on the table. "How do you know that?"

"And they received the Lifetime Achievement Award this year at the Grammys."

I look at Bethany, who's smiling from ear to ear. "I told you, he loves pop culture."

Chuckling, I lean toward him a little bit. "And how is it that you know so much about Queen—wait, how do you know who Queen is at all?"

He glances at Bethany. "My sister listens to them sometimes," he explains. "She listens to a lot of music."

My eyes widen with surprise. "Does she, now? I had no idea." I look at Bethany and our eyes meet for a brief moment. "This gets more interesting by the second."

Bethany rolls her eyes. "Oh, please. It can't be that surprising. You barely know anything about me."

"I guess." I know enough, though. I know that every time I think I have her figured out, she throws me a curveball, and that every time I tell myself I'm *done* thinking about her, she does something surprising that hooks me in again, making thoughts of her inescapable.

I lean back in the booth, my sundae long gone. "All right then, so you guys are awesome and like my favorite band, but what about this Indiana Jones business?" Watching Jesse lick his fingers, I settle in for another debate. "Which is your favorite—wait, let me guess . . . Raiders of the Lost Ark?"

Jesse's blue eyes meet mine and hold for a brief second. "How'd you know that?"

Suppressing a triumphant smile, I shrug. "Maybe a lucky guess. Or, maybe I figured that since you like dinosaurs"—I nod to his Jurassic Park shirt—"you're partial to the snake scene—reptiles, that sort of thing."

Jesse smiles a little, but I've lost his gaze again. "Yeah, you're right."

I clap my hands together. "What can I say, nothing gets by me."

"But," Jesse continues, "paleontologists say dinosaurs were a mix between warm and cold blood. So, they weren't actually reptiles, like snakes."

Bethany smiles again, with pride this time, and shakes her head. She's beautiful when she's like this, when she opens up and lets her walls down. It's her crinkled, stormy gray eyes that have stuck with me all these years, making it nearly impossible to forget about her, no matter how many times I've tried.

"So, you're a smart guy, huh?" I say. "I dig it."

Jesse shrugs. "I read a lot." He stirs what's left of his sundae around in his glass.

My phone buzzes on the table beside me, and Savannah's name fills the screen. I frown down at it. "Uh . . . Give me a sec, would you?" I look at Bethany, whose eyes are on me as I excuse myself from the table and make my way to the door.

I answer the call as I step outside. "Hello?"

"Hey!" Savannah shouts, laughing into the phone. It's her drunken laugh, her *happy* laugh. "Happy New Year, Nicky!"

I let out a relieved breath, glad she's just tipsy and not crying or depressed on the other end. Leaving Saratoga Falls—me, her job, and her friends—to go back home to take care of her parents has been more difficult for her than she'd expected, and for *me*, if I'm honest. "Happy New Year, Red. Where are you?"

"Umm, I'm at a bar in Hannington Beach with a couple of new acquaintances. It's my new hangout. What about you? Is Brady being a mean ol' bastard and making you work all night or did he let you off the hook to meet up with Mac for New Year's?"

I glance inside the restaurant, through the window at Jesse and Bethany as they sit, tucked away at our booth. "I'm at Denny's, actually, of all places."

She laughs. "That's . . . unexpected."

"Yeah, it is." Savannah has no idea.

There's movement on her end, and she's huffing and puffing before the commotion dies down in the background. "I miss you,

Nick," she says quietly. "I just—I wanted to hear your voice. It's weird being here, when I really just want to be there, with you."

I clear my throat, the timing of her call while Bethany is inside, waiting for me, shrinks the world in around me a little, and I feel uncomfortable. "You didn't want to do the long-distance thing, remember?"

"Yeah, but . . ." she sighs. "That was before."

"Before what?"

"Before I knew how hard this would be."

I peer out at the dark street, watching what few cars are on the road pass, at a loss for words. We've gone around and around about this so many times, and it always ends the same. We try it out, it's too hard for her, so we put an end to it. We take some time apart and somehow, we keep ending up where we started. I can't do it anymore. As much as I care about her, I need some sanity too. "It'll just—it'll take time to get used to everything," I tell her. I feel like a broken record, but she's buzzed, and I'm not sure anything I say will matter all that much. "But I'm glad you called, and I'm glad you're having fun . . . You deserve that, at least."

"It's not the same though," she says sadly.

Shoving my cold, free hand into my pocket, I glance inside again to meet Bethany's curious gaze. She quickly looks away and brings her phone to her ear.

"Nick," Savannah says, "I miss you."

"I miss you, too, Savannah."

"Do you, really?" she asks hesitantly. "You sound . . . different tonight."

"Yes, of course I miss you, but this is how things are now." *You're the one who left.*

Whether it's my tone or that she knows deep down this isn't a helpful conversation to be having, she finally says, "You're right. I'll let you go." After an exhale, she adds, "Happy New Year, Nick. Tell everyone I say hi, would you?"

"Of course I will . . . Happy New Year."

We hang up after a few seconds pause, and just as I'm about to head inside, the door swings open and Bethany and Jesse step outside, adjusting their coats.

"What's up?" I ask, glancing inside to see what the rush is all about. "Everything okay?"

"Yeah, everything's fine. We just need to get home. My mom's worried." There's an unexpected distance to Bethany's voice and all the walls she'd let down earlier, all the laughing and openness, is gone. "I already paid, so you don't have to worry about it."

"You didn't have to do that."

"It was Jesse's idea to come here, and it's the least I can do for all your help tonight." She flashes me a smile, but it's a smoke-screen. The distance she's putting between us is too reminiscent of the past. I don't like it, not after everything that's happened tonight.

"Our ride's here," she says and gently urges Jesse toward a blue sedan parked at the curb. "Climb in where it's warm, J." Her tone brooks no argument as she pulls her blonde hair out of the collar of her jacket.

"So, you're leaving, just like that?" I'm not sure if I'm more upset or confused.

"I need to get Jesse home," she says, digging around in her purse. "It's late, and my parents—well . . ." She shrugs.

"They didn't seem too worried earlier," I remind her.

She's tapping something into her phone as she walks to the sedan.

"Hey—" I say, and reach for her arm. "What's with you all of the sudden?"

Finally, she looks at me. Her lips are pursed and her delicate eyebrows are drawn together. "Thank you for your help tonight, Nick. I don't know what I would've done without you. I mean that." But her brow furrows even more and she gets into the car without another word and shuts the door.

Just as suddenly as she appeared in my life this evening, she disappears again. And like always, I'm left standing there with my mind spinning and the all too familiar sting of disappointment.

## SEVEN YEARS AGO

"SEE. *I told you it was a good idea to come." Walking into the kitchen, in a new track home with fancy furniture and large rooms I've never been in before, I peer around at the swarm of people, appraising the party. Everyone is here—the jocks, the skaters, the theater geeks—but it's not surprising; it's the first party this school year. With a couple pre-game beers already in me, I smile at the possibilities. Baseball . . . girls . . . beer. . . If this party is any indication of how Junior year will be, I'm already loving life. "This place is crackin'."*

*"Sure it is," Reilly grumbles behind me, but I just smile at his typical Reilly response, Mr. All-American Good Boy, who doesn't like living anywhere near the edge. I don't give him any grief, though. Knowing what he has to go home to every day, I don't blame him for being less rebellious than the rest of us.*

*"You only live once, Rye. Try to have some fun. You're staying at my house tonight, anyway, so you don't have to worry about anything. My parents will be in bed by nine." I pop a potato chip into my mouth. "Want a beer yet?"*

*With reluctance, Reilly nods, his eyes scanning the room like he's looking for someone.*

*"Sam's not here," I tell him. "She and Mac don't come to parties." My words register, and I frown. "At least, I don't think they do." Now that they're freshmen, I really don't know what to expect. The pseudo big brother in me hopes they won't come to the party, anyway. I shrug, grab Reilly a plastic cup, and pump the keg.*

*"Why would I be looking for Sam?" Reilly asks, but he's an*

15

*idiot if he thinks I don't know there's some sort of attraction between them lately. Either he's trying to keep it from me for some reason or he's in denial about it himself, so I leave it alone.* "Go say hi to a girl and make her swoon or something. You don't look like you're having any fun."

*Reilly just rolls his eyes.*

"Fine, be that way, but you're the DD," *I tell him and shove his cup at his chest with a grin. The slow-as-molasses rate in which he pounds beer is embarrassing anyway.* "I'm happy to be the delinquent for the night," *I say and pour one for myself.*

*Finally, Reilly gives up a smile, and despite my jokes and gibes, I allow myself to relax a little bit for the first time tonight. I just wish Reilly would have some fun, too. I want him to forget his life for just a little bit and be a teenager with me.*

"So," *Reilly says above the surrounding conversation.* "What's up with you tonight?" *He takes a sip from his cup and raises his eyebrow. I* hate *the eyebrow raise. It means he sees too much.*

"What do you mean?" *A guy bumps into me and I try not to spill my beer.*

"You seem really into this party tonight. It's weird."

*I laugh because it's what I do. I laugh and play the role of the happy one. The jokester and tension-breaker who tries to keep the peace all the time. It gets exhausting, which is why I love nights like this.* "It's my parents," *I grumble.* "And Sam."

*Reilly takes a step closer. Ever the serious one, he leans in so I can hear him clearly above the music.* "What do you mean?"

*Shrugging, I take a drink of my beer, forcing myself not to grumble at the shift of the mood. It's too much to get into with all the noise and the nasally, teeny-bopper voice emanating from the speakers, but Reilly won't leave it alone if I don't give him something. So, I hedge.* "Sam and Aunt Alison are at it again," *I tell him. Although Reilly has been friends with Mac and Sam since elementary school, like I have, he's missed a lot, on account of his dad being such a dick. So, over the years I've become the girls' sounding board and confidante, especially now that my aunt and Sam's dad are together.*

*"And your parents?" Reilly prompts, and all I can do is laugh.*

*"Nothing new there. My dad's pressuring me about college. About my future at the firm."*

*"No baseball scholarship then?"*

*I shrug his question away. "I don't want to talk about it." Opening my arms, I peer around the room. "We're teenagers! Partying is an excuse to act our age." My smile widens. "You should try it sometime."*

*"Yeah, and go home to my drunk dad," he mutters and takes a step back. I pretend I don't hear him over the laughter and music, and I take another gulp of my beer.*

*I hate Reilly's piece of shit dad, and I hate that Reilly is too proud to ditch his misery and live at my house. I hate that I have to accept it and that there's nothing I can do to make his life even a little bit better. So, I chug the rest of my beer down, then pour myself another one.*

*"Hey, Reilly! Turner!" Rod Slinsky shouts from across the room. I nod as he bumps his way through the crowd toward us.*

*"Don't indulge him tonight," Reilly warns. "Slinsky's a dirt bag."*

*"Yeah, but he's on the team. I can't ignore him. Besides, he's probably a lot more fun than you are tonight," I say with an elbow to his side.*

*"Whatever. Come find me when you're ready to leave," Reilly says and makes his way through the crowd. He lifts his cup to Slinsky as they pass each other, but they don't exchange more than a what's up.*

*"I was wondering if you'd show up tonight," Slinsky says with a shit-eating grin on his pockmarked face. He moves in for our team handshake and a clap on the back. "Praise Jesus for short skirts, huh? This place is poppin' with hotties." As he peers around the kitchen, I can't help noticing that for all his talk about chicks*

*and the high life, I've never actually seen him with one. He appraises everything, eyes wide and indulgent. "Whose place is this, anyway?" He grins at a group of girls on the other side of the kitchen, like a hungry wolf.*

*"Uh, I think her name is Anna Marie something-or-other, but I don't even know what she looks like. Just that she's a freshman."*

*"That's what I love about being a jock. You get invited to all the parties. Even silly little freshmen want the dick."*

*"Yeah, well, keep it in your pants, Casanova. That's a horror for another night." I laugh at myself and pop another chip into my mouth.*

*"You're hilarious," Slinsky says, and he pours himself a beer. "Where are your girls tonight, huh? Shouldn't they be here, making the rounds, getting to know the school and the jocks?" When his eyebrows dance at the thought of Mac and Sam, I resist the urge to punch him in the throat.*

*I glare at him warningly instead. "They're off limits, Rod. Don't even think about it." I wouldn't let Slinsky anywhere near them, even if my life depended on it.*

*He studies me for a minute, looking me up and down like he's trying to figure out how serious I am. I'm more than serious, and he seems to get the idea. His palms fly up. "Hey, I hear ya, Turner. Loud and clear. You can't blame a guy for lookin' though. The blonde is so sweet and—"*

*When I notice another familiar blonde with long hair hanging over her shoulders, standing in the mouth of the kitchen, my breath hitches unexpectedly, and it's easy enough to ignore whatever bull- shit Slinsky's spewing.*

*Bethany's here. I've seen her around campus a few times since school started, but I haven't talked to her since that day in Mr. Silverman's class a few years ago.*

*She's grown up . . . a lot. I know people change, but her tight jeans and tank top make it clear just how much. I swallow thickly. She's come a long way from the sad mystery girl she was when we were younger. She's tall and beautiful and stands out in a crowd, and she clearly doesn't even know it. I've wanted to talk to her so many times over the years, especially after I'd heard about social services. I'd wanted to apologize about what happened, but too much time had passed before I saw her again, like she'd been avoiding me. It felt weird to bring it up after so long. But now, she's here.*

She probably hates me. *I tell myself I should look away, that I don't want to be a creep in a room full of horny dudes, but when her eyes meet mine and her gaze lingers, there's nothing I can do. My body's on autopilot, and I make a decision.*

*Ignoring Slinsky, I shuffle through the crowd, my feet moving faster than my mind can process what I'm going to say when I get to her.*

*When I'm only a few feet away, she half-smiles. "Hey," she says and crosses her arms over her chest. It's a casual hello, an awkward one, even, and so soft I barely hear her over the music. But she's talking to me, which means she doesn't hate me, not completely.*

*"It's been a while," is all I can think to say.*

*Pulling her bottom lip into her mouth, she glances around the room. "Yeah, it has."*

*I've never struggled to come up with a witty remark or some-thing to say, but my mind draws a blank. "What are you doing here?" It's a stupid question, one that earns me a confused expression.*

*"Well," she says, eyebrows raised a little. "It's a party, so . . ."*

*Laughing nervously, I shake my head. "Right. Of course." My game is officially off tonight.*

*Her pink, glossy lips part and her expression softens, like she's decided to throw me a bone and help me out a little. "My best friend is throwing the party," she explains and drops her hands at her side, welcoming our conversation. "So, here I am."*

*"Oh,* that's *Anna Marie—your friend. Yeah, I've seen you around school with her."*

Bethany *nods and peers around the room. "She's really embracing the high school experience, as you can tell. Her parents are out of town, so of course she has to throw a party."*

*"Of course she does."*

*Her eyes shift away from mine nervously, and I'm glad it's not just me that's awkward, though I'm confused why it's so impossible for me to act normal. I'm not sure if it's the beer or all the time that's passed since I've talked to Bethany last, but this is important to me. Seeing her, talking to her. This is my chance to apologize after all this time and maybe even get to know her a little better.*

*I lean closer. "Well, I'm glad you're here." If I'm not mistaken, her cheeks redden. I appreciate the way she licks her lips and that I have some sort of an affect on her. The cool, calm, collected Nick starts settling back into place.*

*"Do you want a beer?" I ask, holding up my cup.*

*She nods eagerly, and with a chuckle, I take her hand and lead her over to the keg. Someone bumps into us, quickly apologizing, but I barely notice. Her hand is soft and warm in mine, and as much as I try to understand why I'm so attracted to her, I'm just glad she's here and that she's talking to me.*

*Quickly, I pour a cup of beer and hand it to her.*

*"Thanks."*

*We bump our beers together. "You're welcome."*

*"So," she says. "You come to all the parties?"*

*I shake my head. "No, not all of them. Tonight just seemed like a good idea."*

*"You didn't want to be the only player on the team not here?"*

*I wink at her. "Something like that." We talk for a few minutes about things that don't really matter, and I try to hear her, but it's hard to stay focused with the increasing noise within the room.*

*There are a few drawn-out moments of people laughing around us and bumping into us—of us pretending to look around the house* and appraise the party—before I force myself to say something else.

I lean closer again, inhaling the sugary scent that clings to her. "Do you want to find somewhere to chill? It's kinda distracting with all these people."

Bethany nods, more quickly than I expect. "Follow me." She turns and leads me through the crowd. I have no idea where she's taking us, but I follow her willingly.

I'm not much of a drinker, and since I'm three beers deep, my mind starts running away from me a little, and I get inexplicably giddy. I wanted to have fun tonight, so I don't think too much about it. I just let it be what it is.

As she leads me through the living room, I spot Reilly across the room, talking to a couple guys from the team, and a cheerleader hangs on his arm, though I can't tell if Reilly even notices. When his eyes meet mine and he sees Bethany, he frowns a little. He knows how bad I felt after I got her in trouble in middle school and that she's proceeded to dodge me ever since.

I flash Reilly a big, pleading smile, willing him not to kill my buzz, and he doesn't. He smirks instead, and then I'm accosted with a scent of something potent and expensive.

"Oooh, what did you find?" Anna Marie purrs, her shoulder-length, brown hair curled and bouncing as she shimmies in place.

Bethany rolls her eyes and glances back at me. "As if you don't already know. This is Nick."

Anna's cheeks lift with a simpering smile. "Hi, Nick." She reaches out her hand. "I'm Anna Marie, your generous hostess this evening."

Smiling, I shake her hand. She's wearing a lot of makeup and looks good in her tight black dress. She looks older than she probably is, too, which is likely the point. "Nice to meet you." I glance at the crowd. "And thanks for the invite."

She winks at me and looks to Bethany. "By all means, carry on."

*Bethany smiles and rolls her eyes again as she continues toward the hallway. A few people stop us to talk to me, and Bethany patiently waits, but I brush them off, trying not to be a complete asshole, and continue into the den.*

*I stop in the doorway and notice the books that line the walls, and the couch situated under a window with three girls sitting on it, happily gossiping. Bethany walks toward a love seat against the far wall, black and white landscape photos hanging in clusters around it. The music is noticeably quieter in this room, so I understand why Bethany chose it.*

*"Romantic," I tease and step down into the room. "Is this where you and Anna have sleepovers and gossip into the late hours of the night?"*

*Bethany plops down on the couch, careful not to slosh her half-full cup of beer. "Well, while we do giggly, girl things and have half-naked pillow fights until all hours of the night," she says with a hint of a smile, "we don't do it in here, where her father works. We do that in her bedroom." She winks at me, and I like this frisky side of her. I wonder if the beer is starting to get to her or if this is just the Bethany I don't know.*

*"Now* there's *a spectacular image," I say playfully. "You shouldn't have told me that. I won't get any sleep tonight." I sit down beside her on the love seat, not too close, even though I wouldn't mind it. Despite barely knowing each other, it feels like Fate has once again thrown us together, and it feels right this time. Like I'm getting a second chance.*

*"In case you couldn't tell," I say before taking a quick gulp of my beer, "I'm surprised to see you here."*

*Her lips draw up in a cocky grin. "Really? Well, seeing how Anna is* my *friend and a freshman, I'm surprised to see* you *here."*

*"Yeah, well, what can I say? I'm a sucker for free beer." I waggle my eyebrows and take the final swig from my cup.*

*"Well, if that's all it takes . . ." She hands me her cup with a smirk, but I shake my head.*

*"Nah, I'm good . . . now that you're here."*

*She nearly bursts out laughing. "Wow. That's so cheesy. Of all the guys at this party, you are the last person I thought would try to smirk his way into my pants."*

*She's right, and I sober a little. She's not just some chick I want to make out with. She's different, fragile, even if that was who she was a long time ago. It's how I know her.*

*Bethany Fairchild isn't just some girl, she's the girl—the first girl I ever looked at differently and wanted to get to know. Even if it was because she was so sad at the time.*

*"I was just kidding," she says, bumping her shoulder against mine, but I shake my head.*

*"No, you're right." I straighten. "That was stupid."*

*"And flattering," she adds, coming to my rescue. She smiles again and it's sort of hypnotizing, like I've never noticed it until tonight. Or maybe I've never seen her smile before.*

*"So," I start, unable to continue without addressing the elephant in the room. "You don't hate me anymore?"*

*She frowns and leans back into the couch cushion, putting distance between us that feels almost cold. "Hate you?"*

*"You know," I say, wishing she wouldn't make me actually say it. "For what happened. I know my mom told someone, she's a psychologist, she has to do certain things when—"*

*"No, I don't hate you," she says quickly. "I shouldn't have said anything to you that day. It was my fault."*

*"Your fault? Because your parents traumatized you? Who sends their kid to school that freaked out? I don't blame you for being upset. I don't even have a brother and I would've been a mess too."*

*Her eyes shimmer, and right when I'm about to apologize for bringing it up, her lips part. "And you were the only person to ask me what was wrong," she says, like she's dumbfounded.*

*That comes as a surprise, and her eyes fill with the sadness I've seen in them before.*

Shit.

*Bethany blinks and clears her throat. "I don't want to talk about it, though, okay?"*

*I nod. "Yeah, sure." It's silent for a few seconds, and I scratch the back of my head, wondering why I had to open my stupid mouth. Now the silence isn't just awkward, it's charged with everything I want her to forget. "So, what have you been up to," I finally ask. "I mean, I feel like it's been a really long time since I've seen you around. You avoid me at school and this is the first time I've seen you off campus . . . ever."*

*"I don't avoid you," she starts, then rubs her hand over her jeans. "I've been busy with life . . . and school. What about you?" She smiles. "You're a big baseball star, I hear. MVP last year, even."*

*Flattered, I tilt my head. "How'd you know that?"*

*"I'm on your turf now. I hear a lot of things."*

*"Too much, probably," I say, and I think of how crazy the past couple years have been, how different high school is than I'd expected. The games, the hangouts, the parties. I like to have fun, but high school is the rumor mill, and the stuff I hear, even about myself, is mystifying sometimes.*

*"Maybe, but it sounds like you're pretty popular."*

*My smile grows into a full-ass grin. "So, you've been asking around about me, huh?"*

*Her cheeks turn red, and she rolls her eyes. "No."*

*I nudge her a little and lean closer. "Come on, you can tell me. It's flattering, really. Is it my eyes that you like? I've been told they can see into a girl's soul." I bat them at her, too buzzed and high on her smile to care how ridiculous I'm being. "Or is it my rugged exterior—I work out, you know? This throwing arm doesn't just happen on its own." I flex my bicep, laughing when I earn another eye roll.*

*"You're so full of yourself and ridiculous," she says through her laughter. "It's embarrassing."*

*"Yeah, but making you laugh is worth it."*

*Her eyes shift up from her hands to my face, and I hold her dusty gaze. I like the way she looks at me. I like the curiosity and the uncertainty. It mirrors mine. My mom always told me there's a lot to learn about someone by looking into their eyes, and Bethany's eyes are like storm clouds that are bursting with emotions I can't even grasp.*

*"I wanted tonight to be epic," she whispers, like she's confessing or maybe reminding herself. I don't know what she's talking about, but her eyes don't leave mine. Her chest is heaving. She licks her lips. Everything is charged between us.*

*Then suddenly, her lips are on mine, and I freeze.*

*They're soft and glossy, and they taste like beer and berries as I inhale her. I hadn't expected this, but I welcome it. She kisses me more deeply, and in a blissful blur, I reach for her side, wanting to pull her closer to me, to feel her warmth, when she grabs hold of my hand and breaks away.*

*"I'm—uh," she says, breathing heavily against my mouth.*

*I lick my lips and my eyes shift over her, taking in her every look and movement. I have no idea what just happened.*

*She stands up. "I'm—uh—going to use the bathroom. I'll be right back."*

*"Yeah," I say, nodding. "Sure." But she's already walking out the doorway and disappears around the corner. Did I do something wrong?*

*Taking a deep breath, I glance around the room. Whatever that was, it was strangely liberating and horrifying at the same time. The girls are still huddled on the couch across the room. They glance over at me but when I catch their eyes they glance away again, like the little gossip queens that they are.*

*Leaning back against the couch, I let out a deep breath and hope to God I didn't just fuck everything up somehow. Bethany barely knows me, and whatever that was that just happened, I'd like it to happen again sometime.*

"*There he is!*" *Slinsky appears in the doorway. I groan inwardly. He looks around the room, totally overlooking the girls on the couch to my annoyance. Something to keep him occupied would be nice right about now.* "*Where's that cute blonde you disappeared with? She was smokin'.*"

"*She's in the bathroom,*" *I say, wondering if I should make sure she's okay.*

"*Dude, you're the mac! First Brenda and Rachel, now the hot freshman? And those are only the girls I know about. My man gets around.*" *Slinsky laughs, but I stop listening to him. He doesn't know what he's talking about. Rachel is Mac's friend, and I was doing her a solid by posing as her date at the beach. Brenda's cool, but we only made out a couple times before I found out she likes Reilly, and he's not even into her.*

"*. . . can tell The Rodster all about it.*"

"*Yeah, sure, later,*" *I tell him, standing up.* "*I'm busy.*" *I walk past Slinsky and head for the door. The last thing I want is to be is trapped in a room with him while Bethany's having a panic attack or whatever.*

*I glance down the hall in search of the bathroom, and find the door's open. Knowing there's probably a private one somewhere else, I head back toward the living room so that Anna Marie might point me in the right direction. That's when I spot Bethany's purple tank top and long blonde hair among a group of people. At first, I think she's been pulled into an unwanted conversation, but then she pulls some guy's mouth down onto hers. Her kiss is more needy, more eager than the kiss I shared with her only minutes ago, and my blood burns in my chest.*

*What. The. Fuck.*

*When she finally pulls away, she licks her lips. The moment she sees me, I swear, a glint of something shimmers in her eyes, and her mouth sets in a firm line. She said she wanted tonight to be epic, maybe mind-fucking me and making out with multiple dudes is what she meant.*

*She takes the dude by the hand and I stand there dumbly, watching as they disappear into the throng of people.*

*I'm not sure I've ever felt used by a girl before, but I think I just got played.*

*Crushing my empty cup in my hand, I head for the keg.*

*Fuck this.*

# FOUR MONTHS AFTER NEW YEAR'S

# ONE
# BETHANY

## PRESENT DAY

"COME ON, Jesse! I'm so serious right now. We *cannot* be late," I call up the stairs. My professor is going to drop me from his class if he doesn't think I'm taking it seriously. Another late arrival or absence might throw him over the edge, and I'm so close to graduating, I can almost taste the effervescent splendor of freedom.

I plop down on the overstuffed couch in the living room and pull on my black leather boots. Just as I finish zipping them up my calf, there's a crash upstairs. "Jesse?" I hold my breath a moment. "Shit."

Jumping to my feet, I take the stairs two at a time to the landing and hurry two doors past mine, into his bedroom. "Are you al—"

"I spilled the water," he says, frantically wiping at the floor. A glass rolls on its side over the hardwood. "I just—I can't find my shirt—it's my *favorite* one," he reminds me. "It was on the chair, where I always leave it, but I can't find it—"

"Hey," I say calmly and crouch down beside him. I place one hand on his shoulder and hand him one of his dirty socks to wipe

31

up the spill. "It's okay. I put your Jurassic Park shirt in the dryer last night. I'll go get it, all right? No need to panic."

His agitation with himself disallows him to think of anything other than the droplets of water beaded up on the floor, and my chest tightens a little. This is when it's the hardest, when he's so riled up. I worry he might lash out and hurt himself.

"Jesse," I say softly and reach for his hand to ground him. He stares at our fingers and I squeeze a little in reassurance. "It's okay. I know exactly where your shirt is, and the floor will be fine. See —" I motion to the bare wood between his organized piles of laundry and toy figurines. "They're cleaner now than they were a minute ago." Standing, I nod to the doorway. "Come on, let's get your shirt out of the dryer and get you to school in time for that field trip. The Exploratorium is super cool, you're going to love it. Aren't you excited?"

He taps his fingers on the floor, finally pausing long enough to nod.

"Then, let's go. Your lunch is on the countertop. Grab your jacket, and I'll bring you your shirt."

Jesse climbs to his feet, which is all the answer I need. I rumple his hair and nod toward the bedroom door. "Your breakfast is in the toaster, okay?"

"Kay," he mutters and reaches for his backpack.

Exhaling, I try to will the tension twisted in my neck and shoulders away, and I hurry back down the stairs, toward the laundry room. I pull his shirt out of the dryer and give it a once-over. Knowing how upset Jesse is when he can't find his favorite shirt, I worry what will happen when it becomes threadbare after another ten washes.

"Focus, Beth," I tell myself. The shirt is a worry for another day.

Walking into the kitchen, I nearly run into my mom. "Careful," she says, almost regal in her skirt suit, in an ice queen sort of way. She walks over to the coffee pot to pour herself a cup.

I ignore her and hand Jesse his shirt. His anxiety dissolves the instant it's in his hands, and his red cheeks twitch in an almost-smile as he pulls his shirt over his head.

"That thing is still around, I see," my mom says, and though I know she understands why and accepts Jesse for how he is—unlike my dad—sometimes she sounds too much like him, and it scares me.

I push the prickly words that itch on my tongue away, sparing Jesse from having to listen to us bicker. Hurrying over to my bag, I ensure I have the books I need for my classes today.

"Have you had breakfast yet, Jesse?" my mom asks. They are the words of a doting mother, but it's more of a pleasantry—a routine request—than an actual question.

"It's in the toaster," he tells her, smoothing his hands over his shirt.

She smiles at him, if a little stiffly, and wraps his strawberry Pop-Tart in a paper towel and hands it to him. When was the last time she made breakfast, or even put his Pop-Tart in for him? I'm not even sure how long it's been since she's stopped to have an actual conversation with either one of us. Conference calls and meetings with her design clients are in the forefront of her mind, most of the time.

"We gotta go, like"—I glance up at the oversized, whitewashed wall clock, hanging in the living room—"crap, like *now*." Donning my coat, I look at my mom. "Can you pour me a cup, please?" I ask her, nodding to my travel mug by the coffee pot.

She tops her cup off and then fills my mug. The sound of coffee being poured in the morning is like music to my ears. It's calming and promises the energy I need to get through the day. I take my travel mug with a quick thanks and doctor it up into yummy, caffeinated goodness, since she has zero idea how I like it, nor did she bother to ask.

"Remind me, Jesse," my mom says, "where is the school taking you today?"

"The Exploratorium," he answers with a mouthful of food. He finishes eating the crust before he takes a bite of the gooey filling.

My mom gathers her shoulder bag from the counter stool. "Good."

I hand Jesse a napkin and gesture to the corner of his mouth. "Strawberry filling," I tell him.

"Bring him home straight from his after-school program, okay? No errands or ice cream stops today," my mom says, and I heave my bag over my shoulder.

"Why not? He's going to do homework at a friend's today," I remind her. "It's been on the calendar since last week."

She ties her coat over her suit and looks at Jesse. "I want to have a family dinner tonight, since your father will be back in town."

I glower at her. "But socializing is good for him—"

"So is spending time with the family," my mom scolds. "Don't argue, Bethany. Just do it." And just like that, she turns on her heels and disappears into the garage, the sound of the power door rattling open before the backdoor bangs shut behind her.

"God, parents suck," I grind out. I have no idea why she cares about my dad being home, it's not like *he* does. "Let's go, J," I say with a stifled curse and we step out the door.

I'm going to be late, again.

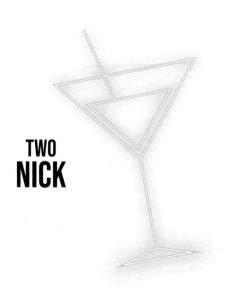

# TWO
# NICK

AFTER APPROXIMATELY 750 days of Construction Management and Architecture courses, nearly 240 project hours, and every elective I've thought to take in between, I sit in my Integrative Design class of my final semester at Benton University, wondering why graduation in two months' time feels so goddamn depressing.

Benton U is a decent school, home of the Timber Wolves and the best college hockey team on the west coast. It's not Yale or Princeton in the academia sense, not by a long shot, but its accreditation in the Arts and Architecture grad world is topnotch. In May, I'll be graduating with above-average grades, even if it did take me longer to complete my certification than most, and I'll be ready to work beside my dad at the firm. Someday, I think.

It's what I've always wanted, at least that's what I keep telling myself.

For months now, something's been nagging at me, but I can't quite put my finger on what. The closer I get to graduation, the more depressing it is because none of it feels right. Everything I've worked so hard for feels like a complete waste of time, making the idea of bartending at Lick's the rest of my life sound more and more appealing. It's fun, easy, and I'm really good at it.

"Good morning, pupils," Professor Murray drawls, as he steps inside the lecture hall. It's exactly 7:55, and I'd expect nothing less from him than to start class early.

*"Being on time is average and expected, and in life, you can't settle for less than anticipatory and extraordinary. Clearly, many of you have yet to embrace the notion of 'quality' in your work, much less extraordinary. That's why I'm here, to raise the bar."* I've gotten that spiel from him exactly three times in my academic career, and it hasn't grown on me yet.

Professor Murray walks over to his desk, opening his briefcase and pulling out a stack of papers, intent on ruining what remains of our weekend buzz. Pushing his glasses up the bridge of his nose, he peers around the room at expectant, anxious faces. By the severity on his face, you'd think this was a rocket science class, instead of a mid-level survey class for architectural and design students, who definitely aren't saving the world one pretty rug or dramatically arched window at a time.

"I hope you're caught up on your reading," he says, and I'm not sure how the promise of being rid of him seven weeks from now doesn't elicit some sense of relief.

Listening to him, a retired, know-it-all architect who moved here from San Francisco eons ago, condescendingly droning on and on the way he does, is unbearably grating, especially first thing on a Monday morning. And yet, part of me finds his class dependable and familiar. I doubt it's his winning personality, though. I glance at the empty seat in the front row. I hate noticing that she's not here or that I care.

Having Bethany in this class seems more probable a reason to look forward to Monday mornings, even if I hate to admit it. I spend half the class unsuccessfully convincing myself that I don't care she's in here, and on days like this, when she's late, I can't help but wonder if she'll show.

"Let's get started, shall we," the professor says with zero affect. He's a tall, spindly man who addresses the class like our mere existence is an affliction he has to manage the best he can. There's always one student that gets singled out each semester, and once he picks his victim, he's like a rabid dog with a meat-covered bone. This semester, that person is Bethany, and part of me hopes she doesn't make it to class today, for her own sake.

The room rustles with turning pages, and I shuffle through my notes from last week. Quickly, I scan my chicken scratch before deciding this test is going to be difficult, regardless of a few seconds of studying; it's not worth an aneurysm so early in the week, so I resign myself to my fate and close my notebook. My eyes find the clock again. Professor Murray is no longer starting class early; Bethany is officially late.

Having her in one of my classes, during my final semester of my final year, especially after her ditching me on New Year's at Denny's, seems almost poetic in the cruelest sense of the word. The one girl that's haunted me for ten-plus years is the one girl I can't have, and is the one girl I'm forced to see two days a week and pretend that life isn't pissing itself in laughter.

Bethany's tardiness is not my problem, but that doesn't matter, because I always care when she's late. I always wonder why. Elbows resting on the desk, I scrub my hands over my face, on the brink of laughing out loud at my insanity. It's a timeless question: why? Why do I care about any of it?

"Put your books away," Professor Murray drawls, and he licks his fingers to separate the stack of quizzes. "Your results today will not be graded on a curve, and I will not be offering extra credit to bump up grades for those of you graduating this semester. And don't think for a second that the rest of this semester is going to be a breeze, either. There will be a project announcement on Wednesday"—the class gasps—"so don't be late. And do *not*—"

The door creaks open, echoing in the cavernous room. Bethany pops her blonde head in, then hurries inside. Her hair's damp, her chest is heaving, and her cheeks are rosy. She's not wearing any makeup today, which would be surprising if that wasn't the case every time she's late to class.

Professor Murray glares at her. "Ah, Miss Fairchild." He crosses his arms over his chest, the remaining tests in his hands crumpling against his suit jacket. "How nice of you to attend class today and act like you even remotely care about graduating. Now, the forty-seven of us who were on time today are going to continue with class, if you don't mind."

"Sorry," she utters quietly, and slips into a seat at the end of the front row.

"And yet, this keeps happening," the professor mutters.

Bethany blushes and her mouth opens, like she's going to say something in her defense, but she purses her lips closed instead and sets down her notebook.

Professor Murray lifts an eyebrow, and I want to request that, for once in his miserable existence, he shove his commentary up his ass.

I wouldn't say I'm protective of Bethany, per se, but I've seen sides of her no one else has. No matter how complicated our non-friendship is, I know what it looks like when she's scared and vulnerable, especially when it comes to Jesse. I also know he's the most important person in her life, and I have a feeling that, whatever her morning routine might be, Jesse is crucial to it. The size of her heart when it comes to that kid melts the frustration and anger away, like it was never there.

"As I was saying," the professor continues, and he walks to the other side of the room to finish handing out the exams. "Your final project is coming up, and I want you to start thinking about what you want it to be . . ."

I try and fail not to look at Bethany or notice her profile two rows below me, as I wait for the tests to reach my row. Tapping my pen on the table, I make myself think about what I'm going to do for my project in this class that I haven't already done, especially given my final externship project I'm already working on for Sam.

Bethany runs her fingers through her hair, capturing my attention again, then she leans down to pull a pencil from her bag. She pauses, unlocks the screen of her phone and checks it one last time, before she straightens in her seat and removes a test from the stack as it passes.

Even through the whispers of the classroom and Professor Murray's voice droning on and on, I can hear her exhale, or at least, I think I can. Maybe I just imagine it as she settles in to take the test.

Like she can feel my eyes on her, she glances over her shoulder at me. Her gaze shifts away from mine just as quickly as it found me, and she practically turns her back to me. I should be self-conscious to be caught staring at her, but that was the first couple weeks we had class together. Now, it is what it is.

When my test finally reaches me, I'm grateful for the distraction.

# THREE
# NICK

AFTER MY THIRD and final class of the day, I arrive at my parents' house, back in Saratoga Falls. This is how it is every Monday: school, family time and home cooking, then bartending for the night at Lick's—a nice ease into a week of chaos. It's a great balance, actually, one I'm used to, and I appreciate the routine *and* the guaranteed home-cooked meals. Between my mom and Sam, I get to eat like a king all week, and I barely have to crack open the cupboard.

The door's unlocked and I step into the foyer. "Knock, knock!" The house smells like roast beef and my stomach approves with a rumble.

"In here!" my mom calls from the kitchen. "I'm just pulling dinner out of the oven."

I head toward her, stomach gurgling again. "I'm frigging starving."

Stepping into the newly remodeled kitchen, I inhale the savory scent of deliciousness and spit my nicotine gum into the garbage.

"Is the gum still helping, sweetie?"

"Meh." I open the fridge and stare inside, looking for leftover spaghetti or pot pie and mashed potatoes, but it's empty.

"Let me guess, you didn't eat lunch again," my mom says, tugging her oven mitts on.

I laugh at her naiveté. "Oh, I've eaten, Ma. You know me better than that. I'm a growing boy. Me like food. It's the oral fixation thing, I guess. And the fact that I'm always hungry."

"Well, I'm proud of you for quitting."

"Thanks, Ma." I glance around at the pristine granite countertops and the dish-less sink. "How is it that the kitchen is so clean, and yet, I know you've been cooking for hours?" I ask her as I lean in and kiss her cherub-smooth cheek.

"It's called practice, sweetheart. If you ever cooked, you would know how to multitask."

"Me not know this word, *cook* . . ."

She smiles despite herself and cracks open the oven door. Heat whooshes through her hair, sending the blonde-gray wisps dancing. "It's my own fault for spoiling you," she says under her breath. "I'll take the blame."

I chuckle and pour myself a glass of water to chug.

"How's the apartment?" she asks, always worrying about me.

"Great. Quiet." Five or so years ago, before I moved out, I didn't think my parents' house was very large. It has always just been my childhood home. Living in an apartment less than a quarter of the size, though, was a big eye-opener, but I love it. There are no parents to fuss about my old boxers and undershirts that are worn through.

"And the ladies?"

At first, I think she might be referring to Mac and Sam, but then I comprehend. "Ah, yes, the ladies. Marilyn and Monroe are doing just fine. I think they really like the new plant you got them for the tank."

"It's plastic," she says.

"Yeah, and they're fish and don't know any better. Trust me, it's a hit."

"A point for Mom then," she says, and I sneak a soft roll off the platter and tear off a bite. "Where's Dad, still at work?" I scoot a hot plate closer to the stove for the roast pan as she pulls it out. My mouth starts to water. "That looks deadly delicious, Ma."

"Thank you. I hope it's as edible as it looks. I've never been able to pick out a decent roast to save my life. Too much fat, not enough fat. Too dry, too small . . ." She lets out a frazzled breath. "And I'm not sure where your father is. Work sounds about right. Now, take the carafe of water to the table, would you?"

I nod, grabbing the sweating pitcher from the counter in one hand, a stack of napkins and the silverware resting beside it with the other. My weekly contribution to family dinner: setting the dinner table. I'm great at it. I don't know what my parents would do without me.

"Oh! I made iced tea for you, sweetheart. It's in the refrigerator door."

"You're spoiling him again," my dad says from the hallway, and I hear the front door shut and keys hit the entry table. I set my armload back on the counter and meet him in the doorway.

"Hey, Pop," I say, wrapping my arms around him with a quick hug.

"Hey, Nicky." He's got a bouquet of flowers in his hand, another family dinner tradition.

"How's the Wyman property coming along?" I ask and take a step back, strangely comforted to see him. "Looks like it's still keeping you busy." So busy, in fact, I feel like family dinners are the only time I see him anymore at all and he's barely at half of them.

We walk into the kitchen.

"It's, uh, good. It's coming along just fine. You know Judd, he's a demanding son of a bitch, as usual."

"Language," my mom says under her breath.

"For you," my dad says, and hands her the flowers.

"They're beautiful." She takes them with a tight smile and nods to the dining room. "Put them in the vase, would you?" Then, she glances over her shoulder at me. "You were setting the table," she reminds me.

"Oh, shit. Sorry, Ma." I can feel her piercing glare without even looking at her, and I can't help but laugh. "Language, I know. Sorry."

The usual cream cloth covers the table, and the vase for the lilies is set off to the side, on the buffet behind it. My mom and dad hustle around, getting the remaining items on the table and setting out the food. I put the extra napkins in the center of the table as my mom pulls out her chair to sit. "All right. Dig in."

My dad takes his place at the head of the table. "You can change out of your suit, Pop," I tell him and fill my mom's glass with water. "We can wait."

"Nah," he says, hanging his jacket on the back of the chair. "I'm fine." He smiles. "Starving, actually. Your mother made this beautiful meal. Let's eat."

I fill his glass with water, then pour some iced tea for myself and sit down. "Thanks for the tea, Ma."

"You're welcome, sweetheart." She unfolds her napkin.

My dad cuts into the roast. "Extra done, just the way you like it," he says and places the end piece on my mom's plate.

"Thank you." She doesn't even bother to look at him, ravenously eying the meat.

We plate the rest of our food in silence, the sound of clanking dishes and the ticking wall clock are all that fills the lack of conversation. I plop some potatoes and a heap of salad onto my plate.

"Oh!" My mom starts. "Did the property manager get your faucet fixed in the kitchen yet, sweetie?"

"I told you I'd fix it, Ma—"

"Nick, that's their job."

I shrug and take a monster bite of my roast. After a quick chew, I explain it simply. "They take forever. It's just easier if I fix it myself."

"Hutch, they should at least reimburse him for the cost, shouldn't they?"

He looks up from his plate, fork and knife in hand, and glances between us. "Yes, they should, but he's a grown man, Leslie. He can take care of it himself."

She glowers at him.

"Don't worry," I tell her. "I've been talking to Eddy, the manager. They'll reimburse me. I had them swear in blood."

"Don't be foul, Nicholas." She sighs, and I smile. These are the moments I miss most, when I still feel like my old self—a kid with only his parents' reprimands and cross looks to worry about.

"It's just," she continues, "you have so much else going on with work and school and the ranch . . . You don't need to take on anything else, sweetheart. You're too nice and people take advantage of that."

"I told you, it's already worked out." I inhale a few bites of potatoes. "I'm twenty-five, I don't need you worrying about the small stuff, Ma, especially when I can take care of it."

"Whatever you say." She cuts into her meat like it's rubber, and I know she's getting riled up.

"Mac sends her love," I tell her, trying to change the subject.

My mom's face brightens and she looks at me. "Oh, how is she? I've been thinking about her all alone in her new place. Does she need anything? I'm going to make a Costco run this week. Let me know what I can get her, would you?"

"Why are you making a Costco run, Leslie?" my dad asks. I almost forgot he was at the table.

"Because," she says flatly. "There are things I need."

"But, it's just you and dad. I don't need anything. And Mac doesn't expect you to buy stuff for her. In fact, I'll probably get a right-hook if I bring her anymore house warming gifts from you."

With a dab of her napkin, my mom straightens and gives me *the look*. "I know she doesn't need or want anything, silly. At least, she's too polite to ever ask. I just—I worry about her with

Katherine back in her life, is all." She shakes her head as if she's still trying to wrap her mind around it. "Mac probably doesn't know what to do with herself half the time. Familiarity is important and *we're* familiar. I'd like to help, if we can."

"You're meddling again," my father tells her.

She scowls at him. "Fine. I just wanted to help." The air in the room feels heavy as we continue eating in silence. I'm not sure when our family dinners became such a stressful meal, but it feels off, for some reason. It feels wrong.

"Your Aunt Alison says the ranch is doing really well," my mom finally says. "That new girl they hired over the holidays, Sommer, is working out fine, I take it?" She looks at my dad. "I'm not meddling, I'm just asking," she clarifies, but my dad ignores her.

"Uh, yeah. She's great." I glance between them, uncertain if my dad is even listening as he stares down at his plate. "Sommer's only part time," I continue reluctantly. "But, she helps Sam out with the menial, daily tasks so that Sam can focus on the clients and the projects, with me."

"Yeah, that's what Alison was saying."

After a gulp of iced tea, I fork another cut of beef onto my plate. "The barn remodel is almost finished," I add, looking at my dad.

Since high school, my dad has pressed me to go into business with him to uphold the family name and run the company when he's gone. Even though I'd been torn between architecture and baseball, I wanted to make him happy and proud. A part of me wanted to work with him as much as he'd wanted to work with me. At least, that's how it was at first.

It started off as avoidance. My dad didn't seem interested in talking to me about architecture anymore, and he didn't ask me about my classes either. Then, he began to express worry about what his associates might think and questioned the ethics and lack of professionalism in giving his son a handout. But I was willing to start at the bottom and work my way up to the top. That had always been the plan, after all. By the beginning of my final school year, everything was muddled. My plan—*our* plan—had completely changed, and my final school project was no longer my initiation into the firm.

It felt like I was being handled more than leveled with. My dad was the reason I was getting this degree to begin with, and changing up the plan on me so late in the game was a slap in the face. I'm not even sure what the plan is now.

He pours dressing into his bowl and mixes his salad around. "I'm glad the remodel is coming along nicely," he says, oblivious. "Did you use the contacts I gave you for the materials? Fred's a hard-ass in every sense of the word, but that's the reason he's the best."

"I contacted him for the joists, but I didn't use him. He was too expensive."

"No?" My dad's brown eyes finally shift to mine. He's silently judging me for going with someone else, or maybe he's wondering if I didn't go with Fred out of spite.

I shake my head. "I have contacts of my own. That's what five-plus years of design projects and externships gets you."

"Well then," he says, "I guess it's a good thing you're doing your own thing. I would've used Fred." It's a dig, a slight one, but enough to piss me off. I'm in the program because he wanted me to be and now he's acting like he didn't blow me off and leave me hanging to "do it on my own". I don't want to sound like a spoiled kid who didn't get his way, so I let it go.

"I know you don't see it now, Nick," my dad continues, "but this is good for you. I think the barn rehab you're doing for Sam is a great way to start your career, and it's one hundred percent on your own. You can be proud of what you're doing, knowing no one handed you anything."

"I'm not rehabbing a barn into an office for me, dad. It's Sam's project, I'm just executing it. It would be the same if I were working for you, only it would be an actual architecture firm to put on my resume. How do you not see the difference? This was supposed to be *our* thing."

He drops his fork, the sound of it clanking through the dining room.

My mom clears her throat and takes a sip of water from her glass. Her kind, amber eyes meet mine, conveying something I can't quite put my finger on in her silence.

My dad wipes his mouth with his napkin. "What do you want me to do, Nick? Things changed. This is real life, son, and a handout won't get you anywhere."

"I'm not asking for a *handout*," I grind out. "But it would be nice if you'd acknowledge that the past seven years of schooling— to be an accredited architect to work for *your* firm—was all for nothing."

"I didn't say you'd never work with me, Nick."

"All right, you two," my mom simpers. She offers me the bowl of roasted vegetables. "I hope you don't think you've gotten out of eating your veggies. Plate up." She nods to both me and my dad, and I grumble inwardly.

She nudges the bowl toward my dad. "Hutch—"

"I've got some work to do at the office," he says, tossing his napkin onto his plate. "I need to get back."

I gape at my mom. "What the hell?"

She shuts her eyes and rubs her temple.

Without another word, he grabs his wallet and keys from the entry table and shuts the door behind him.

I'm surprised my mom's expression is so blasé as she leans back in her chair.

"What the hell just happened?"

"He's had a rough couple weeks," she says, though it's half-hearted and she sounds exhausted. "Time for wine, yes?"

# FOUR
# NICK

SETTLING INTO MY EVENING SHIFT, I turn the classic rock up on the jukebox and survey the mess Brady left for me to deal with. I'm about to put a clean rack of pint glasses away in preparation for the after-work craze, when the door swings open and a familiar face comes into view.

"Oh boy, here comes trouble," I mutter, just loud enough so Bobby can hear me.

"You know it," he says, grinning from ear to ear. By the looks of it, Mac finally convinced him to fix his broken tooth, so other than a faded scar above his right eyebrow and the hidden tattoos beneath his work clothes, Bobby *almost* looks like a clean shaven, blue-eyed pretty boy.

"What, no hockey practice today?" I ask, grabbing a clean pint glass.

Bobby shakes his head. "It's off-season, which means I'm stuck with these jokers." He nods to his sister and the rest of our friends trickling in behind him.

Mac bats playfully at Colton's arm as the door shuts behind them, and when her eyes meet mine, I wink. "Sup, girl?"

"Hi, sweetness," she says, flashing me her megawatt smile. Her high heels clack against the linoleum floor. "Thank God for you," she says and leans over the bar to give me a peck on the cheek. As usual, she's in her signature look: bright, curve hugging designer attire you're more likely to see on a fancy lawyer, than an office manager at a mechanic shop. "These guys are driving me crazier than usual today."

I raise an eyebrow and glance between them as everyone takes a seat at the bar. Reilly and Colton sit at the end, forming an L to face us.

"We're driving *you* crazy?" Reilly asks with an incredulous smile. "Us? These guys right here?" Mr. All-American motions between the three of them. It's nice to see he's officially claimed his spot back in the group after being gone for four years, deployed overseas. "*You*, my friend, are the dream crusher," he tells her.

Mac scoffs. "I'm just trying to save Bobby money," she says, exasperated, and looks at her brother as she peels off her blazer.

"Babe, so what if he wants to super-charge the Mustang," Colton says. "What's the big deal?"

I pour the gang their usual drinks, Black IPA for the guys and a cider for Mac, since Savannah introduced it to her a few months back.

"The *big deal*," Mac says easily, "is everything that comes with it. Bigger fuel pump and injectors—more money *and* distractions." She looks pleadingly at Bobby. "I thought you were supposed to be focusing on the NHL this year, not cars. God knows you've had plenty of time to play with hoses and fan belts your entire life. Hockey is what you've been working towards. It's finally your chance to take the next step. Why add all of this to your plate?"

"Because it's fun." Reilly smirks, but Mac isn't amused, and I get the impression her frown isn't about souped-up hot rods, but something else entirely.

"Fine, whatever. I'm just the big sister. Don't mind me, like always." When Mac's eyes meet mine, she shakes her head. "They only want my opinion when it's what they want to hear."

"Typical," I say and hold up her pint glass. "To take the edge off."

"Perfect," she says. "I need a little sanity in my life."

"Ha! Then you came to the wrong place," I tell her with another wink.

Bobby takes a gulp of his beer and turns to face her fully. "When are you going to man-up and graduate from drinking *cider*?"

"Oh boy, here we go," I mutter, mentally settling in for a typical sibling squabble session.

"First of all," Mac starts. "I'm not a man, nor will I ever be one, thank God. You all take no pride in your attire, and you always have dirt under your fingernails."

"Hey now," Colton says. "Don't lump me in with them." Of course, given how many showers he takes a day between work and the aftermath of Casey, his five-year-old daughter, he's probably cleaner than Mac most of the time.

She leans in and presses a kiss to his lips. "Except for you, babe. Though," she glances down at his hands. "Your hands—"

"Doesn't count. I just got off work," he says flatly, and she leans in and kisses him again. "I know, and I secretly like it when you're dirty." She smiles against his mouth and we all look away.

"Get a room," Bobby groans. "You guys are gross."

"Your face is gross," Mac retorts. "Anyway, I'll consider venturing into the hoppy world of piss tasting beer when it stops tasting like, well, piss. Until then, cider is fine with me."

Always a glutton for punishment, Bobby eggs her on, but I'm not about to engage in another battle of the wits with her about the delicate craft of brewing, which I know I'm gonna lose.

"So, Nick," Colton starts, resting his elbows on the bar top. "Where've you been lately? I haven't seen you around the complex." Being my neighbor and all, Colton and I are used to running into each other at least a few times a week, especially when Casey's around. She likes to make special trips to my house to play Mario Cart or look for Mac, even though Mac hasn't lived with me for a few months now.

"Mostly up at Sam's, helping to de-winter the place now that the snow's gone," I tell him. "I'm still working on the new office space, too. And I have classes."

"*De-winter*?" Bobby asks. "Is that an official ranch term." He chuckles.

"It is now." I grin. "How's the leg, by the way? The last time I saw you, you took quite a beating on the ice."

Bobby shrugs and glances at his sister. He's never been a complainer when it comes to pain, none of the Carmichaels are, but in Bobby's case it's because Mac worries about him too much as it is.

"It's still attached," he says reluctantly. "Annoying as hell, but it hasn't stopped me from playing." He looks sidelong at his sister again.

"Yes, you did say that out loud in front of me," Mac says, distracted as she digs through her purse. "I'm doing my best to pretend I don't care."

Bobby looks sheepish. "You can care, Mac. Just don't be so overbearing. I play hockey. I get hurt. I can't help it."

She turns on her stool to face him. "Don't give me that crap. You can help it."

"Dude, it's *the code*—it's part of the game. I'm an enforcer, which makes it one of my jobs, literally. Sorry if you don't like it."

Mac's mouth draws up in the corner, and I can tell she's trying to play it cool even though she worries endlessly about him getting an injury one of these days he won't bounce back from. "I know. I just . . . If the NHL is what you really want, screwing up your body now—ignoring the pain and brushing off your injuries—it's going to hurt you in the long run. That's not overbearing, Bobby. It's common sense."

"Maybe if you started coming to my games again, you wouldn't worry so much," he mutters. "You'd see that I'm fine."

Mac living in her own place seems normal now, to me at least. Meeting there for a beer or a game night a couple times a month is a nice change of pace. I never stopped to think how her moving out of the Carmichael house has affected Bobby, though. They've always taken care of each other, and now that her dad, Cal, is dating my Aunt Alison, I wonder how often he's home anymore either.

"You're right," Mac says, smiling. "Dad's been telling me to hire help for the front office for a while now. I'd have more of a life if I did." She rolls her eyes. "Maybe even make it to a game or two."

"See!" Bobby's eyes brighten. "It's a win-win. And you guys can bring Casey along—it will be a family affair."

"I don't know about that," Colton says, shaking his head. His blue eyes shadow as he imagines something. Probably Casey sitting through a whole game while Bobby and the boys go to town on the visiting team. He clears his throat. "She's not big on hockey quite yet," he justifies.

Colton's tattoo barely pokes out above his shirt collar, and what Mac once told me flashes to memory. His accident. He's probably not very keen on violence after what happened, having covered up his burns with the tattoo to try and move past it all.

"Casey's still in a Little Mermaid phase," Colton continues. "So, unless you have sing-a-longs and talking fish, we'll have to take a rain check for the kiddo."

"Shiiit," Bobby says with a grin. "If singing and talking critters are all she needs, she'd love it! We have the national anthem—*everyone's* favorite sing-a-long—and a giant, fuzzy wolf running around on the ice and driving the Zamboni during intermissions. She'd have a blast!"

Colton chuckles and shakes his head. "We'll see."

I eye the guys' beers, still half full, and glance at Mac's cider, barely touched. She's still digging around in her purse. "What are you looking for, Mac?" I ask her. "You're stressing me out."

She grumbles and blows a strand of dark hair from her face. "My mom gave me the number of a sports medicine doctor in Benton . . . I wanted to give it to Bobby before I forgot again, but I can't find it."

Bobby shakes his head and looks at me. "See what I have to deal with? A bunch of nagging ninnies. And they wonder why I need a little fun in my life. Hence, the Mustang."

Mac tosses a peanut at his face. "Oh, stop it. You love the attention."

A grin creeps between his lips. "Yeah, I do kinda love it."

With the evening crowd trickling into Lick's and the lively conversation with it, I turn the jukebox volume down and snag a fresh bar towel to wipe down the remnants of the afternoon wave.

"So, Nick," Reilly drawls and shoves his phone into his back pocket. I recognize that tone and brace myself for whatever topic he's going to breech that I've been avoiding. "What's up with graduation? We throwing you a party in May or what?"

With a little elbow grease, I dominate a particularly stubborn sticky spot around the taps and glance up at him. "Yeah, I guess. Once we get the office finished and Sam and Aunt Alison situated in there, I'll feel more like I'm home free, I think." I want to be excited about graduation, but I can't seem to rally.

"We still working on the windows this weekend?" he asks. "I picked up the skylights yesterday."

"You know it." I tear open a fresh bag of pretzels. "Hopefully with a bit more light, that space won't be so depressing. Which reminds me," I say, glaring at Reilly. I slide the refilled bowl toward them. "I have to work Friday night, which means I won't be at Sam's until late Saturday, so you *better* leave me some breakfast this time."

"No guarantees." Reilly smirks and pops a pretzel into his mouth.

Sam's breakfasts are the best part of my weekend, and I try not to let him rile me up. "You're such a bastard," I grumble, earning a deep-throated laugh from him.

"Oh, you guys!" Mac says over all the banter. "We have to talk about our trip to the beach."

"Babe, it's barely April." Colton scoops a pile of peanut shells into his hands.

"Yeah, and the weather is beautiful." Mac's green eyes are bright with excitement. "I've already unpacked my summer clothes. We can thank global warming for that. Besides, the timing's perfect. We get to have a nice beach day, maybe play some volleyball—"

Bobby laughs. "Yeah right. I bet you and Sam don't budge from your towels."

"Oh, hush," she says and glances around at us. "Plus, there won't be hordes of people yet." Mac smiles, and I forget how happy group trips always make her. "How about the 22nd?"

"I'm in," I say. "Call the boss lady and get it in my calendar."

"That's the problem," Mac says, gaze fixed on Reilly.

He glances around at us. "What did *I* do?"

"We need to make sure boss-lady Sam takes the time off," Mac says. "Every year she tries to tell me she's too busy for our trips. You have to start prepping her *now* and get it on the calendar."

"Well," I say, tossing a clean towel over my shoulder. "You guys figure out the details and tell me what to bring. Other than beer, obviously." I head into the back to grab the last couple bags of peanuts and pretzels and add a new order to Brady's ownerly list of to-dos this week.

When I step back out to the bar, Bill and Franky, a couple of regulars, have slid into their normal seats at the other end of the bar, handfuls of snacks already in their mouths.

"Gentlemen," I say by way of greeting. "The usual?"

They both nod, and I grab two Bud Light bottles from the small fridge, tucked beneath the counter, and pop the caps off. "It must be that time," I say.

"What, beer time?" Franky asks.

I nod. "The hordes tend to follow you in, Franky." He's in his late forties, has a graying goatee, and comes in with dirty clothes and a construction vest on Mondays, Tuesdays, and Fridays, like clockwork.

"Does that mean I can collect a finder's fee for everyone who walks in after me?"

"Oh, sure. Brady would love that."

Franky grins and tips his beer at me. "Put it on my tab."

"You got it."

As I take a five spot from Bill, the door opens, the breeze coming with it, and I know it's Bethany before I see her. Her sweet, sugary scent's been branded to memory strongly enough to smell her coming a mile away. When I look up, her gray eyes meet mine. She nods in a surprising yet underwhelming greeting, before heading toward a round cocktail table in the corner of the room.

"Hey, Nick," Anna Marie purrs as she saunters in behind her.

"Sup, girl?" I flash her a toothy smile. I barely got a head nod from Bethany, but Anna Marie's an all-around cool chick—a flirt with a killer smile—but always easy to be around and I'm almost relieved she's here.

I'm surprised, however, when her gaze settles on Bobby. "Hey," she says and bats her eyelashes at him. A lot of chicks dig Bobby, it's probably his hotshot, jock appeal and cocky smile, which I used to relate to.

"Hey." Bobby smirks, acting cool and unaffected as Anna takes a seat at the table across from Bethany. The two of them together actually makes sense, and I suppress a grin.

Of course my gaze lands on Bethany, it always does. I tear my attention away, only to meet Mac's. Her green eyes are fixed on me, filled with sympathy and uncertainty. I know what she's thinking all too well when it comes to Bethany, and I quickly look away.

I don't need any more reminders of just how bad this chick

screws with my head when she's in the same room, despite my best efforts. Sometimes I turn into an asshole. Sometimes I feel like a pitiful fool. Most of the time, I'm just confused by the past and distracted. Either way, it's a mess—*I'm* a mess—and I have no idea why.

Grabbing a couple coasters, I pin my carefree, fun-loving smile into place and head over to their table.

Anna Marie's smirk widens to a full-fledged smile when she sees me. "Looking good tonight, Turner. I thought after baseball you might lose your appeal, but those long days on the ranch really do you some good." She winks at me, like a woman after my own heart.

I can't help but wink back. "It's all for you, darlin'."

"Sigh," she says longingly and bats her eyelashes at me. She's really good at the playful banter, a worthy opponent that always makes my day a bit brighter. Part of me wonders if it bothers Bethany, though she never shows it. She's really good at acting indifferent around me, even after our years of awkward run-ins and regrettable moments.

Anna folds her arms on the table and settles in. Like Bethany, her fingernails are perfectly manicured, her makeup and hair perfectly in place.

"So, where have you been?" I ask Anna. "I was starting to get a little offended—thought maybe you found a different hole in the wall to drink at the past few months." No Anna Marie at Lick's generally meant there was no smiling, drunken Bethany dancing beside her. A weekend staple I'd apparently grown used to.

"Are you kidding? I'd never ditch this place—too many memories," she says, and with a feigned glare, she looks at Bethany. "Someone hasn't been up for it much—plus"—Anna shrugs—"There's exams and graduation," she grumbles. "You know the drill."

"Well, then," I toss a napkin down for each of them, "I guess today's a special occasion."

"It sure is. Just a quick drink to celebrate my parents being out of town for a couple weeks, so I closed the salon tonight."

"So, you'll be the big boss lady for a while, huh?"

Anna Marie tucks her thick brown hair behind her ears. "Yep. And you know what that means."

"Trouble," I say easily. "Nothing but trouble."

She giggles. "Yep." I know exactly three facts about Anna Marie, other than she likes hanging out in Saratoga's renowned dive bar: her mom owns the only tanning salon in Saratoga Falls, Anna loves Champagne, and she's the only consistent person I've ever seen around Bethany since middle school.

Bethany clears her throat and starts digging in her purse like it's a black abyss. I'm not sure if she's really searching for something, or if this is her way of ignoring me. "Are you avoiding me?" I ask, surprising myself.

Her hands freeze in her purse. "What?"

"After class, when you come in here on the weekends—you avoid me. Now"—I glance down at her purse. "You're avoiding me."

Bethany scoffs and shakes her head. "I don't avoid you," she says flatly.

I eye her carefully. "Are you sure? Because I get the feeling that you are."

"I've got a lot going on, Nick. It's nothing personal."

"Sure it's not," I mutter.

"*I'd* never avoid you, Nick," Anna Marie chirps. "You're too sweet." She tilts her head, her smile stretching from ear to ear, and I appreciate her trying to keep the mood light.

With a wink at her, I cross my arms over my chest. "So, what celebratory drink will it be? A whiskey sour for you?"

Bethany nods. "Please."

"And, let me guess," I say with a knowing smile. I wink at Anna. "A bottle of bubbles? You know, Brady only stocks that stuff for you."

"He better," she says, matter of fact. "If it weren't for me, he'd be out of business." She laughs at her own gibe, and I like her all the more for it.

Bethany glances between us.

"All right, bubbles and a whiskey sour, coming right up." I wink at Anna one last time and head back to the bar. I can feel Bethany's eyes on me this time.

Good.

# FIVE
# BETHANY'S JOURNAL

## APRIL 9TH

*Yep, it's me, Beth. I was going through a box of things in my closet yesterday, searching for my old scrapbooking stuff so I could help Jesse with his theme park idea board, and I stumbled across you. The last time I wrote was over ten years ago, according to my last entry. I don't know if I'll find the same comfort writing my thoughts down as I used to, but I figure it's worth a shot. I refuse to call you a diary anymore, though. Hope you don't mind. I have a half hour before my next class, so now is as good a time as any to start up again, I guess.*

*I was just a kid the last time I wrote. Mom and Dad had arguing been arguing and I was certain they were going to send Jesse away. I was a mess. Unfortunately, that's also the day I met Nick for the first time. I'd seen him at school, but I'd never talked to him before. Nick was the boy I didn't know but decided to confide in that day because he cared when no one else did. He asked me why I was crying, so I told him the truth, at least as I saw it at the time: my parents were horrible people, they didn't care about us, they didn't even want Jesse, and I wanted to die. When social services showed up, I knew it was because of what I'd shared. They interviewed all of us and treated my dad like a criminal, especially when they saw Jesse's bruises from one of his tantrums. My dad is a lot of things, but he's not violent. I looked like an idiot for thinking they were actually going to get rid of my brother when really, they were arguing about sending him to an Applied Behavioral Analysis program for Autistic children, which never happened because my mom was against it from the start anyway. I'd blown it all out of proportion, and while my mom had smoothed everything over, my dad made sure I knew I'd made a mess of things. It's been a scarlet letter I've been branded with since.*

*I was esctatic ecstatic the day my mom first told me I was going to have a baby brother. I didn't think at eleven-years-old I would have a sibling. My mom was happy, too, I could hear it in her voice, but there was a sadness in her also. I could see it in her eyes. It was weird, and she's been sad ever since. Now, I can only assume it's because Jesse toggles the spectrum, but shouldn't a mother love her son unconditionally, like I love him?*

*My parents can barely be in the same room together, and my dad jumps at every opportunity to leave town. He comes back from a two-week trip today and we're having a family dinner. It's laughable. We aren't a family. We're people living in a house together. That's why family dinners are pointless, and my mom making them a priority only pisses me off. Every stilted conversation or wordless minute that goes by is a glaring reminder of how much I fucked everything up. The weirdest part of it all is that I hate that Nick knows about so much of it, but I also hate that he doesn't know the half of it, either. – B*

# SIX
# BETHANY

## SEVEN YEARS AGO

THE AUTUMN NIGHT *air is cool, but I'm glad I didn't bring a jacket. It feels good to be outside, away from the stuffy house and my parents. I hate them sometimes. They're never satisfied.*

*Jesse might not be an easy kid, but his speech is getting better and he's barely five. At least he's forming words when the doctors weren't sure he ever really would. And, I might be struggling with my grades, but I try. I try* really *hard. It doesn't matter that I practice Jesse's numbers and letters with him all the time, when I should be doing my own homework or hanging out with my friends, like a normal freshman.*

*My footsteps quicken down the street. The further away I walk from my block, the lighter I feel. All I can hear is my dad's disappointment. I want his voice out of my head for one single night.*

*I try and fail to keep his scathing words from my mind, and I wrap my arms tighter around me. I wish he knew how much it already bothered me that I scored badly on my history test, espe-*

61

*cially since I studied. He doesn't always have to make me feel worse.*

*As soon as Anna Marie's house comes into view, the tightness in my chest goes away a little, and, gratefully, my mind starts to wander. There are a ton of cars outside, which means Anna got her wish—her party is clearly a hit, even if her parents will freak if they ever find out.*

*Pushing every thought of my parents away, I hurry up to the porch.* Tonight *is* going to be epic, *I remind myself as I step inside the house. Britney Spears's nasally voice punctuates the electropop bumping inside, and I nearly giggle when I see all the people.*

*The house looks the same as it always does, only with a mass of bodies. The sitting room is filled with freshmen and upperclassman, chatting and laughing and bouncing to the music.* This is a house party. My parents would freak. *I feel giddy, thinking about the possibilities of the night. Cute boys. Booze. Dancing . . . Tonight, I want to be brave and do something fun and crazy. I want tonight to be epic.*

*I scan the crowd for a comforting face, but when I see a few of the baseball players laughing by the window, my easiness fades. Reilly is standing among them, and my heart skips a beat.*

*If Reilly's here, that means Nick's here, too; they're best friends. I didn't stop to think about who might actually be at the party. I haven't talked to Nick since that day he found me crying in Mr. Silverman's class. It was too awkward and embarrassing to talk to him again after that, after everything that happened as a result. I don't want to feel that shame tonight. I knew being at the same high school would make it harder to avoid him, but I didn't expect to see him at a freshman party—not tonight when I'm supposed to let loose and feel happy and light and free.*

*I let out a heavy breath and re-center myself in the room. This house is big, it's filled with people, and it will be easy enough to avoid him. I'm content with that train of thought, until I step into the kitchen and see him over by the keg. I turn to leave the kitchen, or at least I plan to.*

*"Hey, Bethany," The girl who sits next to me in my World History class stops beside me.*

*"Hey, Cami."*

*"Shitty test this week, huh?"*

*I groan inwardly. "Yeah. It sucked."*

*Cami lifts an indifferent shoulder, like a grade is only a grade. Maybe it is in her household.*

*"Anna knows how to throw a great party, huh?" She holds up her plastic cup. "I didn't think I liked beer, but . . ." she shrugs.*

*Uncertain what else to do, I laugh. "Yeah, I know, right?"*

*Her smile grows. "Well, have fun." Cami leads her date through the crowd and heads for the family room.*

*When I look at Nick again, he's talking to Slimy Slinsky, one of the guys on the baseball team, and he didn't get his nickname because of his oily skin. Slinsky's cringe-worthy in a lot of ways, and it bothers me that Nick's his friend, even though I know it shouldn't. Nick's one of the nice ones, or at least he used to be. I realize I don't know him anymore—I never really did, actually. And he has a reputation now at school. He's a jock and a flirt, and even though I know that's a dangerous combination, I want Nick to still be good, too.*

*"There you are!" Anna Marie chirps as she hurries over to me.*

*"You look hot," I say, taking in her short black dress.*

*She looks me up and down. "And you look . . . like yourself." She sounds disappointed.*

*"Hey, I'm here, aren't I?"*

*"True." She hands me her cup. "But you're late and you look like you need a drink. Here, chug the rest, it's getting warm anyway."*

*I glower and take her beer. "Gee, thanks." I take a couple sips, realizing I'm not a beer person whatsoever, but I'd never complain. Licking my lips, I hand her cup back to her. "So, a warm beer, huh? That means you're not drinking it fast enough. Do you have a fever?" I feign concern and rest the back of my hand against her forehead, only for her to bat it away.*

*"Ha. Ha," she deadpans. "It's hard work being the hostess of such a fabulous party."*

*"Yeah, about that." I glance around the room at all the flushed, smiling faces. "I noticed the whole baseball team is here."*

*Anna's brow furrows and then it seems to click and her eyes twinkle. "Oh! Yes, Nick." The corner of her mouth draws up conspiratorially. "Of course I invited them. Why do you think all of these people are here?"*

*"Why didn't you warn me?"*

*"Why, so you could bail?" Anna lifts a shoulder, practically beaming with pride. "It's your first party, I wanted it to be special."*

*I don't pretend to understand Anna's schemes all the time, even if she thinks they're always in my best interest. "Whatever. You better not disappear on me all night."*

*Anna waves my threat away. "Go get a drink, chat with some people, make some friends—you do know how to be at a party, right?" she jokes.*

*"Yes," I sneer. "I might not get out much, but I don't live under a rock."*

*"Great, then I'll catch up with you in a bit. I have to make sure my parents' room is still locked. Don't do anything I wouldn't do." She winks at me and makes her way through the crowd.*

*I notice Steve Hilman, a hotshot running back from our rival school in Benton, behind her in the hallway, and he winks at me. I immediately glance away. His sister was my math tutor over the summer, and he'd texted me a few times and told me he'd "formed an attachment" to me. It was a bunch of crap; he just wanted me to be another story to tell his teammates, all jocks usually do, and I wouldn't give him the satisfaction.*

*When I turn back around, my gaze find Nick's. He's staring at me and my entire body freezes in place, even if my instinct is to turn around and disappear into the crowd. His eyes are set on me, and he steps past Slimy Slinsky. My heart pumps triple-time when I realize he's walking over. I can't tell if I'm excited or going to have a panic attack, until he reaches me. The moment he smiles, some of my unease fades away.*

I PEER AROUND THE DEN, *at the books lining the walls and the antique bookends. I don't know what I was thinking bringing Nick in here, away from everyone. I've never been good at filling silences, unless it's with Jesse.*

*Nick settles back into the couch, completely ignoring the girls giggling across the room, to my relief.*

*"So," he finally says, "what have you been up to? I mean, I feel like it's been a really long time since I've seen you around. You avoid me at school and this is the first time I've seen you off campus . . . ever."*

*"I don't avoid you," I lie. "But, yeah, I've been busy with life . . . and school." Even if talking to Nick is unexpected, it's not exactly unwanted. The more he talks, the easier it feels to keep the conversation moving. "What about you? You're a big baseball star, I hear. MVP last year, even."*

*Nick's toothy grin fills his handsome face, and I feel lighter again. "How'd you know that?"*

*"I'm on your turf now," I tell him, and Anna Marie likes to know everyone's business. Like, I know Nick has never had a serious girlfriend but he's been seen at parties and games with girls. I know he's flirty and makes friends everywhere he goes. I'm not sure what that means for me, though, sitting here with him. But I know he could be hanging out with anyone right now, but he's not. "I hear a lot of things."*

*"Too much, probably," he admits.*

*I shrug. "Maybe, but it sounds like you're pretty popular."*

*He must like that observation because his grin widens. "So, you've been asking around about me, huh?"*

*I smile and roll my eyes. "No." Yes—maybe a little.*

*He nudges me and leans in a bit closer. "Come on, you can tell me. It's flattering, really. Is it my eyes that you like? I've been told they can see into a girl's soul." He flexes his bicep and lifts his chin. "Or is it my rugged exterior. I work out, you know? This throwing arm doesn't just happen on its own." He's teasing, but it's all true.*

*"You're so full of yourself and ridiculous." I nearly snort with laughter. "It's embarrassing."*

*"Yeah, but making you laugh is worth it." His eyes are smoldering and my laughter dies away.*

*I know he's had a couple beers, but maybe that's a good thing. Part of me wishes I'd had more to drink so that I wasn't sweating in places I'd rather not say, especially not now, of all times.*

*Nick's eyes shift to my lips, and I feel brave again. His attention makes me feel like a pretty girl, and I want to know what it tastes like to kiss him. He's sitting here with me, isn't he? He's flirting with me. "I wanted tonight to be epic," I breathe, and the reminder comforts me. Without allowing myself to think any more about it, I do something for myself. My heart races and my skin tingles as I lean in and press my lips to his.*

*Everything seems to freeze in an instant. His mouth is hot and soft against mine, but he doesn't kiss me back at first. My heart pounds and I briefly panic. When I start to pull away, he presses his lips harder against mine.*

*His kiss is more urgent, but I don't stop him. It feels right and good, and I wish it would consume me so that I never have to think about anything else again.*

*The girls laugh on the couch across the room and the warm cocoon around me falls away. Reality seeps back through my mind-numbing haze, and I realize what I'm doing. I feel the girls' eyes on*

*us, and I question what I've just set into motion. I start to panic
again.*

*Nick reaches for my side to pull me closer, but I pull away.*

*I breathe in deeply, uncertain if I should open my eyes.*

Was I really just kissing Nick? *Not a drawn-out peck on the
lips like I've done before, but a tongue-in-my-mouth, hot-breath-
against-mine sort of kiss, and it was with Nick. I'm not sure if I'm
bubbling with glee or if my stomach is upset and I'm going to
throw up.*

*"I'm—uh." I rush to say words that don't form in my brain.
"I'll be right back."*

*He nods, but his eyes are hazy and round, and he's breathing
heavily. I can tell Nick wants to say something, that he's confused.
So am I, but the last thing I want to do is throw up on him.*

*Refraining from smashing my head against the wall, I exit the
room. Nick's going to think I'm crying again or running away. Or
maybe he just thinks I'm pathetic, which I am.*

*Thankfully, the bathroom door is open, but Hilman stops me
just as I'm about to go inside, his cocky-ass grin spread from ear
to ear. "Haven't seen you in a while, Beth."*

*"There's a reason, Steve," I say with more bite than I mean to.*

*He smirks and lifts an eyebrow. "Whatever you say, but you
know where to find me when you change your mind."*

*I wave him away, too impatient to deal with him right now.*

*Once I get into the bathroom, I shut the door behind me and
stare at my pathetic expression in the mirror. I'm a wreck. I lean in
and fix the pink smudge of my lip gloss and imagine Nick's mouth
on mine again.* He kissed me back. *The realization is huge. Kissing
him was a euphoric high and felt right, like it was a long time
coming. He's the only boy I've ever cared much about and, somehow, he's sitting out there, waiting for me. It's just a kiss, but I feel
alive for the first time. I chock my nausea up to nerves, which seem
to fade the more excited I get.*

*Giddy, I turn on my heels. I fling open the door and head back down the hallway, ready to laugh off my near-meltdown, when I hear Slinsky's boisterous laugh. I pause outside the doorway.*

*"—you're the mac! First Brenda and Rachel, now the hot freshman?" With each name my heart sinks a little. I don't want to be a name on a list of other girls.*

*"And those are only the girls I know about," Slinsky continues. "My man gets around."*

*My chest tightens. Am I going to be a locker room conquest story?*

*"I want all the gory details." Slinsky's voice spins round and round in my head. "Come on, you can tell The Rodster all about it."*

*"Yeah, sure, later," Nick says and the backs of my eyes begin to burn. Nick's voice replays through my mind. "Is it my eyes? I've been told they can see into a girl's soul." Mortification turns into white-hot anger and I let it consume me. I'm an idiot. I've been so busy fawning over Nick, I didn't stop to think about what was really happening. This wasn't the sort of epic I'd had in mind.*

*My feet start moving, carrying me through the crowd with no specific destination as long as it's away from them. I need to numb the sting. I need liquid courage to say or do something that will liberate me from the humiliation and anger that scorches my skin.*

*I stop at the keg and pour myself a half-filled cup, too impatient to let it fill completely. I chug it down, then refill it just as quickly. The foam tickles my lips and the carbonation almost burns going down, but I do it again. Pour and chug.*

*The sound of laughter taunts me, and the thrumming music in my head is almost too distant against the sound of my heart, beating in my ears. My blood is rushing.*

*I'm not sure what comes over me, but when I see Hilman talking to a group of people in the kitchen, I head straight for him. Nick and Slinsky want a story to tell, so I'll give them one. It will be about the night Bethany Fairchild decided she was done being the good one, or the one that isn't good enough.*

Draping my arm over Hilman's shoulder, I take his cup from his hand, earning a surprised frown as I down the rest of his beer. It tastes like crap, but I don't care.

When his eyes shift to my mouth and he smiles, I do what sober, less impulsive me will regret tomorrow. I lean in, close to his ear. "I changed my mind," I tell him, and when Hilman looks at me with amusement, I don't hesitate. I pull his mouth against mine and pray his kiss will chase the memory of Nick's away. And if my dad thinks I'm a disappointment, I'll give him something else to be disappointed about.

I kiss Hilman harder and with more need than I expect, but I embrace it and I don't stop until I can no longer breathe.

Finally, when I pull away, Hilman blinks his eyes open. He looks more than surprised, he looks pleased. "Damn, girl. You're better at that than I expected."

I hated it. I hated every second of it. I want to scream, but the look in his eyes and the power I feel, knowing I can make fancy-footed, star running back Steve Hilman blush, emboldens me.

When I see Nick's face across the room, when I see the shock in his eyes, I can't help myself. I take Hilman's hand and lead him from the room so that Nick's gaze won't burn so badly.

Here's a story for you, Nick.

# SEVEN
# BETHANY

"I'LL TAKE bed number three—oh, and I'd like a flamingo sticker this time, please."

I fake-smile at Carol Goode because it's about all I can manage, and hand her a pair of tanning bed glasses and a small flamingo sticker I can only assume she'll put in some secret place on her body.

"My boyfriend is taking me to Hawaii," she says, all smiles and boasting glee. "I want to make sure I'm ready." She shimmies her shoulders, and I force another grin. "How fun. Let me know if you need anything else."

Carol traipses into room three and clicks the door shut.

"Your favorite person," Anna Marie quietly sings as she comes in from the back, armed with a large bottle of disinfectant spray. "Who's she dating this week?"

"I didn't ask," I grumble and flip my textbook open again. I hate that my life has resorted to nonstop studying.

Anna nudges the disinfectant closer. "Make sure Trent refills all the bottles when he's finished, would you? I have a dozen boxes of inventory and supplies I have to receive in the back today."

"Sure." I'm listening but also not really at the same time. I have a quiz tomorrow in my Developmental Psych class, which is more pressing than bad tans and Clorox spray. I peruse the high-lighted tidbits in my book, scanning for the field studies I need to spend the most time reviewing. Had I not accidentally fallen asleep last night, working on the essay Professor Murray expects me to have completed tomorrow in order to pass his class, I wouldn't be panicking right now.

"Hey," Anna Marie says, leaning on the desk. She taps the countertop to get my attention.

"Hmm?"

When I don't look at her, she covers the open page with her hand. "Hey," she says more coolly, and I meet her blue gaze. "I know you've got a lot going on right now with graduation and your brother, but I need you to work, too."

My cheeks burn, and I swallow thickly. She's completely right. "I know. I'm sorry." I clamp the book shut. I need this job, even if I barely have time for it.

"Why are you working here anyway?" Anna asks. "I mean, I know your parents are loaded."

I bark out a laugh. "And what makes you think any of that money is mine?" I work when I can so I can move out, though going to school full-time makes an apartment feel like a pipe dream at this point. The closer grad school gets, the more I dread the impending cost. "I'm the black sheep, remember?"

"I thought Jesse was the black sheep."

I laugh again, more saddened by the reality of it all, but still highly amused. "He is—we both are," I clarify. "It's complicated." My parents don't give me handouts like hers do, but I would never tell her that to her face. She's been a good friend, even if she's gotten me into more trouble than I'd care to admit. "I'll put my book away."

"I'll tell you what," she says, steadying her hand on my book.

"Trent needs to learn the register anyway. Why don't you take your break? That way you can get some studying in now, feel a little better about it, then actually carry on a conversation with me later, when we're really slow and I'm about to lose my mind."

I smile at her, a real smile this time. A *grateful* smile. "That would be awesome, actually."

"All right, I'll go grab Trent. Mrs. Folen should be coming in any minute for her three o'clock appointment. Stay up here until Trent's ready, okay? I can't have him scaring our best customer away because he's inadequate and awkward in just about every single way."

"Why did your mom hire him again?" I ask, realizing Anna's right. Trent is a nice enough guy, but he's a twenty-one-year-old violinist that should be working at the music warehouse or at a grocery store, not cleaning tanning beds and folding towels.

"A favor for her friend, I guess. The perk of being the boss's daughter: I get to deal with all the crap my mom doesn't want to." She rolls her eyes. "Just stay up here with him for a bit, would you?"

"Yeah. Sure."

Just as Anna Marie turns down the hall, she pops her head back into the room. "And amidst your crazy schedule, plug me in for Friday night. I know you're busy and all, but Bobby is going to be at Lick's, and I told him I would meet up with him."

"So?"

"So, we're going out, girl. You need some pep in your life. And bubbles."

"Always more bubbles," we say in unison, and I can't help but laugh.

"Put me in your calendar!" she calls down the hall. "Don't forget."

Since the misery and recklessness of my breakup with Mike wore off, I've tried to keep a low profile. My nights of freedom have been few and far between, anyway, but I'm generally okay with that. Distractions, it would seem, are my kryptonite.

After shoving my textbook back into my bag behind the counter, I settle in at the desk again. It's warm for a spring afternoon, and I knot my hair up on my head and breathe out the tension in my shoulders.

Turning my phone over, I'm happy to see I have no missed calls from my mom or Jesse, which means today went by without a hitch. Every time she has to pick him up from school, I worry she'll run late, and send him into a tailspin. Her design business is the most important thing in her life, that and a strange need to please my dad, which makes me resent her even more.

A woman's trill laughter reaches my ears from outside in the breezeway, and I assume it's Mrs. Folen. So, I'm shocked to see a familiar red-headed bombshell, laughing with her arms around Nick as they walk past the windowed storefront. Savannah hasn't been at Lick's in a while, and I heard she moved away. I assumed her and Nick were over, but apparently, I was wrong.

I want to look away from how sickeningly sweet they are together, but I can't. I can control very few things in my life, and I wish my back and forth feelings for Nick were one of them.

The way his hand rests at her lower back, leading her into the deli, is a painful reminder of all the what ifs. What if I'd never left Nick on the couch the night of our kiss? What if Nick hadn't been friends with Slinsky? But I did, Nick was, and the rest is history. So, we're left with a big heap of stilted conversations and utter awkwardness over the years that makes everything a complicated mess.

Nick laughs, a deep throaty sound that enlivens his whole face and makes his eyes crinkle in the corners.

Savannah's smile widens and she laughs along with him as they step inside.

I force myself to look away.

The way Nick was with Jesse on New Year's rekindled something I'd assumed was only a smoldering crush from years ago. But like last time, I was dumb enough to allow myself the slightest bit of hope, only for him to jump to Savannah's beck and call the moment his phone rang. It was a blessing, actually. I needed the reminder that kindness is not the same as affection.

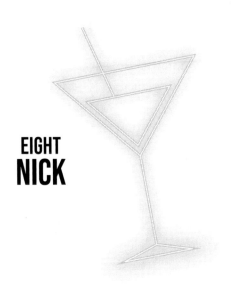

# EIGHT
## NICK

SAVANNAH GRABS us a table in the back corner of the deli, and I head up to the counter to order our favorite sandwiches. Having Savannah visit is nice, I've missed her laughing at all my jokes, and she's always felt like one of the guys in a way, too. Even if we've become more than that—*had* been more than that? It's hard to tell sometimes when we're together. We're easy and too comfortable, which makes my friends without benefits rule difficult, even if it's necessary. Things don't need to be more complicated between us than they already are.

Without thought, I glance out the window at the Range Rover parked in the lot. Bethany's working today, which doesn't help my muddled thoughts any. Gratefully, my stomach grumbles and Schmitty hands me my salami and Savannah's veggie sandwich, nicely wrapped and ready on trays.

When I slide into the booth with Savannah, I notice she's already got our drinks and chips set out, like she usually does, and she smiles up at me knowingly.

"Aw, you remembered," I say. I scoot her sandwich tray to her and pop open my Dr. Pepper.

"Of course I did. I moved away, I didn't lose my memory.

Squirt during the summer, *only*, and Dr. Pepper the rest of the year. It might be warm out, but it's not technically summer." She winks. "I remember all your quirks. That's why I come back every now and again, someone needs to make you feel special. Plus, I miss your smile."

"Yours isn't too bad either," I tell her and take a bite of my salami sub. "I could live on these," I groan.

Savannah takes a bite of her sandwich, more primly than I do.

"So, what's new with the parents and Hannington Beach?" I ask. "You haven't talked about them much since you've been back." I try to be somewhat of a gentleman and wipe the mustard from my mouth.

She shrugs and crunches on a chip. "What's there to say? It sucks not being able to hang out with people my own age on my days off."

"Just give it time, you've only been there a few months."

"Being at home with two retired parents is—let's just say I didn't think this was going to be my responsibility yet, especially since I have other, more qualified siblings. You know?"

"Ah, yes. But you're the most available one."

"Yep." She growls out the word and takes another bite of her veggie sandwich. She glances at me, but I try to keep the conversation light and continuous, or risk a long silence that ends in *should haves* and *I wishes* and more *I miss yous*. "Bill's dating someone now," I tell her. "I haven't seen him around Lick's as much."

"Really? So, our regular isn't so regular anymore, huh? What's new with the crew? Have you finished your project yet?" Savannah's eyes light up in the afternoon sunlight. "Is Sam micromanaging you?"

I shake my head. "No, actually. She's pretty far removed, in this part of the process, at least. She and Aunt Alison will dive in when it's time to decorate. I'm just externing for a 'highly-rated, horse boarding facility in need of an office remodel.' At least, that's what I'm telling my instructor."

"Well, you're not claiming anything that isn't true." She pops another potato chip in her mouth. "They don't have to know that you're related."

"True." I wink at her. "I like the way you think."

"That's because I'm awesome."

"Also true."

She smiles and my heart warms a little. "So, what do you want to do tonight? I'm only here for a couple days."

"That depends," I say, leaning back in my seat. "How much trouble are you planning on getting into? I'm getting old. I have responsibilities now."

She laughs. "So dramatic."

I take a couple gulps of my Dr. Pepper. "So, what's the bar like where you're working, anyway? Is it at all like Lick's?"

Her eyes linger on mine, and she sighs. "It will never be like Lick's, sadly."

"What, no strapping young men to ogle during your shift?" I tease but the look in her eyes is anything but playful. She sobers, and her face is almost crestfallen. "I miss you, Nick. I miss you a lot. I wish—"

"You've still got me," I tell her, putting a quick end to any talk about *us*. "I'm just a little further away now."

I can tell she wants to say more, but to my relief she resists. I don't want to have that conversation again, not today.

Savannah puts both of her pickles on my plate as a peace offering.

Happily, I take a bite of one, savoring it. "Now *this* I miss."

# NINE
# BETHANY

I SHUFFLE in through the front door after work, bags, books, and my purse in hand, greeted by the familiar welcome of Jesse shouting my name excitedly as he rushes down from his room.

"Hey, J!" I call back, strangely glad to be home. While this house might make me crazy, it's also familiar, and my memory foam mattress awaits me upstairs. "I have something for you," I tell him. "Well, it's from Anna Marie, actually, but—" The patter of his footsteps turn to slow creaks on the stairs. I smile over my shoulder to find him standing on the final step, staring into the kitchen.

Following his gaze, I straighten. "Hey, Dad." He's standing in the kitchen in his "casual" business attire, though nothing is ever casual about Charles Fairchild. He doesn't go by Chuck or Charlie, it's Charles, always. His shirt is perfectly pressed and his jeans look brand new.

I discard my coat and purse on the couch.

It's the first time I've seen him in almost two weeks. He didn't make it for family dinner last night because his flight was delayed, and not surprisingly, he didn't bother coming up for even a hello when he finally arrived home, late last night. By the look on Jesse's face, it's the first time Dad's come out of his office today.

"How was New York?" I ask because it's the scripted way this conversation goes.

"Arduous but productive." He pours himself a glass of iced tea. "How was school today?" It's a blanketed question meant for both of us.

"Good," I lie, because *fine* is his least favorite word. "I had three lectures today, so I'm glad it's over." I lean against the kitchen island. "And, I just finished my shift at the salon."

Jesse is quiet, as usual, and when he doesn't say anything, I glance over at him. He's sitting on the bottom stair and staring at the ground as he runs his finger along the smooth wood floor.

"J?" I give him an encouraging smile when he meets my eyes, and, slowly, he makes his way over, dragging his feet until he reaches the barstool beside me. Jesse looks everywhere in the kitchen but at my dad.

"And you?" my dad prompts, leaning against the counter as he brings his glass to his mouth and looks pointedly at Jesse. "How was school today?"

Jesse shrugs. "Fine."

"Just fine?"

"Yep." He starts drawing invisible circles on the marble countertop, retreating into a safe place in his mind. It only takes someone with ears and a heart to know my dad's tone is anything but loving, and Jesse doesn't do well when my dad's home.

"Hey," I say softly. "Tell Dad about your trip to the Exploratorium yesterday."

My dad sets his glass on the counter. "A fieldtrip, huh?" His words don't resonate with Jesse, they're too stiff and unyielding, like concrete. Each word is leaden with an unspoken censure, and Jesse shuts down every time.

So, I change the subject. "What did you and mom do after she picked you up from school?" I ask and brush his sandy-brown hair from his eyes.

Jesse's entire demeanor changes in an instant, and he looks up excitedly. "Mom bought me new trading cards today!" The solemn drum of his voice is suddenly a falsetto, and he climbs down from the bar stool and runs for the living room. He stops at the coffee table and looks frantically around. "Where are my trading cards?" he asks in a panic. "Where are my cards?"

"I had the cleaning lady put them away," my dad says with no affect.

"Where are they?" Jesse nearly shrieks.

The garage door opens and my mom fumbles in, paper bags in her hands and her purse and briefcase hanging from her shoulder. "Evening, everyone," she says with an exhale. She's oblivious to Jesse's turmoil and the brewing storm she's just walked into. "Since I went back to the office for my briefcase, I stopped for takeout." She sets the two paper bags down on the countertop.

Mom meets my gaze first, then peers out at Jesse, who's riffling through the living room in a whirlwind.

Frowning, my dad watches him. "Calm down," he says, but Jesse can't help himself. In a panicked flurry, he opens the entertainment center drawers and the blanket chest. He looks in the cubbies under the coffee table and then in the writing desk by the bay window.

"Where are they?" he demands, and runs up the stairs.

My mom's gaze shifts from me to my dad. "What's going on?"

He shakes his head, clearly annoyed. "Why don't you ask your son?" he says, and he walks into his office.

"Great," she grumbles and drops her purse onto the floor. My sentiments exactly.

She hurries upstairs after my brother. As meltdowns and spin outs go, that one took less time than usual, thanks to my dad. I bite back every caustic remark that comes to mind. We've seen him all of five minutes and the house is already in unrest.

My dad's chair squeaks from inside his office, and I hate him for acting so indifferent. No, he's not acting, he *is* indifferent when it comes to his own children, and it's sickening.

Jesse's muffled shrieks carry down the landing. I hear my mom's low murmurs of reassurance, but it won't help, nothing will —not until she finds his cards. I consider taking a shot from the bourbon bottle staring at me from the wet bar, before I brave the crap storm I'm likely going to start as I walk into my dad's office.

"You seriously don't know where his cards are?" I ask him, storming into his office. He sits in his overstuffed office chair, like I imagine a pompous, self-absorbed politician would, pouring over documents in front of him that are clearly more important than my standing there.

"No, Beth, I seriously don't." He doesn't even bother looking up at me. "Probably in his room with all his other toys."

"Why couldn't you just leave them where they were? They weren't in anyone's way."

That earns a narrowed look from him. The angles of my dad's face are sharp, his face clean shaven, and despite the way his fingers flip through stacks of papers on his desk, his eyes are always fixed on something, always focused and thoughtful. And now, they're fixed on me. I swallow thickly.

"I told her to straighten the living room because that's what I pay her to do. So, that's what she did. Despite what you and your mother think, it's not a personal attack on your brother."

"Whatever," I grumble and decide retreating upstairs with the rest of my family is probably best. Just as I turn on my heels, he says my name.

"Beth?"

I stop in the doorway. I know big-wig investor and hard-ass extraordinaire, Charles Fairchild, doesn't want to have a father-daughter moment, so I brace myself best I can and slide my armor into place for his impending lecture.

"What is this your mother tells me about your grades slipping?" He stares at me, expectant. I like it better when he's busy shuffling through paperwork.

"They're fine," I tell him, my first mistake.

"Fine?"

"Yes."

He sits back in his chair. His gray hair is slicked back, and I can smell his expensive aftershave. It's probably the most comforting thing about him. "I told you when you double majored this wasn't going to be easy for you."

"Yeah, I remember the vote of confidence."

"Well, is it?" he counters.

"No, it's college. It's not supposed to be easy." I can't help my tone, even if I know how this is going to end. I hate bullies, and my dad is a bully of the worst kind because I can't escape him.

"You're right, it's not, and by doing exactly what I told you not to do, you've set yourself up for failure."

"Bs aren't the end of the world, Dad. They're above average—they're *passing* grades." And there's my second mistake. Mediocre is unacceptable in my house, that's why Jesse and I are both black sheep; we're both less-than in his eyes.

Shaking his head, he clasps his hands in his lap. "So," he says, deceptively calm. "*Average* and *fine* are still words in your vocabulary, I see."

My hands clench to fists at my sides, my nails digging into my palms as I try and fail not to bite my tongue. "It's better than failing," I point out to him.

He glowers at me. "Well, Beth, when you're forking out $20,000 a year for your brother's private school and $35,000 a year in college tuition, you can stand there and tell me what's acceptable and what's not. You wanted to do both of these programs, even though I told you it was too much for you. You promised me you would make it work, that I wouldn't be disappointed, yet here we are." He rests his elbows on his desk and exhales like his life is so painfully hard, like my average grades are a blight on his existence—like *I* am.

His stare cuts into me and his attention burns, just like his constant disappointment.

Like so many times in my life, anger gets the better of me, and I take a step closer to him. "So, you're upset because I have a job *and* I'm double majoring while sustaining a B average?" I clarify and grit my teeth.

"Watch your tone."

"How is it that we've all failed you so miserably? We do everything to please you, and God knows, Jesse and I try. Even Mom does. Yet, we're all failures in your eyes." I throw my hands up. "I'm not sure why we even bother." A voice in the back of my mind is telling me to reel the anger in or he's going to explode, but everything about him enrages me. His presence alone makes my mom look like Parent of the Year. "What do you want from me?"

"What do you want from *me,* Beth? Do you want me to be easy on you so that you have more time to party? So that you don't have the pressure of keeping your grades up and actually doing something with your life? Why is it that everyone in this house thinks that I owe *them* something. After everything I've done for all of you."

"What is it that you give us, exactly? Money? Because it's not love and affection—you can't even make it home for family dinners. I don't want your money, if you're going to hold it over me the rest of my life."

He stands up, leaning his fists on the desk. "That's enough," he warns. The papers crinkle under his weight. "If you don't want my money, then pay for grad school on your own."

I swallow the prickly ball rising in my throat. I've been expecting this—wanting the liberation of it, in a way—but the logical part of me wonders what I've just done.

"Do whatever you want, Bethany," he says, cinching the knot rapidly forming in my stomach. He sits back down, no longer able to look at me. "If you don't care about your grades, then neither do I."

His easy dismissal of me and my life is like a serrated edge against my skin. It cuts and aches, and I want to scream.

"Close the door on your way out."

Without a word, I slowly turn for the door. I don't want to cry over him, not anymore, and I hate that I can't stop the tears from forming.

I close the door and stand outside his office for a minute, numb and exhausted from this constant battle. I'm not so spoiled that I don't know other people put themselves through college all the time—students who have it harder than I do. I could figure out a way to pay for school without him, even if putting my apartment on hold for a little while was the compromise.

Straightening, I take a deep breath, but it hitches when I notice my mom, standing in the kitchen watching me. Ignoring the tears quickly forming, I walk past her and up the stairs. I'm about to shut myself inside my room when Jesse opens his bedroom door.

"Beth," he whispers. There's concern in his voice, even if his face shows no sign of it.

I smile, hinging it into place. "Hey." I walk over to where he hangs out the doorway and rumple his hair. "I was just going to find you."

"Mom found my cards," he tells me. "Want to see?"

"I'd love to see your new cards, J."

# TEN
# BETHANY'S JOURNAL

## APRIL 10TH

~~Mom and Dad, thank you for asking about my day. My professor singled me out yesterday in front of the class, like always, because he doesn't know that I have a controlling mother who only wants to talk to me in the mornings as I'm rushing out the door, making me late. And remember how I was so worried about him failing my paper I worked so hard on for extra credit? I actually did better on it than I thought I would. Oh wait, you don't remember any of it because you've never asked.~~

*Maybe one day I'll actually write this. - B*

# ELEVEN
# BETHANY

LYING BACK ON MY BED, I stretch the stiffness from my body and flex my fingers and toes. Sitting cross-legged isn't as easy as it used to be. With a sigh, I glance at my alarm clock and want to throw up. It's nearly midnight, and I feel like I've only retained half the information I've processed over and over for the last three hours.

My Graduate Records Examination is coming up—only a couple weeks left before I know if I make a score decent enough to get me into an accredited psychology program . . . and I feel sick to my stomach.

I hate to admit that my dad is right in a sense. Double majoring seems like the dumbest idea on nights like these, but then, psychology is what I really care about. It's what I want to do, and it wouldn't be so stressful if that wasn't the case. Design, that's more for my parents—for my mom's firm. I enjoy design, but I don't want to work for her, and that type of work, well, it isn't my passion.

*School can't be this difficult for everyone.* Even double majors. *Can it?* I don't understand why I struggle so much. It's not for lack of trying. Too much on my mind and too many distractions, maybe . . . or, too much pressure. I heave out a sigh. *All of the above.*

I stare at my highlighted notecards and open textbooks. All I know for certain is, I need a break. Trying not to let my precarious notecard piles slide around, I climb off my bed. Milk and peanut butter cookies sound magical, and it just so happens, we have both.

When I open the door, I'm happy to see that Jesse's bedroom light is off, which means he's finally sleeping. Sleep isn't usually a problem for him, except for nights after a big upset. Jesse's always less predictable when my dad is home; his presence is a disturbance in the Force and Jesse is all about routine.

Tightening my ponytail, I make my way down the stairs and into the kitchen. I relish the quiet hours when the house is silent, and I feel like I'm in my own little bubble. I hear a few muffled words in my parent's master suite, though, and I'm not the only one awake. My parents rarely argue these days—they barely talk to each other—so when they do, I know things are bad. Unable to resist, I take a step closer.

" . . . you be a little more understanding?" my mom asks, and I like that she's annoyed with him, even if she'd never confront him in front of us.

My dad doesn't say anything, and for a minute, I panic that they know I'm outside their door.

"If I'm easy on him, he'll stop trying to do better," my dad finally says, and I roll my eyes. For being such an intelligent man, he's stupid in so many ways, it's actually cruel. I wonder if he's ever once stopped to think about how his actions translate to Jesse.

"It doesn't work like that, Charles," my mom says evenly. "If you were around more, you'd actually see how well he's doing. Every time you come home, you get him all riled up—" She stops abruptly, and I hear muffled movements before she speaks again. "If you're angry with me, Charles, be angry with me. Leave the kids out of it. It's not their fault," she says more softly, maybe even a little desperate. "Jesse's a boy, he needs a father, not a drill sergeant."

"This is who I am, Laura. You knew what you were signing up for when we decided to make this work. I could've left, but I stayed—for you. For *them.*"

While the sharpness in his tone doesn't surprise me, his words do. My parents are dysfunctional, but I didn't realize my dad had made a decision to *stay*.

"You can't make me a man I'm not, not after everything that's happened. If you want Jesse to have a different father, then go find one. This is me, this is how I am. Period."

My heart beats fervently, and I'm not even sure why. We'd all be happier if my mom left my dad, but something about this conversation doesn't feel right.

"What about Bethany?" my mom asks.

"What about her?" The knot in my stomach returns and tightens at the coldness in his voice.

"You weren't home ten minutes and you nearly had her in tears." He doesn't say anything.

I straighten and wipe away the unexpected dampness from my cheek.

"She's still struggling, Charles."

A dresser drawer closes, and my father finally speaks. "She's always struggling."

"She's *trying* to make you happy." My mom's tone is almost frantic, and I can tell she's exhausted, trying to make him understand, like me.

"No, she's doing whatever the hell she wants. If she wanted to make me happy, she'd listen once in a while. She would've quit her job when she decided to double major—she wouldn't have assumed she could handle a double major in the first place. Her grades would be up. She's been fighting me the whole way, and look where it's gotten her."

"Maybe if you'd help, instead of throwing money at her—"

"Oh, and your relationship with her is so much better? When was the last time you even had a conversation with your kids? You work just as much as I do, so don't try to make me the asshole."

"You don't need any help in that department," she mutters.

"Excuse me?"

"You heard me."

I take a step backward, caught somewhere between shock and fear of what they might say next.

"I'm trying to make this work," my mom finally says, wearily.

"Yeah, since when?"

There's a sudden chill in the air as I back further away from their room. The acid in my dad's voice—the desperation in my mom's—makes my heart ache for them. For me, and for Jesse. I don't know how it came to all this, but we are beyond broken.

# TWELVE
# NICK

IF MY DAD hadn't stormed out of our family dinner a couple nights ago, I wouldn't have taken his blowing me off for breakfast this morning so personally. Should I be worried about him? The more I think about it all, the angrier I get. He hasn't just been distant, lately he's been almost absent.

As I pull into the parking lot at the U, my phone rings again, his fifth attempt to reach me this morning, and I finally pick up.

"Nicky?" he says, and I hear the surprise in his voice.

"I'm heading into class," I tell him and shut the Explorer off. "I can't talk right now."

"Well, we need to, and soon."

"We could've talked this morning," I remind him. "I was there, waiting for you."

"I know. I'm sorry, son."

"What's going on with you, Dad? This isn't like you, at all."

He heaves out a breath, and I can practically hear him shaking his head. "There's a lot to say, and now's not a good time, okay? I'm at the office. We'll talk tonight."

"Yeah, okay." I don't expect him to bear his soul in a room with his subordinates, so I don't push him. "I'm gonna be late for class, I gotta go." I end the call, staring at the darkening screen for a moment and wondering if I shouldn't try harder to get some insight out of my mom. Thinking back, I wonder how I couldn't tell something was wrong sooner than this. Clenching my hands, I let out a deep breath. Whatever is going on with them, it isn't good.

When I look at the dash, my mom and dad fade away, and I grab my bag. "Goddammit."

I hop out of the Explorer and slam the door shut behind me. I'm fucking late. I jog through the parking lot toward the quad. I know I won't make it there in the two minutes I have until Professor Murray's class officially starts, but I haul ass anyway. By the time I get to Building C, there are only a few students hustling around, which means I'm officially screwed.

When I get to Professor Murray's lecture room, I brace myself and open the door. He's addressing the class, writing down names as they shout them out. He glares at me as I hurry to an open seat in the second row, his eyebrow raised. "Nice of you to join us, Mr. Turner." He looks back to the rest of the class.

"And, Miss Martinez, who will your partner be?" he asks as I pull out my notebook and peer at the person's desk next to me to see what they're talking about. There's no handout and no one's books are open yet.

"Debra Hess," she replies, and the young women exchange a grin. Professor Murray calls out a few more names before the lecture room door opens again. Everyone stops chattering as Bethany walks in, her chest is heaving and her hair mussed, probably a lot like mine.

Professor Murray looks from Bethany to me. "Since you and Mr. Turner don't seem to care who your project partners are, the two of you can work together." He smiles with false amusement and writes what I assume are our names down on his paper. "We'll see if between the two of you, you can get your project completed on time."

Heaving out what little air is left in my lungs, I lean my head down on the desk and silently groan. There are worse things than being her partner for a project, but this isn't what I need right now.

I can smell her perfume before I hear her footsteps and apologies coming down my row. She slides into the empty seat beside me and pulls out her things.

"Partners?" she whispers. "For what?"

I look at her, already exhausted from this day. "I have no idea."

Bethany glances at her phone, adjusting it to silent, when I see a text message pop up on her screen. I don't mean to pry, but I read the message without thought.

> Mom: Your father and I have late meetings tonight. I need you to pick up Jesse after class.

Heaving a sigh, she shoves her phone into her purse.

"If you've learned anything in this class this past semester," Professor Murray begins, "it's that design is mostly about planning. It's about the bigger picture and, even more than that, it's about making your client happy. Luckily for you, there is no real client, however, I expect a full mock-up of a room design, as if there were. I want a written proposal, an estimate, and a budget of no less than ten thousand, complete with an image board, list of possible vendors—the whole gamut. I want to know what your project is, what purpose it's serving, and what it's going to look like and cost in the end."

"Professor Murray?" one of the students asks a few seats down.

"Yes, Mr. Mallory?"

"When's this project due?"

"I want everything on my desk by May first."

The class groans and his eyes narrow. "I'm happy to move the deadline up a little, if you'd like."

"No, May first is great," Chuck says regretfully. "Just checking."

"Good. Three weeks should be plenty of time for this, especially given you all have partners." Professor Murray's eyes land on Bethany and then on me, and I glare back at him. This is an elective for me, and I don't have the patience for this today.

"This is going to act as one of two final grades for this class," he continues. "So, prioritize it accordingly. I'm going to give you the rest of class to meet with your partner to outline and plan. If it looks like you aren't using your time wisely, we'll dive into the next chapter in your Integrative Theories coursework and focus on historical architecture trends in modern societies."

Everyone groans.

"Riveting, I know." His gaze shifts around the room. "Well, then, get to it."

*This isn't happening.* My tolerance has reached its limit this morning after only two hours of sleep, spilled coffee on my jeans, my non-breakfast with my dad, and because of him, being late to class. I don't have the bandwidth to deal with Bethany right now, too.

She turns to face me fully. "Well," she says, her voice as prickly as I feel, "this is going to be interesting."

"Yep." I lean back in my seat and cross my arms over my chest. Then, we stare at one another. Her eyes are duller than I remember, with dark shadows, like she's exhausted. "Late night?" I ask, though I'm not sure why I care.

"Something like that," she says, brushing off my comment. She picks up her pencil, poised for note-taking. "We're going to need time outside of class to work on this. Maybe we should start by figuring out a meeting schedule." She pulls her teal-cased phone from her bag and scans her calendar. "Thursdays are out, those are my nights with Jesse. I could do Saturdays, though—mornings are best."

I nod. "Fine. I'm assuming we should meet at the Falls Library?"

"That works. We should meet this weekend so we can get started, if you're available. We can divvy up the tasks and just check in through email or texts after that."

I only half-hear her as I make a note to meet up with her this Saturday, then a text pops up from my dad.

> Dad: Crap. I can't do tonight.

Of course he can't. I shove my phone into my pocket.

"Study date on . . . Saturday," Bethany mutters and her fingers flutter over the screen. "I'll bring the coffee." She clicks off her phone.

A study date, really? The absurdity of our situation is too much, and I can't help but laugh, which only makes Bethany's frown deepen.

"What?" Her eyes turn to slits, and she heaves out a breath. "What's the problem?"

"This is hilarious. Me and you—partners—planning *study dates*. It just proves my theory."

Bethany lifts a perfect eyebrow and pulls her glossy bottom lip between her teeth. It only irritates me more. "Do I even want to know?" she asks.

"Sure—it's like a game. The powers that be are toying with us. They're testing me. It's really funny, if you think about it."

"You know what, Nick? You can laugh about this all you want, but this isn't a joke to me. I need a good grade on this project, and if that means we have to suck it up and get over our shit, then I'm willing to do that. Are you?"

I'm a little stunned by her severity. "*Our* shit?"

"Yes," she bites back. "*Our* shit. This—you. Your attitude."

"*This* is because of you, one hundred percent." I gesture between us.

"Really? And what did I do, exactly?" Bethany huffs and leans back in her seat.

"I have a whole list," I tell her easily. "How much time do you have?"

She almost looks disgusted with me. "What are you, five?"

Knowing she's feeling an ounce of the frustration I feel around her gives me a teensy bit of satisfaction, even if I know it's juvenile. I'm tired of her indifference toward me, and right now she's a captive audience.

When I don't say anything, a sneer parts her lips like I've never seen. "You're unbelievable. Did you drop your rose-colored glasses this morning, and on top of that, you have to have me as a partner? I've made your mood worse, haven't I?" She tsks, mocking me.

"You don't know anything about my morning," I grind out.

"Yeah, your perfect life must suck." She leans forward again, a venomous gleam in her eyes. "I'll figure this out on my own. I don't have time for this . . . Find a new partner."

It all happens so fast, I don't realize she's gathered her things and exited the room until the door slams shut behind her. I don't even have time to process anything before Professor Murray walks toward me.

I silently curse myself.

"Mr. Turner," he drawls, glancing around the room at the students huddled in pairs. "Is there going to be an issue working with Miss Fairchild?"

I can't bring myself to say yes, so I shake my head and stare out the door, wanting to go after her, if only to set the record straight. "No, sir," I say instead. "We just had a misunderstanding."

"See that it gets straightened out, Mr. Turner. Both of your graduations depend upon it."

I nod again. It's all I can do without losing my shit.

# THIRTEEN
# NICK

## THREE YEARS AGO

HIP-HOP AND LAUGHTER *reach my ears before the roaring fire comes into view beyond the dunes. People collect around it, students and post-graduates alike, excited for the first official summer bonfire of the year. Despite Sam's frown and slow footsteps, I think tonight might actually be fun, which we all desperately need.*

*I glance back at her and Mac. "Sam, if you keep making that face, no one is going to talk to you tonight," I warn. "Which defeats the purpose of getting out and living a little."*

*"Yeah, come on, Sam," Mac says, nudging her a little. The wind picks up, catching Mac's dark hair in a frenzy. She smooths it down and leans in to loop her arm through Sam's, tugging her closer. "You need to join the land of the young, wild, and free again at some point. Tonight's as good a night as any, right? Booze, shadows to hide in, enough people-watching to keep you distracted . . . Besides, you love the beach, and it's a beautiful night." I can hear the concern beneath layers of pep and joviality in Mac's voice, a concern we both share. But, whether it's a girl*

*thing or just their friendship, Mac has a way with Sam that I never will. So, I walk a little further ahead, trying to give them more space.*

*"I know it's hard, Sam," Mac continues, "but it's been months. You can't stay holed-up at the ranch forever. Your dad wouldn't want you to miss out on your life because of him." Her voice is low but soft, and she's got Sam this close to the land of the living again, which is saying something.*

*"Look, I appreciate your intervention, you guys," Sam says loud enough for me to hear. "But this isn't about Papa right now."*

*"It's not?" Mac glances between us.*

*Sam shakes her head. "No—well, not really."*

*Shoving my hands in my sweatshirt, I stop and wait for them to pass me, curious to hear her answer.*

*Sam shrugs. "What if they're here?" she finally says. Her gaze shifts from me to Mac, and then to the fire on the beach. "Mike and Bethany—together—is the* last *thing I want to see tonight." She looks down at her feet, trying not to stumble in the sand.*

*I don't want to see Mike—or Bethany, for that matter—any more than Sam does. Looking back into the throng of partiers, I search for familiar faces in the dying sunlight. There are some, but none unwanted, that I can see.*

*"I doubt Mike will be here," Mac finally says, and we stop at the outskirts of the party. "At least, he better not be." She grumbles the last part.*

*"And if he is?" There's a plea in Sam's voice, one I've grown familiar with over the past five months, even if I'll never get used to it. It's the tone she uses when she's not ready for us to leave her with her thoughts; the desperate side of her that can't understand why Mike would treat her the way he did when they were so happy. It's a different Sam, a broken Sam.*

*"Then, we'll leave," I promise.*

*"At least I don't have to worry about Reilly," she grinds out. I'm still getting used to the brittleness in her tone when she speaks*

*about our best friend. She might think Reilly is to blame now, in all her rage and broken heartedness, but I don't blame him for stepping in and breaking them up, especially not after learning Mike was cheating on Sam with Bethany. Sam distanced herself from all of us while she was with Mike, so I might not have been completely in the loop, but even I could see he was bad news. The chaos Mike created in his wake will haunt all of us for the rest of our lives, and the son of a bitch could care less about all of it.* What asshole doesn't return your calls after you almost die in a car accident— after your father *does*?

*Mac peers around at the crowd. "This town is getting too big, I don't think I know everyone here anymore." She's only partially joking. "So many people came this year."*

*Sam groans. "I already feel sick."*

*"Deep breath, Sam," Mac says.*

*"Here. I have just the remedy," I say happily. I pull a beer out of my ice chest and hand it to her. She just needs a little something to loosen her up, we all do after the year we've had.*

*"Hold the bottle tight," I tell her and pop the cap off with the butt of my lighter. Sam's face scrunches and my smile widens. "Pretend it's a wine cooler. Go on, take a big swig."*

*Her grimace is very Sam-like, and it makes me happy that there's still part of her in there somewhere.*

*"Yo, Turner!" Slinsky shouts. I nod at him and second baseman, Chet Tompkins, as they make their way over from the other side of the bonfire. Although I have nothing against either of them, I don't want to reminisce with them about baseball tonight, especially when half the team went on to play minor league or coach, one of them was even drafted to the Dodgers. Me, on the other hand, I stayed behind to go back to school, the farthest thing from living my dream, even if I do like architecture.*

*I meet up with the guys closer to the bonfire, knowing Slinsky is one of Mac's least favorite people, so I try to spare her. The guys are grinning, their eyes enlivened by firelight and they seem almost giddy to be here tonight.*

*"Dude, what's it been—a couple years since I saw you?" Tompkins says as I grab a beer from my handheld ice chest.*

*"Something like that," I say and situate my Igloo in the sand. Save for a few waves around town, we haven't seen each other in a while. It's definitely not like it used to be.*

*Tompkins comes in for a side clap on the shoulder.*

*Then Slinsky. "What's new man?" he asks.*

*"Not much. Same shit, different day." I nod to Slinsky. "You still painting with your dad?"*

*"Yeah, it's temporary," he says and takes a gulp from his plastic cup.*

*I glance over at Mac and Sam as they wade further and further into the group. Mac is all smiles and flirty laughter as familiar faces surround them, but Sam's eyes dart around the party, and she really does look like she might puke.*

*"And you're at your dad's firm now, huh?" Tompkins says. "That's cool."*

*I shake my head, taking a swig of my beer. "No, not yet. I'm still working on my degree. What about you? Still coaching?"*

*He nods. "And getting married this winter," he adds. "But I have to say, I thought I'd hate it, but surprisingly I don't."*

*"What, getting married?" Slinsky says. "I could've told you that."*

*"No," Tompkins chides. "Coaching little league. I actually like coaching the little shits. They remind me of us, only they're half the size, and I'm pretty sure they're bigger assholes than we ever were."*

*We all laugh, but it feels forced and a little awkward, like time has stolen our comradery, which used to be the most dependable part of our lives.*

*"So," Slinsky says, "What's up with Reilly, is he still deployed?"*

*I nod and take another swig of my beer. "Yep, I'm not sure where, but I got an email from him a few weeks ago."*

*"Yeah, I bet he's somewhere miserable," Tompkins mutters. "Does he at least like the Army?"*

*Reluctantly, I nod. "I don't know if he'll be back anytime soon," I say sadly. Although I get to take the Rumbler out every now and again for a tune-up, I miss my best friend.*

*"It's crazy. It's like we're all adults now and getting old or something," Tompkins says with a sigh.*

*"Hey now, speak for yourself," Slinsky laughs. "I'm in my prime." He winks at a young blonde who's probably still in high school, and I shake my head. Some things never change.*

*Peering around the bonfire, I realize Mac's right. There seem to be fewer people I actually know at these things anymore. I meet Mac's wide eyes and register her "come save us" look as she nods to the guys standing around her and Sam. With a smirk, I pull out a beer for Mac since she's bottleless, and plan my escape.*

*"Hey, I'll catch up with you guys later." I nod to Mac and Sam. "Duty calls."*

*Slinsky winks at me, which I ignore.*

*"See ya, Nick," Tompkins says over the sound of the music. "Let's grab a beer sometime!"*

*"I'm working at Lick's now—stop by anytime!" I shout back.*

*Jogging up to Mac and Sam, I wonder when, exactly, I became their cock-blocker. It was gradual, but I don't mind it, especially when Sam is out of sorts and Mac might as well be flying solo.*

*"Ladies," I say, stopping beside them. "I hope I didn't keep you too long." I look at the two guys talking to them. They give me a once over. "Hey, I'm Nick," I say, introducing myself with an affable smile.*

*They nod at me, and I hand Mac a beer. "My lady."*

*She smiles, grateful, and looks at the two John Does. "Any-way," Mac says sweetly. "It was nice meeting you guys. Enjoy the bonfire." To anyone else it's a polite smile, but I see it for what it* is, painted on and desperate to be unhinged. The guys glance between Mac, Sam, and me, clearly confused before they turn and walk away.

Mac sighs and chugs some of her beer. "Thanks," she says, letting out a deep exhale. "I don't even care that this taste horrible. I needed a drink. My wingman is MIA tonight," Mac says, nudging Sam playfully.

But Sam's eyes widen before they narrow and a familiar laugh catches my ear. Sam's face says it all, burning red, even in the darkness. When I turn around, Bethany is lip locked with a guy I've never seen before, sucking on his face like she's rabid.

"Homewrecker's already moved on, I see?" Mac mutters beside me.

But when Bethany comes up for air and sees me standing there, her expression surprises me. I'm not sure if it's my frown or the fact that she's clearly wasted, but for a fleeting moment, I think I see the sad-eyed girl from middle school. Her glassy eyes are fixed on me and her grip on the dude she's hanging on loosens.

"That was fast—" Bethany's gaze darts to Mac, like she hadn't noticed her until now. "Mike too boring for you already, or is this the other guy?" Mac sneers.

"Let's go," Sam says, turning for the dunes again. Mac is all too willing and they head toward the pathway. Bethany's date tugs on her to follow him to the fire, but Bethany's eyes narrow on Sam and she tugs her arm away from him as she watches the girls walk away.

All I can do is shake my head, and I follow after the girls. When I reach the top of the first dune, I peer back to find Bethany is straddling the guy's lap at the fire, lips locked on his again. I don't know what happened to the Bethany I thought I knew, but she's long gone. The girl I see now is lost.

# FOURTEEN
## NICK

"BRADY!" I shout above the noise. "I need a margarita on the rocks for the young lady in the pink sweater." It's Friday night, which means Lick's is where it's at. The city kids come out of the woodwork, teachers let loose, and Saratoga Falls becomes a college town on 'roids. The locals, well, they come in for an after-work drink and stay for five.

Taking the ID from Pink Sweater's friend, I glance between the hottie and her license. She doesn't look old enough to buy cigarettes, let alone drink, but it's legit, even if my gaze lingers on her bright blue eyes longer than it needs to. I might even call them mesmerizing, if it weren't for a pair of smoky gray eyes I haven't been able to get out of my head all week.

I wink at Pink Sweater and her friend as I return their Oregon IDs, because that's my thing—I wink and smile and, mostly, the ladies eat it up. Then, I rest a pint glass against the Lagunitas tap to fill 'er up.

"And . . . what can I get for you, sir?" I ask the man at the end of the bar. With a quick tip, I pour the excess foam from the glass in my hand and slide it over to the woman patiently waiting for it. I take the guy's order and everything else is automatic.

My hands move swiftly, wiping wet spots from the bar, and my eyes scan the other patrons' drinks. I check on the man at the end who's been sipping his beer for what feels like an hour, and then on the guy with an empty tequila shot, hitting on a girl who's clearly not into him.

The girl he's with leans over the bar when she catches my eye. "I'll have a whiskey this time," she says. "A double." At the rate this date of theirs is going, I'd say she's going to need it.

I nod. "We talking top shelf or—"

"JD, please," she says, checking her watch.

"A woman after my own heart." I flash her a smile. "Coming right up."

I flip a highball in my hand and clank it down on the bar top, pouring two shots for her before she can even get her wallet out.

"Seven-fifty," I say, sliding her shot over on a black, square napkin. I glare at the guy next to her who hasn't moved for his wallet once tonight. He's clueless.

The woman slides me a twenty. "Keep the change and keep them coming," she says. It's getting late, and at the pace the night is going, it's going to end one of two ways. Either a bar fight is going to break out and/or someone is going to puke. I'm hoping it's only the latter.

"You're it," I tell Brady, cashing Miss Jack Daniel's out. I give him "the look" and nod at her as she downs her double shot.

Brady glances down the bar at her, sweat beaded on his brow, much like mine. He shakes his head. "Not a chance."

"Dude, I'm not on barf duty tonight," I say, stepping closer.

"*Dude,*" he says, mocking me. "I'm your boss. You'll do whatever I say."

I smirk at him and wring out a wet towel. "Whatever you say, *boss.*" I make a mental note to keep my eye on Miss JD tonight as I scoot her another shot and a bowl of pretzels.

If I hadn't been a fixture in this place for the last few years, I wouldn't push my luck with Brady, but we go way back, and I know he would never fire me. Not unless he closed this place down, which would be a true-life sob story.

With a whistle at Brady, I nod to the floor and head out from behind the bar to make the rounds. Peanut shells and half-full, forgotten beers litter the room and tables. *A damn waste and shame.* Shaking my head, I glance over at the jukebox in the back corner where Mac, Sam, and Reilly are hanging out. I notice Bobby and Anna Marie standing by the dartboard, separate from the group, but I don't see Bethany anywhere. I try not to think about her as I clear off the tables, but that doesn't last long.

I'm gathering discarded pint glasses, when a vision of tussled blonde hair, long legs, and a black fuck-me dress consumes every ounce of my attention. Bethany saunters into the bar, wearing those goddamn pink heels I can never get out of my head, with her arms wrapped around some guy I've never seen before.

Bethany's all smiles, her eyes are glassy, and her lipstick is smeared a little, and I know she's feeling good. She's a temptress tonight. By the look of her now, you'd never know how angry she got in class on Wednesday.

I walk back to the bar with the dirties and submerge them in the suds tub. I do a quick drink check around the bar, pour Miss Jack Daniel's a *single* shot, and ask Brady to get another line of margaritas going for Pink Sweater and her friend.

"How did I get stuck on margarita duty?" Brady asks.

"You want to play bus boy?" I'm more than happy to switch with him.

Brady shakes his head. "You missed some glasses over there," he says happily, and pours a line of tequila shots for one of the groups at a cocktail table. I head back around the bar for another load and try to steer clear of Bethany when she sees me.

"Oh, Nick!" she calls over the noise.

"That's my name," I drawl and grab an empty glass before finally looking at her.

"Can you get us a drink?" Her date nuzzles the side of her face, like he can't take his grubby hands or eyes off of her. I'm not a jealous guy by nature, but I don't like the way her date stares at her lips, like he's a predator and hungry.

"Uh . . ." I hesitate. She's pretty drunk.

"I'll take a whiskey sour," she says, oblivious, and her friend with the bad hair asks for two shots of tequila. "Top shelf," he clarifies.

"How about some water," I tell her, ignoring her date's request completely.

"What? No, that's not fun."

I laugh. "It looks like you've had plenty of fun tonight already."

Her easiness vanishes, and her hands fall away from her date and to her sides. "I'd like a drink, Nick," she bites out. Her posture stiffens and she takes an unsteady step closer to me.

"I'm not serving you tonight, Bethany. You're already lit."

She looks shocked. "Are you screwing with me?"

I grab a few more empty glasses from the wall bar beside them, winking at a chick who bumps into me and giggles with apology. Bethany's date steps closer, his greased black hair slipping into his even darker eyes. "What the hell is your problem, man?" he growls.

"I don't have a problem, but she's cut off." I glare at her friend. "And if you keep pushing me, so are you."

"Nick, stop it," Bethany says, glancing wild-eyed between us.

"Stop what? I'm the bartender. It's illegal for me to over-serve someone."

Bethany grabs hold of my arm and pulls me toward the door. She wobbles on her feet, but she's too determined and angry with me to trip and fall. When we get into an empty pocket of the bar, she grills me. "What the hell is your problem? Why are you being an asshole?"

"I'm not being an asshole," I say coolly, even if I'm not sure that's entirely true. "I'm doing my job."

"I've had a few drinks, so what? It's not like I'm belligerent or something."

"Or something," I mutter. "Just have some water for a bit, Bethany, it wouldn't kill you." I turn to leave.

"Wait," she demands and reaches for me again, her fingers tight around my forearm this time. "Is this some joke to you—are you getting back at me for walking out of class the other day?"

"No." I take a step closer to her. "But what the hell are you doing? Why are you out with this creep and acting like—"

"Like what?" she asks sharply. Her eyes narrow on me. When I don't say anything, she takes a step closer to me. "Go ahead, Nick. Say it. I know you and your friends have been stewing in resentment toward me for years now." She flings her hand in my direction. "Why don't you just get it out of the way. A slut? Trash? Homewrecker? I couldn't possibly just want to have a fun night out and act my age like everyone else, right?" Her eyes glisten and her face reddens even more.

I'm not sure how to respond as I register the hurt in her eyes. When I don't say anything, she peers around the bar, like she's suddenly worried she's making a scene.

"Thanks for ruining it," she says, and without another word, she pushes through the door and disappears outside, the door swinging open and shut in her wake.

Bad Hair comes up behind me and glares. "Hey, dip shit, you just cost me my date."

I stare at the door settling back into place. The look on her face confuses me, but the offense in her voice was real. I turn back for the bar. "Tell someone who cares."

# FIFTEEN
# BETHANY'S JOURNAL

## APRIL 13TH

*So, I've been staring at my ceiling for a couple hours, trying to sort out what happened at Lick's tonight. My night out was ~~was~~ supposed to be fun. I ~~supposed~~ was supposed to go out with a flirty guy I met at the coffee shop and live with wild abandon. That's how it is for most people my age, right? They go to parties and ~~going~~ go dancing and live like they'll never be twenty-something again. What makes me so different? Is it Nick and Lick's? Is it this town and the past it holds? Is it a deep-seated shame I will never be able to shake because of my parents? Why is it so impossible to be happy for one fucking minute? -B*

# SIXTEEN
# NICK

MY HEAD'S FUZZY, but the sheets feel like melted butter around me, and I don't want to move. It takes me a moment to realize I'm only half asleep and someone's pounding on the front door.

Peeling my eyes open, I force myself to sit up in bed. I'm tired and drained, and whoever is knocking on a Saturday morning is going to get a knee in the scrotum. I told Reilly I was sleeping in today, and, according to my alarm clock, it's only nine. It might as well be 5AM after going to sleep around four.

More pounding scatters what remains of my haze, and with a curse, I climb out of bed. My apartment is dark, the drapes drawn and only a few slivers of morning sunlight filter in, illuminating a path to the door.

Reilly knocks again as I reach for the handle. "Yeah, I'm awake," I growl and fling the door open. The sun's like acid on the backs of my eyes, and I stagger back. "Jesus, could you—"

"Sorry, not Jesus. It's me," a bored, female voice says, and I blink my eyes open to see Bethany standing on the landing. She adjusts her book bag, slung over her shoulder, and offers me a tall to-go coffee. "Latte?"

"What the hell are you doing here?" I groan as last night comes flooding back to me. Then, I remember our study date. "Ugh, I'm too tired for this." I step out of the way so she can come inside.

"Hence, the coffee," she drawls and offers it to me again.

This time, I happily accept. "Thanks." As she glances around my apartment, I take a sip of coffee and appraise her jeans and long sleeves. Her hair's damp and she looks surprisingly put together for an early-ish Saturday morning. "How come I feel worse than you look?" I ask. "Shouldn't you be nursing a hangover or something?"

"I wasn't that drunk, you were just being an asshole."

I laugh bitterly. "Yeah, sure, if that's how you remember it."

"Can we, just, not talk about any of that?" She bristles, and I walk into the kitchen to add a bit more sugar to my coffee.

"Fine. But, I thought we were meeting at the library."

"Yeah, well, we never decided on a time—"

"Because you ran out of class like a crazy person," I reminder her, and lean my palms against the counter.

"*And*," she continues, "I wasn't sure you'd even show up after last night." She says it with a little bit of humility, so I let it go.

Bethany drops her bag on the sectional and peers around my dark apartment before she walks over to the window. With a quick tug, my navy drapes are open, light brightening the living room, and she sighs. "Now it doesn't feel like I'm on How to Catch a Predator," she mutters.

"Wow. Please, make yourself at home. By all means . . ."

Bethany looks at me, her eyes shifting over my body. "Not that I have anything against half-naked men, but do you mind?"

I glance down at my pajamas, or mostly lack thereof. "I was hoping to sleep in a bit longer, but clearly that's a pipe dream." I take another swig of my coffee, in no rush to make her feel more comfortable, and set it on the counter before I disappear into my bedroom.

"So," I call into the living room, "I take it we're working here this morning?" I hear a zipper and crumpling papers.

"If you don't mind," she says. "Since we're already here."

I pull a fresh t-shirt over my head. "How did you know where I live, anyway? Do you stalk me or something?"

"Yeah, I have been for years." She says it so nonchalantly, I have to laugh. "Brady told me," she amends. "He owed me a favor."

"That sounds intriguing."

"It's not. I introduced him to my dad so he could get some investment advice," she explains.

"Oh, I didn't know that."

"Yeah, well, there's a lot you don't know," she mutters.

"Yeah, like what?"

"Ginger tea and a shot of whiskey."

"What are you talking about?"

"Something you don't know about me," she explains, but I'm still confused.

"Okay . . . Care to add any context to that?"

I hear her rustling around in the living room. "Hangovers—it's what I take for hangovers."

"Ah, got it." I finish dressing in silence, not wanting to bring up last night again. After I brush my teeth and run my fingers through my hair, I head back into the living room. She's sitting on my couch with neatly stacked piles of books and notecards spread out in front of her. She looks like she belongs there with her legs folded under her and her hair in a knot on top of her head.

A rush of gratitude washes over me, seeing her in my apartment, and I quickly fill the silence. "Better?" I ask, gesturing to my more appropriate attire.

Her mouth tilts in the corner and her pewter eyes meet mine. "It's an improvement."

# SEVENTEEN
# BETHANY

NICK'S EYES linger on mine a bit longer than I'm comfortable with, so I'm forced to fill the silence. "Nice place, by the way."

"Thanks." He drops his notebook onto the other side of the sectional.

His apartment is a total bachelor's pad, complete with a mountain bike hanging on the wall, dirty boots, and a cowboy hat by the door. I like the grays and browns that color his apartment, though —they're subtle and sleek, yet still masculine. "Did your mom help you decorate?" The rug beneath his dinette table catches my attention. Its black and white geometric trellis shapes add a bit of noise to all the drab.

"Is it that obvious?" The Nick-ness of his voice is gone, and when I look at him, so is the brilliance of his eyes. It's clear I've hit a nerve.

"I'm a design major, remember? It's sort of what I do—notice things. Don't take it personally."

Nick walks into the kitchen without saying another word about it. "You want a Pop-Tart or something?" He reaches into the cupboard and pulls out a box of blueberry.

"Pop-Tarts are Jesse's favorite," I tell him and unwind myself from the couch. With a little extra pep in my step, I walk into the kitchen.

"What can I say, the kid's got good taste." His eyebrows waggle at me, and just like that, his Nick-ness is back. "So, is that a yes?"

"Sure." I unwrap a pack for myself and hand it to him to stick in the toaster. Our hands have touched before, but this time, it's different. It's the first time we've touched since New Year's in his car, and here, in the privacy and quiet of his home, it feels more intimate than it should. I take a step back and smile, nodding to the PlayStation on the floor by the big screen. "Video games?"

A grin envelops his face. "Hell yes, video games. I'd love to kick your ass in Mario Kart."

"Actually . . . I'm more of a Duck Hunt kind of girl."

His eyes widen. "That's literally the worst game ever. There's a reason it isn't around anymore."

I nearly snort a laugh. "What can I say, I bought an old Nintendo at a garage sale when I was little. It only had one game but it kept me busy before Jesse came along. Let's just say it holds sentimental value. I'm down for some Mario Kart though."

His eyebrows lift. "Yeah? I thought we're supposed to be working?"

Nodding, I run my fingers through my hair. "You're right. I'm easily distracted when I'm anxious."

He smirks at me and lifts an eyebrow.

With an internal groan, I retreat back to the couch. "This *whole* project makes me anxious. This is the worst timing possible."

Nick pulls out two Pop-Tarts from the toaster and moves around his kitchen with ease. He tears off a paper towel and opens and closes a drawer, and I wonder if this is what it would be like to spend every Saturday morning with him. If we might have a cup of coffee, eat breakfast, and banter back and forth about childhood hobbies.

"Are you okay?" he asks. "You're making a face."

Deer in headlights, I force a smile. "Yeah. Great. Thanks." Even as I remind myself how complicated we are, I find it incredibly easy to be around him, too.

"You said 'worst timing' . . . What did you mean?" His eyes are on me, expectant and probing.

"Well," I start, not certain how much to tell him, let alone how much he cares to hear. "I'm taking the GRE in a couple weeks, and I need to focus on that exam so I'll be able to get a good score." I dig for a pen in my book bag, suddenly desperate to keep myself busy.

"A GRE?"

I blow a loose strand of hair from my face. "It's like a rite-of-passage for psychology students thinking about a master's degree. The better your test score, the better your chances are of getting into a good school. Kind of like the SATs, but more important."

"But . . ." Still standing, he leans against the counter and crosses his ankles, a perplexed look on his face that's almost comical. "I thought you were an interior design major, thus our Integrative Design class."

"Yeah, well, I'm a double major," I say quickly, and I reach for my coffee, hoping he'll avert his gaze.

"Wait, why the hell would you want to do that to yourself?" he asks, and the laugh that bubbles out of me sounds almost lunatic.

"I don't know," I admit. "I mean, I do, but, no, I don't know what I was thinking. I'm crazy."

"Kinda cute-crazy," he says lightly, and my eyes meet his.

Both of us sober.

"Oh," Nick says quickly and hands me my two Pop-Tarts. "Ugh, sorry. They're getting cold." That's the least of my worries right now. "No worries, thanks." Tapping my pen on my notebook, I take a bite of my breakfast. "We have a lot to discuss, we should probably get started."

With a nod, Nick plops down on the couch across from me. "Sure."

"So," I say, pointing to the doodles on my notebook. To the average person, they might look like scribbled gibberish, but to me, they're a necessity. "I came up with a few project ideas to run by you, but I don't know how you'll feel about them. First, I was thinking we should pick a local spot, maybe a business we think needs a remodel so we can actually go inside, check it out, make some informative decisions—"

"Actually," Nick says, and takes a long pull of his coffee. "I've already decided on our subject matter—well, I might have."

"I see. That's . . . surprising, and a little presumptuous." I fold my legs beneath me, settling in to hear his revelation.

He watches me skeptically.

"Are you going to tell me what it is? I'm on pins and needles over here."

Nick smirks and scratches the side of his face. When his lips purse, I start to worry a little. "I don't know if you're going to like it, but it's a really good idea."

That's somewhat frightening. I tuck my hair behind my ears. "Might as well come out and say it."

"I'm still working at Sam's ranch a couple days a week," he says.

My palms begin to sweat, even though I have no idea where he's going with this. "Okay . . ."

"Look, I know the two of you don't really get along, but I'm remodeling her barn for my final project—converting it into an office, actually—and while I was just going to do the conversion for my final, we could work on the interior together for Murray's class, doing Sam a solid *and* getting our project finished with bonus points on top of it."

I blink at him.

"We already have my plans and schematics of the structure, and we could throw in before and after photos, not just a mockup from AutoCAD." He leans onto his knees and looks me in the eyes. "You were worried about your grade the other day, and I heard you. So, this is my proposition. I have to get this project done anyway, and Sam is going to need all the help she can get." He shrugs. "I think it's a no brainer."

"But?" I hedge. He seems too hesitant for there not to be a hitch, other than my issues with Sam.

"We'd just need to make sure everyone is on board." He drapes his arm over the back of the couch and waits for me to respond.

"Ah, got it. Sam knows nothing about this proposition."

"Not yet. I wasn't going to ask her until I knew you were in."

Tapping my pen against my notebook, I peer around his apartment. I do need this grade and, as much as I dread having to interact with Sam, an easy project would be a lifesaver right now.

"You know your stuff, Bethany," Nick adds, and even though I know he's trying to butter me up, his expression is sincere. "You might not ever make it to class on time—"

"You just had to sneak that in there." I roll my eyes.

"*But,* I've seen your vision boards and I think Sam would like your style, which makes it ten times easier on you." He tosses down a stack of barn photos, what looks like 'before' the remodel. It's a big space, and depending on the changes he's made, it has a lot of potential.

Sam and I have *never* been friends. I hated her for the Mike thing, she hated me, but even before that I knew she didn't like me. "You realize she's going to hate this idea, Nick. She's gonna say no."

He shakes his head. "No, she won't. I'm going to use my charm to get us this job. Consider it taken care of."

I doubt Nick batting his eyelashes at her will soften her up enough. I try to ignore my curdling stomach at the thought of having to work with her and her hateful stare. "You better get her liquored up first."

"You don't know Sam like I do," Nick says, almost defensively, like he can read my thoughts. "She has her reasons for feeling the way she does about you, but she'll overlook them to help me out."

His resentment toward me is obvious, even if it's misplaced. I meet his gaze. "She thinks she does, anyway."

Nick stares at me, his eyes narrowed, like suddenly my presence is riling him up. The last thing I want is a repeat of the other day in class.

"Look, Nick, let's get something crystal clear. In spite of what you all seem to think, I did *not* steal Sam's boyfriend—I got screwed over, too. And I think you know that."

He frowns. "Do I?"

I grit back my instinct to curse him for thinking I would do something like that to begin with, but then, if the years we've known each other have proven anything, it's that we've never really known each other at all.

"I believe your exact words the first and only time I brought Mike around my friends were, 'Looks like your new boy toy is awesome. He's already hitting on Sam.'"

The creases in Nick's brow deepen. He might have a difficult time remembering that day, but his words have haunted me because, apparently, they were true.

"You said he wasn't your boyfriend," he finally says, and I'm shocked he remembers.

"No, I said he wasn't my *boy toy*. There's a difference."

"Not to me—not then, anyway."

All I can do is shrug. "Well, it was the truth. I don't know what to tell you. So, you can get over me and the Mike thing, because it wasn't a bright, sunny spot in my past either." I try not to dwell on just how dark of a time it was for me. "I did a lot of things I regret then, but being a *homewrecker*, as Mac would call me, wasn't one of them."

Nick's eyes don't leave mine, but I'm not sure if he's really looking at me or if he's thinking. Eventually, his eyes refocus on me. "So, you think all of this is about Mike?" he asks, almost incredulous, and I bristle a bit more.

"It's definitely part of the problem," I admit. "But no, Sam and Mac have been giving me death-stares longer than that. Probably before high school even—"

"Yeah—I'd say after I tried to help you, and you blew me off. You blew me off at Anna Marie's party junior year, too, only that time you decided to run off with that running back, Hillard or Hill—"

"Hilman, and I didn't blow you off, Nick. You were being an ass."

"What?" He sits forward on the couch. "You're going to somehow turn this around on me?"

"Hell yes, I am. The last thing I wanted to be was the '*hot freshman*' on your list of locker room conquest stories. Sorry to thwart your plans, *Turner*. I'd expected it from Slinsky, but not from you."

Nick laughs, but it's an incredulous, overly amused laugh. "*Slinsky?* That was about *Slinsky?*" He stands up and begins pacing. "Let me get this straight, you ditched me because of *him?*"

I rub my hands over my face, feeling this conversation spiraling too quickly into dangerous territory. "Why are we even talking about this," I groan. "Nick, none of this matters anymore. We have a project we need to work on."

"Oh, it matters," he bites out, more exasperated and surprised than I'd anticipated. "Wow. I mean—wow."

"Will you stop saying that, please."

"You disappeared to make out with *Hilman* because of something Slinsky said?"

"I didn't disappear to go make out with him, Nick. I was angry —it just happened."

"Oh, well, in that case I forgive you," he says hotly. "I can't believe you thought I would tell Slinsky *anything*," He walks over to the sliding glass door and stares out at the balcony.

"And New Year's—I helped you find your brother and you ditched me at Denny's."

"Give me a break, Nick! Your *girlfriend* called."

"What? You mean, Savannah?"

Rolling my eyes, I inhale a deep breath. "Yes, of course, Savannah. The whole town knows you guys are together."

He smiles, like all of this is simply too amusing for him not to. "She and I haven't been together for months. She moved away and now, we're just friends." But the waffle in his voice tells me he's not one hundred percent certain about that.

"I saw you guys together on Tuesday, Nick. Even if you're not 'together' you're still *together*."

His frown returns.

"Look, Nick. We could go back and forth about all the other instances too, or we can try to forget about it all and focus." I'm not sure why, but what's happened or hasn't happened between Nick and I over the years feels unexpectedly raw. Especially now that I know what he's thought of me all these years.

"Well," Nick breathes. "This is all very . . . enlightening."

"I told you we should've stayed on topic. Now it's just going to be weird."

He makes a self-deprecating sound and grabs his phone. "I'll call Sam." He reaches for the sliding door handle then spins around. "Do me a favor, would you?"

I peer up at him, into eyes darkened by more emotion than I expect.

"Don't assume I'm like Mike or Slinsky, or any of the asshole guys you've dated, okay? You'll be wrong one hundred percent of the time."

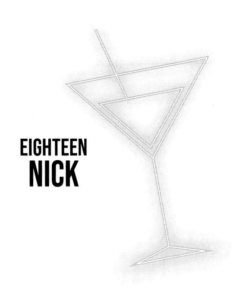

# EIGHTEEN
## NICK

AS I STEP onto the balcony to call Sam, all I can think is that I've got a lot more in common with Reilly than I realized. Not only are we like brothers, but I probably hate Mike as much as he does right now, differently than I hated him before. I hate him for breaking Sam's heart, and for the mess he created of her entire life. And I hate him for hurting Bethany, too, because clearly, he did. Mike, Slinsky, and all the dirt bags in between, are pieces of shit, and Reilly and I have to sift through their aftermath.

When I glance through the sliding glass door, Bethany is peering out at me. Her lips purse, and it's obvious she's anxious. Hell, I am too, but not for the same reasons. Talking to Sam is the easy part. It's spending the next few weeks working with Bethany that worries me. If today is any indication, it's not going to be easy.

I wink at her. It's a peace offering to break the tension that's already rooted between us, and she's barely been in my living room an hour.

Shaking it off, I press CALL, and settle in to talk to Sam.

As it rings, I realize, had it been a few months earlier, I'd be out here lighting up a smoke to take the edge off, because Bethany, sitting on my couch, being irritatingly soft and natural, like she belongs there shouldn't matter to me, but it does. That's how I know I'm screwed.

"Morning," Sam's voice finally comes on the line. Clanking and scraping echoes in the kitchen.

"Sup, girl? Did you save me some breakfast?"

"No."

I grin. "Liar."

"Well, there won't be, if Reilly eats it all." She huffs and the background noise falls quiet. "So, what's up. Are plans changing for today?"

"Not exactly." I eye the empty ashtray on the patio table, long-ingly. "I need your help with something. It's a project for one of my classes."

"Wow, you sure have a lot of projects."

"It's my own fault. I shouldn't have taken another one of Murray's class. I knew better."

"What's the project?"

"Well, my partner and I have to present a fake design project from start to finish—vendors, cost analysis, the works. I was thinking we could use the barn project to take it a step further."

"What do you mean?"

"Help you and Aunt Alison with the interior, that sort of thing."

She nearly snorts. "That sounds amazing, actually . . . What's the catch?"

I bark out a laugh. "Dammit, Sam, you know me too well."

"You're not a tough case to crack, Nick, charming as you are."

"So, you think I'm charming, huh?"

She's shaking her head, I know she is because I know her like the back of my hand; she might as well be sitting beside me. "You're incorrigible." With a deep breath, she continues. "So . . . the catch . . ."

I glance inside at Bethany curled up with her notebook on my couch. "Bethany's my partner and you'd have to present her with a budget, agree on décor style—you get the picture."

"What?" It's a breathy, skeptical sound more than an actual word, and I let that sink in for a minute, uncertain what else to say. "You mean like she will be coming to my house and working on this project—with me?"

"Something like that," I say tentatively. When Sam doesn't say anything, I continue. "You would really be helping me out, Sam."

"Well—of course it's fine. Whatever you need." I can tell it's difficult for her to say, but I know that she means it, which is what matters most to me. "I'm not even going to ask how this happened."

I lean forward, resting my elbows on my knees. "Thanks, Sam. Since I'm going to be there today, working on the barn, do you mind if she drives up to see it?"

"Uh, I guess?"

I laugh a little. "Way to sell it, Sam."

"It's fine. I told you, whatever you need, I just—"

"Thanks." I stretch in my seat, about to say goodbye when she says, "Nick?" Her voice is cautious.

"Yeah?"

"I know there's a weird connection between you guys, and I also know you don't need me to tell you this, but . . . just be careful, okay?" Although I don't need a warning or for her to worry about me, I appreciate the hell out of it.

"I know . . . Thanks, Sam."

"See you later."

"See ya." A weight lifts from my chest when I press END, and I peer into the living room again to find Bethany watching me, worrying her bottom lip. She's beautiful and looks innocent, even if I know she's a siren behind those soulful eyes. I've never understood her hold over me, but it's moments like these, when she's vulnerable and real, that become etched in my mind and stick with me for days after.

I give her a thumbs-up and flash her a smile that's a bit more enthusiastic than I feel. Whatever the back and forth between us has been over the years—the misconceptions and run-ins and arguments we've had—it's all come at a cost: distraction – curiosity – a slew of unanswered questions and an inexplicable desire.

Bethany's phone rings, and when I look inside again, her eyes are wide with worry, then narrow. "Jesse, slow down," she says and tucks her hair behind her ear. "What?" Her words are muffled through the door, but when she rises to her feet and begins pacing the room, I know something's wrong.

I head inside, quietly sliding the door shut behind me.

"I don't think that's what she meant, Jesse." Bethany's voice is calm, but her demeanor is anything but. "Mom wouldn't do that." She walks a line from the kitchen through the living room and back again.

Growing more anxious, I take a step closer. It feels like I'm in middle school again. I want to help her, even if I don't know how, but if history's taught me anything, it's to stay out of it. So, I hang back and give her space.

Abruptly, she stops. "Wait, what?" Her mouth's agape, and when she registers me standing a few feet away from her, she turns her back to me and her voice quiets. "I know, J," she says, placating him, and even though I get that this isn't my business, I can't help the sting of her snub, knowing she's blocking me out, again.

# NINETEEN
# BETHANY

"DAD SAYS the Sunset program isn't worth it—he's gonna pull me out, Beth!" Jesse cries. It's the most desperate he's been in a while, and my heart breaks for him. "They're my only friends."

"I know, J," I say unsteadily and pull at my hair. "I'll figure something out, okay?" My grip tightens around my phone. The fact that this is happening makes me want to scream. The kid can't catch a break when it comes to my dad, and I'm done with it all. "Is Mom home?" I'm already shoving my things into my bag before he can answer.

"They're arguing downstairs."

"All right, well, I'm on my way. I won't let them pull you out of your program, okay? Just stay up in your room—stay away from Dad, and I'll be there in ten minutes."

He sniffles in the phone.

"Okay?"

"Yeah," he says, sniffling again, but it's going to be hours before he's feeling like himself again. "Love you, J." I hang up the phone and drop it into my bag. When I look up at Nick, concern creases his brow.

"I—uh—I have to go. Sorry. I know we have a lot to do, but I have to get home."

"What happened? Is Jesse okay?"

I shake my head. "Nothing's ever okay," I bite out, but I know Nick isn't to blame. Taking a moment to pause, I clear my throat. "Jesse struggles a lot in school for obvious reasons. I've talked to his teacher and she's pretty cool, I mean, she tries to be understanding, but Jesse isn't very social—he wasn't making friends until we put him in this after-school program for kids with developmental issues. It's small, so he feels comfortable there, which is *huge*." I shake my head, still struggling to accept that my dad is so detached from our family's reality. "My dad wants to pull him out."

Nick frowns. "Is it a money issue?"

I freeze, my hair falling into my face. I forget Nick doesn't know my dad, though I'm not sure why I'm surprised. No one does, not really. "It's not the money. There doesn't have to be a reason for my dad to be a dick." I finish gathering my things and peer around Nick's living room. "I take it Sam agreed to the project?"

"Yeah," he says with a nod. "We're good to go."

"Thanks for doing that. Text me, okay?" I write my number on his notebook and turn to leave.

"Just meet me at the ranch tomorrow," Nick says. "Ten o'clock? I'll text you the address, and we'll figure it out from there."

Finally, I look at him, into his hazel eyes, and see his kindness and his worry. "Sure." I reach for the door handle. "Thanks, Nick."

"I hope it all works out," he says. "For Jesse's sake."

"Me too," I mutter, and shut the door behind me.

WHEN I GET HOME, I drop my bags at the door. The living room is empty, and I hear commotion in Jesse's room. He's gone from hysterical to angry, but my mind is only on one thing. My feet move so fast, I'm in my mom's office in the den before I can think of a strategic approach to the situation.

Morning light filters in through the large windows, and the strands of gray in her perfectly combed, blonde hair shimmer in the sunlight. Her glasses rest on the bridge of her nose as she stares down at the invoices spread across her desk, and she doesn't bother to notice me.

Eventually, when she's tired of me hovering, she peers up over her Neiman Marcus frames. "I thought you had a project to work on?"

"I did, until I got a hysterical call from Jesse. What the hell is Dad thinking? Are you seriously pulling him out of Sunset?"

"Your father wants to."

"And you're letting him?" I nearly screech. "Jesse's *happy* there, or doesn't that mean anything to you?"

"Hey!" she shouts. "Of course it matters to me, and watch how you speak to me." She splays her hands over her desk. "I won't let your dad him take him out of program. Calm down."

"Have you told Jesse that? He's in tears."

"No, I haven't. He's destroying his Lego jungle by now. He won't listen to me."

"So, you just let him spiral?"

"Just because I don't coddle him like you do, doesn't mean I don't care. And, don't forget for one second that *I'm* his mother, Bethany. Not you. You don't always know what's best for him, despite what you may think." She leans forward. "Maybe if you spent more time worrying about yourself and your extra-circular *activities*," she snaps, "your grades would be better, and I wouldn't have to put out *that* fire as well."

I grit my teeth, choosing my battle carefully. I know how much she hates my drinking and going out, but my free time is none of her business and I barely get any of it as it is. "If you're Mother of the Year, then why do you let Dad treat him like that?"

"Treat Jesse like what? Jesse overhead us talking and had a tantrum. I'm not rewarding that kind of behavior."

"Yeah? What about explaining it to him in a way he can understand, instead of letting him go down a black hole?"

She removes her glasses and pinches the bridge of her nose, like my very presence is an inconvenience. "Bethany—"

"*You can't do this right now*, I know." I throw my hands up.

"I have two accounts I need to close Monday. I'll deal with your brother when he calms down."

I don't bother pointing out to her that if she spent half the time with Jesse that she spends on work, he might actually like her and be less defensive. Shaking my head, I turn to leave, but I only get a few steps before I force myself to turn around again. "You'll push him away, just like you pushed me, and then you'll have no one, like Dad."

I stalk from her office and through the living room, up the stairs to Jesse's bedroom. I might be reactive when it comes to my brother, but it's better than indifference and allowing him to feel like more of an outsider than he already does.

"J?" I say, peeking my head inside his room.

"Go away," he growls, but I know he doesn't mean it. He's crouched down beside his crumbled Lego world, angry.

He can try to push me away all he likes, but unlike my parents, I won't let him. "No way. I came home to make sure you're okay and that's what I'm going to do. You called me, remember?" I step inside and take a seat on his bed. "Well, since you ruined your jungle, what are we going to work on tonight?"

"I don't care." His bottom lip pinches as he frantically puts the colored Lego pieces in piles. He's more upset with himself now for ruining his masterpiece than at my parents.

"Mom will make sure you stay with your friends, J. You don't have to worry about that, okay?"

"I don't care." He's all movements and concentration. "I *don't* . . . care." He spits out the words as he fusses over his piles, organizing the mess he's made. It's the only thing that will reel him back in—order in the chaos of his mind—so, I wait. I wait for his hands to stop fluttering over the mass of broken pieces and for his stimming sounds to cease. I wait for him to feel comfortable in his own skin again before I speak.

"If you don't care, maybe we can make a boat this time, or a house, instead of a jungle."

Jesse shakes his head and rests his chin on his knee, bent over the green Legos. He holds up a plastic palm frawn. "I want to make a jungle."

With a smile, I join him on the floor. "Sounds good, but we're adding a waterfall this time. And a unicorn."

His face scrunches. "There are no unicorns in the jungle," he says, distracted. But his mouth tugs in the corner. At least it's something.

# TWENTY
# BETHANY'S JOURNAL

## APRIL 14TH

*I'm not sure when I became this manic person on the brink of freak-out mode, but I've been feeling particularly agitated lately. The older Jesse gets and how little my parents seem to change or come around to him and his needs doesn't help. I have a feeling Nick is more the cause for my mood, though.*

*Being around him more frequently after years of awkward, off and on encounters is hard to wrap my head around. Today, he was kind, if a little grisly when I showed up at his door. We might've argued, but it felt good in a way. It needed to happen, I think. He's different when it's just us—him with me and Jesse, or just me. Different from the cocky, smirking Nick that I've run into at the movie theater when he's with a girl or when our friends meld together during summer camping* ~~trisp~~ *trips.*

*But working with him AND Sam on our project has taken things to a whole other level. I've been thinking about what happened with Mike a few years ago more than I'm comfortable with, now that the past seems to be catching up with me. Being with Mike distanced me from Jesse and my parents . . . maybe that's why I cling so tightly to my little brother. I want to make up for lost time and for Jesse to know that I will never choose a guy over him again. And I won't be like my parents who think work is more important.*

*Being with Mike also sent me into a spiral I don't like to think about—a lot of drinking and late nights, and guys I surrounded myself with because they noticed me and made me feel something other than pain. A lot of wandering and darkness, but thank God for Anna Marie, my saving grace and the devil on my shoulder. She cared more than anyone else did.*

*The night I called Mike and heard Sam's voice in the background was the night my heart was shredded in two. It went from "Sam and I are just friends" to the gut-wrenching truth that came pouring of out of him when I started to freak out. Something in him snapped and he laid it all out there, not a single grain of sugar to coat the truth. Yes, he'd been with Sam. Yes, he was seeing us both. He was also tired of high school girls and their needy emotions. He'd spent over a year telling me I was important to him and that my parents shouldn't treat me like garbage, only for him to discard me the moment I was no longer worth his time and energy.*

*I wanted to blame Sam for it all. I did, for a while. She was the other woman. She'd ruined everything, and that's why I maliciously flirted with Reilly last summer during our camping trip. I knew it would piss her off, even if they weren't together. Despite what I can only imagine she's been through after losing her dad, she got her happily ever after.*

*If only my parents would move on too. They never cared that I was devastated about Mike, only that my grades were slipping, among other responsibilities—yet another reason my dad is permanently disappointed in me, even if my mom is the one who hurt me the most. Her calling me a slut one night when I came home drunk has stuck with me ever since.*

*Last year, at the Hughes holiday party, I realized for the first time that Sam not might not have been the conniving bitch I thought she was. Maybe she was just a gullible teenager, like I'd been. If Mac's words from that night are all I have to go on, then I'm supposed to be the bad guy in all of this. Go figure.*

*So, yeah, I guess being around Nick and Sam . . . it's not something I want to do but needs to be done. Especially if I'm going to get through the next month. -B*

# TWENTY-ONE
# BETHANY

SUNDAY MORNING FEELS like a fresh start. I'm not sure if it's the sunshine or the fact that I crashed last night after work and slept like a rock for the first time in forever. Or, maybe it's because Jesse is at a play date with one of the kids from his program, acting like eleven-year-olds generally do.

Sunshine and happiness aside, driving up the dirt road, toward the boarding facility, it finally *really* hits me that I'm not just working on this project with Nick, which is a minefield of its own, but I'm working with Sam on this, too. And, it's on her turf. My palms are sweating, thinking about it, but if Nick's right, technically, this will be an easy project, and if I allow myself to hope just a little bit, it might even be fun.

Pulling up the drive, I take in the vast ranch surrounding me. It's impressive, with a large stable and a menagerie of horse heads and rumps sticking out of the stalls. There's a pasture with a gray horse, grazing, and a stately white farmhouse with navy blue trim, situated opposite of it all.

I park my Rover next to Nick's Explorer and climb out, notebook and pencil in hand. *Sam runs all of this?* Her dad was somewhat of a legend in Saratoga Falls, a renowned horseman that I'd seen a couple times at the County Fair growing up. I remember the buzz around the accident and being sad for her, even if I hated her at the time. It's only now, though, being at her home secluded up on the mountain, that I can almost feel the loss of him.

A lukewarm breeze hits my face, and I smell dirt and nature, and I hear birds chirping and chickens clucking somewhere off in the distance. The ranch is its own world, and I can't even imagine what it's been like for Sam to take over this place. It's admirable, even.

Since Sam and Nick are nowhere in sight, I follow the sound of drilling, coming from the barn. Banjo and harmonica riffs meet my ears along with it, and I know I've found Nick. Creedence Clearwater Revival is one of his favorite bands. I know this from many summers being in the periphery of his life.

I weave between buildings, imagining how much Jesse might like to visit a place like this one day. He'd love the horses and animals, maybe all of it a little over-stimulating, but in a good way for once, I think.

The barn looks like the oldest building on the property, perhaps the only original structure that's left, and I admire how rustic it is, how rich in history it might be and the possibilities of what we can do with it.

Lingering in the blinding yet rejuvenating sunlight a moment longer, I let it soak through me for a final dose of serenity, before I step into what could potentially be the definition of a bad situation.

I walk through the large open doorway. There's nothing inside that would warrant the leathery scent that fills my nostrils, but I inhale deeply. It's a little musty, but I like it, strange as it is to me. There are tools in some areas, fresh wood and building materials in others, but other than that, the space is relatively empty of anything resembling a barn. It's a big space, though. Large enough to house a few tractors, and definitely large enough to transform into an office space.

Finally, my eyes rest on Nick, standing on a ladder and drilling something into the skylight a few yards away. His back is to me as he whistles to the radio, unaware of my presence, and I enjoy the clandestine moment.

With his arms extended above him, his abdomen shows just enough to elicit my appreciation and a fleeting curiosity of what his skin would feel like against my fingertips. He shifts his weight to his other foot and his arms strain against the sleeves of his t-shirt, his muscles flexing.

"See something you like?"

I spin around to find Sam behind me. Her eyes, the color of chestnut and whiskey, shift from Nick to me. I swallow, imagining my face the color of a ripe tomato. "Uh—hi," I say automatically. "Just checking the place out."

Sam lifts a delicate eyebrow. She's petite and pixie-like with her wild blonde hair and tanned skin, but the look in her eyes is prudent, like she's seen a hundred lifetimes over the years, and the set of her jaw makes her surprisingly formidable, too.

Sam shoves her hands in her back pockets and steps a little closer. "It's obvious you like him," she says, though I barely hear her over the sound of the drill. "So why do you play games with him all the time?"

"I don't play games," I say quickly, a dozen other, more self-preserving replies come to mind, but I grip my notebook more tightly instead. "I . . . it's complicated." The years of wondering and wishing things were different make my true feelings difficult to separate. I'm not sure I do like him, or if it's the idea of him.

To my relief, Sam lets it go. "So," she says, gesturing to the space. "This will be my new office."

"It's a good size," I say, easily slipping into design mode. "Do you mind if I ask what you used it for before the remodel?"

"Well . . ." Sam gazes around, like she's trying to remember. "The back corner was old stalls that were rotted out. They were holding old tractor parts and rusted tools that were my grandpa's, which Papa was holding onto." I glance from the corner of the

133

room to her face, wondering if it's difficult for her to speak of her dad.

"And this area," she continues, gesturing to the middle of the barn, "had my dad's old John Deere that didn't run. Nick pieced out the parts and sold it for me so we could use the space. And, over here," she says, gesturing to the area where Nick's installing the windows in the pitched ceiling. "This is where we were storing most of the horse feed. We've moved it all to the stables though, which is working out better," she muses. "Anyway, that's the gist. Reilly helped Nick with all the demo, but the biggest challenge so far, was Nick replacing the load bearing support beams that were rotting."

"Yeah, this place looks pretty old, but the bones seem good."

Sam nods, admiring the transformed space. "Yeah, I'm really happy with it. Other than a few spots on the roof that need some mending, which Reilly is taking care of, it's just about done."

I nod, but my mind is swirling with possibilities. Rustic chic, antique accents, and understated furniture. "I really like the old windows up there, it looks great." I meet Nick's gaze, and he winks. Remembering his taut abs, I flush and clear my throat. "So," I say, jotting down inconsequential notes, "what are your must-haves for the space? That will make it easier for me to wrap my mind around this."

"Well . . . " Sam tucks a stray wave of hair behind her ear and peers around. "I know I need a desk."

When she doesn't say much else, I smile. It's clear this isn't Sam's forte, which gives me a bit of a confidence booster. "Are you worried about privacy or sectioning areas off? I'm not sure what exactly you'll be using the space for."

"Meetings with boarders, and my stepmom will be out here, working on accounting. I know this space is bigger than we need, but it seemed like the perfect opportunity to get all of the crap that's taking over the house out here. Plus, I want us to look more professional. We have twelve boarders now, and I hate them having to call the house number or come inside if they need something and I'm not out here."

"Got it. Are you thinking you'd like to keep it practical and open? Maybe an open floor plan?"

"That's kind of what I imagined."

I walk over to the loft to check out the stairs. "I'm thinking maybe we use the loft for the bookkeeping—it's separate, but it's still open, too. Nick might have to run additional wiring up there, but it could be done." I quickly sketch the layout of the barn, wondering how we should use the open floor plan to suit Sam best.

"I like that," she says, staring down at my sketch. "I think Alison will too."

"Do you have any décor themes in mind—a style you're partial to?"

Sam shrugs. "I have a few things I've bookmarked. I'll send them to you. I like simple, and I stay away from shiny things. Alison would be a better person to ask. She's not as excited about all of this as I am, but she knows what she likes. She'll be more helpful than I will. She already has a running list—no dirt floor and definitely an air conditioning system of sorts for the summertime. Reilly's working on ventilation instead, but Alison is skeptical. And the concrete floors are going in next week, I think." Sam shrugs. "Anyway, she's the picky one."

Sam glances around at the space, and I can't help addressing the elephant in the room. Holding my notebook up to my chest, I look at Sam and steel my nerves. "About Reilly . . . Sam, the whole thing last summer—"

She puts her hand up and squeezes her eyes shut in a silent plea. "I don't want to talk about any of that," she says. "This"— she extends her arm in a brief wave around the room—"is manageable for me. I'm not, however, good with—" she gestures between us.

"Ladies," Nick says lazily as he climbs down the ladder. "Glad to see there's no fur flying in the air or claws out."

We both glare at him, and he holds his palms up. "Aye! 'Twas only a joke."

"We were just talking about what to do with the space," I say, choosing a more neutral topic.

"And," Sam says, glancing between us, "I have to jump on a call, so you guys let me know what your plan is and what you need me to do. Nick, you should wrangle Alison in at some point, she should have a say." With a quick turn on her heel, she heads out of the barn. "Make good choices!" she calls over her shoulder, and Nick salutes her.

When he looks at me, wood shavings clinging to his shirt and dust smudging his face, I smile. His eyes are more green than brown in the sun, filtering in through the skylight, and I wonder if he knows how sexy he is.

I decide that's a firm *no* when he smacks his chewing gum with a grin, completely oblivious, and steps closer. "So, that seemed to go well enough." He rests his hands on his hips, amusement bright in his eyes. "I didn't want to interrupt you two, but my arms were about to fall off, tightening those screws over and over again."

Laughing, I shake my head. "No, it definitely wasn't as horrible as I would've thought," I admit. "But I wouldn't say we're on hugging terms or anything."

"Ha! You never will be. Sam isn't a hugger. Not really. That's Mac. You know you're 'in' with Mac when you get a hug." He spits his gum out in the trashcan by the door.

"I can see that about Mac, but don't worry, I won't hold my breath for that, either."

Nick casts me a sidelong glance, a sparkle of something mischievous or knowing in his eyes, but he doesn't say anything. Instead, his gaze shifts to my lips, lingering. The *something* that lives in the air between us at all times is sometimes impossible to ignore, and letting it hang in the silence is more than I can handle right now. Being this close to him, seeing him here in his element with the easygoing air I've always admired about him, is too much, too, and it makes it easy to forget why I'm here in the first place.

"I'm sorry about yesterday," I blurt. "I know we didn't get much work done. I left kind of abruptly, but I'll make it up to you. You've already done so much—" I peer around, imagining the barn before. "I have a lot of catching up to do."

"Don't worry about it," he says, kicking at a stray piece of hay. "I hope everything worked out okay. You seemed pretty upset."

I stare out through one of the old, single-paned windows, like there's something more noteworthy outside than the concern on Nick's face. "Yeah, it's fine."

"Are you sure about that?" I notice him reaching for my face from the corner of my eye, and my eyes dart to him. I'm not sure if it's possible to pale while your cheeks burn, but my eyes widen, and his mouth quirks up in the corner.

"You have something in your hair," he says quietly and gently plucks a flake of sawdust or straw from it, but I don't notice which. It's not important, not when his eyes are locked on mine and the silence grows.

"There he is," Reilly calls, causing me to jump. I spin around as he steps into the barn. His smile is wide, and he lifts his chin at Nick before his eyes shift to me. "Hey, Bethany." Reilly's easy expression never falters.

With a tightlipped smile, I nod a hello and offer him a quick wave of uncertainty, knowing the last time I saw him I was laying the flirting on pretty strong.

"I figured I'd find you riding out in the pasture," he says with a face-engulfing grin.

"Yeah right," Nick mutters.

Reilly glances at me. "Nick's petrified of riding," he explains with a smile. "But you didn't hear it from me."

Nick glowers but Reilly ignores him. "So," he says, "did you get the breakfast I left for you yesterday?"

"What?" Nick's eyes widen. "No. Sam said you ate it all."

Reilly winks. "I did. I was just screwing with you."

"Not cool, Rye."

With a chuckle, Reilly rests his palm against a support post, leaning his weight against it. Then, he looks at me again. "You here to keep this guy on track?"

"No, not at all," I say easily, impressed with all they've done already. "I'm in awe, actually. I saw the before photos, and it looks amazing in here. You guys have done a really great job so far."

"Thanks. It's mostly Nick. I'm in charge of the Honey Do List." Reilly chuckles and looks up at the new skylights. "They look legit."

While the guys chat back and forth, I can only think of how strange all of this is. Maybe it's the high schooler in me, but I'm standing in a room with two guys I've always known about but never really *known*, and it's surreal to be a temporary fixture in their circle.

*So, this is what is feels like . . .*

## TWENTY-TWO
# NICK

I PULL up to the curb outside my apartment and glance into the rearview mirror as Bethany pulls her Rover up behind me. She gets out of her car, hauling her book bag over her shoulder. I try and fail not to notice how good she looks in a simple yellow dress and sandals. I didn't tell her at the ranch that she'll likely regret that next time she's up there working. I was too distracted, staring at her legs the whole time, but I make a mental note to tell her, eventually.

With a smirk, I open the door and get out of the Explorer. "Fancy seeing you here," I say and collect my thermos and flannel jacket from the backseat.

She runs her pale-pink, painted fingernails through her hair. "Yeah. Are you sure you want to spend the rest of your Sunday working on this? You already spent your morning at Sam's and—"

"Bethany," I say, climbing up the stairs to the second floor. Her footsteps are quiet compared to mine. "You don't have to feel bad. It's my project too."

"Yeah, well, you've already done so much."

"For another project that I *have* to do. I'm not making you do Murray's final on your own." Plus, I want to spend time with her.

Pushing away all the reasons that's a foolhardy idea, I find my house key, deciding to let the cards fall where they may.

When we reach the landing, Casey's standing outside her door, two apartments down from mine. Her brown hair is braided on both sides, and her favorite doll is clutched under her arm. When she sees me, her eyes light up. "Nick!"

"Hey, squirt." I flash her a big, toothy grin.

Casey takes in the sight of Bethany. "Hello," she chirps, and she seems almost mesmerized.

"Hi, cutie," Bethany says in a voice reserved for little kids. "That's a very pretty doll you have there."

"She's my favorite," Casey explains. "Her name is Pickles."

Bethany's eyes widen. "Oh?"

"Yep! Nick named her for me."

I burst with laughter, more than amused by the look on Bethany's face, as I unlock my front door. "What can I say? Pickles are my favorite."

"They're mine too," Casey explains.

"For now," Colton mutters as he steps outside. He glances between Bethany and me and pulls the door shut. "Hey there."

"Hi, I'm Bethany." She waves slightly.

"Colton," he says. "And this munchkin here is Casey."

Casey waves shyly at Bethany, like she's awed or nervous, and I can't help but love the kid all the more for her innocence. "You look like Cinderella."

"I do?" Bethany peers down at her sundress as she smooths it down a little. "The cinder girl or the princess version?" she asks wryly, though her insecurity is lost on Casey.

I can't help but chuckle as I set my stuff inside the door.

"Uh . . ." Casey considers Bethany's question seriously. She glances between her face and her clothes. "Both, I think."

"Well, I hope that's a good thing," Bethany mutters.

Colton shoves his wallet into his back pocket. "It is."

"Yep! Yep! Yep!" Casey's head bounces with the syllable.

"She's my second favorite Disney Princess in the whole world." She displays a number two with her fingers.

"I see. Well, in that case, thank you very much, Casey. It was lovely to meet you."

Colton takes her hand. "Come on Casey baby, we don't want to make Cal angry for being late."

"Oh boy, family dinner with the Carmichaels? That's going to be . . . fun."

Casey nods emphatically. "We're having spaghetti."

"Yep, and it's going to be gone if we don't get there on time," Colton warns. "You two kids have fun." He looks at Bethany. "It was nice to meet you."

"You too," she says with a little wave at both of them, and we watch father and daughter hurry away.

"Grandpa Cal would never be mad at me." Casey's chirps carry on the breeze as they make their way down the stairs.

"Yeah, I know. Lucky."

I laugh at Colton's reply and head inside my cold apartment.

"She's cute." Bethany wraps her arms around her middle as she steps into the icebox.

"Yeah, she's a kick." I flick the lights on and hand her one of my sweatshirts from the laundry basket. "It's clean, I promise."

She lifts a playful eyebrow but accepts it. "Thanks."

"This place stays pretty cool, so when I don't let the sun in during the day it's a bit chilly. I'll get the fire going. The sun's going down soon."

"You don't have to do that—"

"It's gas and gets the living room warm in seconds. Trust me, you want the fireplace on." I pull off one boot and tuck it out of the way by the door.

Bethany doesn't argue. Instead, she sets her bags on the couch and checks her phone. It's a habit of hers, I've noticed. She keeps it on her at all times and looks at it regularly. I have a feeling Jesse has something to do with that.

"So . . ." She drops her phone on to the couch cushion. "Your neighbor's dating Mac, huh? It makes sense, I've seen them together at Lick's."

"Yep." I pull off my other boot then walk to the kitchen. "They've been dating since Christmas. He works at Cal's, that's how they all met."

"Is that complicated—them working together and him being your neighbor?"

"Not anymore." I set my thermos on the counter, glad Mac and Colton figured their shit out. It was getting awkward there for a minute. "You can set up shop at the table." I nod to my small-ass dining room and set my bag in the chair.

"Great. Do you want me to order a pizza or something? I'm getting a little hungry."

"Actually, that sounds mouthwatering right now."

She smiles and picks up her phone. "I can't believe you named her doll Pickles," she mutters, and I like the easiness and amusement in her voice, and that I put it there. Then, her eyes shift to me with a measure of concern. "You don't by chance put pickles on your *pizza*, do you?"

I bark out a laugh. "No, I don't, but now that you mention it, I'm not sure why. Maybe I should try it."

"Maybe we should get two pizzas."

"I'm kidding. If you can live with pepperoni and olives, we'll be golden."

The corner of her mouth lifts. "That's what I usually get—sometimes with mushrooms for Jesse."

"Cool," I say, though it's more than cool, it's perfect. She rubs the backs of her sweater-clad arms, then types into her phone. "It should warm up quickly. But here's a blanket in the meantime." I grab the throw draped over the other end of the sectional and walk it over to her until I'm so close, her perfume fills my nostrils, like I've stepped into a candy shop.

"Thank you." Her gaze shifts to me, and she takes the blanket.

Her gray eyes are so soft and captivating in the shadows of the room, I feel the rumble of something more dangerous than flirting awaken inside me.

"Uh, yeah, you order the pizza," I say, turning for my room. "I'm going to jump in the shower."

## TWENTY-THREE
# BETHANY

MY NECK ACHES, and I cringe as I stir awake. Though I'm sitting upright, I'm in a cocoon of warmth and in a semiconscious haze that tries to pull me back to sleep. But my neck . . .

When my eyes finally open, a half-eaten pizza blurs into focus on the coffee table, project notes, blue prints, and photos strewn around it. The fire in the hearth is still blazing, lighting the room, and I realize I fell asleep. I half expect to find Nick's left me on the couch and gone to bed, but I register his steady breathing and find he's asleep beside me.

I glance around the room as everything in my mind's eye sharpens. I have no idea how long I've been asleep, but when I see the microwave clock reads nine-forty, I figure I'm an hour away from dirty looks and condemnation from my parents, when I get home.

My eyes find Nick again on their own accord, and a claw of panic rakes over me. My instinct is to sneak away before he wakes up and things get awkward, but the subliminal part of me—the part that feels curiosity and desire—keeps me just as I am, only inches away, admiring him despite myself.

*You're bordering on dangerous,* I tell myself. But I can't look away. Nick's face is almost bronze in the low light of the room, and my gaze traces the scruff shadowing the outline of his jaw, appreciating the masculinity of it. I've only ever seen him freshly shaven, and my fingertips are itching to feel the roughness of his skin. I imagine how his perfect lips draw up into a contagious smile—it's so Nick, so carefree, and it intimidates me in ways I've never understood.

Daring to close my eyes, I lean in and inhale the scent of wood and male skin. I know now without a doubt that I'm neck-deep in an impossible situation. Nick and I are oxygen to a flame, combustible and all-consuming. Whether it's hatred or desire, the end result would be the same. He would ruin me, and I'm barely holding on as it is.

"That tickles." He rasps the words, and my heart gallops. Lazily, he peels one eye open.

I'm too close, too obvious. I've been busted. "I was checking to see if you're awake," I whisper, but only because I can barely find my voice.

Nick peels his other eye open, and if I'm not mistaken, there's a self-satisfied gleam in them. He tugs slightly on my hair, and when I look down between us, he's playing with the ends that brush against his bare arm.

"Sorry," I breathe, and when I meet his gaze again, it's fixed on me, soft but focused. Searching and leaving me feeling exposed.

Just as I'm about to lean away and put some distance between us, he presses his mouth to mine, a bit roughly, as if impulse compelled him to, but I don't move.

His kiss is entrancing, casting a spell over me, and I can't keep my eyes open. A weightlessness, that feels a lot like relief, floods my senses and I kiss him back.

Despite my racing heartbeat, any apprehension I have fades when his palm cradles my cheek, warm and strong and surprisingly soft. My mind melts along with my body, becoming a malleable heap beside him to do with as he wills. *This* is right. This is perfection. Our muddled history dissolves to nothing. He pulls me closer, kissing me more deeply.

I've never felt so calm and ravenous at once, but I know I want more from him than I should. I'm overreaching. I'm setting myself up for disappointment and something too closely resembling another heartache. I can feel it as I let him in.

My hair falls in a veil over us as I lean closer, letting him consume me. All that exists in the room with us is a burning need and the crackle of the fire. I grab hold of his biceps and urge him even closer, down and over the top of me. I want to feel his warmth and weight against my body.

Our chests heave together, and I run my hands through his hair. His groan makes my fingers greedy and my body hum. I want to feel him alive and virile and like he's mine, just for a little while.

"Wait, what are we doing?" he rasps against my mouth, then pulls away. Nick leans back against the cushion. He scrubs his hand over his face, and his chest rises and falls as he tries to catch his breath. "This is a bad idea."

My lusty haze diminishes, and the warning signs I've been ignoring begin to flash again. The warmth of the room becomes a cold vacuum, assaulting my exposed skin. The burn of rejection and my erratically racing heart feels too much like I've lost control, and I can't allow that right now. There's too much at stake —it's too similar to shadows of my past.

I shake my head and rake my fingers through my hair. "You're right," I breathe. "That was the stupidest thing we could've done." I rest my elbows on my thighs and let out a deep breath.

Nick leans forward as well. "I don't know about the stupidest, but—"

"I'm gonna go," I say quickly and hurry to my feet. I start shoving all my notes and the project materials into my bag, no rhyme or reason to any of it.

"Hey, wait." Nick reaches for my arm. "Don't go yet."

I laugh desperately. "Why not, we're clearly done working."

"Because," he says, peering up at me, his green eyes shimmering in the flickering firelight. "We have to make whatever this is between us work. Don't run away and make it weirder and more complicated than it already is." He runs his thumb over my arm, a reassuring gesture that only makes staying more difficult.

I pull my arm away. "You're right, things are definitely weird and complicated, but my staying won't change that, Nick," I admit. "It was an impulsive kiss, probably something we needed to get out of our system. But, it *is* late and I need to get home. We have class tomorrow."

"I think you know it's more than just an impulsive kiss."

"Whatever it was, you were right." I haul my bag strap over my shoulder. I'm not going to get mixed up with Nick, not now when I have enough to deal with. "We shouldn't have done that."

"That's not what I said."

"You know what I mean."

Nick shakes his head. "Why do you think it's like this with us?" he asks, eyes fixed on my arm where he held it. "Being drawn together only for you to push me away." Finally, his gaze shifts to me, expectant.

"Push you away? You make it sound like I'm playing games with you all the time or something. You ended that kiss, Nick, not me. And I need to focus on graduation right now. I can't keep falling into this trap." I know Nick isn't Mike, but the risk with Nick is even greater, I know it, deep down in my bones, and I *cannot* do that again. "I have more to lose this time," I remind myself.

Nick's expression hardens. "We already discussed this. You make a lot of assumptions about me—I'm not like Mike."

"I'm not saying you are but—" I turn to face him fully, my patience thinning. "What is this between us, Nick?"

"I don't know. I wish I did, so that it would stop haunting me."

"Exactly. We're not ready for this, not right now."

"Speak for yourself," he bites out. "I think we should see what happens."

"What—why? In what world is *us* a good idea?" His friends don't like me, I barely like them, and Nick knows next to nothing about me. Then there's Savannah who's "not" his girlfriend.

"What's the alternative, ignoring whatever this tension is between us?"

"We've been doing it for this long," I say with what patience and willpower I have left.

"Yeah, and look where it's gotten us." His gaze is fixed on me, pinning me in place and willing me to see his point of view, and I do, which is why I know anything more between us is a risk.

"Fine, then. *I'm* not ready for this. I don't have room in my life for the outcome of a *see-what-happens* relationship."

Nick's brow furrows. "So, what, you've already got it in your head that it won't work? Instead of trying, you're going keep surrounding yourself with douchebags, like the one in the bar the other night?"

"Just because you don't know Ryan, doesn't mean he's a douchebag, Nick. Stop assuming you know *me*." His judgement only magnifies the years of narrowed looks and snide comments he's made. That my parents have made. That all Nick's friends have always made. They don't know me, and I'm tired of everyone assuming that they do.

Nick shakes his head and groans. "God, this is so dysfunction-al," he says with a laugh. "And I thought I was always the level-headed one. Yet here I am, trying to *convince* you to, what, go out with me?" He laughs and leans back on the couch. "I didn't see this coming."

Nick's words are like a prick to my heart and my ego. Does he even know what dysfunction looks like?

"Then let me spare you the hassle of worrying about *any* sort of dysfunctional relationship with me," I say and open the front door.

"Let's just focus on being partners and getting through this with our sanity intact, shall we?" I don't bother looking back at him as I shut the door behind me. He's right, this is dysfunctional and I have enough of that in my life, I don't need Nick thrown in the mix, too.

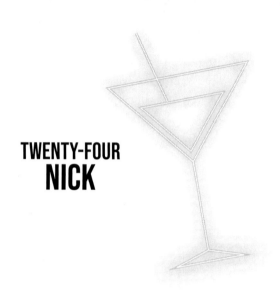

# TWENTY-FOUR
# NICK

"LET'S see which one of you can tell me the difference between modern and postmodern architecture in two sentences or less." Professor Murray glances around the room expectantly. A few people raise their hands, but he calls on Bethany.

"All right, Miss Fairchild, why don't you take a stab at it."

She taps her pen against her notepad, a tick I've noticed since our first class together. "Uh, well," she starts, clearly searching her memory for the answer. "Modern architecture was dominant after World War II through the 20th century, and incorporated new construction technologies, like reinforced steel and glass. *Post*modern architecture expanded the movement, introducing a more high-tech aspect."

"And," Professor Murray drawls, "what do you mean by high-tech, exactly?"

I'm not sure why Bethany always seems to look like a deer in the headlights of an oncoming car when the professor singles her out, but she does. You'd think after four years of lectures and classes she'd be over it by now. She always knows the answers, even if she has to think about them for a second first.

"Uh," she starts again, tapping her pen more fervently, "architecture wasn't just about the exterior, but the interior too—the steel and glass and concrete all became a major part of interior design in postmodernism, not something ugly that was meant to be hidden. At least in larger buildings. It was more 'outside of the box' design, so to speak."

"And the year of this transition to postmodernism?" he quizzes her.

I see a twinkle in her eye this time. "It's a gray area, Professor Murray. We're not exactly sure. It's a bridge more than a *new* era of design."

I'm not sure if it's amusement I see playing on the professor's features or surprise. Maybe a little of both. He nods then addresses the rest of the class. "Who can tell me which major architects played a role in this *bridge* Miss Fairchild speaks of?"

Hands go up, but I can't look away from Bethany. She stares down at her notes, doodling and no longer paying attention. Half the time it's like she's not even present in class. Like she doesn't even want to be in here, but I know how important her grade is to her, even if she doesn't seem to show it all the time.

She glances at me from the corner of her eye. When she finds me watching her, she blinks and looks away, but I can't.

All I can think about is last night and how it felt to have her in my apartment and in my arms—to feel her warmth and how real she is when she's always seemed so far out of reach.

I'm not sure if it was calling her dysfunctional or simply the tug and pull of being in the same room, but I saw something in her —a pain and anger that gave me pause.

Bethany is a whirlwind, to say the least, and I'm not sure what sort of mess I'd be getting myself into if something did happen between us, more than just a kiss, but I think I actually hurt her feelings last night, and I can't live with that.

Knowing I will have Wednesday nights and Saturdays to make it up to her over the next few weeks makes me feel a little better. Despite her walls, I'm not ready to give up on her completely. That desperation in her, the quietness mixed with the passion and fury that I sometimes see, is enough to hook me in, wanting to know more. Wanting to *see* more of the real Bethany. Needing too so that I'll really know what it is about her that I can't seem to live without, if anything at all.

She glances at me again, and I know I've been staring way too long. I should be more embarrassed than I am. Her eyes linger on me for a few more seconds, and I purse my lips and nod some sort of awkward greeting, the only thing I can think to do as I sit up in my seat. I have no idea how I'm going to get through the next few weeks, but I better figure it out.

I ARRIVE in Saratoga Falls after my last class of the day, with a half hour to spare before I need to be at my parents' for dinner. So, I decide to visit Mac. She's more removed from the Bethany situation than Sam is, and I could use her advice. Even if I think I know what I want, I also know I'm walking a fine line between possible stupidity and liberation after years of pent up curiosity.

When I walk into Cal's Auto, the doorbell dings but Colton and Mac barely notice me as they engage in an animated conversation at her desk.

"I know she's a pain, but you're the best guy for the job. You could run circles around Bobby with this one." Her perfectly straight, dark hair brushes against the middle of her back as she turns to look at me. "I'll be right with—" Her face lights up when she sees me, and I know instantly that it was the right decision to come here.

With exaggerated adoration, she clasps her hands against her heart, her green eyes smiling. "Oh, my love, where have you been all my life?" Mac steps out from behind her desk and hurries over to me, high heels clacking against the tile, and she throws her arms around my neck and kisses my cheek. Her lips are glossy, as usual.

"Gross," I mutter.

"Oh, you love it." Mac wipes away the sticky remnants.

"Hey now," Colton mutters, but his blue eyes twinkle with amusement.

I shrug. "What can I say? The ladies love me."

"Clearly," Colton says, shaking his head. "She never hugs me like that." He lifts a dark eyebrow.

"Lies," she tells him with a playful shush. Not for the first time, I realize how much I like them together.

"Hmm." His mouth quirks in an almost imperceptible smile. Colton's dry, reserved humor is an equal match to her lively banter. He's patient and thoughtful, while she's a pistol, to say the least. Then again, everything Mac is and does is fierce, making Colton one of the luckiest men alive to have her undying love and loyalty.

"Well, I *am* pretty irresistible," I tell him.

Mac bats my shoulder. "Don't get a big head, now. You'll make me look bad." She takes a step back, all seriousness now with squinty eyes as she studies me. "Now, Nicholas Turner, you rarely come visit me at work, especially lately . . . Is everything okay?" She asks it hesitantly.

"Yeah, fine-ish."

"Uh-oh," she says, hands on her hips.

"That's my cue." Colton salutes me. "See ya, Nick."

"Wait!" Mac hurries back to her desk for a sheet of paper. "You didn't think I'd forgotten, did you?" She holds it up with a smirk. "Chop. Chop."

He takes the paper with a sigh. "You owe me big," he grumbles.

With a shoulder lift, Mac winks at him. A grin pulls at his lips again as he heads back into the shop, leaving Mac and I alone in the office with the mechanical, high-pitched sounds of the warehouse echoing into the room.

"So, I take it life is good?" I ask her, unable to resist a smile.

She shuts the door to the shop, closing us inside.

Though it's been four months or so, it seems like it was yesterday that Mac's dad told her to do some soul searching. I've missed her living on my couch, and the pure entertainment in watching her and Colton trying to decide if they even liked each other.

"Yes, life *is* good, actually. Who knew my dad was such a sage, old man?"

"It's not weird being with Colton and working together?"

"No, it's nice, actually." She points to the chair by the window for me to sit. "I get to see him every day, but he still gets 'Casey time' when he has her at his place. Things are pretty perfect, for now." She crosses her arms over her chest and leans back against her desk. "But you didn't come here to talk to me about Colton. So, spill. What's brought you onto my turf?" She puts her palm up. "And before you ask me, I will not move back in with you. I can't handle your snoring."

"I don't snore. You do."

Mac laughs. "Fine, a soft, dainty snore, *sometimes*. I'll grant you that. But still, I know you miss me, and as much as I love you, I'm happy to be on my own, thank you very much."

I shake my head with a mock sigh. "You really are a dream crusher."

"That's what's on my name tag," she mutters and nods to the two chairs again in the pseudo-waiting area by the large window. "Now, sit."

Frowning, I glance from her to the chair. "That feels too much like a therapy session. I have my mom for that."

Mac chuckles softly. "And given your new project partner, a session or two would be a bad thing?"

"Sam told you, huh?"

"And Colton told me Bethany was at your house," she adds.

"Damn this town," I grumble and take a seat. Something tells me this won't be a quick in and out, so I might as well get comfortable.

Mac plops down in the other wingback chair with a euphoric groan. The leather creaks as she settles in. "Fine, suit yourself, but I've been running around like a madwoman all day. These heels are killing me." She toes them off, and I recognize what she's doing—giving me time to gather my thoughts and muster up the nerve to tell her whatever it is I've come to say. That's what comes with twenty years of friendship, and I appreciate the hell out of her for it.

"I need help with her," I blurt out. "With Bethany. I need help thinking this through."

Mac leans back in her seat. "Hey, no judgement from me." She eyes me, though, waiting for me to continue.

"She's—we're—" I don't know where to start, exactly. "Ever since New Year's, things have been complicated."

Mac snorts. "Things've *always* been complicated between you."

I lift an eyebrow.

"Sorry. That's not helpful. Continue." She clasps her hands together and sets them in her lap for dramatics.

"Fine then, more complicated than usual," I revise. "Except, I realize now that everything that's happened over the years is way more complicated than I thought—so many assumptions."

"Oh?"

I nod. "The high school party, Denny's, our run-ins over the years. I don't even know what other stories she has in her mind that keep her at a distance all the time. She has so many walls," I realize.

"Trying to get along, I get," Mac says. "But, you seem very concerned with her letting you in all of the sudden." She leans closer. "Which means you've invested something," she says slowly, like she's working out the kinks—filling in the holes. "You really like her all of the sudden—wait, did you guys kiss?"

When I don't say anything, her eyes widen. "You kissed her?" I can't tell if Mac is amused or horrified.

"Well, yeah. It sorta just happened. I stopped it, though, so it's not like it went further than that."

Mac squeezes her eyes shut. "Hold on a sec. You kissed her and then put a stop to it, and now you don't understand why she's putting up walls?"

I look at her dumbly. "Well, yeah. I guess."

She chuckles again, more animated this time, like she knows a secret as she massages the bottom of her foot. "This is where guys and girls are clearly different. If *I* were at a guy's house and he kissed me, then pushed me away, I'd put up a few walls, too. I'd likely take it personally and feel rejected, especially if he didn't take the time to explain *why* he kissed me and then pushed me away." Her eyes meet mine.

I want to tell Mac that I put more thought into my reaction, but the truth is, I didn't. It was honest and it just came out the way it did, whatever it was I said.

When I don't say anything, Mac leans forward, her gaze leveled on me. "Look, Nick, you said yourself, you have a history with Bethany. And, in reality, you barely know her. You need to be friends before you screw things up worse than they already are by jumping into something that could blow up in your face, permanently this time." She pauses. "You need to trust each other so that you're no longer operating on the misunderstandings of the past."

She lets her words sink in for a minute, but I already know Mac's right. It's one of the downfalls of not having a sibling as a sounding board and always relying on my friends to talk me through everything. Getting out of my head helps me to see everything differently.

"This is what happened between Colton and me," she continues. "You saw what a shit-show it was. We totally missed the friends-first step, and the first six-plus months we knew each other were based on assumptions, and bad ones, at that. I'm now one hundred percent pro friends-first. And I know you, your feelings for her aren't going to fade until you've exhausted them. They've been percolating too long. So, you might as well embrace it, but just be smart. You've got the perfect opportunity with this whole project situation, especially if she's trying to keep her distance. Take your time. Get to know each other. You owe it to yourself so that you can move the fuck on if it doesn't work out in the end and you can say you actually tried."

Mac's right. Mac is always right about these things, just like she was right about Sam and Reilly needing each other again to move on with their lives. I won't be able to let whatever exists between Bethany and me go until I know what it actually is.

"So, what are you going to do?" she asks.

"Try to be friends," I say. "Make a grand gesture." Though, I don't even know where to start.

## TWENTY-FIVE
# BETHANY

I'M PUTTING a fresh load of laundry in the washing machine, when I hear the doorbell.

"Jesse, can you get that please!" I shout toward the living room. "It's probably Mrs. Franklin, picking up the Goodwill from Mom." I pour the detergent into the tray and listen as Jesse barrels down the stairs. "The bag is by the door!"

Slamming the washer shut, I press the digital timer and head back into the kitchen to wash my hands.

"Hey, kid." Nick's familiar voice carries in from the doorway, and my heart skips a beat.

"Hi," Jesse replies, and I hear the door shut. "My sister's in the kitchen."

"Cool. Nice digs you guys got here."

"It's all right." Jesse's voice is so small compared to Nick's, and I watch them in the foyer. The fact that Nick is in my house is strange, and part of me wonders if I should be angry that he assumed he could show up uninvited, especially after what happened the other day. He knows I want to focus on this partnership. But another, bigger part of me is surprisingly grateful he came by. Especially after I had to cancel and didn't think I was going to see him tonight.

"How'd you know where we lived?" Jesse asks as they step into the kitchen.

"A friend told me."

My gaze meets his as I wipe my hands off on a towel.

He lifts three bags. "I come bearing gifts," he says, sounding uncertain, even if his voice is light and his expression easy. "A peace offering for the other night," he adds. "You brought coffee the other day, so I figured I could bring some food since I'm crashing your movie night."

I smile at the gesture. "Thank you." I've been thinking about our kiss and the argument we had, nonstop, but no matter how I looked at it, things would remain awkward and complicated. Yet, here Nick is, somehow able to make all that uncertainty go away, for now.

His true Nick smile falls back into place. "I hope you like BLTs and cheeseburgers. I got both from Harley's Diner on my way over. I wasn't sure what you guys might want. I even got a salad, in case grease or meat aren't really your thing." He sets the bags on the island.

"You didn't have to do this," I tell him, and pull a handful of napkins from the cupboard.

"It's not a problem. We need to eat, right? And since you had to babysit and couldn't meet, I figured I'd come to you—talk about the project and stuff." We stare at one another for a few breaths, what feels like an unspoken truce passing between us, then Jesse steps up beside Nick.

We both look down at him. With wide, excited eyes, Jesse glances from me to the bags that emanate the comforting scent of deliciously warm, fried foods.

Nick grins and pulls a couple of wrapped sandwiches out and sets them on the counter. "So, kid, what'll it be?"

Jesse takes the cheeseburger without a second thought and greedily unwraps it.

"Then you're definitely going to need some curly fries." Nick scoots them closer as Jesse climbs onto a stool at the counter. "And if you're at all like me, you like extra pickles on your cheese-burger"—Nick winks at me—"and lots of dipping sauce." He pulls out a few BBQ, ranch, and honey mustard containers and sets them by the fries. "Super fancy, I know."

"Ranch, please," Jesse says and takes a bite of his burger, way too big to fit his mouth around.

Jesse loses himself to a mess of special sauce and cheese strings as Nick steps around the counter, closer to me. "I'm sorry if I'm intruding. I took a chance, hoping you were hungry, and we might still be able to get some work done, or at least . . . talk."

"Talk?" I ask, fishing for a glimpse into the inner workings of Nick Turner's brain.

"Yeah, or watch a movie or whatever."

"Oh, you're staying for a movie now, huh?"

Nick winks at me, then looks at Jesse and pulls two DVDs from a plastic bag. "Now, Jesse, you have a very important deci-sion to make. Are we watching Raiders of the Lost Ark, a movie you've likely seen a hundred times, *or* are we branching out and watching The Goonies?" He holds both cases up for my brother to see.

Jesse's eyes dart between them before he finally nods to The Goonies, sauce coloring the corners of his mouth.

With a hoot, Nick celebrates with a ridiculous dance in place, and I find it impossible not to be happy that he's here.

"Here, J, wipe your mouth, would you?" I hand him a napkin. "Believe it or not, you still have to act polite in front of Nick; he's still considered a guest, even if he did invite himself over." I smile to soften the jab, while careful not to encourage Nick, but I know I've failed when he's grinning from ear to ear.

"Admit it," he says, leaning in closer. "You're glad to see me."

"Ha! And why would I be glad?"

"Because, you'd be stuck cooking and wouldn't get to watch The Goonies, a *classic,* remember?"

"If I admit it, are you going to do another jig in the middle of my kitchen?"

He shrugs. "Most likely." He winks and peers into the food bags. "So, you fed the kid, now it's your turn. What will it be, a salad, a cheeseburger, or a BLT?" He looks at me expectantly.

"Which one do you want?" I ask him, not wanting to take his favorite. I pull a few Squirts from the refrigerator and set them on the marble countertop, along with a few glasses, then slide one of each to Jesse.

Nick shakes his head. "Nope. I asked you first."

"Well, it's a hard choice. You see, I'm both a grease and a meat sort of girl. So . . . I think I'll take the BLT."

"Ooh, good choice. But their burgers are by far the best." He points to Jesse's messy face as proof, then slides the sandwich over to me. "Don't worry," he says. "I'll share with you if you change your mind." Popping a fry into his mouth, Nick glances at Jesse and settles onto one of the barstools. "So, what's new with you, kid? Staying out of trouble at school?"

Jesse nods, fiddling with the corner of his cheeseburger wrapper.

I sit on the stool beside him and take a bite of my BLT. The bacon is perfect, the sourdough bread still warm in my mouth, and I groan. "This is so good." I glance at Nick's burger, then remember our pizza. "Why is it I always eat crap food when I'm with you?"

"What? BLTs are good for you—you have every food group. And pizza isn't crap food, it's a staple."

"I'd like to see you try to convince mothers everywhere that's true."

Nick's smile grows again. "Moms love me, you know. I might actually be able to."

"I wouldn't doubt it. Everyone loves you, it seems." His eyes shift to mine. "You know what I mean."

"So, quickly," Nick says, swallowing, "before I decide I don't want to do any work whatsoever tonight, where are we at with the furniture orders and delivery? The floors will be ready Friday."

I swallow and wipe the crumbs from my mouth. "Well, I emailed Sam a bunch of links. As soon as she chooses, which she promised would be tomorrow since our deadline is creeping up on us, I can get the furniture ordered. The only issue is, delivery will likely be a week from then, give or take. So, I think we should go to Benton on Saturday and pick out the accents, like the rugs and wall pieces—essentially make it a mall day so we can get started on at least part of it. What do you think?"

"Other than I hate shopping?"

I nod.

"Sounds like a plan." A pickle drops from his burger and he pops it into his mouth. "Anything else?"

Breaking off a wayward piece of bacon, I take a bite, then wipe up his pickle splatter with my napkin. I can't help it, and when I feel his eyes on me, I look at him sheepishly. "Um, no, I don't think so. Not right now. I figure once the hard stuff is decided, we can worry about putting the portfolio together. That won't take much time, and I could really use this in-between-time to study for my GRE."

"How's that going, by the way?"

I shrug. "Slow going, but that's expected. I just wish I wasn't so stressed out about it."

"I can see why you would be," Nick says, balling up his wrapper and dropping it into the bag. Jesse watches him, though he's still working on his burger, falling to pieces in his hands. "It's a big deal."

"It's like every test has led up to this moment, and I feel like I should be more prepared, but I'm not. It just gets . . . frustrating."

Nick dumps the rest of his fries out on a napkin and deposits the garbage in the compactor. "What are you doing tomorrow?" he asks. "Do you have class?"

"Thursdays? No. I work at four, though. Jesse's off this week for Spring Break, so we'll likely run errands or something." I stick the last bite of my sandwich into my mouth. "Why?" Part of me wants to be prim and proper while I'm stuffing my face, but it's too good to care.

"I think I know how to help you with your exam," he says thoughtfully. He glances around the counter, looking for something. When he finds a note pad and pen, he jots down an address and slides it over to me. "Meet me here tomorrow around ten or so. Bring Jesse."

I reach over to their fry pile and snatch one for myself. "Why are you being so cryptic?"

"Because, if I tell you where you're going, you won't show up," he admits, and I don't like the sound of that. "Bethany, just trust me, okay? I want to help you, and I can. So, let me."

"You should do it, Beth," Jesse says.

"Are you still on my side or his?" I ask playfully.

Jesse shrugs. "You've been stressing out for, like, ever."

I pop another fry, drenched in barbeque sauce, into my mouth and eye Nick closely as I consider his offer. "Trust you, huh?"

He nods. "Yeah. Trust me." His gaze is steady, sincere.

"Okay," I finally say.

Jesse balls up what's left of his cheeseburger, like Nick did, and he drops it in the remaining garbage bag. "Before you touch *anything*," I tell him, "you better wash your hands, J. I'm serious."

"I will," he grumbles and walks toward the bathroom. I pop one last fry in my mouth with a guttural groan. "You're right, these are pretty awesome."

Nick winks. "Told ya."

Unable to stand a messy counter, I pick up what's left of the fries and the garbage and toss it into the trash. I wet the sponge and start wiping off the counter, all while Nick's eyes are on me. I feel them. I always feel them. It used to make me uncomfortable in class, like he was judging me, but here, after all that's transpired between us, it sends a tingle through me. "You're staring again—you're always staring." I finally look at him.

"No, I'm thinking," he clarifies and leans against the counter beside me.

"Oh yeah? Well, then, what are you thinking about?" I scoot the salt and pepper shakers out of the way and scrub the island harder.

Nick clears his throat and crosses his arms over his chest. "That I shouldn't have kissed you the other night."

My scrubbing falters before I remember myself and turn toward the sink. I wasn't expecting him to say that.

"I don't mean it like that, Bethany. Don't take it personally. I just—I think I messed things up, especially with what happened after, and I want you to know that I'm sorry."

With my back to him, it's easy enough to shrug off everything that happened, like we'd simply chosen a subpar movie on Netflix last night, not that we'd shared a groping session. It was more than that to both of us, though, that much was clear.

"It's totally fine," I tell him. I have no idea what I'm doing as I fidget around the kitchen. All I can think about is that kiss. "I over-reacted. We were both tired and stupid—"

Nick steps up beside me, waiting for me to look at him. After a few seconds, I force myself to meet his gaze.

"It was more than that to me," he says with certainty. "But I heard what you said. I know this isn't something you want right now, and I'm not going to make everything harder on you by throwing more complication into the mess . . . Nothing has to happen until you're ready." His eyes never leave mine, and he takes a step back, somehow sensing the havoc that descends over my senses when he's around. "I promise. The next move will be yours, whatever you decide it might be. But I'm not going to leave you alone, either."

Grateful, I lick my lips. "No?"

His head shifts ever so slightly to the left. "I want to be your friend."

# TWENTY-SIX
# NICK

BETHANY BRINGS the Range Rover to a stop outside my parents' house, her and Jesse natural and oblivious to me watching them from the window as they talk and walk to the door. I have no idea if bringing them here was a good idea or if it was completely idiotic, but they're here now, and if nothing else, I know my mom can help Bethany study.

"I don't think I've ever seen you like this," my mom says, startling me. She steps up to the window beside me, just as the doorbell rings.

I cross my arms over my chest. "I'm not sure what you mean."

"Well, you seem a bit nervous, for starters." My mom's makeup is perfect and natural looking, her hair is perfectly done. There's even a twinkle in her eyes.

I scoff. "Not nervous, just . . . hopeful," I say, surprising myself. "And if *I* didn't know any better, I'd think you were a little bit *excited*."

"Well, of course I am. It's not very often I get to meet your friends, not anymore at least, especially the pretty ones." She smiles knowingly and walks to the front door.

"You know Bethany, Ma. Remember, the whole debacle in eighth grade with her parents?"

"Well, she's not a little girl anymore, is she?" She winks at me, and I laugh, completely creeped out. "You're being weird."

"Just trying to loosen you up," she says, and nods to the door. "Well, are you going to be a gentleman and answer it, or do I have to do it for you?"

"I got it," I say and my mom turns for the kitchen.

"I'll pull out the pitcher of iced tea."

Bethany's smiling at Jesse when I open the door. I love her smile, I realize, and I don't see it nearly enough. "Hey," she says happily, if a little bit uncertain.

"Hi." I open the door wider. "You guys came."

"I told you we would." There's a hint of amusement in her gray eyes, like she's surprised I questioned it. Truth be told, I'd assumed something would come up with her parents or she would decide she didn't want to trust me after all.

"Yeah, you did." I glance at Jesse and wave them inside. "Hey, kid."

"What's up?" Jesse says, and I silently rejoice a little bit at the hope that he really is warming up to me.

"Not much, just excited to hang out with you for a bit," I admit. Knowing his penchant for collecting things, I have a feeling he'll be the only one to appreciate my childhood assemblages upstairs.

They both peer around the entry, into the living room, and up at the landing. "This is a beautiful house," Bethany starts. "But where are we exactly?" The hesitance in her voice tells me she has a good guess already.

"This," my mom says from the kitchen, "would be Nick's childhood home." She steps out of the kitchen to join us. "And you must be Bethany." She hurries over. "It's so nice to finally meet you, sweetie." She wraps her arms around Bethany's shoulders, pulling her into a tight hug.

Bethany's eyes meet mine, and I can tell she's contemplating fight or flight.

"I'm Leslie or Mom, you can call me whichever you like."

"Oh, okay. Thank you." Bethany takes a step back from her and smooths out her t-shirt.

"And you, young man . . ." my mom continues, and bends slightly to Jesse's level. I've told her about his Autism, so she doesn't expect him to look at her, but she treats him as she would any kid all the same. "You're a handsome one. Look at those pretty blue eyes." My mom's voice is soft and affectionate, reminding me of when I was younger.

"Do you want to introduce yourself to Nick's mom?" Bethany urges.

"Hi," he says, distracted as he processes all the new things in the house. "I'm Jesse."

"It's wonderful to meet you, Jesse. Now," she straightens. "Before we get down to business, why don't we snag a chocolate chip cookie? I made them fresh this morning."

Jesse nods, more emphatically than I've ever seen before, and follows my mom into the kitchen without a second thought.

Bethany grabs hold of my arm. "What am I doing here, Nick? At your parents' house, really?"

"Remember I told you my mom's in the psych field? She's a retired professor, she's offered to help you study for the GRE."

"What?" she whisper-shouts. "Nick, you didn't have to do this. Why—" she shakes her head, and I know where her mind is going. I know she's spiraling back to before, to the mess created and probably the residual embarrassment of it all. Not only does Bethany not like asking for help, she's a private person.

"Hey," I say, resting my hand on her shoulder. "I know it's hard for you to accept help unless your brother is missing," I say, hoping the playful jab will loosen her up. "But my mom wants to. She needs something to do anyway. Trust me, you're doing her the favor." I shrug. "Besides, who better to help you study than someone who's taken it before, albeit a hundred years ago."

"I heard that, Nicholas."

Bethany's face reddens. "I can't believe this," she whispers, and I can tell she's torn.

"Leave if you want, but I had a fun day planned for me and Jesse, so you'd be screwing him and my mom over by leaving."

She glowers at me.

With a wink, I nod to the kitchen. "Come on. Have a cookie, it will make you feel better."

Taking her hand, I lead her into the kitchen. Jesse and my mom are sitting in the nook, macking on giant chocolate chip cookies, each with a glass of milk. "I hope you didn't eat them all, Jesse," I say. "These are my favorite, you know?"

"I didn't eat them all . . . yet."

I laugh. "Oh, funny guy. I better hurry then." I grab one off the plate. "Are they any good?"

"They're *really* good," he says with a mouthful. He looks at his sister. "They're even better than peanut butter."

I pull out a chair for Bethany to sit beside him. "I'm not sure about that," she mutters and sits down, taking her first bite.

"She likes the peanut butter cookies best, huh?" I ask, taking the opportunity to learn a bit more about her. I sit down beside my mom, the four of us enjoying a cookie around the card table. "What else does your sister like?"

"She likes the Amazing Race," he tells me. "She yells at the TV all the time when she's watching it. And she threw a pillow at a hockey game once."

I glance at Bethany in time to see her blush. I'm not sure if it's the purity of her light skin, but her flushed cheeks are the first thing I notice whenever she's embarrassed.

"It was a bad call," she mutters.

"Yeah? Note to self—don't watch sports with Bethany. Or, at least wear a helmet." I look at Jesse, eager. "What else?"

"She sings Britney Spears in the shower."

I burst with laughter. "Really?"

"Okay, that's enough," my mom chides. "Leave the poor girl alone."

"Isn't it bad enough I'm going to gain fifteen pounds hanging out with you?" she holds up what's left of her cookie.

"He's still eating junk food, I take it." My mom purses her lips, as if she didn't already know.

"Only when I don't have leftovers," I tell her. "It could be worse."

Bethany smiles. "According to Nick, cheeseburgers and BLTs have all the necessary food groups, so they're good for you."

My mom wipes a bit of chocolate off her thumb and shakes her head. "Does he?"

"Well, that's our cue, Jesse." I shove the rest of my cookie in my mouth. "Let's go upstairs and let the ladies study. I'll show you my comic book collection, among other things." I like the intrigue in his eyes. "Holler if you need anything, ladies." I nudge Jesse. "Time to show you the *bachelor pad*."

# TWENTY-SEVEN
# BETHANY

"JUST REMEMBER, Bethany, you know this stuff." Mrs. Turner closes the test book. "How long have you been at this, three years?"

"Yeah, of specific study, anyway. Though it seems like a lifetime."

Mrs. Turner smiles at me and tilts her head. "You're very passionate about this," she says, as if it's only just occurring to her. "Do you mind if I ask what it is that draws you to psychology?" She sighs and leans back in her chair. "For me, it started out with a handsome professor who was offering a beginner's course." She smiles and removes her reading glasses. "I guess I decided I liked a lot more than his smile. I changed my major and never looked back."

"Well," I start. "When I was a freshman, I took a Psychology 101 course and found it fascinating. More so than interior design. I knew I couldn't quit design, my parents would've freaked, so I decided to double major." I drop my pencil and sit back in the cushy, dining room chair. "It was because of Jesse, too" I admit. "Ever since he was born, I've wanted to understand the mind and how it works." I stare down at the thick textbooks that have weighed me down over the past four semesters. "I want to understand and help families that struggle with issues they don't understand. I don't want other kids with social anxieties and learning disabilities to struggle the way I watch Jesse and my parents struggle."

Mrs. Turner's gaze is long and thoughtful. "Well, I think it's a field that really suits you, even if it's difficult. Passion is all you need to succeed, really. And that's not something you're lacking. Nick on the other hand . . . Well, let's just say I think he's finally starting to question what he's passionate about, which makes me happy."

Mrs. Turner stares out the window, into the backyard, and I don't know if she's thinking about Nick or maybe her own passions in life. Maybe even her disappointments and regrets.

"Well, thank you for your help," I tell her. "I appreciate you taking the time to meet with me. I feel like I've retained more in the past few hours than I would have with another week studying on my own."

"It was my pleasure. You've got Cognitive down, you just need to take more time to think through the syntax of it all. I know it gets confusing, especially if you overthink a question, but keep in mind, as complex as some of these questions are, they will always be straight forward. There are no trick questions on this test." She smiles at me, and her kindness seems to seep into me. "You're going to do great. You should have no problem getting a 600 on this. Just stay out of your own head, if you can." She winks at me, and I see where Nick gets his charm from.

I nod, grateful that she's sitting across from me, eyes smiling with pride and encouragement.

"There's no need to rush either," she adds.

"I hate to ask this, since you've already helped me so much," I rush to say before I change my mind. "But . . . do you mind running through this with me again next week, before the exam?" I stand up to collect my things.

Mrs. Turner's head bobs with an enthusiastic nod. "Yes! Yes, I'd love to. You let me know when, and I'll make sure we have plenty of snacks. We'll run through it, like it's the real thing."

Uncertain how to show my gratitude, I lean down and wrap my arms around her.

"Oh," she chirps and hugs me back, more tightly than I expect. She rubs my back soothingly, the way mothers do, and she's soft and warm, and it almost brings tears to my eyes. My mom would never have the time to sit down and study with me. My dad wouldn't even consider it.

Remembering myself, I pull away. I straighten with a smile, and stack my books and notecards on the table. "I wonder what the boys are doing upstairs."

"Getting into trouble, I imagine," Mrs. Turner says, and when I'm about to crumple up my doodle paper, she reaches for it. "I don't mean to pry, sweetie," she says hesitantly, and my shoulders tense. Her expression is curious and tentative. "But, have you ever been tested for dyslexia?"

Shaking my head, I glance between her and my doodle paper, not getting the connection. "No. I've never considered it."

"You know the material we went over, but it's connecting the ideas that you struggle with," she muses. "It would make sense why some of these ideas get a bit mixed up in your mind. You speak about it all so clearly, but the process . . ." She points to my doodle page. "You doodle when you're thinking."

"Yeah, it's just a habit."

Mrs. Turner smiles. "Good, you're very creative." She rises from her chair. "I was just thinking, it might be good to know, moving forward. Perhaps learn a few tricks to help you with school. There's no sense in struggling more than you need to."

Most of my life, I've worried about Jesse, never stopping to think that I might have a learning disability and that's why I've always struggled so much. "My parents would freak," I say, partially amused.

"Would you like me to give you the name of a clinician friend of mine? Her name is Katy Richters. I referred a few patients to her when I was practicing, and I believe she's still at it. She would be able to give you a screening assessment—a profile of sorts to show you your strengths and weaknesses. You'd know what tools you need to make your academic career easier."

It's easy to fantasize of a day when school is a little less daunting. "I'll think about it," I tell her. "Thank you, Mrs. Turner."

"Please, sweetie, call me Leslie. I feel old enough as it is without the added formality." She slides the books she referenced during our quizzing back into place on the bookshelf in the living room.

"I'll try." I glance up the stairs, hearing Jesse's muffled laugh, and smile.

"Nick and Reilly used to spend hours up there, playing video games and who knows what else," Mrs. Turner muses.

I imagine Reilly and Nick in their teens, running up the stairs after baseball practice. It's the perfect house for having friends over—big yards and lofty rooms. I can almost see Nick in the den, sprawled out on the floor, watching Indiana Jones and the Last Crusade, and eating popcorn with his friends.

"Nick's been really good to Jesse," I tell her. "Which is everything to me. You raised a very good man."

She looks at me like she can see into my soul. "Yes, he is a good man, and a good friend to have." With a dip of her head, Mrs. Turner excuses herself from the room before I can reply. I'm not sure if that was a semi-sweet, sugar-coated message, or if it was a simple statement, but I'm left wondering as I drop my bag off by the front door. According to the wall clock, I have a few hours before work and errands still to run, so I head up the stairs in search of Jesse.

Family photos line the wall as I meander up the staircase, and the carpet is off-white, a little shaggy and outdated but well taken care of. The upstairs of the house is just like downstairs. It's perfectly furnished and matching, everything in its place, much like my house. Though Mrs. Turner's taste isn't like my mom's. It's soft and plush where my mother's design is all sharp angels and monotone colors. The fact that there are happy family photos —photos of Nick and his friends, and framed animal paintings and artwork instead of abstract pieces hanging on the walls—make it seem like a different world than what I'm used to living in.

I smile, a little envious but pleased that Nick's childhood seemed like a happy one, like I'd imagined.

The floorboards creak as I explore the landing, passing by what looks like an extra bedroom, lightly furnished with a light wood dresser set and a floral comforter on the bed. I pass a bathroom and upstairs office, everything bathed in the light that filters in through the large wall of windows in the front of the house.

I hear Jesse's laugh through the door at the end of the hallway and creak it open. Peeking inside, I find the two of them sitting on bean bags in front of a large but boxy television, both of their faces contorted as they twitch and squirm in their seats. The cars they're driving screech and burn out down empty, digital streets.

A neon green convertible flips across the screen and Nick groans.

"Dude!" Jesse says, truly smiling for the first time in a long time, and it makes my chest tighten. "You died, again."

"Yeah, thanks, kid. I appreciate you rubbing it in." Nick turns to him and offers a high-five. "Good job, though. You schooled me."

"It's all right, you haven't played in a while."

Nick chuckles and rubs the back of his neck. "True. Let's go with that." When he notices me, his eyes widen. "Hey, how did it go? Do you feel smarter?" he teases.

"A lot, actually. Thanks for asking." I look past him at Jesse. "Come on, J. We have to run a few errands before I take you home. Get your stuff together, okay?"

"Nick's letting me borrow his comics," he says, climbing to his feet. He shakes his hair out of his eyes and places the comics on the floor into a large plastic bin.

"He is, is he? All of them, I see." I eye the storage container.

Nick smirks. "That's only the first box."

"Wow. Lucky me." I bat my eyelashes and walk over to him. Jesse's cleaning up the piles he created, and I stop beside Nick. "Thank you," I say wholeheartedly. "Your mom is really wonderful, and I—I seriously don't know how I would get through this test without her. Without you." Everything he's done hasn't just been for me, it's been for Jesse too, and the knowledge of that makes my heart melt for him and me question why I've been so worried about being around him to begin with.

Nick shoves his hands in his pockets. His eyes don't leave mine, but his brow furrows ever so slightly. "I'm just glad my mom was able to help."

"She did. I feel a lot better. She gave me some great tips and some things to think about."

"Good." He winks at me and grabs the container of comics. "Well kid, you heard the slave driver. We better get these loaded up."

"Okay," Jesse says and he and I file down the stairs behind Nick. "Go say goodbye to Mrs. Turner," I tell him, and Jesse hurries into the kitchen, with more pep than usual. Although I know he's had fun today with Nick, I'm sure the plate of cookies waiting inside has something to do with it.

"Nick," I say, resting my hand on his arm. "I'm sorry for assuming you were an asshole."

He looks at me with a cocky grin. "Are we talking about high school again?"

"No—yes. The past ten years, actually. I think a part of me wanted you to be a jerk, so I jumped to conclusions."

His eyes shift from my eyes to my mouth and back again. "Why would you want me to be a jerk, Bethany?" The confusion in his eyes hurts my heart.

"I don't know," I tell him honestly. "Maybe I was scared to let you in again."

He sets the bin down, never taking his eyes off of me. "And how do you feel about that now?"

"It's not as scary as I remember," I admit.

"Good."

Mrs. Turner and Jesse laugh in the kitchen, and Nick takes a step closer. "I was wondering something," he says. "Jesse mentioned he wanted to take an equine class but your parents won't let him."

"Oh, the equine therapy? Yeah, they've sort of been putting it off." I fudge the truth a little. My dad said no, but my mom is thinking about it.

"I know I'm not a therapist"—he laughs at the thought—"but let me take you guys to the ranch Saturday. He'll love it out there."

I know Jesse will love it—he'd be ecstatic—but that's a bit more intrusion in Sam's life than I'm sure I'm comfortable with.

"Don't overthink it," he urges. "Just say yes."

In that moment, I know my heart is in the most danger it's ever been in. I suddenly can't say no to him. "Okay. Sure. What about shopping for Sam's décor?"

"Darn, I guess we'll just have to reschedule."

## TWENTY-EIGHT
# NICK

AFTER BETHANY and Jesse take off, I decide it's time to talk to my dad. It's Thursday afternoon, and I know he's working, so I head to his office. I turn into the Turner and Tillman Design and Development parking lot and pull up next to my dad's Tundra. The distance between us has happened so gradually and quickly at the same time, I'm not sure I noticed it until recently. First, blowing off my final project, then missing dinners and our breakfast . . . it's like he doesn't want me to be an architect anymore, or maybe *he* doesn't want to be an architect. I'm not sure if he's planning on selling the company, or if maybe he's rethinking life decisions and doesn't want me to walk down the same path, but it's time to find out.

I step out of the Explorer and head toward the entrance. The fact of the matter is, I need my dad right now. I have no idea what the hell I'm going to do once I graduate, now that my plan to work with him is all but dust in the wind.

As soon as I step inside, I see a few familiar faces, and the sound of ringing phones and muffled conversations fill my ears. It's more nostalgic than I'd expected. I used to walk here after school on the days I didn't have baseball practice. Sometimes

Reilly would come with me and we'd hang out while I waited for my dad to finish up. My dad's enthusiasm and passion for his work seemed almost superhuman and inspiring. Now, he feels more like a stranger.

"Hey, Nick!" Thomas, my dad's right-hand man, waves me over to him as he packs up his briefcase.

"Hey, Tom." I shake his hand. "It's been awhile."

"Yeah, it has. You look great, kid. You been eating your Wheaties?"

Laughing, I nod and hope I haven't been eating too many of them. "Something like that."

With a pat on my back, Tom nods to my dad's office. "He's just finishing up a meeting."

"Hey, thanks."

"Catch you later, Nick."

I wave a goodbye, and Tom heads for the door. As I continue toward my dad's office, I admire his firm. I take in the large, square building, single story with exposed beams in vaulted ceilings. Drafting tables are spread about, milling bodies scattered around. It's rejuvenating, in a way, and awe-inspiring. The older I get, the more I appreciate the work my dad has put into this place, a new, modern building, nothing like the old historical brick and stone structures in town he remodels for a living.

I smile politely at the employees I've never seen before, introducing myself as Hutch's son, Nick. Some of the staff are busy, others are closing up for the day, and for the first, time I get a sense of how large the company's grown and it makes sense how busy he's been. I had no idea. This was his vision. Now it's his company and responsibility. He built it and made it all happen and I feel hopeful that I might still be a part of that.

My dad's secretary isn't at her desk when I get there, so I bypass it. With a quick knock, I open the door to his office, and my heart stops beating. "What the fuck?"

A red-headed woman scrambles to smooth out her clothes, and

my dad straightens, but not quick enough. I saw her mouth on his and her fingers wrapped around his tie—his goddamn hand was on her ass.

My stomach curdles, and I clench my hands to fists.

"N—Nick . . ." My dad fumbles out my name and pushes the woman away from him, nearly knocking her over.

She glares at him. "Hey—"

"What the fuck are you doing?" I shout.

"Watch your mouth," he orders, but I don't give a shit what he's saying.

"You're screwing your secretary?"

"I'm a partner in the firm," she corrects and tugs down the hem of her shirt again for good measure.

"I don't care who the hell you are." I glare at my father. "Is *this* why you've been blowing me off? You didn't want me to find out?" The guilt slackening his features tells me all I need to know. "I can't believe this." I turn for the door.

"Your mother already knows, Nicholas," he calls after me, as if that makes any difference to me whatsoever, and I stalk through the building. Everyone and everything around me is a blur, and I head straight for my car. My blood is boiling. My heart is hurting. And I have no idea what I'm going to do next.

"Nick!" I can hear my dad behind me, but I don't stop for him. I fucking *hate* him. "Nick, stop for a minute."

"No," I bite out. Each step against the asphalt is punishing and not nearly quick enough.

"You don't understand—"

I whirl around to face him. "Are you kidding me right now? You're fucking around on your wife—on *my mother*. You *are* still married, right? Or, is that bullshit too, just like all your late nights, working on big projects, while Mom's at home, waiting for you." I'm disgusted even looking at him. "I can't believe you. *You*, of all people." There's an anger inside of me I've never felt before and it burns in my muscles, a searing pain so raw I want to haul off and punch him in his slack-jaw face.

"Nick, things haven't been right with me and your mother for a long time."

"Then get a goddamn divorce!"

His eyes light up, like I've given him permission to be a decent person. "You're right, Nick. We should've gotten a divorce a while ago."

"No shit." I turn and hurry to the Explorer.

"You need to hear the whole story before you do something rash. Nick—we did this for you, don't you see that?"

I laugh and fling open my car door. "Seriously? I'm not a ten-year-old kid. Don't put any of this on me."

"I'm not trying to, Nick. I'm just telling you the truth. None of this is easy."

"Yeah, it looked real hard on you a few moments ago." I climb into my car, barely slamming the driver's side door shut, before I throw the Explorer into reverse and get the fuck out of here.

I see the woman rush over to my dad in the rearview mirror, her red hair bouncing.

Yeah, life's been really fucking hard for him.

# TWENTY-NINE
# BETHANY

AFTER THE LAST customer leaves the salon, I lock the door and hurry through the night-end, cleaning routine. I toss a load of towels in the washing machine and sterilize all the beds. Anna Marie already set up the spray tanning booth for tomorrow, so all that's left is a quick register closeout and I'm home free. For the first time in a very long time, I'm actually eager to get home for a reason other than Jesse.

Since talking with Mrs. Turner earlier, all I can think about is the possibility that I might have a learning disability. For some people, it might not be something to get excited about, but for me, it means there's hope it can get a little easier. It means that I'm not crazy and perhaps I have been studying the best I can. Maybe my dad won't be so disappointed in me, or maybe it will only solidify how broken he thinks I am.

I've thought about it fleetingly over the years—that something could be wrong with me, that is—but so many people struggle with school and on their exams, I never thought about it much more than that. Everything Mrs. Turner said, though, makes so much sense, and now I want to know more. A cup of tea, pajamas, and my laptop sounds like the perfect night to end a really good day.

My phone rings as I shut all the lights off and step out the door. I pray it's not my parents with some sort of emergency, so I'm pleasantly surprised to see that it's Anna Marie.

Juggling my purse, my phone, and my clanking keychain, I answer. "Hey, I'm just closing up." I pause with the key in the lock. "Did you need me to do something before I leave?"

"Hi. No, but you should come down to Lick's."

"Uh—I kind of need to get home to do some homework," I say, fidgeting with the door.

"Trust me, Bethany, you need to get down here . . . Nick is here."

"Okay, so?" Manhandling my things, I make it to the Rover and toss them all inside.

"He's not working, Bethany. He's literally at the bar, drunk, like the drunkest I've ever seen him before."

I start the engine and sit there for a breath. "That seems weird. Is he alone?"

"Yes, he's alone, and I know it's weird, that's why I'm calling you."

"No Reilly or Mac—no one's there with him?"

"No, something's clearly wrong. I thought since you guys are all buddy-buddy now, you should know."

An unexpected panic takes hold of me. "Yeah. Thanks. I'm on my way." In all the years I've seen Nick at the bar, he's never been wasted, and I've never see him drinking, alone.

As soon as I get to Lick's, Anna's outside on her phone. She hangs up when she sees me and smiles. "He's still in there. I think he's even flirting with the guys at this point."

"What?" I know she's probably joking, but I head straight for the door. "How long has he been here?" I ask over my shoulder.

"I have no idea. I got here an hour ago. Sorry."

Nodding, I head into the bar. It's relatively dead, but it's a Thursday night so I'm not really surprised.

Nick's at the bar with a water glass in front of him, which is a relief, but when Brady looks at me, his eyes are pinched with worry. Nick's resting his elbows on the bar, spinning a coaster around and around on the countertop.

"Hey," I say and sidle up beside him.

When Nick looks at me, his eyes widen. "Hey! Fancy meeting you here."

I can't help but smile. "Yeah, I know. What a coincidence." His eyes are veiled with drink, and I think sadness. His words are a little slurred, and I can tell his happy-go-lucky Nick-ness is forced tonight. "Where's the crew at?" I ask.

He shrugs and looks back at the Anchor Steam coaster he continues to spin. "Home, I guess. Hey, do you want a shot? All shots are on me tonight."

Brady gives me the look, as if he even needs to. "No, I'm okay, thanks. I was just heading home. Do you want me to drop you off at your place on my way?"

He shakes his head. "Nah, I'm not ready to go home yet, even though *Brady* cut me off." He chuckles to himself. "He's such an asshole sometimes, but I love 'em." He raises his palm. "High-five, dude, for being cool."

I stifle a laugh as Brady gives Nick a high-five. "Thanks, brother."

Pulling out the stool, I slide in beside Nick. "You want to tell me what happened?" I ask quietly.

A shit-eating grin parts his lips. "Life," he says. "But it was my turn anyway."

"What do you mean? Did something happen after I left your mom's?"

When I look at Brady, he shrugs and gives us some space. "Let me know if you need anything."

"Ha!" Nick takes a sip of water, his eyes only half open. "Not exactly." His smile disappears as his thoughts drift, and I want more than anything to say something that might make him feel better, but I know he's beyond that now.

"Nick," I say, reaching for him. I rest my hand on his arm and squeeze, hoping he'll look at me. "Do you want me to call Sam?" Her number is the only one I have, and I know she'd be here in a heartbeat if Nick needed her.

"No. No, don't call Sam," he says, adamant, and he shakes his head. "She's busy."

"I doubt that. It's almost eight. She'd love to come hang out with you."

He shakes his head again. "No," he repeats. "She's had enough bullshit to deal with in her life. She doesn't need mine too—they all have. This—" He peers around the bar. "It was bound to happen, sooner or later. Life's not perfect, you know," he tells me, then he laughs. "You already know that." He stares at my hand on his arm. "Are you flirting with me, Bethany Fairchild? I thought we had a deal."

"I just want to help, Nick," I tell him. Whatever happened, he's more than hurt, he seems to feel guilty, and I have no idea why. "Why don't you let me take you home. It's better than stewing in this stinky bar—no offense, Brady."

He smiles and hands another patron a beer.

"You *are* flirting with me. Trying to get me in bed, huh?" He laughs at himself again and slides off his stool. "All right. I need to get back to Marilyn and Monroe anyway. I haven't fed them today."

I glance up at Brady. "What do I owe—"

"You're good, don't worry about it," he says and waves my question away. He mouths a *thank you*, and I reach for Nick's hand to steady him. Instead, he wraps his arm around me and we head out the door.

"You know, Bethany, you and me—we're a good team. We're killin' it on our project. And look, you can even carry me." He motions like he's going to jump in my arms, and I nearly have a heart attack.

"Let's *not* try that," I say desperately, bracing my hand on him. "I think I'd hurt us both."

He just laughs and we make our way out to my car.

Nick's silent the entire ride home, and at one point I wonder if he's sleeping. When I pull up to his apartment, though, I realize he's just staring out the window. His eyelids are drooping, but he's awake, lost somewhere in his mind.

"We're home," I say softly, and shut off the engine.

"I like the sound of that," he says with a languid smile and opens the door to climb out. Hurrying around the car, I let Nick lean on me, praying for an eventless climb up the stairs. Thankfully, other than his added weight against me, we make our way effortlessly to the front door.

I help Nick with the lock, and the moment we're inside his apartment, he sighs. It's cold, like always. "Do you want a fire or do you want your bed?"

"Is that a proposition?" He tries to waggle his eyebrows, but I can tell his heart isn't in it anymore. It would seem the fun-loving Nick Turner can't turn off the charm, even when he's drunk as a skunk and miserable.

Taking his hand, I lead him into his bedroom. I've never been inside it before, but it's much like I'd expected. An oversized queen bed, dresser, and side tables to match. Perfectly coordinated sheets, drapes, and an accent rug, but his clothes are scattered around the room. I imagine it might mirror whatever is going on in this life right now.

Pulling back the covers, I motion for him to get in. He looks at me, but I'm not sure he really sees me as he starts to undress.

"I'm—uh—gonna get you some water. I'll be right back." I head for the kitchen, searching his cabinets for a barf bowl, just in case. I grab some ibuprofen and fill a glass of water. When I'm certain I've given him plenty of time to climb into bed, I head back in.

Nick's already between the sheets, lying on his side with his eyes open. It's surreal to see him so still and quiet. "Are you thirsty?" I stop beside his bed.

He shakes his head, but I put the glass to his mouth anyway. "Just a few sips, at least."

Nick doesn't argue and shuts his eyes as he takes a gulp, then another. I'm not sure I'd be as obedient if I was as drunk as he is.

When he's finished, he looks at me. "I didn't feed the fish."

I set the glass down on his side table. "I'll feed them for you before I leave." Smiling, I sit on the bed next to him. "Don't worry, your guppies are in good hands."

"Only give them a pinch," he says quietly. His voice is low but soft. "They're greedy bastards."

"One pinch—got it." I run my fingers through his hair, unable to resist Nick like this. He seems so fragile and vulnerable when he's not smiling and laughing and putting on a show for everyone. I wonder who Nick really is beneath all that, then I realize, I already know.

"That feels good," he says with a little moan.

"Jesse likes it, too. He always falls asleep."

Nick sighs. "Jesse's awesome."

A small smile pulls at my mouth. "Yeah, he is." The way Nick cares about him makes my heart so full, the backs of my eyes sting, just a little. "You're pretty awesome, too," I whisper.

I watch the way his hair falls from between my fingers, and after a few breaths, I think he might even be asleep.

I stand up to go.

"Stay," he whispers. "For a little bit?"

He has no idea how badly I want to, despite myself. "Yeah, sure."

Walking around the foot of the bed, I crawl on top of the comforter next to him and pull up the folded blanket at the bottom to shield me from the cold. "I'll lay right here, for a little while."

Nick doesn't turn over or say anything else, he just lets me be, and I watch the way his body moves with each breath. It's like a lazy metronome in a room of silence.

If I hadn't been spending so much time with him over the past couple weeks, I would think my being in his bed like this would be so far out of my comfort zone, I'd turn tail and run. But whatever's between us now becomes easier and more comfortable each day, and this, being in here with him, feels right.

"I saw my dad with a woman today," Nick whispers, and I hear the raw emotion in his voice. Having met his mother just this morning, my heart breaks for her, and I can only imagine Nick's devastation, whether it's for him or his mom, or both.

"I'm sorry, Nick." I roll onto my side, staring at his back. There's a hitch in his steady breaths, and I know all too well what that means. Scooting closer, I wrap my arm around him. Neither of us say anything more. We just lay there in silent company until he finally falls asleep.

# THIRTY
## BETHANY'S JOURNAL

APRIL 19TH

*Today was unlike any day I've ever had. It was a revelation of sorts. Not only did I discover that I'm not a complete failure, like my parents seem to think, but I've discovered my true feelings for Nick, complicated as they may be.*

*Tonight, I saw the real Nick that hides ~~all~~ behind all the smiles and playful banter. That's the guy I want to know more. I can't help but think that with the family issues he's going through, and knowing how fucked up my own are, he might confide in me again. I hope he will. For whatever reason, he seems hesitant to lean on his friends, which surprises me. So maybe, I can give him something this time, the way he's given me so much the past couple weeks.*

*His mom thinks I have dyslexia. I've tried so hard for so long to be as good as my parents want me to be, at least as far a school is concerned, but I always miss the mark. At least now it makes a bit more sense. I wonder if my parents ~~ever~~ have ever considered my having a learning disability and they just pushed the idea away, not wanting it to be true. Or, maybe they've never considered it and think I enjoy my father's disappointment.*

*At least I feel better, knowing what I do, and that whatever happens, whether I'm dyslexic or not, it won't matter to Nick. He's one less person I have to be someone I'm not for.*

*-B*

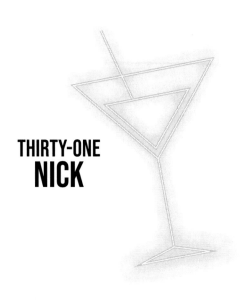

# THIRTY-ONE
## NICK

I'M NOT sure how many minutes pass, or if it's been closer to an hour, but I sit outside my parents' house, thinking how I barely recognize my life the past twenty-four hours. When I woke up this morning, it took me a while to remember going to Lick's and why there would be a bottle of whiskey, ibuprofen, and a ginger teabag sitting on my nightstand. Then I remembered Bethany. I pull out my phone and re-read our conversation.

> Me: Thanks for last night. I didn't even have to kick you out this morning
>
> Bethany: You're hilarious . . . and welcome.
>
> Bethany: How are you feeling?
>
> Me: Decent. Thanks for leaving me your hangover remedy.

I've wanted to ask her a million questions about last night and let her know how much I appreciate her taking care of me, but nothing I type feels adequate enough, and I can't bring myself to press SEND. I put my phone away and decide to worry about it later. I have a mother to worry about right now.

I stare up at my bedroom window—the one I gazed out of as a child, watching my dad work on his cars. I stare at my mom's rose bed, imaging her bent over it with a giant hat and too much sunblock on her face. I stare at the green, perfectly landscaped lawn where my dad and I practiced my pitching—where he taught me how to hold a bat properly and how to throw a proper punch. I stare at the driveway, where we helped Reilly rebuild the Rumbler. We were a normal, happy family. Now, it all feels like complete bullshit.

I can't get the image of that woman's hands on him out of my mind, and I try not to think about how many times he's probably cheated on my mom—just once? A dozen times? All with that woman? The thought that there might be others makes what bile's left in my stomach churn.

*Does she really know he's cheating on her?*

Reluctantly, I get out of the Explorer and make my way inside. This is going to be one of the most difficult conversations I've ever had, and I try to brace myself for it, even if I have no idea how to. I'm not sure if my dad called to give my mom a heads-up or not. I don't know if it matters.

Grabbing onto the doorknob like it's a lifeline, I slowly open the door and step into the entry. The house is quiet. I know she's here, her Mercedes is in the driveway, but the house feels empty. Every single thing is in its proper place, but I see it now for what it is: spotless and unlived in, cold and unwelcoming. It feels lonely.

"Ma . . ." I step further inside and shut the door behind me. "Mom!" I call more loudly. When I notice the screen door is open in the kitchen, I make my way to the back. The kitchen is spotless, the granite countertops barren and the vase that's always filled with flowers is empty and turned upside down by the sink.

If I were still living at home, she'd be starting dinner by now.

She'd have the radio on and the sound of pots and pans would be echoing through the house. Her light footsteps would patter around on the tile floor and she'd curse when she didn't think I was listening.

"Mom?" I say again, stepping up to the screen door.

"Nick, sweetheart?" she says, and I can hear the surprise in her voice as she pushes her chair away from the patio table. Her eyes are wide and she smiles when she sees me. "Sweetie, what are you doing here?"

"I need to talk to you," I tell her, and step outside.

She comes up to me and wraps her arms around my shoulders. She's short and petite in my embrace, and I hug her more tightly. When I open my eyes, I see the bottle of white wine on the table and a half-eaten chocolate chip cookie.

She takes a step back. "Well, this is a nice surprise. Do you want some dinner?" she asks, smoothing out her green blouse. She's not wearing any makeup. She has nothing cooking. She wasn't expecting me so there's no charade in play.

"Is everything okay?" I ask. It's obvious my dad didn't call her, which I'm partially grateful for. Part of me needs to know how far she's really willing to go to save face and protect me from the truth of their relationship. Another part of me wants to be mad at her, too, for lying to me—for doing this for *me,* if any of what my dad said is even true.

"Of course, everything's fine. I didn't have any plans today, so I figured I'd just . . . relax." She laughs anxiously, and I can't stomach her veiled truths.

"I know about Dad," I bite out. My words are angry and clipped. I don't want to sound like a petulant kid, but I want to shout at her to stop pretending.

"Excuse me?" She pales a little but has the nerve to seem affronted at the same time.

I hesitate, lost in the gaze of a mother who has loved me more than life itself for as long as I can remember. Only now do I see her pain and loneliness. "I know about Dad," I repeat. "I saw him with her."

Slowly, understanding fills her eyes, and her cheeks turn a burnt red. Deep lines crease around her lips. Her amber gaze doesn't leave mine as she swallows and sits back down in her chair. "Sit, Nicholas." Her voice sounds like a stranger's, distant and maybe a little bit relieved.

"So, how long has he been screwing his partner?" I force out, unable to wrap my mind around this fake life they've been living.

"Language, please," she says, clasping her hands in her lap. Despite how frail she seems, her tone brooks no argument.

I scrub my hands over my face and squeeze my eyes shut.

"I'm sorry you had to find out that way, sweetheart." She takes a sip of her wine and rests her palm on the table. "And, to answer your question, I didn't know it was a partner. I mean, I'm not surprised, but we don't talk about his extracurricular activities."

"How can you be so cavalier about this?" My words are strained and desperate, and I hate how small I sound.

My mom stares at me, sympathy in her expression, like she's worried about me when it's her my heart breaks for right now. My stomach roils in what feels a lot like guilt, and I hate my dad all the more for making me feel like I had some role to play in all of this. "And don't tell me you did this for me. I would *never* want this."

She nods and doesn't say anything at all.

"I can't believe this is happening." I stare into the crystalline pool. Reilly and I used to compete for the biggest cannonball. Was my dad cheating then? My gaze shifts to my mom, but she's fixated on the stem of her wine glass. "How long has this been going on?" I finally ask.

"A few years," she admits, a bit reluctantly.

"A few years? You've been lying to me for *a few years*?" I grit my teeth. "This whole time you were putting on a show?"

"It wasn't a show, Nick."

"Of course it was a show, that's all it's been. Every family dinner, every time you've stopped by my apartment or we've gone out to dinner, acting like everything is fine. It's all fake."

"We didn't want to burden you with—"

"The last three years have been a complete lie—it's insulting. You knew why he wouldn't work with me on the project—I feel like an idiot. My friends ask about you, and I tell them you're doing fine. I tell them Dad's working late and busy, not that he's screwing his partner." I hit the tabletop, sending her white wine sloshing over her glass.

"That's enough," she grinds out. "I know it's difficult to accept all this, and I wish you didn't have to find out this way, but this was our choice, Nicholas. This is what we chose, and that's just the way it is."

"Fine," I say. I know her situation isn't simple, but it seems black and white enough to me. "I'd like to know why. You're a psychologist, for Christ's sake. How could you possibly think lying to me is better than the truth?"

She doesn't bother reprimanding me, she looks too exhausted. Her eyes glaze over until they begin to shimmer, and she looks away. Still calm and collected, she says, "Adults don't always make the right decisions, or the best ones. But being a parent changes things. Sometimes we get ourselves into situations we're not sure how to get out of, at least that's how I've felt at times. One lie turns into five, then it turns into a lifestyle. It's hard to break out of, even if you want to."

She takes another sip of her wine. "When you were born, I was so happy. I kept telling myself that I didn't need to go back to work because I had you, and you were my life, and I needed to spend as much time with you as I could. I knew one day you wouldn't want your ol' mom around, and I wanted to enjoy you while I had you."

She offers me a sad smile. "I missed work though. I missed having a purpose in life outside this house." Picking up her glass, she swirls her wine around and around, watching the liquid whirl. "When you and Josh became friends, I was so happy for you. Old

Mr. Reilly was such a lost soul, so I was happy when you and Josh found each other. You were inseparable—such sweet boys—and you brought me so much joy. It helped me to forget that a part of me felt like it was missing.

"Then," she continues, "you met Mac and Sam, and Sam's mom had just died. The girls started spending almost as much time here with us as Josh did . . . It was nice, having a full house."

"And now that we're all living our own lives, you decide to live yours like this? You could go back to work if you miss it so much."

She looks at me again. "You know as well as anyone that change is scary," she says, but I'm not sure what she means. "You have how many certificates now and how many degrees? All because you've been putting off graduating."

I frown. "This isn't about me," I remind her.

"Isn't it? Your heart is broken, and I don't blame you, sweetheart."

While she may be partially right, I have too many questions about them to focus on me. "Then, what are you scared of?"

She takes a contemplative moment, what feels like a lifetime. It's enough time for me to realize I'm not around as much as I should be, that she feels alone, and I probably could have prevented that much at least.

"I'm scared of failing at a different life," she finally says. "I would like to think I can do anything, and that I could start over if I wanted to, but I'm not as young as I used to be, and I'm not nearly as brave."

"Ma, you'd rather stay here and be miserable than even try? I'm older now, and you can have it all—the job and you have me . . . Is it him—do you still love him?"

"No," she says, easily. "I fell out of love with your father the moment I found out he was having an affair, or maybe it was before, given how easy it seemed to be to deal with it, looking back." She eyes me closely, but I can tell she's contemplating, maybe even reliving the past few years before she continues. "Of course, I felt betrayed, but I remember feeling a little bit of relief, too, which isn't healthy," she muses. "We worked a few things out. There are rules, and while I know you think that's stupid or wrong, it's helped, believe it or not."

"He doesn't even live here, does he?" It took me a while to figure that out, but it's glaringly obvious as all the pieces start to fall into place.

"No, not really. He sleeps in the guest bedroom downstairs, occasionally—"

"When you have to keep up appearances," I say, raising my hand to stop her. "I get it." I lean across the table and clasp her hand in mine. It's soft and delicate. "I want a better life for you than this."

With crinkly ocher eyes, she offers me a small smile. "I know you do, sweetheart, that's why I didn't tell you. I don't want you worrying about this. When I'm ready, I'll figure everything out. I have my freedom too, you know? I have my friends and this place, which keeps me more than busy. And it's filled with happy memories I couldn't bear to part with."

"But, Ma—"

She leans forward and cups my face with her hand.

"This was our decision," she reminds me. "My only regret is not telling you myself."

I shake my head, helpless and angry and hurt. Yesterday, my biggest concern was what size railings I needed to order for Sam's office loft. Now, I feel like I've been hit by a fucking truck.

# THIRTY-TWO
## NICK

SITTING on my balcony as dusk descends, I light a smoke for the first time in two months and let the cool night air calm my senses. Light barely filters in over the mountains, and I try to think if I've ever felt more conflicted than I have today, than I do in this moment.

I know I have every right to be pissed off after three years of bullshit lies, but do I get to hate my dad when my mom has been just as deceiving? Would I still hate him right now if he'd told me what happen three years ago, or just be disappointed instead of both? Either way, he's not the man I thought he was.

I take another drag of my cigarette and revel in the simple, familiar things, like the burn of the menthol in the back of my throat. I've gone two months without a smoke. I almost caved a couple times, but today I didn't try to fight it.

Leaning my head back, I shut my eyes and exhale into the breeze. I feel like there's a paper I should be writing or book I should be reading, but that's as far as my memory serves me. A crow caws from the redwoods that line the back of the lot and the final patch of setting sunlight is warm against the cool night air.

A recognizable rumble accelerates up the street, and I know

there's a lifted, red Chevy pulling to a stop outside my house. I didn't think I was up for company, but knowing Reilly's here comes as a relief. When the engine shuts off, I stab out my cigarette and make my way to the front door.

Bobby peers up at me as I step out onto the landing. He climbs out of the passenger seat and lifts a six-pack and a brown paper bag. "Party time!"

"You up for visitors?" Reilly asks and tugs the hem of his shirt down as he steps up to the curb. I don't answer because it's not really a question. They're both already on their way up the stairs.

"Who told you?" I ask as they make their way to my front door. I haven't told anyone about my dad, too ashamed or angry I guess.

Bobby ignores me and steps inside my apartment.

"Alison told Sam—"

"Ah, my mom," I finish for him. "Got it."

My apartment is dark, still closed up from my being gone for the day. Marilyn and Monroe's tank is the only offering of light.

"This is depressing," Bobby mutters and flicks on the light switch.

"I just got home." Sort of. It's hard not to notice the stuff filling my apartment, purchased with guilt money or whatever it is—mats and towels and blankets my mom's bought me, picture frames, top-of-the-line cooking sets I never use—so it was easier to leave the lights off.

Together, my friends fill my apartment the way jocks fill any room. The silence humming around me is stomped away by boot steps and throaty quips. It's a liveliness I didn't realize I needed.

"You didn't think we'd let you stew alone, did you?" Reilly pulls a bottle of Dr. Pepper out of the mixed six-pack of soda on the counter.

I smile. "I might've hoped."

"Ha!" Bobby plops down on the couch. "No way. It's initiation night, my friend."

"Initiation night?"

Reilly hands me a Dr. Pepper.

"What, no beer?" I ask, surprised.

"Do you *want* beer?" he asks.

I shake my head. "No." Especially not after last night.

"Good," Bobby says with a fiendish laugh. "Because we brought something way better." He dumps the contents of the paper bag out on my coffee table: beef sticks, Sugar Babies, Whatchamacallits, and every sugary thing I remember from my childhood, are splayed out in front of me. "Wait, there's more!" Bobby jumps up and heads out the front door.

"Although this is all very touching and . . . interesting, I'm a little confused. Is this about my parents?"

"Not really about your parents," Reilly says. "It's more about you being one of us now."

"One of you? As in a part of the crew?" I laugh. "I thought I was the ringleader."

Reilly clasps my shoulder with a chuckle. "That you are, my friend, but that's not what I meant." Reilly takes a swig of his soda. "All my life you've had to listen to me bitch and complain about how shitty my life was. I've never wished any of that on you, but you're not so much an outsider anymore, are you?"

I shake my head. "That's a fucked-up thing to say, Reilly."

His chuckle deepens.

"But you're right, it feels a little different."

"Exactly. Now we can all be miserable together. Plus, we have years of advice and support to give back to you."

"Wow, I even get reused material. I feel like royalty."

Reilly kicks off his shoes and plops down on the sectional. I do the same, strangely happy. We clink bottlenecks, and Reilly raises his Dr. Pepper. "Welcome to the club, buddy."

"Oh, there's a club? How fancy."

We both take a gulp, and Reilly heaves out a sigh. "Yep, the Fucked-up Family Club." He smirks.

Bobby comes back inside with an old-school Nintendo console, and I burst with laughter. "No way!"

"We're going back to our roots, baby," Bobby says. While my childhood begins to resurface—late nights at my house, playing Super Mario and eating junk food from the nearby 7-Eleven—I can't imagine what any of this would mean for Bobby, being like five years younger than us.

"He's here for moron support," Reilly confides, winking at me.

"Hey," Bobby says. "I might not be as thick as thieves as the two of you, but I've been a part of the club longer than Nick, so I'm an elder, in comparison."

"Oh, there's a ranking?" I clarify, glancing between them. "Good to know. I'll start planning my coup then."

"Yep!" Bobby plugs the console into my big screen. "And it's boys only, too."

"Perfect." I clap my hands together and lean forward on the couch. My palms are itching to hold the rectangle controller in my hand again.

Reilly does the same, elbows resting on his knees. "Seriously though, why didn't you call me?" he asks more quietly, and I wonder if he's even a little hurt.

"It's nothing personal," I tell him. I'm not in the mood to have another heart-to-heart today. "I'm trying not to think about it right now, Rye. That's all. It's hard for me to wrap my mind around, you know?"

I don't look at him, but see him nod from the corner of my eye. "Yeah, I figured as much. That's why we showed up, even if all I do is whoop your ass in Tetris."

"Tetris! My day just got even better."

With a no-mercy expression, Reilly hands me a controller. "Shall we get to it then?"

"Hell. Yeah."

# THIRTY-THREE
## NICK

"I CAN'T BELIEVE you're doing this, Nick." Sam's voice is one of awe and surprise as she puts Shasta's halter on in the stall across from me. "Are you sure you don't want to ask for a rain check? You've sorta got a lot going on right now. Maybe you're not thinking clearly."

"Thanks, Sam, but I'm sure. The last thing I want to do is dwell on my parents' shit."

"So you're just going to ignore it?"

"Trying to," I tell her, peering over Target's mane. "Someone keeps bringing it up."

"Fine. Sorry. I just can't believe you're actually going to ride."

I lead Target out of his stall and follow Sam and Shasta to the hitching post. "I can't say I'm all that excited about it," I admit. The horses' hooves clomp against the cement floor, a familiar sound that fills at least two of my workdays every week.

"Shasta will be fine with Jesse in the arena. You don't have to physically get on a horse."

"I have to do this," I tell her. "I want to." I'm determined to conquer this fear I've had for the last ten-plus years; a seemingly small and insignificant one compared to the hurdles Jesse has to face each and every day. And maybe I'm trying to prove to myself that I'm not like my mom; I don't want fear to hold me back.

"But Target, of all horses?"

"You told me Target needed to be ridden, so, I'm doing you a favor."

She runs her fingers through his dark mane. "He's the wiliest of them all. I think you should start with training wheels, that's all."

"Keep talking, Sam. You're really helping me relax."

She snorts a laugh. "Good. You razz me all the time. It's nice to dish out a little payback."

Shaking my head, I give her what she wants, a smile. "Touché. Well, you're going to get plenty of material today." I head back to Trinity's stall. Between my parents, Bethany on her way, and riding for the first time in forever, Sam will have plenty to divulge to the crew later.

When I slide the stall door open, Trinity's tan and white head pops up and she walks toward me. "No food yet, girl," I tell her and slide her halter on. It's purple and bedazzled, like only Sarah, her owner, would do. "You do get a ride, though."

Trinity follows me out of her stall, the lead rope draped around her neck instead of in my hand, and we make our way toward the other horses at the post. Today is going to be interesting, and although I know how to ride, I'm still anxious about doing it. Call it an irrational fear after falling off as a kid, but the last thing I want to do is look like an ass in front of Bethany and Jesse, especially after the drunken state she saw me in the other night. Other than a text to confirm she's coming, I haven't talked to her since.

Sam picks up the horse's hooves to give them a quick check. "Shoes look good." She pats Trinity's rump. "You know, this might go without saying, but it's strange seeing you and Bethany together."

"Yeah? Well, we're not together. I think you know things between us are a little more complicated than that."

"Do I?"

"We're just friends, Sam."

"Right. Well, it could be worse, I guess. I'll get some carrots."

"Wait, wait, wait." I drape my arm over Trinity's back. "Are you saying you don't hate Bethany anymore? Are you starting to *like* her?"

She doesn't turn around to answer me. "Don't get all worked up," she mutters.

I barely hear her over the clucking chickens and the horses. "You'll have to speak louder. I don't think I heard you right, Sam."

"Screw off!" she shouts this time, and I laugh at the turn of events. "This week really is full of surprises," I tell Trinity, and she blinks lazily at me.

Bethany's Range Rover hums up the gravel drive a moment later, and I steel my nerves. Today I have to act like I have my shit together. "What could go wrong," I breathe out and head toward her car.

I'm not sure what I expected her to be wearing today, but she takes my breath away as she steps out of the car in a pair of hip-hugging jeans and her cowboy boots. It's easy enough to forget my nerves as she smiles at me.

Jesse ambles toward me in jeans, a pair of boots that look brand new, and a well-worn Star Wars t-shirt—one of his favorites, I imagine.

"Hey, kid." I give him a friendly tip-of-the-hat.

Both of them eye me up and down, but while Jesse's look is more curious, Bethany's seems appreciative, and I flash her a smile. "Hey, good lookin'."

"Hi." She rests her hands on Jesse's shoulders, almost like she's using him as a shield. "You sure look the part today."

I tip the brim of my hat to her with a wink. "Why thank you, mi'lady. You two don't look too bad yourselves. I'm glad you came out." I nod to the horses behind me. "Want to meet your trusty steed for the day?"

The screen door to the house swings open and shut, and I hear

Sam's boots on the steps before she appears around the corner of the stable.

"Howdy," she says, her blonde waves catching in the breeze. Her eyes land on Bethany first, skirt quickly to me, then she locks eyes with Jesse. He quickly looks away. "Hi. I'm Sam. Welcome to the Miller ranch."

Bethany squeezes Jesse's shoulders. "Go on, J. Introduce yourself. This is Sam's ranch and her horse you'll be riding."

"I'm Jesse," he says, but he peers around at the horses, and the ranch, and the chickens walking around outside their coop. There's a lot to see out here, and I can imagine he's anxious to take it all in.

"Well, Jesse, it's nice to meet you. I brought you something that is going to make Shasta your best friend in the whole world."

"Sam knows horses better than anyone I know," I tell Jesse. The easiness between us from the other day at my house isn't gone, but tampered in this new place with a stranger standing in front of him. "She must have something really special for you."

She holds out a few large carrots. "Why don't we give the horses a snack and get to know them a bit better?" Sam hands Jesse and Bethany a carrot each. "This will put them in a good mood." Sam smirks at me. "And Nick's going to need all the help he can get on ol' Target today." She shows Jesse how many times to break the carrot and Bethany steps closer to me.

"I thought you were the horse guy," she says, curious. She glances from Sam to me.

"Oh, I'm a horse guy—I groom them, and muck their stalls, and exercise them—but I don't actually *ride* them."

Her brow furrows. "Why not?"

"Just isn't really my thing," I tell her, not wanting to go into too much detail and scare Jesse away from riding.

Her eyes widen. "Oh yeah, I do remember something Reilly said the other day about you riding."

"Yeah, bad experience once, but I'll make an exception today." I wink at her.

Bethany doesn't press for more information, but I can tell she's curious.

"So, Jesse," Sam says. "Have you ever been around horses before?" She's trying to gauge his interest and experience, like she does with potential boarders who think they're interested in buying a horse.

"When I was younger, I rode a pony," he tells her. "But I don't really remember it. I like horses though."

"Then you're in for a treat." She stops in front of her gray mare. "This is Shasta. I've had her for years. She's very special to me—I think you're really going to like her."

Sam runs her hand down Shasta's muzzle, then down her neck. "You can pet her if you want. She's gentle, just be aware of her feet." She pats Shasta's shoulder blade. "Shasta's big and can't always see you. Okay?"

Jesse nods, staring at her leg like it's going to stomp on him.

Bethany steps in and begins to follow Sam's lead, running her hand down the length of Shasta's girth. "Try it, J," she says. Bethany's presence alone helps put Jesse more at ease, though it would seem he needs little encouragement.

Jesse reaches out his hand then smiles with awe. "She's soft."

"And she's strong," Bethany adds. "You can feel her heart beating."

"Here, put your palm out like this," Sam says and demonstrates how to feed a bit of carrot to Shasta. Jesse only hesitates a moment before his curiosity is too much for him to ignore and he steps closer and opens his palm by Shasta's mouth.

I nudge Bethany and break off a piece of my carrot, nodding to her horse for the day. "You'll be riding Trinity." I give the palomino a pat on the neck.

"She's beautiful," Bethany says, running her hand down the curve of Trinity's back.

"Yeah, and she's a sweetheart. I thought she'd be a good fit for you. And she'll love you forever if you give her a piece of carrot."

"Oh, she's an easy one, too, huh?"

I laugh. "Yeah, she is."

Bethany stares at the carrot in her hand. "Sam and Jesse made it look easy," she muses. Then she looks at me. "I've never actually fed a horse before." Impatient for her treat, Trinity turns to Bethany. Startled, Bethany takes a step back.

"Here," I say gently, and I take her hand in mine, cradling our palms together. "Keep your fingers open, and she'll pick it up with her lips. It won't hurt, trust me." I squeeze her hand reassuringly and slowly ease it toward Trinity's mouth.

In less than a second, the deed is done. The carrot crunches loudly between Trinity's teeth, pieces of it falling to the dirt, and Bethany laughs. "That actually tickled a little."

"Yeah, horse whiskers are like that." I'm still holding her hand, though, and I know I should let it go. I promised I wouldn't make this harder on her, but her nearness makes it almost impossible to take a step back. I'm supposed to be her friend, but I want more. I always have, even if I didn't understand why until now.

Bethany looks at me, her eyes shifting over my face momentarily, then she removes her hand from mine and moves to the side.

"Yeah, so," I nod to what's left of her carrot. "Go ahead and give her the rest." I pick up the curry comb. "We should probably get started."

# THIRTY-FOUR
# BETHANY

ANY OTHER SATURDAY, I'd be working on homework and studying in my pajamas all day, doing chores intermittently, and keeping an eye on Jesse while my mom's lunch turns into a shopping trip, then dinner and drinks with a client. But here I sit, on top of a butterscotch-painted beauty, finally comfortable in the way her body moves with each jostling step beneath me. In this arena, covered in dust, I feel strangely relaxed and at peace.

It could be that I finally feel like I know what I'm doing and that Sam is no longer watching from the sidelines. While any feud between us, I guess you could call it, is on hold during this project, I can tell she's wary of my being here. This is more personal, and yet she's opened up her home to us, which makes me hopeful, even if she has a watchful eye that rests on me more often than I'm comfortable with. Jesse looks happy, though, which makes it all worth it. He seems taller and even a little proud on the back of Shasta, and I have Sam and Nick to thank for that.

Jesse slows Shasta to a stop and whispers praise in her ear. Patting her neck, he straightens and looks around the arena, still taking it all in.

"Well, kid, I think she likes you," Nick says from his dark, coffee-colored horse beside Jesse. Although Nick hasn't ridden in years, he seems natural and confident enough to me.

"Should I give her some water?" Jesse asks as he stares at the trough.

"Sure, just a little."

I ride Trinity up beside him so she can dip her nose in for a quick drink, too. "So, what do you think about all this horse stuff, J?" I ask him.

Jesse smiles to himself, watching Shasta's ears flick back at us as she slurps down some water. "It's cool," he says modestly, but I know he's giddy inside.

"Yeah, it is pretty cool," I agree. I nudge Trinity away from the water, not wanting her belly to get too full, and Jesse follows.

Scanning the hillside, I admire the land that surrounds us as we clomp over to Nick. "Is all this Sam's property?"

"Yep. It's a bitch to take care of, too." Nick cringes at his words and mouths a *sorry* as he glances at Jesse, but my brother's heard me say worse, and he's too enthralled with Shasta to notice anyway.

There's a whistle from the railing. When I look over, Sam is on the other side of the pasture and climbs up. "Anyone interested in a quick trail ride? I need to go to Reilly's to let Petey out."

"Uh, I dunno if we're ready for that yet, Sam." I glance back at Jesse. "It seems a little soon."

"I'm more worried about Nick," she says with a wry smile. "Jesse can ride with me. I don't take up much room."

"I'm okay with that. Jes—?" He's already nodding before I can finish. "Well, there you have it."

"Great." Sam flings her leg over the railing effortlessly, like she does it all the time, then she jumps into the arena and meets us in the middle.

"Yeah, don't worry about me, Sam. I'm happy to go on a trail ride. Thanks for asking." Nick winks at me, and I wonder if this is how it always is between them. Playful and easy.

He jumps down from his horse and helps Jesse move to the back of the saddle so Sam can climb up. Once everyone's back in the saddle, we head out of the arena, Sam and Jesse taking the lead.

She opens the gate, and Nick closes it once we're through. We make our way around the pasture, toward the hills that line the backside of the property.

"Hold onto your reins," Nick says, coming up behind me. "They're going to get excited with all the green grass. Once Trinity goes down for a bite, you might not get her head back up," he teases. Or, at least I think he's teasing. Trinity perks up and her ears pivot around at the change of scenery. "They love going off-road."

"I don't blame them. I'd get bored running around in circles, too," I say.

We ride in companionable silence, and every so often, when Jesse looks back at me, I wave in reassurance.

"So, are you going to tell me why you don't like riding?" I ask, unable to resist a smirk. I can tell it's a touchy subject, but he has to know I was going to ask.

Nick looks at me askance. "I had an accident when I was seven. Totally not a big deal, I just never wanted to get back on again."

"It sounds like a big deal if you didn't want to ride."

Nick shrugs. "It is what it is. I barely remember it, actually. I think it was the fear that became the monster, more than the memory, if that makes any sense."

"It does," I say, knowing my fears rule me more than I'd like them to sometimes.

He peers out at the rolling hills as our horses start up the incline.

"But, you're riding today. For Jesse?"

He shrugs. "For Jesse. For me."

He's quiet for a while, and I worry I've hit a nerve until, finally, he speaks again. "Thank you for the other night."

"What, for taking you home? It's the least I could do."

"But you didn't have to stay," Nick adds quietly. "I appreciate it."

I blush. "I wasn't sure you even remembered any of that."

Nick doesn't say anything else, and once again, the silence between us stretches as we make our way toward a large oak tree on the crest of the hill. Sam and Jesse veer off and make their way down toward the lake.

"We can wait up here," Nick says, anticipating me. "Jesse will be fine. We can see Reilly's place from up the hill. There's an outlook Sam's dad used to take me to a long time ago. You can see most of the property."

I stare out at the glinting water. Growing up here seems like a dream, one I might not have appreciated in another life. We make our way through the woodsy hillside, twigs and leaves and debris crunching beneath the horses. Every now and again, Trinity tears a long green weed from the ground, growing too tall to resist.

We weave around trees and up and down the landscape, over logs and around rocks, until we finally come to a small clearing. As our horses come to a stop, I admire the way the blue skies kiss the tops of green and the rolling hills and oak forest that stretch out beyond the outlook.

"This is all theirs?" I ask. The beauty of it is humbling in a way that living in town has never been. "I feel so small."

"It's not all theirs, but a lot of it is. Reilly has some of it, and there are fence lines Sam's never crossed, up in those hills further back."

I scan the property on the other end of the lake and find Jesse and Sam making their way up to the house. Sam helps Jesse down and when she opens the pen, a black and white dog runs up to him, tail wagging excitedly.

"So, Sam and Reilly live in houses across the lake from one another, huh?"

Nick nods, dismounts Target, and wraps his reins around one of the low oak branches. "Pretty much." He glances back at me. "You might want to stretch your legs. You're going to be sore, if what I'm feeling is any indication." He winces and does a quick lunge.

"That's . . . not hilarious at all." I try to stifle my amusement.

"You laugh, but this shit hurts." He walks over to the big oak and rests his palm against it, staring out at the swelling hills. I follow suit, finally finding the courage to ask him something I've been wondering about all day. "You seem . . . okay about everything that happened the other day," I say, even though I know that's highly unlikely. "Have you talked to your parents about it?"

Nick takes a deep breath and looks at me with a sheepish sort of smile tugging at his lips. "Yes. No. But, it could be worse. Let's just say that I feel like I'm part of the club now, too."

"What club is that?"

"The Fucked-up Family Club." He leans against the tree with a smug smile. "According to Reilly, I'm a member of the 'guys only' chapter."

"Cute," I say, glad his friends finally know what happened. "Well, I extend you an official welcome, from the 'girls only' chapter." I startle when my phone buzzes in my back pocket.

"You're a squeaker, huh?"

"Pardon me?"

Nick barks a laugh. "That sounded wrong. I mean, you squeak when you startle." He shrugs. "Good to know."

I lift an eyebrow and peer down at the text message.

Dad: Where are you?

"What's wrong? Is it your parents?"

"Yeah. No big deal. My dad probably wants to lecture me about school."

"Hmm. Speaking of school, have you thought about which

grad school you'll apply to after you get an awesome score on your test?"

"No," I say with a grunt, and I straighten my back. "What about you? Where are you going to work after you graduate, some big firm in Benton?"

Nick's easiness fades, and he plucks up a long piece of grass. "No, probably not. I like working at Lick's, to be honest."

"Yeah?"

"Sometimes I think that's what I want to do, just work there my whole life. I'm good at it, and I like people, most of the time." He twirls the grass between his fingers.

"Maybe you should buy your own bar," I tell him.

His eyes shift to mine again. "Now you're just talking crazy."

I push him playfully. "I'm serious. If you love it, you could get your own place, turn it into whatever you want—you have the capability. You could run your own bar in your sleep."

His amusement turns to something more enlivened, and he smiles. "Sounds kinda nice, actually."

"You could call it Pickle Juice. Or Nickel's, for Nick and Pickle."

He chuckles. "I think you should leave the naming to me."

"Well then, what would it be?"

"I dunno. I've never thought about it before."

"You have to have a signature drink with pickle juice, at least," I tell him. "It only makes sense. You named a doll Pickles for crying out loud."

Nick laughs, more boisterous this time, and I think I could listen to him laugh all day long and never get tired of it. "That sounds delicious but I don't think people would go for it."

"You'd be surprised. It would be a good marketing strategy. It would make you stand out. I think you should seriously consider it. I can picture it perfectly."

I have to resist the urge to do a lunge or two, knowing a deep hamstring stretch would be euphoric with all the tension in my backside. Knowing I wouldn't be as cute as Nick doing it, though, prevents me. The last thing I want is to look like an idiot.

He chuckles beside me. "Just do it, Bethany. Stretch it out. You know you want to."

"No, I don't," I lie through a smile.

"Just do it. Come on, I'll do it with you—"

I push him, snorting out a laugh. "Stop being weird."

He pushes me back. "I'm not being weird, I'm making you laugh. It's the best part of my day."

My cheeks flush, and after a long, drawn out, sideways glance, I decide making him smile is the best part of my day, too. With a smirk, I do a quick, awkward lunge, earning me another hearty chuckle, and I revel in the sound.

# THIRTY-FIVE
# BETHANY

AFTER RIDING, Jesse and I go out for an ice cream before heading home to lock ourselves upstairs in the game room and watch movies all night. My dad's Jaguar is parked in the garage with no sign that my mom is home, which isn't surprising.

Exhausted, Jesse and I shuffle up to the front door, my legs so sore, I can't imagine what tomorrow will be like. "Wait," I say as Jesse reaches for the doorknob. "Your shoes. Leave them on the tile entry. Mom will *freak* if you track horse shit into the house."

He smiles down at his feet, as if he's contemplating it.

"You wouldn't get to drink Squirt for a month, buddy. Your life would be miserable."

Flinging the door open, I step inside and balance the best I can as I pull off one boot and then the other. My hope to go in and decompress, though, is short-lived.

"Beth," my dad says, eerily flat from his office. I've barely gotten through the front door, and I already have a bad feeling.

"Take off your shoes and head upstairs, J."

Jesse's eyes meet mine, his brow furrowed in question. In worry.

Flashing him a reassuring smile, I nod toward the stairs. "Jump in the shower so we can start our movie."

Finally, he nods and jogs up the stairs. Dropping my purse onto the couch, I make my way through the living room, to my father's office.

When I step into the doorway, he sets the document in his hand down, pissed or troubled, I'm not sure which, then he rubs his brow. "Did you have fun today?" he asks, but there's no real curiosity in his question, no inflection or interest at all. He's upset with me, and I'm damned no matter what I say.

"It was successful." I decide it's the safest answer. "Jesse had a blast and learned a lot. Nick was really great with him." I almost smile at how good the day felt, but any lingering joy diminishes as my dad continues to glare at me.

He leans back in his chair, his eyes not leaving mine. The fact that he's giving me his full attention is a telltale sign that I should be worried. "How's your project going?"

"It's going fine. Why?

His expression is unchanging, and he clasps his hands together in his lap. "I ran into Edward Murray this morning."

Confused, I shake my head. "Edward Murray . . . You mean, *Professor* Murray?" I'm not sure how my dad knows my professor, but I'm not that surprised. My dad knows everyone in this community. Benton—Saratoga Falls, it's like they're one in the same. I hate it.

"He mentioned you and your final project partner were having some problems."

"We were, in the beginning, but we're not anymore."

"So it seems," he mutters. "Your mother told me you were working on your project today."

"We were supposed to, but plans changed. I *was* with Nick, but we—" The absurdity of the conversation stops me short, and my blood begins to boil. "I'm twenty-three, Dad. I don't need you micromanaging my school work *or* my life."

"No? Well, if history is any indication of the direction this *partnership* of yours is going, you're only distracting yourself again from what's important."

"What the hell is that supposed to mean?" I cross my arms over my chest, barely able to contain the annoyance bubbling beneath the surface. He sits there high and mighty, like he knows anything about me, my life, my distractions . . .

"This is Mike, all over again," he grumbles. "I'm not doing this with you again."

The color drains from my face, and my heart skips a few beats. "Nick is nothing like Mike," I tell him. "You don't even know him."

"No, and I don't need to. You barely graduated high school with Mike whispering in your ear. Now, so close to graduation, you and your boyfriend—"

"His name is Nick, and he's not my boy—"

"—are spending a lot of time together."

"Yes, that's what partners do," I bite out. "They spend time together, they work. Nick and I happen to be friends, too. And he likes to be around Jesse."

"And sleepovers, how do they fit into the project—excuse me, the friendship?"

"You have all of this *so* wrong," I growl with disdain. I'm tired of him always assuming the worst. Bored with having this same conversation over and over, I turn to leave. "I'm done talking about this."

"Don't do something you'll regret, Bethany."

"You don't know anything about me or Nick," I snap and look back at him, eyes narrowed and a thousand curses desperate to pass my lips. "If you want me to graduate, stay out of my business."

Surprisingly, he doesn't say anything else as he watches me walk away, silently fuming. When I notice my mom standing by the couch, her arms crossed, eyeing me like I've done something wrong, I can't resist. "Don't even start with me," I say and head upstairs.

I'm relieved to hear the shower water running and Jesse inside as I slam my bedroom door shut.

I only remove my dirty pants before I collapse on my bed with tears in my eyes. Why does this all have to be so hard? Once again, the constant conundrum of an apartment or grad school overwhelms me and I know I have to make a decision—I have to come up with a plan.

My phone buzzes in my pants pocket on the floor, and I scramble for it. When I see Nick's name on the screen, my chest aches a little under the weight of it all—of seeing his name and the relief I feel and what it all means. I force myself to answer. "Hello?"

"Hey, how are you feeling? Sore yet?" He laughs on the other end of the line, and I wish I could, too.

"Ah, yeah, a little. Now's not really a good time, Nick." The backs of my eyes begin to sting. I hate that I let my dad get to me, but he's like poison, bleeding in.

He's quiet for a heartbeat. "Are you okay?"

His sincerity and concern makes it difficult to breathe, but I force my vocal chords to work. "Yeah. I'm fine."

There's movement on the other end of the phone. "Jesse forgot his jacket, I just thought you should know."

"Oh, okay. Thanks." I can barely manage the words as I let out a suffocating breath. "I'll get it later."

"Hey, I know you said you were going to work on our summary tomorrow, but—do you want to do something fun?"

"Something fun?" I ask, wiping the moisture from beneath my eyes. All I can think about is the look of censure on my dad's face at the idea.

"Yeah, the gang wants to go to the beach tomorrow. What do you say? Feel like acting your age for a day?"

I nod, eyes blurred with tears. "Yeah, actually, that would be really great."

# THIRTY-SIX
# BETHANY'S JOURNAL

## APRIL 21ST

*I'm not sure why I keep trying to please people who will never be happy. I'm tired of having to explain myself. I'm tired of their assumptions. Sometimes I feel like my parents ~~done~~ don't care much about me one way or the other. But, if that's true, why do they micromanage my life so much? How can they not see that they're pushing me away, or is it that they don't care? I don't even think their anger with me is about grades anymore. Not really, anyway. It's about how far I've somehow fallen in their eyes, and how I'll never live up to what they want.*

*Leaving seems like the only thing to do, and I know I would be happier, even if I'd hate being away from Jesse. But, I have to get out of ~~her~~ here, and that's what I plan to do, after I take the GRE. If I can wait that long. –B*

# THIRTY-SEVEN
# NICK

THE MOMENT I walk into my parents' house, the tension in my body triples, despite the smell of homemade cookies that fills the air. Normally, it's a comforting scent that makes my stomach rumble and my smile stretch from ear to ear. After my phone call with Bethany, though, and hearing the reediness of her voice, something tore open inside me. I've heard her scared and angry and frustrated, but never desperate to hold herself together like that. I know it had something to do with her parents, especially after seeing that text from her dad, which makes me think of my own and how screwed up this situation is. It's hard to imagine how this family dinner will go.

"Nick, sweetheart, is that you?" My mom's voice rings from upstairs. "I'll be down in a minute. I'm just freshening up."

"No prob." I head into the kitchen to snoop. There are chocolate chip cookies on the counter, some on a small, decorative plate, and two Tupperware containers beside it—one for my dad and one for me, I assume. I wonder if it's easier for her now, not having to hide the truth.

Opening the fridge, I reach for the carton of orange juice. It's light and almost empty, so I spin the cap off and chug what's left.

"I see not everything's changed," my dad says from behind me, and I nearly choke in surprise.

Wiping off my mouth with the back of my hand, I glance over my shoulder. He's in his workout clothes, like he's just coming home from the gym. But then, this isn't home anymore, not for him. He sets the newspaper on the counter and walks over to the cabinet and pulls out a glass.

"Nope, not everything." I toss the empty carton into the recycling.

My dad eyes my ranch clothes. "How's Sam?"

"Good." I don't feel like elaborating, not while there's no trace of remorse on his face.

He pours himself a glass of water. "I'm glad. She's a good kid."

"We're not kids anymore," I remind him. "We've been adults for a long time now."

My dad shakes his head, as if he's amused. "You'll always be our kids, Nick. We'll always want to protect you."

I step over to the sliding glass door, biting back my resentful comments. I'm not sure if I should start in on him now or wait until my mom's present so we can hash it out together and be done with it.

"I wasn't sure you'd join us tonight," he admits. The laughter in his voice I remember so well as a child has been gone for a very long time, I realize.

"Yeah well, here I am."

When my mom strides into the kitchen, she smiles at me, wraps her arms around my shoulders as best she can on her short little legs, and then she squeezes me tightly. "Hi, sweetheart."

I squeeze her back. "Hey, Ma."

"How much time do I have before dinner gets here?" my dad asks and chugs down the rest of his water.

My mom looks at her watch. "Ten minutes or so," she says,

sparing him a glance. But it's not awkward the way I'd expect it to be. "You have time for a quick shower."

My father excuses himself to run upstairs.

"You'll be happy to know," my mom says, rinsing out my dad's glass, "that I decided to spend my time baking cookies today instead of worrying about dinner."

I tilt my head, confused.

"I've order dinner from Giovanni's. It should be here soon."

My stomach rumbles at the thought, and her smile widens. "I thought you'd like that." She hands me the two cookie containers. "One's for Bethany and Jesse. Make sure they get it, okay?"

Surprised, I take them from her. "Sure."

"I mean it, Nicholas. You," she says, pointing to one container. "Bethany." She points to the other one. "Don't touch."

"I got it, Ma," I say with a laugh. "I'll make sure she gets it. I have *some* self-control, you know."

"Good." She smiles at me. "I really enjoyed having them here the other day. I hope Bethany decides to come back for another tutoring session."

"I do too," I admit. "She said it helped her a lot. I think she really appreciated it."

"I'm glad I could be helpful." I can see it in my mom's eyes—a sense of purpose. It lightens her expression and her eyes smile. I don't know if my dad notices those things anymore or if he even cares, but it makes me happy.

"So, this cookie business," I say, inching closer to the cookie plate. "Are they strictly an after-dinner snack or . . . ?"

"You can have *one* now." She chuckles softly and pats my shoulder. "How can I resist that handsome smile of yours?"

"I wish everyone thought that," I semi-joke.

My mom's brow furrows, and I don't like the sudden sympathy in her expression. "So, you're still not dating then?" she asks, folding her fabric napkins just the way she likes them for the table.

"No, we're not dating," I say easily enough. "I don't really know what we are."

"I see."

"You do? Because I sure as hell don't."

"Language, Nicholas." My mom opens the fridge and pulls out two brand new jars of pickles.

My salivary glands kick into overdrive. "Are those for me?"

"Of course they are. Do you think I'm going to eat two jars of Claussen's on my own?"

I snort. "*I* could."

"I'm aware," she grumbles. "They were on sale at the grocery store, so I picked up a couple." She nods to the cookies. "Put them with the rest of your things. I don't want you to forget them."

"Oh, I won't. You got the best ones."

"So you've told me."

I scoot my to-go pile to the end of the counter, out of the way, and my mom points to the cupboard. "Pull out plates and glasses for dinner, Nick, and set the table, please." She holds out her fabric napkins. "Use the nice ones this time."

I do as she says, but part of me thinks pretending we're going to have a nice dinner together is stupid. They don't have to keep up the charade anymore, it just makes me uncomfortable.

"Did you see the roses your father brought me?"

I glance at the vase on the buffet and the white roses that fill it.

"Are you guys working things out or something?" I ask, because it's weird that he's still getting her flowers and they're acting so normal, when everything is anything but.

Then the doorbells rings and my mom hurries toward the door; my dad jogs back down the stairs.

"Just in time," he says and pays the delivery girl. He brings the takeout into the dining room and sets it on the table. Clapping his hands together, he says, "Ravioli, salad, and pesto bread sticks. Dinner is served."

"It smells delicious," my mom coos. "I'm ravenous." She

opens the plastic lids. The smell of rich Italian herbs waft over the table and my stomach rumbles again. "Serve yourselves," she says and disappears into the kitchen. She returns with an uncorked bottle of rosé, and I feel a pang of sadness, remembering how things were just a few days ago, how they used to be.

"Would anyone care for a glass?" she asks as she opens the curio cabinet.

"Please," my dad says, scooping food onto my mom's plate for her.

I glance between them, awed by whatever is going on right now, and shake my head. "No, I'm good, thanks."

"Suit yourself, it's Saturday after all." She pulls out a glass for her and my dad. "Are you going to work tonight, sweetheart?"

I smooth my napkin in my lap. "Yeah, at eight."

"Well then, I won't be a bad influence on you, not tonight, at least." She smiles at me, knowingly. I like to have a glass of wine with her now and again, but only with her. It's sort of our thing.

"So, Nicky," my dad starts, "how is your project going up at the ranch?"

Shrugging, I take a sip of my water. "It's going fine."

"Just fine?" He stabs his lettuce onto his fork, like it's just another dinner.

"Yeah." I set my fork down on my untouched plate. "So—why did you buy Mom roses?"

They look at each other, confused. "I always buy your mother flowers before family dinner."

"Yeah, but why? You guys aren't really together and I know that now, so it's weird." When they exchange another glance, I can't take it anymore. "Why am I here, exactly?"

"You're here for dinner, of course." My mom takes a bite of her ravioli.

"Are we really going to sit here and pretend like we're a happy family—asking me about my projects . . . Dad's dishing up your food for you, like that's normal."

"It is normal, Nicholas," my mom says.

"Yeah, but, aren't we going to address the elephant in the room, because it's creeping me out that we're pretending I didn't see Dad groping some woman in his office."

"Nick, that's enough," my dad says, and the grasp I had on my emotions when I walked in loosens, it's almost overwhelming.

"You two have been lying to me for, what, three years or something? You want to just brush it all under the rug and that's supposed to be okay?"

"We're not brushing anything under the rug, Nick." My dad's voice is stern and demanding, but it doesn't faze me. He lost that power over me when he started screwing his coworker.

"What do you want to talk about, Nicholas?" my mom asks. "What do you want to know?"

"I want to know why you are both still acting like you're married when you haven't been for a long time. What happens now? Dad, are you moving out—*really* moving out?"

"We haven't decided what we're going to do next," he explains, but it's not a satisfactory answer.

"Are you sorry about what you did?" I ask.

"Yes, of course I'm sorry about what happened. I never wanted to hurt your mother, or you."

"Nick," my mom says, "we just wanted a nice dinner with you. We wanted to make sure you're okay."

"Well, I'm not okay," I tell her honestly. I see the hurt fill her eyes, but I'm not sure why she's surprised. "How did you really think this was going to go?" I shake my head and sit back in my chair. "I feel like I'm in The Twilight Zone."

My dad folds his hands and rests them on the table. His expression is unmoved, and it feels like I'm talking to a wall.

"Do you have anything else to say?" I ask him.

He clears his throat and glances at my mom. "I don't expect this to be easy for you, Nick, and I understand why you're angry, but your mother has forgiven me—"

"I wouldn't go that far," she says into her wine glass.

"Look," he says, impatient. "Nick, I wish you knew how sorry I was. I didn't want this to happen. It just did. I can't undo it, no matter how much I want to."

My mom fingers the edge of her napkin.

My dad rubs the side of his face.

I stare between them, and the three of us sit wordless for what feels like eons as the grandfather clock ticks back and forth, measuring the silence.

"You know what I wish?" I ask him. "I wish you could see yourself the way I've seen you my whole life. I wish you knew how shitty it feels to know the man you've aspired to be is really a selfish asshole who blew off his son and broke his wife's heart. I wish you knew what it felt like for me to walk in on you with another woman. Or that you acted like it was nothing more than some awkward misunderstanding. You cheated on your family—you lied."

"Yes, I know I cheated!" he finally says with some emotion. "I know I screwed up and I'm sorry. I truly am, but I can't undo it, Nick. I know you wish we could rewind and go back, but we can't. This is just how it is now, even if it's uncomfortable for you."

I blink at him, processing.

"And she's more than just another woman," he says more quietly. "I care about Carrie, even if that's difficult for you to hear."

I glance at my mom. She's staring into her wine glass like she wishes she could crawl inside and lose herself to a sea of oblivion. I don't care what she says, she's not completely over what he's done to her. Maybe my dad's not either and this is how they're handling it—pretending or wishing things were different.

"Fine. You guys do whatever you want. It's your lives and if you want me to accept it, I won't bring it up again, even though this feels beyond wrong." I try to formulate my final words, but all I can think about is anger. I glance at my dad. "But, let's be really clear about something. If you still want a relationship with me, I'm not going to make it easy for you, like Mom has." I stare into his eyes and tell him as fervently as I can. "You don't get to just show up and pretend. I'm not a kid anymore. If you want my respect, you actually have to earn it this time."

His eyes shift over my face and he looks away.

"Remember that the next time you blow me off or drum up some lie about why you can only act like my father when it's convenient for you."

My mom's eyes are wet with tears when I look at her again, but as much as it hurts to see her upset, I'm upset too. "Sorry, but I'm not really hungry anymore." I stand up from the table as my phone vibrates in my pocket. When I pull it out, I expect to find Brady's name on the screen, but it's Savannah's. "Enjoy your dinner," I say and head for the door. "See you next week."

I accept the call, thankful for a distraction. "Hey, Red."

# THIRTY-EIGHT
# BETHANY

I GLANCE AT MY PHONE. The hour-long drive to the beach has been quiet. Nick and I don't say much, but then, I didn't sleep last night, and Nick is in a strange mood today. I try not to let the fact that I'll be spending the day with the entire crew get to me, but it's daunting, no matter how I look at it.

"Your destination, my lady," Nick says as he pulls into the parking lot. I see Reilly's big red truck and Mac's Jeep and know they've likely been here for a while. Nick isn't an early riser, I've determined, which, given his job, is understandable.

"Do me a favor, would you?"

I blink at him.

"Shut your phone off. I don't want anything ruining your day. This is supposed to be fun."

I roll my eyes but do as he asks, because he's right. Today is supposed to be fun.

We unpack our things from the Explorer, and steadying myself for what will probably be a trying but hopefully fun day, I hang my beach bag over my shoulder and grab the other end of Nick's ice chest.

I blow an errant strand of hair from my face as we lug it

through the parking lot and over the grassy dune, to the path leading down to the beach. "What did you put in here, exactly? Bricks?"

"No, ice," Nick says with a smirk.

"You're so funny."

"And our sandwiches and snacks . . . and some waters and a few beers. And a jar of pickles, of course—the usual."

"You can't forget the pickles."

"Nope. Never."

My steps are uneven in the sand, but it's warm and soft as it falls around my sandals and between my toes. The air is fresh and intermittently cool against the heated rays of the sun.

Mac brushes the sand from the back of her legs as she stands up and heads for their ice chest next to the barbecue pit, her dark hair piled messily atop her head. I watch the rest of the gang milling around on the beach, oblivious to us as we make our way toward them. This is the first time I've been more than just an outlier, looking in.

Back in high school, hordes of us would come down here for volleyball games and bonfires. I brought Mike out here one day after meeting him at a dinner party with my family. His dad was a bigwig friend of my dad's, and I'd offered to show Mike around since he was new in town. We flirted and laughed, and the way he looked at me, like I was some precious, intriguing creature worth knowing, had me eating out of the palm of his hand.

To my seventeen-year-old self, Mike was like no other guy I'd ever met; he was older, someone outside of school and Saratoga Falls with worldly experience, and no ties to anyone other than me. I could be myself with him.

But bringing him out here proved to be my first mistake of many. That's the day he'd met Sam. The day Nick planted my first kernel of doubt about Mike, only for me to ignore it so it could bite me in the ass a year later.

I don't know how soon after that day Mike started sneaking

around with Sam, but when I found out, I hated her for it. Even if logic told me she likely didn't know he and I were together. He was older and we did our own thing, always away from crowds, which was my second mistake. Part of me knew Sam was probably duped, like me, but it didn't make the truth less painful. It all seems like yesterday and yet a lifetime ago, too.

Sam shouts at Mac to bring her a drink as she sits up on her woven blanket and tucks a loose wave of blonde hair behind her ear, the rest pulled back in a braid. I imagine her eyes are fixed on the beach festivities, on Bobby, Reilly, and Colton, playing bare-footed volleyball in their shorts.

"Fear not, ladies, the party has arrived!" Nick calls down to them.

Mac and Sam peer back at us, smiles engulfing their faces, though they falter a bit when they see me. I'm not surprised by it, though my reaction to the way my presence affects them stirs my unwanted insecurities back into place.

"It's about time, sleepy head," Mac says, shielding her eyes with her hand.

Nick flashes them a full-faced smile. "It's not easy looking this good. I needed my beauty rest."

"Oh, I've seen you first thing in the morning. I know all about it," she teases and we make our way over to the blanket.

When I meet Mac's gaze, it's more curious than I expect, less thwarted. "Hi, Bethany," she says.

"Hey," is about all I can manage as Nick and I drop the ice chest beside the others on the sand.

When Sam finally looks at me, she offers me a small smile but doesn't say anything. She's still uncertain how she feels about me, I've noticed. Yesterday's civil conversation was for Jesse and Nick's benefit, and she's fine when we talk about design stuff, but the past still lingers, and so does Sam's dislike for me, even if she's trying.

"Oh, look, you got him out of bed!" Reilly says, jogging up to the group. He's all easy smiles and bright blue eyes as he glances between us.

Reilly could make things awkward if he wanted, especially after my friend Claire kissed him and caused a scene between him and Sam last summer. She'd wanted a final summer fling before she moved away, but Sam walking up on them during Claire's brave moment wasn't part of the fantasy. Mortification was what Claire got instead of Reilly. He got his girl, though, and he just smiles and acts like it never happened at all.

Reilly tosses Nick the volleyball. "How are things?" He looks Nick directly in the eye. I get the impression he's talking about Turner family drama, and I busy myself, pulling my hair up into a ponytail.

"Fine," Nick says, tossing the ball back to Reilly. "Annoying."

"Time for another Tetris night?" Reilly lifts his brow, hopeful, and I drop my beach bag onto the sand.

"Oh, you want to get your ass handed to you again?" Nick asks. "Fine, then. Let's do it."

"It's always a competition," Sam says, handing Reilly a bottle of water. He chugs it down, then gasps for breath and glances between me and Nick. "You guys should come play some ball. Brush some of those cobwebs off from being so sedentary and hunched over your textbooks."

"I'm down," Nick says. He glances at me, his eyebrows dancing. "You want to play?"

I look from him to Mac and Sam, situating themselves on the blanket. As much as I'd like to play with the guys to avoid the awkwardness that awaits me here, I know it won't earn me any points with the girls, so I shake my head. "Maybe later, when everyone's ready to play."

Nick nods and jogs after Reilly, toward the net. I'm not sure why I have the sudden need to get Mac and Sam's approval, but I feel like I do, especially if Nick and I are going to be friends. I don't want it to always be weird. Plus, I'm not as indifferent as I used to be. I *want* them to like me, and maybe I'm tired of letting people form their own, misguided opinions of me, too.

"Here," Mac says. She pats the empty space between her and Sam. "Take a load off. Catch some rays—it feels *really* good." She pulls her t-shirt off and then her shorts, revealing a full body most girls would kill for and most guys want to get their hands on.

She stretches back, completely oblivious. "Come on, Sam doesn't bite, I promise." Mac pats the blanket again and adjusts herself, her eyes closed behind her sunglasses.

"Okay, sure." I tug my sundress over my head, feeling the nip of the breeze against my skin, but I like it. It's something else to focus on instead of the thick silence that seems to mask the sound of seagulls and crashing waves off in the distance.

Sitting down between them, I wonder if Mac put me in the middle on purpose as I pull out my sunblock. It doesn't matter why she did it. *Today's about having fun.* That's what Nick keeps telling me, and it's what I keep repeating to myself over and over.

"That lotion smells amazing," Mac says. "What is it, lilac?"

I nod, realizing she probably can't see me against the backdrop of the sun. "Yeah. It's a new product we got in at the salon. It's overpriced, but it doesn't smell like coconut, which is nice. Everything in the salon *always* smells like coconut."

"Yeah, that's annoying."

With a sigh, Sam turns onto her stomach, pulling her braid off her back. "This feels *sooo* good," she groans. "I can't remember the last time I went sunbathing."

"See, Sam? I told you it would feel good to relax." Mac looks at me and shakes her head. "You wouldn't believe how hard it is for me to get this girl to pamper herself once in a while. I've gotten one mani-pedi with her in the last year. *One.*"

I smile, appreciating Mac's easiness around me.

"I guess that happens when you're so busy," Sam says on a sigh.

"No—not true at all." Mac scoffs. "I'm always busy, yet I still find the time."

With a laugh, Sam wipes the sweat from her forehead. "But you're high maintenance. I'm not."

"Take it back!" Mac gasps with feigned fury.

"No way. It's true." Sam's head lolls to the side and she grins. "And that look on your face is priceless."

When I'm finished with the sunblock, I scoot back on the blanket, ignoring the goosebumps over my skin as I ball my beach towel up under my head.

"Well, I think Bethany would agree with me," Mac continues. "It's nice to treat yourself every now and again, right?"

I nod. "Yes, it's nice, especially if you need to unwind. Getting my nails done is sort of my ticket to escape for an hour or so every once in a while."

"I totally get it," Mac says. "I have brothers, too. I think I might over compensate with the girlie thing just so I can remind myself I'm not a greasy slob, like Bobby is."

Sam and I both chuckle and drift into an easy quiet. The sounds of the ocean and the guys laughing and grunting as they hit the ball off in the distance becomes a serenade, and I lose myself to the warmth of the sun on my face. An airplane echoes somewhere far away. "I didn't realize how nice this was going to be," I muse, the sun melting every tightly wound muscle in my body.

"Did Jesse have fun yesterday?" Sam asks, her voice muffled by the blanket.

Recalling the pure joy on Jesse's face as he and Nick brushed out the horses after our ride was priceless, and I know I couldn't have asked for him to have a better experience. "Yeah, he did. He loved Shasta," I say and look at her. "Thank you for letting us come out and ride."

"It was all Nick," she says. "Of course I'd never tell him no." Her eyelashes flutter behind her glasses, and I can feel her gaze on me. "Bethany," she says with a thoughtful pause.

"Yeah?"

She waits a drawn out moment, then continues. "Don't hurt him this time."

I stare at her, shocked and a little offended by her request. Nick and I have had our share of issues, but I can't take credit for all the turmoil that's passed between us. This is the moment I assumed would come, though, and I'd tried to prepare for it.

"I'm not trying to hurt him," I tell her. "I'm not *trying* to do anything. We're just friends."

"What were you before?"

Nick and I have always had a connection, but we've never been anything to one another. "Nothing, I guess."

"That's my point."

"What Sam is *trying* to say," Mac interrupts, "is that even as *nothing* to each other, all the back and forth between you guys has been really hard on him. So, imagine our concern now that you guys are actually friends." I'm too busy trying to ignore the burn of discomfort blooming in my chest and cheeks. I peer up at the blue sky. The sun burns my eyes, but I let it.

"I don't care what you guys say," Sam grumbles. "It's clearly more than just a friendship. He rode a damn horse for you. That's not nothing." She sounds a little awed, even if she doesn't sound terribly happy about it.

"He was just doing something nice for my brother, it doesn't mean anything."

Sam snorts, making me bristle.

"Maybe, but . . ." Mac sprays herself with more tanning lotion then looks down at me. "Nick's never come to me about a girl before, *ever*. So, that's big—that means something too."

My heart beings to hammer against my breastbone, bringing unexpected anger and hurt just beneath the surface. *He talked to Mac about me?* Rationally, I know it makes sense. They are best friends. But, the knowledge makes me feel exposed and a little betrayed.

"See, he's clearly losing his mind already," Sam jokes, but I don't find it funny.

I reach for my dress. "I get that you're protecting your friend," I say, tugging my dress over my head. "But despite what you both think, you don't know me. I don't control what Nick does or feels. I'm not saying that I haven't helped make things complicated between us, but you only know his side of things."

"By all means," Sam says. "Enlighten us."

As much as I want to tell her to shove her judgements up her ass and explain ten years' worth of "my side" of things, I'm not sure there's much I can say right now that will make this situation any better, not while I grow more bitter by the second.

"Why?" I say, rising to my feet. "You've clearly made up your minds already." I straighten my dress and peer around for an escape. "I'm gonna stretch my legs." I head toward the beach, away from them and the group, uncertain how things turned from conversational to toxic in a matter of seconds. My feet sink into the sand, making it difficult to walk away from them fast enough. I'd like to go play with the guys, maybe bat playfully at Reilly and give Sam a real reason to hate me, but that's not who I am anymore. I'm not sure it ever really was.

"Hey!" Sam says, jogging up behind me. "I'm sorry if I made you uncomfortable."

I laugh bitterly and continue walking. "Wasn't that the point?"

"No," Sam says. "Well, maybe a little," she amends. "Look, I'm sorry okay? He's like my brother. He's been looking out for us since elementary school, and I feel like it's my turn."

"I'm not a harpy, Sam. I didn't scheme my way into his life, like you seem to think. Neither of us asked to be project partners. It just happened."

"I get that," she says with a huff. "Will you please just stop for a second?" Sam tugs on my arm. "God, you people and your long legs . . ."

I stop and look at her, deciding it's best to get everything out in the open now.

"You're like his kryptonite," she says, a wisp of her hair floating in the breeze. "You heard Mac. You screw with his head and make him crazy."

"Well, I—"

"You don't do it on purpose, I get it. I just—I don't want him to get hurt."

I shake my head. "Neither do I."

She blinks and bites the inside of her cheek before she speaks again. "I don't know if he's always thinking clearly when it comes to you, and you guys are delusional if you think you're only friends." She shakes her head. "I guess what I'm trying to say is, this is probably going to end badly. I just hope you guys know what you're doing."

No, I have no idea what we're doing, but I don't have time to think about it. Nick comes jogging up the beach. "Hey."

He and Sam exchange a look before she glances at me again, then heads back toward the blanket.

Nick lets out a raspy breath. "Is everything okay? That looked pretty intense." He smacks on his gum, assessing my reaction.

"It's fine," I say and continue walking. "I just need some space."

# THIRTY-NINE
# NICK

"I'M JUST gonna grab my project stuff," Bethany says as we step into my apartment. "I'll finish the summary this week and start putting the binder together so we can focus on moving all the furniture in next Saturday."

"I was going to do that with Reilly this week, but I'll let you do all the frilly stuff."

"'kay." She grabs her book bag off the floor. She hasn't really looked at me since the beach. Whatever was said between her and Sam has caused her walls to go up again.

"What did she say to you?" I ask. "You've been . . . different. Was she rude? Sam can be a little pushy but I'm sure—"

"It's fine," she says. "That talk was bound to happen at some point. Sam's just concerned."

"What is she so concerned about, me and you?" I know Sam doesn't love Bethany, but I thought she was coming around to the idea of her.

"Yeah, and honestly, I don't blame her." She scrambles for her papers on the table.

"What? Don't listen to Sam. She doesn't know what it's like between us—she doesn't get it." For the first time in my life, I'm pissed at Sam. Bethany and I were doing so good, now she's a million miles out of reach again.

"Why do this to ourselves?"

"Do what? Be friends?"

"Is that what we really are?" she asks, surprising me. "It feels more complicated than that."

"Of course it's complicated. It's stupid-complicated, it always has been, and it's annoying as hell. But I told you from the beginning that I would let you steer the way."

"I don't know, Nick—" she says with a groan.

"Know what? Why does any of it matter? Why can't we just be whatever we are?"

"Because it's dangerous," she says.

"Dangerous how, like you might actually be happy for once?"

She shakes her head. "You've got enough going on in your life, Nick. I don't want to mess things up for you. I don't want to risk this turning out badly and—"

"Bethany," I say softly. "Why don't you and everyone else stop worrying about me for a minute. What do *you* want? And it's not about Jesse or your parents, either."

Bethany's eyes are gray embers that burn with something unspoken, and I will them to meet mine. If I could get her to look at me, *really* look at me, she might finally admit what's going on in her head. "Hey," I breathe, and take her hand in mine.

When her eyes shift to mine, they're shimmering, and as she opens her mouth, I hold my breath. Hopeful. "I just want to get through this project."

I watch the way her cheeks redden and her eyes shift over me. "That's all?"

"Isn't that enough, for now?"

I shake my head. "It's beyond that for me, now," I tell her simply. "No matter how much you deny this, you know it's not going to just go away when we're finished with this project. And, I don't want it to."

She pulls her hand from mine and shoves everything into her bag, every one of her neurotic tendencies forgotten. I want to be angry with her for pushing me away, but the pain in her eyes makes it difficult to grab hold of anything other than hope that what she *truly* wants is stronger.

She hauls her bag up over her shoulder. This morning I was admiring the way she looked, standing in my apartment in her sundress. Now, I panic that she's going to leave and might never come back.

"Don't go." It's a plea and I hate how weak it makes me.

She walks over to the couch and picks up her beach bag. "I have to—"

"Bethany," I say, stepping in front of her. "I don't want you to go."

"Please, Nick." She looks everywhere but at me.

I study her trembling lip and can almost feel her reluctance like it's my own. "Fine." It takes all the willpower I have to step aside, knowing I have to respect whatever decision she makes, even if I hate it. "If you really want to go, I won't stop you."

She clears her throat. "Yeah, I do." But she doesn't move, and I can hear the wavering resolve in her voice that only needs to be swayed just a little.

"You like me," I tell her. "Even if it's complicated—I can feel it. I've always felt it, and so have you." I take a step closer. "Screw the past. Screw Sam and everyone else. I'm not going to let you push me away anymore."

"Oh, really?" she says dryly.

I cross my arms over my chest in answer. Her conviction is wavering, and I can't help but allow a quirk of a smile. "If you really want me to play the bad guy so that you don't have to admit to yourself you want to stay, I can."

"And how's that going to work, exactly?"

A dozen ways I might get her stay pop into my head. "I'll force you."

"Are you going to tie me up and hold me against my will?"

I grin. "I'd love to, actually." I'm only partially joking.

She sighs and drops her hands by her sides. "Please stop, you're being ridiculous."

"Nope. It's time we un-complicate this."

"That's impossible, Nick."

"Why?" I step closer and take her beach bag from her hand.

"Because . . . I don't want to get hurt."

Though I assumed she was scared in some way, it's hard to hear her say it's because of me. "I won't hurt you, Bethany," I promise, and run my fingers over the strap of her purse and pull it off her shoulder.

"I don't want to fuck it up."

"Then don't."

"You act like it's that simple," she breathes. "We are never simple."

I drop her purse on the couch, holding her gaze despite how crazy she makes me and the fact that I want to pin her against the wall and show her how good we'd be together. "No, we're not. But all these years have been building up to something. It's time to see where it takes us."

She licks her lips. "It's going to ruin whatever this is between us." It's like she says the words because she thinks she should, not because she means them. They're light on her tongue, almost breathless, and her eyes are locked on mine.

"Or," I whisper, "make it better."

Her head shifts slowly from side to side. "You can't know that."

"I know that you look smokin' hot in those cowboy boots that I've watched you dance in more times than I can count, and that I nearly lost my shit today when you took off your sundress." I take a step closer so that her sandals touch my toes. "I know you've worn the same perfume since high school and that you're neurotic when you need to be in control of something."

I tuck her hair behind her ear and frown. "I know that when I've seen you with other guys, you don't give them any part of you —you barely look at them, definitely not the way you're looking at me."

I lean closer, sunblock and shampoo filling my nose and making my insides ache with desire. "And I know that you're having an extra bad day when you knot your hair on top of your head, and that you'd do anything for your brother, no matter what it costs you. Some nights you go out and want to live with abandon, but it never sates you." I take her messenger bag off her shoulder and let it drop to the ground. "I know that you push me away because whatever this is between us scares you more than anything."

"And it doesn't scare you?" she rasps.

I appreciate her soft bottom lip and the dimple on her left cheek when she swallows thickly. "Not anymore and certainly not enough to let you leave." I want to see what we could be, to prove to myself it's not all in my head. I want to prove that it's not years of tension and distance that's made us feel an attraction to one another, but something real beneath the surface.

No more waiting. I kiss her.

No more games and back and forth. In this moment, she's my life's blood. She's the heat coursing through my veins, the adrenaline that makes my body hum and my heart pound, like I'll explode without the taste of her again. I want her in every way, and all it takes is her lips parting against mine and a whimper before I lose myself.

# FORTY
# BETHANY

I'M LOST in a wave of euphoric surprise and sudden relief as Nick's mouth covers mine. His hands are hot against my jaw and neck, and I can't help but whimper as his tongue slips between my lips. Mint and man fill my senses, and a lightning storm enlivens every nerve ending on my body. Thunder rumbles through his chest and the charge that has always filled the space between us becomes an air supply I can't breathe without. It's what makes him so dangerous. It's what consumes me and stirs something wild awake inside.

My arms tangle around his neck, unable to resist the pull between us that's become a life-support my body can't deny, and I give into him completely.

Hands flutter. Our bodies press together. Nick lifts me up against the wall, it's unyielding behind me. My legs wrap around him, my insides swirling with a red-hot need as his hands grip my thighs and his mouth devours mine.

This is different than our kiss before. It's frenzied and raw and all-consuming.

His hands find the hem of my dress. "Take it off," he commands, tugging at it. "I want it off." My bathing suit top gets in the way, but that doesn't slow him down. It fuels him, filling him with more determination as he tears my dress away. His hands are greedy and he yanks my bathing suit top down, lifting my breast into his mouth.

I gasp and pull his soft hair between my fingers, my body clenching in need as liquid heat pools inside me, yearning.

"Nick," I rasp. "Please."

He bites my lip. "Say it," he growls. "I want to hear you say it."

I'd do anything he asks if it meant he'd fuck me. "I need you." I whimper as his fingertip brushes over my nipple. "I—want you," I gasp, squeezing my legs tighter around him.

Nick yanks me from the wall and walks us to his bedroom. He drops me onto the bed, appraising me, like I'm a prize he's won, watching me writhe with wanting as he pulls away. He tugs his shirt over his head then unbuttons his shorts. "There's no going back," he says. It's a warning, but I'm not sure if it's for me or himself.

Every doubt is gone. Every fear is a fading memory. "I don't want to go back." The chill without him against me makes me tremble, and I run my hands down my body. Nothing matters before this. "I never want to go back."

Nick pulls a condom from the bedside table, and I struggle to keep my eyes open in my anticipation. I feel the bed move and Nick climbs over me. "Look at me," he says. His voice is a distant, alluring rumble, pulling me to him.

I open my eyes, lost in the wild green and brown that stare back at me.

He kisses me again, more gently than I expect, and I memorize this. This feeling. This elation and levity. When he finally eases himself inside me, the weight of the last ten years disperses, and I'm completely undone.

# FORTY-ONE
# NICK

LYING IN BED, with Bethany in my arms, is the most surreal feeling I've ever had. She's not the girl of my past or the girl of my dreams. She's Bethany. She's real. And if the past couple hours are any indication, she's mine. The thought makes me hard all over again.

Her chest rises and falls in soft breaths beside me as she blinks lazily up at the ceiling, her fingertips trailing my arm wrapped around her middle. Her skin is so supple and warm, and I can't keep my hands and mouth off her.

Kissing her shoulder, I sit up on my elbow and peer down at her delicate profile. She blinks slowly. The ruddiness of her cheeks, the sated gleam in her eyes, and the way her hair sprawls out over my sheets is my doing. She looks happy and sated, and I revel in the sight of her.

"How long do you think we could hide out in here before people come looking for us?" I ask.

She smiles, a genuine smile that makes me consider holding her hostage so that she never has to worry about anything ever again. "If I'm not home to get Jesse to school tomorrow, my mom will freak."

I nuzzle into her neck, breathing her in. "That's too bad. I was hoping we could play hooky tomorrow."

She chuckles softly. "I wish. We have to report in about our project progress tomorrow."

I grumble. "Professor Murray is the last thing I want to be thinking about right now."

She cups the side of my face with the palm of her hand, and I immediately relax. "At least I'll get to see you," she says, surprising me. Her soft expression falters. "I should go soon. It's getting late, and I'm already going to get the third degree."

I sigh, watching the shadows creep into her eyes. "Your parents suck."

"You have no idea." She laughs, partly amused, and presses her lips against mine. She holds our kiss, inhales before she breaks away and rests her forehead against mine. "I'm going to move out soon," she says. "I don't know when, but . . . soon."

"And leave Jesse?"

She shrugs. "I won't be gone forever." Her eyes meet mine and I see the pain in them, a pain I know I can't fix, no matter how badly I want to. "I need to get out of there though." She kisses me this time and whimpers against my mouth.

I want to joke that my persistence finally paid off but this—us—is too big for jokes. I can feel it in the words she doesn't speak. Instead of saying anything, I kiss her back, letting my lips linger this time, savoring her. We lie in each other's arms a little while longer before she turns around in the sheets to face me fully.

"What happens now?" she whispers.

I kiss her nose and flash her a wolfish grin. "Well . . . I have a few things in mind."

"I meant what happens with us?" she clarifies with a laugh, then she sits up, the sheet falling from her body.

I groan and bite the back of my hand. "Are you serious right now?"

Bethany peers down at the bikini discarded on the floor, like she's decided it's time to get dressed.

"First of all," I grab her wrist and pull her back down to me, earning a giggle I've never heard from her before. "I'm never letting you go; you're mine now," I tell her. "I mean that in the least creepy way possible." But I do mean it. Now that I've seen a glimpse of what's possible between us, I can't ever let her go. She's the one I want. She's the one I've always wanted.

"What is it?" she asks, concern creasing her brow.

I reprise my smiles and give her a wink. "Just working out the timeline for a quickie after class tomorrow." I bite playfully at her neck, provoking another giggle that makes my heart soar.

# FORTY-TWO
# BETHANY

IT'S eleven when I finally force myself to go home. Though the porch light is on, all the lights are off in the house, which is a relief. I don't think I could handle my parents right now, not while I'm still high on the whirlwind the past few hours have been.

Quietly, I open the door and step inside. As expected, the house is silent, save for the ticking of the wall clock, and I divest my bags in the living room as quietly as I can. Although my mind is more still than usual, my body feels boneless, encouraging an irrepressible smile. It all still feels like a dream, and I can't remember why I'd been so scared to take the leap with Nick. He's different than Mike, I've always known that, even if doubt has inched its way in one too many times. Now, though, I feel it in every fiber of my being. Being with Nick is right.

Desperate to chug some water down before I collapse on my bed, I flick the kitchen light on to find my mom standing at the island. I clasp my hand over my mouth to stifle a scream. "Oh my God," I breathe, squeezing my eyes shut. "You scared the shit out of me."

"Where have you been?" She's scowling and doesn't mince words.

"I've been at Nick's. We were working on our project, and I fell asleep."

"More lies?" she seethes.

I blanch. It might not be the whole truth this time, but I've been nothing but honest until now. "Excuse me?"

"You may think I'm an absentee mother, Bethany, but I'm not blind. I know what the walk of shame looks like." Her words are like acid around my heart. "I defend you to your father and you do *this*?"

"Do what?" Even if she knows about Nick, I can't see her being so angry about it. She's petrifying—even in the middle of the night her hair is perfect and her disappointment drips off each and every syllable. I've never seen her so angry with me.

"Did you forget something today?"

I shake my head, dread clawing at me as I try to remember. "No—"

"You were supposed to pick Jesse up from the movie theater— his friends left and he was waiting there, alone and scared out of his mind for over an hour. How could you do that to him?"

"But, I didn't—"

"It took me all night to get him to calm down. What the hell was so important that you couldn't even answer your phone? *Him*?"

My chest tightens. "It's off," I realize. "My phone's off . . ." My mind is swirling. If I had been drinking, I might think I was intoxicated. It all feels unreal. "I checked the calendar yesterday— it wasn't on the calendar." I rush over to it to find it's written in, but I know it wasn't there the last time I checked. "I didn't know I was supposed to pick him up."

"Well, you were, and this time you get to tell him why you forgot about him and didn't pick up his nineteen calls." She shakes her head.

"I was with Nick, yes," I say, my voice shaking. It feels like the world is cold and rushing in around me, and I can't catch my breath. I would never forget about Jesse. I would never disappoint him. "It's not like that, though."

"So, you're *not* sleeping with Nick?" I don't want to lie, but I can't bring myself to say yes. She shakes her head. "Never mind, I already know the answer." She seethes the words, like I'm disgusting to her, and it tears at my heart.

My mom grabs an empty glass from the counter and walks to the sink to rinse it out.

"Why do you say it like that?" I ask, hating the hurt in my voice.

"Because your father is right," she bites out. "This is Mike, all over again."

"Nick is *nothing* like him—"

"Only this time, your brother gets the shit end, too."

"Stop using Jesse to make your point," I grind out. "I'm nothing like you and Dad. Jesse knows he can count on me."

Her eyes widen and her nostrils flare, but I refuse to be lumped into the same category with her. "I have *never* forgotten him before."

"I didn't either! It was *one* misunderstanding. I didn't know I was supposed to pick him up. If you would communicate better and not leave last minute notes on the calendar, I would have shown up."

"And your phone? Are you blaming that on me too?"

"I had my phone off for one afternoon."

She shakes her head like she can't stand the sight of me and it fuels my anger.

"I wanted *one* day for myself—you're acting like I've ruined Jesse's life."

"No, but you're on the path to ruining yours."

I gape at her, at a complete loss. How has it escalated to this? I don't see her logic. I don't understand what she and my father are so worried about. "You both act like I'm incapable of being a level-headed adult, like I couldn't possibly have a boyfriend and maintain a semblance of responsibility. Mike was almost *four* years ago—I was in high school. It's time to get over it already."

She takes a step closer. "Get over it? You barely graduated high school because of him. You lied—you never went to class. God only knows what trouble you and Anna Marie got into. I half expected you'd come home pregnant. So, you don't get to tell me I'm overreacting when I've seen first-hand how thoughtless and reckless you can be when it comes to your infatuations."

"*Thoughtless?*" I breathe. "*Infatuations?*" I walk to my bag on the couch, pull out my journal, and toss it onto the counter. "Reading material, in case you care to know how *thoughtless* I've been over the past ten years—how *infatuated* I am with Nick," I say, tears dripping from between my lashes. "Since I'm such a disappointment to you and Dad, consider me a burden you no longer have to bear."

I turn for the stairs. I don't know if she picks up the journal or if she even plans to read it—I'm not sure I even really want her to —but it's all I have left of myself to give her, and I'm out of ideas about how to get through to them.

By the time my bags are packed with as much as I can carry, I hurry for the door and I don't look back.

# FORTY-THREE
# NICK

I'M PRACTICALLY WALKING on sunshine when I get to school Monday morning. I wasn't sure I could sleep after Bethany left, but I was out like a light until my alarm went off at seven. I have no idea how this morning's class will go, but I know I won't be able to take my eyes off her, differently than before.

Heading toward class with fifteen minutes to spare, I figure a trip to the vending machine will be a good time-filler. When I see knotted blonde hair and the black and purple messenger bag I've stared at a dozen times, sitting on the bench, I walk over to Bethany, unable to resist my excitement.

"You came early," I say, plopping down beside her. She startles and jumps, and when she peers up at me her eyes are red and puffy, like she's been crying. I hadn't been expecting that.

Bethany pulls her ear buds out one by one and blinks at me.

"What's wrong?" I brush a strand of hair from her face. "What happened?"

She wipes at her eyes and shrugs. "I'm fine. Just tired. I got in a fight with my mom last night."

*About me.* That's the first thing I think of. "About what?"

She shakes her head. "It doesn't matter, but I stayed at Anna

Marie's. She said I can stay with her for as long as I need. I just . . . I can't be at home anymore."

"Does Jesse know?"

She pulls the sleeves of her shirt down over her hands and swallows thickly. "I told him when I picked him up for school this morning. It's not like I won't be around anymore, I'll still pick him up for school and stuff. He didn't have much to say, but I think he understands."

Although I've never met Bethany's parents, I've known since middle school that I didn't like them. "I'm glad you left," I admit. "You can always come to my place."

"Thank you." Bethany smiles weakly and takes my hand, splaying our fingers together.

"You could've at least called me, you know?"

She nods. "I needed some girl time." Bethany tries to downplay it all, but this is a big deal for her, leaving home, and I'm worried what this is really doing to her. "Besides, I don't want my shit to be your shit. Not yet, anyway."

"But I care about you, Bethany, and that means I'll happily take on your shit too."

She laughs but I'm serious. "Speaking of bullshit," she says, and finally looks at me. "How are things with your parents?" Her eyes search mine, like she's not sure it's her business, but I would tell her anything. "I've been wanting to ask, but didn't want to pry."

"So, I got to pry, so now it's your turn?" I wink at her and heave out a weighted sigh. Glancing around the quad, I search my feelings. The anger's only simmering. The hurt is still there, but maybe that's disappointment. Or, are they the same thing some-times? "I don't know." I sigh again, trying to recall exactly where things were left. "For now, the farce continues. I thought they were pretending for me, but I guess it's not only that. I think they're lost. We're having another family dinner next week, which is going to be weird as fuck, but it is what it is." I pause. "I'm more worried about what I'm going to do after graduation. Now that I've decided I *don't* want to be an architect, I don't really have a direction."

"So, you're certain about that, huh?"

"I'm certain," I tell her easily. "It's been a damned waste of time and money, and I hate thinking about it, but I haven't been interested for a while now. I just wanted to make my dad happy. Now it all feels wrong, so . . ."

We sit in silence, my thoughts drifting to possible futures as Bethany sits quietly beside me.

"Everything is skewed when your eyes are wide open," she says. "I've had this story in my head that I couldn't leave my brother for so long, I don't even know why anymore. That I couldn't have my own place and go to school—that moving out was near impossible—but people do it all the time. Nothing is black and white."

"True," I concede.

Bethany groans. "I hate the gray areas though, too."

"Until this year, my life has always been 'white' and my friends have always lived in the gray. Now, they're the ones that are grounded and know who they are. They've already been through their shit. I'm the one that's lost."

Bethany laces her fingers with mine. I appreciate that we can be together like this now, comfortable and easy.

"Me, too," she says. "We can be lost together."

Grateful, I smile at her words and lean in for a soft peck on her lips. "Yeah," I say, begrudgingly, "but we should probably at least find our way to class."

# FORTY-FOUR
# BETHANY

AS I'M PUTTING the clean towels away in the supply closet, I hear the front door bell chime, and I head out to the counter. I'm grateful to see it's Anna Marie come to relieve me. "How's it going?" she asks. "Is it as dead this evening, as I expected?"

"Yep, I'm afraid so." I lift the appointment book up for her to see the blank time slots. "I did book a few sessions for tomorrow."

"That's promising." She stashes her purse behind the counter. "Thanks for covering a few hours for me today."

"Yeah, sure, it's the least I can do since you've let me crash at your place the past couple days."

"I have an extra room, it's no big deal. I'm just glad you got out of there."

"Yeah, me too." I give her a sidelong look and when she meets my gaze, her cheeks are rosy.

"What?" she asks sheepishly.

"How was your make-out session with Bobby?"

Anna rolls her eyes. "It was a *study* session," she says. "We were *studying*."

I raise my eyebrows, biting back a smile.

"Fine," she finally admits. "How did you know?"

"Well, for starters, you guys don't have any of the same classes. You're a business major, and Bobby's doing the bare minimum to keep his hockey scholarship. Therefore, you were *not* studying. Not to mention, I know you guys have been hooking up."

She smacks my arm. "No, we have not."

I gape at her. "Why are you lying again?"

"I'm not lying, I just—"

"You just what?"

"I'm trying not to get my hopes up. He's hot and sweet and funny . . . He's a mechanic and can work on my car when it breaks down—and trust me, it's on its last leg."

I shake my head, surprised to hear the unbridled adoration in her voice. "You really like him, huh?"

Her full, perfectly shimmering lips pull into a giant smile. "Yeah, a little."

"Ha. I think more like *a lot.*"

Anna giggles, and I smile with elation for her. She's been one of us 'lost girls' for a while now, scared to commit after a Mike-esque boyfriend broke her heart, hence her partying and playing the field. Bobby seems like a good one, though, and I'm happy for her.

"So, what's this date *you're* going on tonight with Nicky-poo?"

I laugh. "Don't call him that, please. I beg you."

"I'm happy to call him whatever you want. I'm just glad you guys are finally getting it on. It's seriously been so painful to watch for this long."

Rolling my eyes, I stick my tongue out at her. "Whatever, it's not like it's a fancy date or anything. I just thought it would be fun to actually do something together that didn't involve schoolwork or his friends, for once."

"I like it. You asked him on a date, very assertive. And it's so soon in your relationship, which means you're totally falling for him, but I already knew that. I always like it when people prove me right." She holds up her chin with more self-righteousness than I think she knows what to do with.

"Like I said, it's nothing big. Just dinner and drinks at his house."

"Perfect." Her eyebrows dance. "Quality time with a bed in the vicinity. Always a good idea."

Laughing, I shake my head. "If we decide to use a bed," I tease.

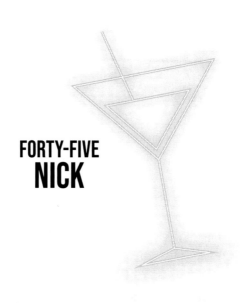

# FORTY-FIVE
# NICK

I'VE JUST FINISHED SHOWERING when I hear a knock at my door. I consider answering it just as I am, naked in all my glory, but decide against it. Wrapping my towel around my hips, I make my way to the door, glancing at the clock. I'm running later than I expected.

Bethany greets me with a beautiful smile as I crack open the door.

"Hey, sexy," I say, moving out of the way.

She holds up two bags of groceries as she steps inside. "Hungry?" She eyes my naked chest approvingly.

"Not for food," I growl and lean in for a kiss. Bethany's lips are smooth and minty, and I press my mouth more firmly against hers.

"Yum," I mutter, and set the two bags on the counter for her. I pry open the grocery bags and rub my hands together. "So, what are we having?"

"Well, I know you love Sam's southern cooking, and I don't pretend to be as good a cook as I hear she is, *but* I figured some homemade mac and cheese, a steak, and salad might be sufficient?"

My stomach rumbles. "You know the way to a man's heart. Just give me a minute to throw on some clothes, and I'll come help you with dinner." I make my way down the hall and into my room.

"No rush," she says and starts clinking around in the kitchen.

"So," her voice drifts down the hall. "You had to work late at the ranch?"

"No, not exactly," I admit. "Savannah wanted to meet up. She's in town for a few days, and she's got some shit going on with her family."

"Oh, I didn't realize . . ."

"Yeah, she needed a shoulder, so to speak." When I'm finished throwing on some clean lounge clothes, I head back into the living room. Bethany is moving around in my kitchen like she knows it by heart—like she belongs there—and it makes me smile.

"So," I ask, leaning against the counter. "What can I do to help?"

She slides the cutting board, a hunk of Gouda, and a grater toward me. "Care to do some grating?"

"Sounds easy enough." I wink at her. I do know how to grate cheese, even if I've only done it enough times to count on one hand.

"You have to wash your hands first," she reminds me, like I'm Jesse.

I'm about to retort with a snide remark, but I stop myself. Her eyes are on me knowingly. "Yes, ma'am." I probably do act like an eleven-year-old most of the time anyway. I smile and flip the faucet on.

"So, what's that other bag all about?" I ask, nodding behind me at the canvas tote on my table.

"*That* is for cocktail hour."

My eyes widen with intrigue. "Say what?"

She pours balsamic vinegar into a large Ziploc bag with a dash of other spices and locks the meat inside to marinate. "Well," she says, lifting her shoulder indifferently. Her scoop neck t-shirt hangs loosely around her, exposing her tank top and soft skin, though I try not to notice.

"I figured that if you ever decide a bar is in your foreseeable feature, you'll need to have a signature drink. Or plural. So," she continues, "I thought it would be fun to experiment tonight, Mr. Bartender." She looks over her shoulder at me, and despite my resolve, I want her in my arms more than I've wanted anything all day.

Drying off my hands, I step up behind her and wrap my arms around her waist. "You wouldn't be trying to get me drunk, by any chance, would you, Miss Fairchild? I don't think that's part of Professor Murray's partnership expectations."

She chuckles and leans her head back against my chest. "I could be wrong, Mr. Turner, but I'm inclined to think none of this is. But I don't want to think about him or the project tonight."

I inhale her and nuzzle at her shoulder, biting down lightly on her soft skin when I can't take it anymore. Bethany moans as I move up the column of her neck and take her delicate earlobe between my lips. When she leans into me, I want to tear her clothes off in the middle of the kitchen, but I remind myself that she's gone to all this trouble to cook dinner, so I make myself behave.

Kissing her jaw, I straighten. "I guess I better stop distracting you," I whisper in her ear, light and alluring, hoping she'll remember this moment in an hour when the stove isn't on and food isn't waiting to be consumed. "We'll continue this later."

"Fine," she grumbles, "but only because I'm starving."

I kiss her lips, silently telling my libido to calm his ass down in my pants, and I clear my throat. "So, about that Gouda?"

# FORTY-SIX
# BETHANY

"OKAY, SO," I say, appraising the half-empty glasses of tester cocktails on the coffee table. "Are we officially giving up on a pickle juice drink then?"

With a heart-stopping smile, Nick lifts a shoulder and glances between them. "You tell me." He hands me his high ball. "I like the dirty pickle martini, myself."

I sniff it, wondering if I'll enjoy it at all, given I don't like martinis to begin with.

"Just try it," he urges, intrigue lighting his eyes.

I take a sip and find I'm pleasantly surprised. "The martini isn't that bad, actually. Then again, it might just be that my taste buds are in shock from the salty dog, pickle drink you concocted."

"Yeah, that one was definitely a bad idea."

I take another sip of his drink and hand it back to him. "The more I drink the better it gets."

He chuckles and holds his pinky out like he's fancy and takes another sip. He cringes. "I think it might actually be getting worse."

I nestle into the couch a little deeper, completely comfortable and at ease as I watch him study the concoctions we've been testing for an hour now. "So, where are we at with the name?" I ask. "We've crossed Church and Nick's off the list. What about Shortstop, since that's the first one you thought of."

Nick stares into the fire with a faraway look. "It was my position on the team for three years, and the nostalgia of it—I dunno. I thought it would be cool."

"I think it's great, and it has a nice ring to it. 'I'm gonna make a short stop by the bar'—no wait, that doesn't really work." I nearly giggle, feeling sated by a few, albeit gnarly, drink choices.

"And you can't forget the hot baseball outfits for the female bartenders, you know, keeping the theme going and all."

I snort a laugh. "Yeah, right."

He winks at me and sets his drink down. "I think that's enough pickle infused drinks for one night," he says.

"Yeah, I'm pretty pickled out."

"But you're right about one thing, every bar needs a signature drink."

Laughing, I wipe the table off where his drink dribbled. "And, of course, gross pickle drinks should be yours."

"Hey, it was your idea." He pulls me to my feet. "Come on, I've tortured you enough. Let's get you a real cocktail."

On bare feet, I follow Nick over to his bar cart, eyeing an array of liquor bottles and mixers. "You're a whiskey sour girl," he says, mostly to himself as he takes stock of the ingredients in front of him. "What I really want to make you is a mint julep."

"You mean like the horse races and big hats kind of mint julep?"

He nods. "That's the one. I think you'd like it, and it's a nice summer drink. Plus, I can totally picture you in one of those floppy hats and a big frilly dress, looking all proper. It sorta turns me on just thinking about it."

I shake my head, amused and filing that fantasy of his away for later. "Well, then, make me one."

"I don't have any mint. Have you had a Manhattan before?" He looks over his shoulder at me.

Digging in the recesses of my mind, I try to remember. Eventually, I shrug. "I don't know—I don't think so."

"Do you like vermouth?"

I shrug again.

"Well, I guess we'll find out." He laughs to himself. "I think you're going to hate it, actually."

"What?" I smack his shoulder playfully. "Then why the hell are you making it for me?"

"Because I want to see your face when you drink it. Women make the best faces when they drink alcohol they don't like."

"We do?"

He nods. "Yes, trust me. I would know. I get to watch it all the time. And you should see Mac's face when she drinks beer. It's sort of magical, actually." He mixes a shot of whiskey and red vermouth together, then adds a dash of bitters.

"I'll have to keep a straight face then, won't I?" I say stubbornly.

"Ohhh, is that a challenge?" His eyes widen with glee as he stirs the contents together. "Where's Mac's camera when I need it." He winks at me and hands me my drink. "Here ya go, mi' lady."

"You wouldn't be trying to get me drunk on a school night, by any chance, would you?"

"Ha! You're the one who brought over a bag of mixers and wanted to create a bar menu, which is really fun, by the way."

Skeptical, I take the glass and sniff the amber contents. My first impulse is to shake my head. It doesn't smell fantastic, sort of sweet and sour all at once, but I don't let it show on my face.

Nick's amusement is enough to bolster my determination to accept his challenge, and I take a sip. I swallow it immediately, without letting it settle on my tongue or fumigate the inside of my mouth. I breathe out and try to appreciate the aromatics of it all.

"What are you, a professional? What are you doing?"

"I saw it on TV once." I lick my lips and shrug. "It's okay, not absolutely horrible." I take another sip to show Nick I'm no sissy-lala who can't handle my booze.

"That's it, huh? That's all I get, a shoulder shrug?" He shakes his head and takes the last swig of his martini.

I hand him my glass. "You should try it."

"Oh, I know what they taste like." He leans back against the counter.

"Then you don't mind having a taste," I say, holding out the glass.

He shakes his head. His eyes are leveled on me. "I'm not a fan of vermouth," he admits, his voice low.

I take a step closer to him. "No? Worried you might make a face if you try it?" I goad him.

"I won't make a face."

I take another step, licking my lips. "Just a taste?" I purr.

Nick sets his glass down on the counter next to him with a clank, but his hand lingers there, waiting for me to make a move.

I stop when my breasts touch his chest and my hips meet his. Feeling the bulge in his pants, I press my hips harder against him.

He lets out a quick, heavy breath, his hazel eyes eager as they scour my face. We don't say anything for what feels like minutes. We stare and gauge one another. I test him. And feel the tension in his body coil against me.

My hand brushes against his erection as I reach down between us, and I revel in the way his body trembles, trying to hold itself together. He purses his lips, and I wonder how long he can manage before he takes me right here on the kitchen table.

I grab him through the thin fabric of his pajama bottoms, letting his warmth seep into my palm. I squeeze my hand softly around him, reveling in my power over him in this moment. I'm winding up a beast; I know that and welcome it. Tonight, I don't want to know what's black and white or up and down.

Untying his waist string, I reach inside. The moment I feel him, his eyes shut and he lifts his face to the ceiling and groans, his hands gripping the edge of the counter. "You have no idea what you're doing to me right now," he grinds out.

"Actually, I think I do." I lift up onto tiptoes to whisper in her ear. "And I'm loving every minute of it." My tongue snakes out and licks his ear before I pull it between my teeth, biting him gently and squeezing him in my hand at the same time.

"Fuck this," he growls, and his hands wrap around my waist and lift me onto the table.

LATER, I wake up, naked. I peer around the dark room, recognizing Nick's dresser, realizing I'm in his bed. I let out a sigh of exhaustion and contentment and turn over to find he's not there.

Sitting up, I glance around for him, but he's not in the room. Soft light filters in from the hallway.

I glance at the clock. It's midnight.

Knowing his night hours are strange, working at the bar a few nights a week, I can only imagine his sleeping patterns are wonky, so I climb out of bed, wrapping the top blanket around me, and walk to the bedroom door. When I creak it open, I hear his voice, low in the living room.

" . . . I care more about her than I realized," he says.

I stop, dead in my tracks, not wanting to intrude but knowing I shouldn't linger in the hallway either.

"No. It's not like that. We're just friends." He pauses a moment and my heart hammers in my chest. *We're just friends?* Is he even talking about me? Or does he just not want anyone to know we're more than what we are? I feel sick thinking about it, but I can't stop my feet from moving toward him.

The floor creaks beneath my feet, and Nick looks up from his hunched position on the couch. He smiles immediately, which calms me. "Hey, man, I gotta go. I'll catch you tomorrow." He laughs at something the person says on the other end, and drops his phone on the coffee table.

"Hey, did I wake you?"

I shake my head. "I don't think so. I just, I woke up and you were gone."

"You looked so peaceful while you were sleeping, I didn't want to wake you, but I couldn't sleep."

He saunters over to me in his pajama bottoms and eyes me up and down. "As much as I like you in my sheets," he says, leaning in for a kiss. "I like you in my bed even more." He lifts me into his arms and carries me back into his room.

His smile is the stuff of romance novels and sweet, dirty dreams. I could get lost in him, in his eyes and the way he looks at me, like he can't believe I'm real.

After Nick sets me in bed, he leans in to kiss me. It's sweet and soft, and his mouth lingers against mine. "Are you going to get back in bed?" I ask more feebly than I like, but I want him in here with me. I want him to lie with me so I know he's real and that he's mine.

"Hell yeah, I am." He tucks the blankets around me and walks around the bed to crawl in beside me. In one swift motion, he pulls me against him, squeezing me tighter as he inhales and kisses my shoulder.

"You should go back to sleep," he says. "You have to get Jesse in a few hours."

"I don't want to sleep," I tell him, turning in his arms to face him. I peer into the dark shadows of his face, wishing we could lie like this forever.

Pressing a kiss to his lips, I commit the feeling of this moment to memory. Parents, school, the future—none of it matters right now because I have strong, amazing Nick, and for the first time in my life, I don't feel alone.

I brush his jaw with my thumb and lean back ever so slightly. "Thank you," I tell him.

"For what?" he whispers.

"For all of this."

Nick stares at me for a few breaths and runs his fingers through the ends of my hair. Then, he kisses me, a featherlight touch that holds an inexplicable promise.

# FORTY-SEVEN
# BETHANY

THE NEXT MORNING IS ROUGH, but not because I didn't get much sleep. I don't want to go to class or deal with real life. Not yet. But want and reality rarely go together, so I roll my ass out of bed and pull on my jeans and a fresh t-shirt.

As soon as I hear Nick shut off the shower, I grab my toiletry case so that I can squeeze into the bathroom to finish getting ready.

"You shower longer than I do," I shout, uncertain if he can hear me.

He creaks the bathroom door open. "What?"

"You shower like a girl," I repeat.

"I already told you, I work hard to look this good."

Smiling, I shove the pajamas I didn't even wear into my bag.

Nick's phone vibrates on his nightstand, making me jump. I wonder if I should get it or not, or maybe take it to him, as I walk over and pick it up. "Your phone's ringing," I tell him.

"It's fine. I'll call her back later."

I stare at the name blinking on the screen and the pretty redhead who's smiling back at me. He knew it was Savannah calling him, which is strange, but I try not to let it bother me. I know that they're friends and they talk sometimes, even if it is seven in the morning.

But even though I know that, it doesn't sit right with me. He saw her last night, that's why he was late getting home, and she's calling him again, already. I know Nick isn't Mike, but his friendship with Savannah hits a little too close to home for me to brush it off completely.

When the call goes to voicemail, I see there are four missed calls since last night, one of them was around the time I woke up to find him out in the living room. Was that who Nick was talking to?

I try to remember what he was saying, but it's a bit of a blur.

*"We're just friends."* But who was Nick talking about, me or Savannah?

His words stoke a smoldering memory from three years ago, and I can't help the churning unease in my stomach, it's too visceral and alive to ignore.

"You knew it would be Savannah," I say.

"Yeah, I figured." He says it so nonchalantly, like her popping up on New Year's, and last night, and this morning after we shared the night together, is something I should get used to.

My grip tightens around his phone. "Why is she calling you so much?" I ask, finally dropping his phone on the bed.

I hear the medicine cabinet open and shut before he answers. "I already told you, she's having a hard time with a few things."

His easiness in speaking about his ex-girlfriend makes me bristle. "Never mind the vagueness of that statement, don't you think it's weird that you guys were together, she broke it off, and yet she's still calling you all the time?" I can't help but wonder if whatever is between him and Savannah isn't over.

"No, it's complicated. It's just how we are."

*And we're complicated and look how we are,* I don't say.

"We didn't break up because we don't get along, it was because of distance. So, of course we're still friends."

I stand in his room, staring at the doorway, my mind and heart telling me two different things. He probably doesn't get it, he doesn't understand how hard this is for me. But, the red flags are too glaring to dismiss just because it's Nick.

He comes into his bedroom and clasps his hands on my shoulders with a grin. "Please don't be weird about this, okay? We really are just friends." He leans in for a quick peck on my cheek and tugs his shirt over his head.

I hand him his phone, wondering what his feelings for her really are, the ones deep down he doesn't admit to. The remnants of the relationship they had that *he* didn't want to end.

"Please stop looking at me like that, Bethany," he says, finally stopping long enough to take this seriously. "I would do the same thing for Sam or Mac, and you wouldn't get upset about that. I hope."

"No, I wouldn't. But you haven't slept with Sam or Mac. They didn't dump you like Savannah did."

He glares at me. "That's a little harsh, don't you think?" He slides his phone into his back pocket.

"I'm sorry, Nick, but it's true. Have you stopped to ask yourself why she keeps calling *you*? Because it seems like she's not over you yet."

He shrugs. "Maybe she's not, but why does it matter? Nothing will happen, and I can't just ignore her. You have to understand that."

"I understand that you don't want to hurt her feelings Nick, and maybe she does need you, *or* maybe that's why you guys need to stop talking—so she can move on. She's going to have to eventually. Now seems like a pretty good time to me. You have to understand *that*, too."

"Bethany," he says, more irritated now. He scrubs his fingers through his damp hair. "Look, it's not that simple."

"Why not?"

"It's just not. I need you to stop making a big deal about this, okay? I promise you, nothing will happen. We're just friends."

It's a familiar story I've heard before, and even though I believe Nick thinks that, I have to know one thing. I follow him into the living room where he plops down on the couch. "Does she know we're together?"

"What?" he pulls on his shoe. I don't repeat myself because I know he heard me. "No, she doesn't. I haven't had time to tell her."

Red fury consumes me. "Are you serious right now?" I bite out. My heart is racing and all I can see is Mike and Sam. All I can picture is another phone call between Savannah and Nick, turning into another and another until it turns into something more. "You've had *how* many conversations with her in the past twenty-four hours alone? In the past few days you couldn't find a single moment to bring it up? After everything that's happened, did you really think I would be okay with that—that there's another girl on the side?"

Resting his elbows on his knees, he glares at me. "Are *you* serious? She's not just some 'girl on the side.'"

"Don't I look serious?" I ask him, causing his brow to furrow deeper.

"I already told you, Bethany. I'm not Mike." He pulls on his other shoe then stands up and brushes past me. "Stop comparing us."

I'm not sure if it's the fact that he isn't even trying to see my side of it, or if I truly am worried he and Savannah might still have feelings for one another, but I head back into his room to grab my things. The more I think about the time they spend together, about how they are together—how I've seen them in public and how comfortable they still are together—the more convinced I am that their friendship might not be something I'm able to accept, not if he's going to act like I'm crazy for simply wanting her to know I exist. I shove my toiletries back into my bag.

"That's not the sort of thing that just comes up in a conversation with your ex," Nick says more forcefully from the kitchen.

"Well, maybe it should be." I pull my phone charger from the wall and grab my hairband. Maybe I'm overreacting and he hasn't had time to tell her. Or, maybe on some level he doesn't want to tell her because he'll drive Savannah away and she'll be gone forever and he can't handle that. Either way, I feel sick to my stomach, and I can't stay here and pretend that I'm okay. "I'm going to get ready at my parents'."

"Seriously?" He stops in the doorway, anger pinching his features. "You're that upset about it?"

I don't bother pointing out the obvious. "I have to take Jesse to school anyway."

"Bethany, nothing is going to happen with Savannah," he says and steps closer. "I promise. Why aren't you hearing me?"

"Why aren't you hearing *me*? It's not only about that," I say and turn around to face him with my bags in hand. "I don't want to be second anymore, Nick."

"There we go with the Mike thing again," he grinds out.

"I know you're not him. But you meeting up with Savannah and talking to her at all hours of the night—her knowing nothing about me—makes me feel like a dirty secret. Maybe if you had the gnawing, rotten feeling settled in the pit of your stomach, like I do, you'd understand why I can't simply deal with it."

Nick looks confused and maybe a little hurt, a lot like I feel.

"I gotta go," I tell him, and shut the door behind me. I need space before I say something I might regret.

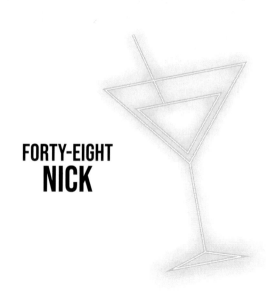

# FORTY-EIGHT
## NICK

I SIT in my Explorer in front of the Fairchild's house for a minute, collecting myself. I'm not exactly sure why I'm here, only that Bethany didn't answer my call this morning and I didn't see her around campus today. I figured something must've happened with Jesse—or, the more I think about it, I've screwed everything up more than I realized.

I should've known Savannah would be a trigger for Bethany; she's the reason New Year's ended with me standing outside in the cold, alone, after all. And, I've thought about telling Savannah about Bethany a couple times, but I haven't wanted to hurt her, especially when she's already feeling alone and struggling with being in Hannington Beach.

Climbing out of the car, I brace myself for whatever awaits me on the other side of the door, and I head up the walkway. I see an unfamiliar Volvo in the driveway, so I know someone's home.

Even if it's pathetic, I can't go through the day not knowing where me and Bethany stand or what exactly happened. So, before I can change my mind, I knock on the front door.

There's movement inside before it slowly creaks open and who I assume is her mom is standing there, eyes red, and blonde hair pulled back out of her face. She's attractive, if a little more haggard than I imagined.

"Can I help you?" she asks, looking me up and down. Not in a judgemental way, but curious, I think.

"Yeah, Bethany's not here by chance, is she?"

Her eyes narrow slightly and she shakes her head. "And you are?"

"Nick," I tell her. "I'm her—project partner, I guess." I'm not sure what we are anymore, and it kills me.

"You don't seem certain."

"Yeah." I let out a breath and run my fingers through my hair. "I'm not," I mumble and turn to head back to my car. "Sorry to bother you."

"Nick," she calls, opening the door fully. Mrs. Fairchild is still in what looks like her pajamas, which surprises me. "She's at the salon until closing."

I nod, grateful. For the first time, I wonder what happened this morning that would leave Mrs. Fairchild's eyes puffy and more rumpled looking than Bethany described. "Thank you."

She clicks the door shut, and I climb back into my car.

The instant my phone rings, my heart races and I pull it from my pocket. When I see that it's Mac, not Bethany, my heart sinks instead. "Hello?"

"Hey, can I move your maintenance appointment from next Monday to Wednesday afternoon? We have a big—"

"Yeah, sure. That's fine." I glance back at Bethany's house.

"Okay . . . Why do you sound weird? What's wrong?"

"Nothing," I tell her and turn the ignition. She and Sam have already said their fair share about my relationship with Bethany, I don't want to hear any more. Especially an "I told you so."

"Well, you're clearly full of shit. Come on, tell me—"

"You've already done enough, thanks though."

"Excuse me? What the hell is *your* problem?" She's quiet a

minute, and I'm not sure what to say, or if I want to say anything. "Is it Bethany?" Mac asks.

I lean my head back against the headrest. "Yeah." The hesitation in Mac's voice stirs up a bit more anger than I expect. "I hope you guys had fun with your jabs the other day at the beach. She would barely talk to me after we left."

"What?" she says breathily. She's surprised and somehow, I feel a little vindicated. "I'm so sorry. Is that what this is about?"

"No, but it doesn't help, Mac."

"Then . . . what is it? What's going on?"

I run my hands over my face and laugh at myself. "I think I just fucked it up."

# FORTY-NINE
# BETHANY

STEPPING out from one of the tanning rooms, I put the spray bottle behind the desk and check the schedule for the next clients. It's been a busy day, one wave of people after another, but I guess busy is good. For the business and for me. It saves me from dwelling on my otherwise looping thoughts about Nick, about Jesse's morning meltdown, and playbacks of my mom's message after I left this morning.

She sounded more distant than usual this morning, different than her rigid, frantic self while Jesse was upset. I'm not sure what's happened since then, but she wants me to come home after work to talk. Nick wants to talk too. I know I need to talk to them both—I *want* to talk to Nick, so badly it's all I can think about. I regret getting angry this morning, but I'm not sure I should. Part of me feels justified, knowing he'd be unhappy if the tables were turned and I were having late night phone calls with an ex-boyfriend.

Another part of me keeps saying that this is Nick we're talking about, and he would never purposely hurt me. Then, darker shadows of the past remind me that the hurt sustained between us over the years started out as unintentional, too. They were misunderstandings that spiraled. What's to stop any of that from happening again?

Feeling a bit toasty in the warm spring air, I pull my hair up into a ponytail in preparation for the next round of clients. Unbidden, my gaze shifts outside to Schmitty's deli. I want more than anything for things between Nick and I to work, but until he decides to tell Savannah about us, I'm not sure I can begin to accept their friendship.

"Thank you," one of our regulars says as she hurries out from one of the rooms. She tosses her towel on top of the overflowing pile. "I have to pick the kid up from school." She says it like she's going to be late, then she waves. "See you next week."

"See ya next time, Brit."

Laundry, a quick rub down of the rooms, cashing out, reminder calls to a select few clients for tomorrow . . . I have plenty to do before we close up shop in a few hours, and I really hope Trent is doing a decent job with the inventory in the back so that I don't have to manage that later too.

I wipe down the counter around the register and try not to think too much about Jesse's morning spiral. It happens sometimes if he didn't sleep well or maybe he had bad dreams. And then my mom didn't have any of his favorite shirts washed for him to wear. I just try not to assume any of it's because I'm not staying at home right now. Jesse knew I'd be picking him up—he knew he'd see me, and our morning routine would be mostly the same. I try to tell myself that, just because I don't live there anymore doesn't mean his breakdowns will be a regular occurrence. I hope.

I try to think about the barn project, instead. I'm happy with how it's turning out, and it's projects like these, albeit generally on a smaller scale, that remind me that as much as I don't want to be an interior designer, I do enjoy it sometimes too. I smile as I realize how close we are to the end of the year and after graduation, I'll never have to see Professor Murray again.

The doorbell dings, and when I look up, I'm astonished. Savannah's standing in the doorway. Her red hair hangs down in waves around her shoulders, and she stares at me, her eyes not leaving mine as she steps closer.

"Uh, hi," she says awkwardly.

I straighten and step closer to the counter, grabbing hold of it to steady myself. I doubt she's here to schedule her first tanning appointment. I have no idea what's transpired between her and Nick in the past five hours. All I can do is wonder if she's here to tell me she wants Nick back.

Whatever the reason, the fact that she's here at all makes my stomach roll. "Hi . . ." I finally manage. It's an uncertain sound. I'm not even sure it comes out as a word.

"So, this is weird, so I'll get right to it," she says, splaying her palms on the counter. "Nick told me that you guys are together." She pauses and her eyes don't leave mine, like she's still processing the news. "I was surprised, *really* surprised, actually, but Nick made it very clear that he wants things to work with you, so I needed to know, whatever that meant for our friendship."

My heart flutters a little at her words, and the tension of the day that's been coiled in my shoulders and neck slackens a little.

"He mentioned our friendship has caused some problems, so— I want you to know that, even though this is strange to say to you, I want Nick to be happy. Right now, I guess that means with you. I'd still like to be his friend, but I don't want you to feel like I'm a threat on top of it—I don't want to be the reason he's unhappy." Savannah's dark blue eyes are piercing and genuine, even if her tone is a little bitter.

Tentatively, I nod. Her admission is surprising, however she may truly feel about it, and it's a gesture I didn't expect.

Savannah purses her lips. Looks around the room then down at her hands before she looks at me again. "Okay then . . . I'm gonna go." Her head bobs awkwardly and then she turns to leave.

"Savannah?"

She glances over her shoulder.

"Thanks."

She lifts a delicate eyebrow and gives me a once-over. "Don't fuck it up," she says soberly. A small smile tugs at the corner of her mouth, then she walks out the door, slides her sunglasses on, and she disappears from sight.

I'm still staring out the window, mind reeling, when Anna Marie comes in from the back room with a box in her hands. "Who was that?"

"Savannah," I breathe.

I look at Anna and her mouth is gaping. "As in *the other woman?*"

I glower at her. "You don't have to say it like that, but yes."

"What the hell did she want?"

Smiling to myself, I turn to face her. "To call a truce."

Anna's surprise mimics what I'm feeling, even if I'm still processing it all. "So, are you going to call Nick, then?"

"Of course, but not now with you lurking." I slide the scissors to her across the counter. "When did you get here? I thought you were running errands for your mom?"

"I just got back—just in time, too. Remind me never to let Trent do inventory again," she says as a tangent, then shakes her head. "But that's not important right now. You need to call Nick. You're *killing* me right now."

"My life isn't some soap opera for your viewing pleasure, you know," I remind her, and tilt my head. "I text messaged him earlier; he knows I'll call him on my break."

"Well, whatever you do, you should make sure he's in your corner *before* you go into the snake pit after work."

"I will. Shouldn't you be more worried about what you're going to wear for your date tonight?" I ask her, and she blanches.

"How do you know about that?"

"The walls at your apartment are paper thin," I remind her.

Her eyes widen. "Good to know."

Laughing, I pick up the laundry basket. "I'm going to put a load in. Stay up front for a sec, would you?"

Anna nods and pulls her phone from her back pocket. No doubt texting Bobby a quick warning about tonight. "Isn't having a roommate so fun?" I ask over my shoulder, and she grumbles something inaudible.

I'm in the laundry room, sorting through the spray tan and hand towels, when I hear the front door ding. Knowing Anna Marie is out there, I leave it to her to deal with the next wave of clients.

I have no idea what exactly my mom wants to talk to me about. It could be anything from coordinating Jesse's schedule to asking me to move all of my things out of the house this week, if she's so inclined. And, as much as I don't want to have a face-to-face conversation with her tonight, I also wish it was over with already.

There's a creak in the floor as Anna comes into the room. "I'm almost finished," I tell her and glance over my shoulder. But it's Nick who's standing there. His hands are in his pockets and an uncertain expression creases his face.

"Hey," he says. His eyes are shadowed and his brow is deeply furrowed. I'm not sure I've ever seen him so drained of everything that makes him Nick, and my heart hurts that it's because of me.

"Hey." I set the towels aside.

"I know you said we'd talk later, but I couldn't wait." He's more solemn than I've ever seen him. "I hope I won't get you in trouble being here."

"Ha. Are you kidding, Anna's in the hallway listening, I'm almost certain." It's a joke, but Nick doesn't smile.

I swallow thickly. "I'm sorry I didn't call you sooner, it's just —it seemed like too important a conversation to have than a quick check-in between clients, you know?"

"Well . . . I'm impatient." He says it lightly, but it's not the same Nick-ness I'm used to.

"Nick, I—"

"I'm sorry," he says urgently and takes a step closer. He runs his fingers through his hair. "You were right about Savannah, I should've told her. Mac painted a very vivid picture for me, and I nearly lost my shit."

I frown. "What do you mean?"

"If you kept talking to a guy—if you were friends, *especially* with an ex"—he shakes his head—"I don't know if I could do it. I just—I wasn't thinking about it like that. All I could hear was you comparing me to *him,* and I hate that you'd think for a single minute that I'd ever hurt you the way he did."

I take Nick's hands in mine, squeezing them as I will him to hear me and understand. "I don't think that. I know you aren't like Mike, trust me. I tell myself that all the time. Sometimes it's just hard not to get lost in the what ifs, you know?"

He tugs me closer, his eyes searching mine, earnest. "I told Savannah," he says. "I wanted you to know. I should've done it from the beginning, but I didn't want to hurt her feelings, because I do still worry about her."

I take a deep breath and nod. "I know you told her."

His brow furrows again. "You do?"

"She was here."

"Savannah was? Why?" He looks almost frightened.

"Because she cares about you," I tell him reassuringly. "She wants you to be happy. *And* she wanted to tell me not to fuck things up."

Amusement pulls at his lips, but he doesn't smile.

Rising to my tiptoes, I wrap my arms around his neck for a hug, because it feels like it's overdue. He's solid and warm and all-consuming as he squeezes me against his body. His strength is soothing and I soak it up for later tonight when I'll need him, even if he can't be there with me.

Like he can feel my anxiety, he leans back and brushes a stray hair from my face. "What's wrong?" he asks softly and rests his forehead against mine.

"I have to stop by my parents after work," I explain. "My mom wants to talk."

He looks at me for a moment, like he's trying to decide what to say. "Do you want me to take you? I could wait outside."

Knowing I have to do this on my own, I shake my head.

"Beth—"

"Really it's fine."

"I don't want—"

Before he can argue, I press a kiss to his lips. I'm not sure if it's him or me that whimpers, but everything falls away as his palm finds the side of my face, his thumb stroking my cheek as he kisses me fervently. "You're trying to distract me," he breathes.

"Is it working?" I press my lips to his again, softly and letting them linger.

Nick smiles against my mouth. "Yes."

With a contented sigh, I rest the side of my face against his chest. "Let's not fight anymore, okay?"

"Sounds easy enough. But you know, *if* we were to fight again —which I'm sure will *never* happen," he says playfully. "I accept pickles as recompense."

I try and fail not to laugh. "Of course you do."

# FIFTY
# BETHANY

I SIT OUTSIDE MY PARENTS' house for a few minutes before I can bring myself to go inside. Seeing Nick has put my mind at ease in a strange way, and although I don't want to have this argument with my mom, whatever it may be, I don't think it will affect me as much as it might have any day before today. Whether it's my parents cutting me off or telling me to move my things, I feel like I'm ready for it. I'll figure it out without them.

Jesse's bedroom light is on, flickering behind his drawn drapes. He's already gone through his nightly routine of reorganizing his special toy piles and brushing his teeth. He's playing his video game before he goes to bed, until he's so tired he can barely keep his eyes open. At least he's still got those small routines to comfort him, and knowing that makes me feel better, too. Being away from him is difficult, but the longer I'm away, the more I know it's for the best.

I walk toward the house, expecting it to be locked like it usually is, but it's not. When I open the door, the house is quiet, and only a side table lamp glows in the living room. A light over the oven illuminates the kitchen and my mother's outline at the center island.

She sets a glass of wine down on the counter and looks at me. I rarely see her drink, so I'm surprised to see a bottle on the counter, half empty.

"You came," she says in a whisper, so quiet I almost don't hear her.

I set my purse down on the couch. "I told you I would."

Slowly, she lowers her feet onto the plush rug, covering the hardwood floor, and walks over to the light switch. She eases the soft glow of the dimmer up so I can see her more clearly.

Her yoga pants and loose sweater are a surprise. Her hair is in a messy ponytail, her eyes red and puffy. I can't remember the last time I saw her like this, a normal mother, mussed and real and beautiful in her own way. Gone is the perfectly groomed Laura Fairchild who has a different skirt and pantsuit for each day of the week.

"Please," she says, "sit down." She walks over to the sink and pours herself a glass of water from the filter. "Can I get you something?"

"Um, yeah, water would be great. Thanks."

I claim a barstool across the island from her, noticing my journal on the marble top. My stomach flip-flops.

When she turns around, she catches me eyeing it. "Please, take it," she says, nodding to the leather-bound book as she slides me a water glass, more than half full. "Part of me . . ." She sighs. "Part of me thought I shouldn't read it, even though you wanted me to. Another part of me couldn't resist." She stares at the book, like it holds some powerful memory. "You're right. I feel like I saw you for the first time." Her eyes shift to mine, shimmering in the low light. "Saw myself, actually."

My grip tightens on the glass of water. "Is that why you wanted me to come over?" I ask, trying to move this awkward and unwanted conversation along. "To talk about my journal?"

She glances at it again. "I'm not quite sure." Her voice is distant, and her uncertainty confuses me.

"Mom, is everything okay?"

Her face hardens with a frown. "No, Bethany, everything is not okay. This," she says, gesturing between us, "is far from okay."

"Well," I bite back, "it's been like this for years, so I'm not sure what you expect me to say."

"Nothing," she says more quietly this time. "You don't have to say anything. But I would like you to listen."

As always, my gaze shifts to the stairs, checking for prying eyes and ears. Jesse's door is shut, and the neon light of the television illuminates that part of the dark hallway.

"He misses you," she says suddenly. She laughs to herself and wipes beneath her eyes. "I know you've seen him every day, but it's different, you not being here." She sits back down at the island. "Things haven't always been this hard," she says. "Not between us. I can see how you might remember it that way, but for a time, things were different."

She fingers the stem of her wine glass, eyes fixed on the beaded charm marker as her thoughts take her somewhere far away. "I've been trying to think back and remember at which point I started to forget what it meant to be a mother. Things have gotten so complicated over the years . . . I wish it was easier to explain it all to you."

She pauses, thinking. I feel like I should say something to fill the void, but I'm not sure what.

"When you were a baby, you were my pride and joy. That's all I'd wanted, after I married your father. He was the prom king, I the queen. It made sense back then. He was prominent in the town and had high hopes and vast dreams. He inspired me." Her eyes shift from a memory in space to me. "I thought that everything would be better between us when I had you. That a child would add a layer of additional love and connection to our marriage."

"But it didn't," I hear myself say. Something stirs inside of me that I haven't felt in a long time—affection for her, I think, and curiosity.

"What they say is true—you can't fix a marriage by adding a room to the house or a child to the mix. And I made far more mistakes than that."

Running my finger over the condensation on the glass, I try to imagine my parents' lives before I was born—how lonely it might've been—and I wait for her to continue.

"There's something you should know, Bethany. I swore I would never tell you, but I would be a hypocrite if I didn't, and it's not fair to your father—for you to hate him and not know the whole story."

Her words surprise me, intrigue me, even, like the past twenty-three years are only a version of him and I might finally get a glimpse at who he might've been a long time ago.

"He's not a loving man, I know that, but he's not heartless, even if he seems like it at times. We'd tried to have another child many times after you were born and it didn't happen. It's part of the reason your father and I grew apart. So, I did something I'm not proud of, my deepest shame and darkest secret. He's a better man than you realize, if for no other reason than he didn't turn me and Jesse away after your brother was born."

"What a saint," I mutter. "He didn't turn his own child and wife away simply because he had a *broken* son."

She eyes me without response, as if she's waiting for me to understand. Her words are muddled in my head, and when they don't register, I frown. "What do you mean, he didn't turn you away?"

She peers into my eyes, only blinking as she inhales a deep breath. "Jesse is not your father's son."

"What?" I lean onto the counter, gaze unwavering.

"I had an affair."

"What?" I repeat. "And you've been judging *me*, acting like I'm such a disappointment?"

"I didn't want you to follow down the same path—I was

scared." Expression unchanged, tears well in her eyes as she sits there, prepared for a verbal lashing, but I can't speak.

I don't know what to say. I don't know if I'm hurt or surprised or simply confused. "Who is Jesse's father?" I whisper and glance up at his closed bedroom door.

She shakes her head. "One of your father's old clients," she whispers and tears stream silently down her cheeks. "I wasn't going to tell your father that I was pregnant. I was going to leave him, but I was frightened. I didn't have a job then. I was home with you at the time and when you father found out—well, the rest is history."

"You cheated on Dad," I say again.

"He tried to forgive me, and that's the man you know today. Angry. Betrayed. Maybe even heartbroken."

The sudden sympathy and respect that swells inside me for my dad is strange and overwhelming.

"He resents Jesse, but not only for the reasons you think he does. There's so much more behind it."

"But—why are you guys still together if you're both so unhappy?"

"I started working my ass off to have a stable career so that I could start a new life for us, but it's been so long, I've lost sight of why I was doing it to begin with."

The late nights in her office, the weekend meetings . . . This whole time there was a haunting shadow following her—a drive in her I didn't understand. I didn't realize how little I know my mother, until now.

A tear trickles down my cheek, for Jesse and my dad, and I wipe it away. Looking at her, I don't know what I feel, but I see her through a lens I never have before.

"I hate myself for what I've done," she admits. "I've hated myself for it since the day Jesse was born, and even more when I realized Charles would never forgive me. There has always been a life-sucking secret between us instead. I ruined us, and I've turned this family into something so far gone, I don't know if I can turn it around again . . . but I'd like to try." Even in her most revealing moments, she's so much in control it almost hurts me to watch.

"I'm going to talk to your father about a divorce when he gets back from his trip. I can go part-time at the firm. I'd like to spend more time with Jesse before I lose him, like I've lost you."

This time, I wipe tears away for me and the mom I never had. For the woman in front of me who's more broken than I ever could've imagined. The mother I'm seeing for the first time.

"I understand if you don't want to stay here any longer, but you will always have a home here, if you decide you want to come back." She eyes my journal again. "I know things are difficult right now for you, that you're worried about school and Jesse, and I don't want you to struggle needlessly about a place to live. I will help you with your graduate program—your father will help you, too, no matter what he says. He's too good not to, even if you've never seen that side of him before."

I nod, unable to formulate any words. In the past few minutes, I've learned that my parents are nothing like I'd always known—or thought I knew. That my brother truly is a black sheep in my father's eyes, but not for the reasons I've always assumed. I've learned the true depths of my parents' unhappiness, and I swallow a sob in my throat.

My mom takes a sip of her wine and folds her arms over her chest again. "I know I've been absent from your life for years now, Bethany, but as your mother, no matter how much you hate me—"

"I don't hate you," I hear myself say.

Her face softens a little. "I'd like to request one thing." She leans forward and rests her elbows on the countertop. "I'd like you to take that dyslexia screening—I want you to get help, for your-self. Not for me or your father."

I feel the creases in my brow deepen.

"Let Mrs. Turner help you. She's a good woman, and she's

better at the nurturing stuff than I am." It's a self-deprecating joke, but I can tell she's trying.

"I will," I promise.

She nods and takes another sip of her wine. A pause turns into a few breathes, and I wonder what she's thinking as the silence stretches between us. The clock ticks. The laundry machine beeps in the other room, and a dog barks outside the house as we're wrapped in shadows and darkness.

"Now what?" I finally ask, wiping the moisture from my cheeks.

"Well, I suppose I should let you get back to, whatever it is you do on a Tuesday night."

"Homework," I tell her, and I step down from my stool.

She stands up and tucks a strand of hair behind her ear. "Bethany," she says, almost urgently. "I know what I've told you doesn't fix anything. I know it might even make everything worse, but knowing what I do now . . . You deserve the truth."

It's the longest, most honest conversation I've ever had with my mom, and it means more to me that she could ever know. "Thank you."

She nods, and I wonder when the last time was my mom had any physical contact. I walk over and wrap my arms around her. She's rigid and unyielding at first, but only for a second before her arms wrap around me.

"I love you," she rasps.

"I love you too."

She cries into my hair and squeezes me tighter.

Her vulnerability speaks volumes, and for the first time in my life, I have hope that things between all of us might actually get better.

# FIFTY-ONE
# NICK

"GOOD MORNING, LADIES AND GENTLEMEN," Professor Murray drones on with his condescending niceties, but I tune him out. Bethany isn't in class today. She didn't even text me, and I'm worried about what happened last night with her mom and that her absence has something to do with it.

"—projects due in just under a week, but I'm certain you're all quite prepared for that," he says sarcastically. "Because we have a few more weeks until the end of the semester, I figured, why not cram in the Victorian Revival period and an exam before the semester is finished. Some of you will be graduating, after all. Consider this my parting gift to you." His eyes meet mine, only briefly, and all I can do is shake my head in disbelief. This guy needs to get laid.

My phone vibrates in my pocket, and I pull it out, anxious to see if it's Bethany. I smile.

> Bethany: Sorry I didn't make it to class. It's a long story. Meet me outside after.

I text her back, relieved.

Me: With bells on.

"Mr. Turner," Professor Murray says. "Is there something more interesting than my lecture?"

I smile at him, barely able to contain myself. "Sorry. I just got some great news about my project."

"Hmm. May I continue then?"

"By all means." He eyes me carefully, his brow lifted like he doesn't know if I'm just being facetious or if I'm that excited. My smile broadens, and he finally gives up and continues to address the class.

The next forty minutes feel like the longest and most drawn out of my life. Once class is finally over, I head to the bench where I've met Bethany once before. She's nestled into the corner when I spot her, her hair up in a ponytail and her book bag at her feet. She hears my approach and glances at me, a smile parting her lips, and my heart flutters.

"Hey," I say, my voice unexpectedly soft. I lean down at kiss her lips, then push her bag out of the way and sit at her feet.

"Hey you." She's freshly showered, her hair still damp and she smells of body wash or soap. I wrap my arm around her folded legs to pull her closer against me.

Her eyes are a bit red, but given the night she's likely had, I'm not entirely surprised. She lifts her phone and shakes her head. "Anna wanted me to play hooky today, but . . ." she shrugs.

"Why am I not surprised?" I smile, but it quickly wanes. "So, how did it go with your mom?"

Bethany takes in a deep, steady breath and her eyes shimmer a little. "It was . . . unexpected."

"Yeah? Are you okay?"

Her head bobs in contemplation. "Yeah, I am. At least, I understand now why my parents are the way they are with one another, and why there's always been a push and pull between my dad and Jesse."

I eye her, waiting patiently for her to continue.

Bethany picks a piece of lint off the knee of her jeans before her eyes meet mine again. "Jesse is not my dad's son," she says.

It takes a moment for the words to really sink in and for me to realize what that means. The age difference between Bethany and Jesse makes more sense now and the toxicity of their family becomes a bit more understandable. "I take it your dad knows, then," I think aloud.

Bethany's chin inclines a bit and she smiles, but it's not a real smile, it's a saving-face smile, like she's not sure what to believe or think. "He knows, and I'm pretty sure that's why both of my parents work so much. I think it's hard for them to be around each other. My dad being away from Jesse so much, though . . . it only puts more distance between them."

It makes sense, but I'm not sure what to say, so I sit silently and wait for her to continue.

"My mom says they're going to get a divorce, which I think is a good thing, for both of them—for Jesse," she says thoughtfully.

"And for you," I add.

She nods, but her thoughts are still somewhere else. "Jesse won't understand, though," she finally says, and her eyes meet mine again. "What if he thinks it's his fault they're separating? He doesn't know the truth. He doesn't understand any of this. I'm not sure if my mom is going to tell him or if he should even know, at least not yet."

"I guess that's something your mom is going to have to figure out for herself," I tell her. My reflections about my own family drama have been in the forefront of my mind. "If my mom is any gauge, there's only so much us kids can control."

Bethany takes my hand in hers. "Did you talk to you parents again?" she asks softly.

"My dad," I say with a nod. "It's official, they're getting a divorce too." I let out a breath and realize I'm actually relieved. "It feels right, strangely enough." A few months ago, I would've been devastated. "I can't believe how much has happened in the last few weeks."

Bethany squeezes my hand in hers. "At least there were some good things," she says.

I squeeze her hand back. "Yeah, I guess you could say that," I say playfully.

This time, she winks at me.

# FIFTY-TWO
# BETHANY

AFTER WEDNESDAY'S CLASSES, Nick and I head back to my house to begin packing my things. Part of me is weary to have him here, knowing my mom will be home after work. Then again, keeping Nick away from my family, as screwed up as we are, would only perpetuate their false ideas of him and make him seem like "just some guy," which is the last thing Nick is to me.

So, imagine my surprise when my mom came home early from work to help us pack and take a load of things to Anna's. She and Nick have been cordial, if a little awkward, but seeing them interacting makes me unexpectedly happy.

"You look more like your mom than your dad," Nick tells me, studying a family photo on my dresser.

"Yeah? I'm not sure if that's a good thing or a bad thing."

Nick glances between me and the photo. "It's a good thing," he clarifies. "Imagining you with a five o'clock shadow is more horrifying than sexy."

The front door opens and closes downstairs, and I assume my mom's brought Jesse home from school.

I pull the rest of my pajamas out of my dresser drawer as Nick picks up one of my bras from a clean pile of clothes and holds it up to his chest. His eyebrows waggle when he looks at me.

I try not to smile, so not to encourage him. Instead, I shake my head. "Are you planning on helping at all or just distracting me?"

With a laugh, Nick sets my bra back on my folded pile and heads for the door. "Helping, of course. I'll grab you a few more boxes." He disappears down the hallway.

"Hey, kid," I hear him say, and I imagine Jesse's probably happy to see him. They chat for a bit, but I lose myself to the memories of this room, realizing that I might never sleep in it again. How many endless nights have I laid awake in here? How many tears have I cried? I stare at my journal, poking out of my book bag and wonder where I'll be in five years and what that version of me will think when reading reflections of the past.

"Hi," Jesse says, and steps into my doorway with one of his favorite T. rex figurines.

"Hey." I finish folding a nightshirt. "How was school?"

"Fine," he says. "Ms. Harding gave me a gold star today for reading out loud."

"You read out loud? That's pretty impressive. No wonder she gave you a gold star. Did you get to read whatever you wanted?"

He nods slightly. I know he doesn't want me to leave, but it's not like I won't still be around all the time. "Let me guess, you read out of your science encyclopedia?"

He nods again and picks at the dinosaur's tail.

"Well, no wonder you did so well. You know it by heart."

When he doesn't engage, I finally turn to him. "Don't be sad, J. I'll still see you every day, like I always have. I'm still going to pick you up from school and help you build your jungle—"

"I'm working on a boat now."

Though to anyone else, it's an insignificant thing, to me, it's all the world. I've always wanted to build a boat, and finally, he's letting go of the jungle and giving it a try. "All right, then. I'll help you with your boat—but only if it has a mermaid," I add.

His face scrunches.

"Hey," I say and step over to him. I tug at his shirt. "This will be good for you and Mom. She wants to spend more time with you. Besides, this way I can be the bad influence and take you out for ice cream when you're with me."

Jesse's blue eyes finally find mine but only for an instant. "Promise?"

I smile. "A cross-my-heart sort of promise. Okay?"

He nods with a little enthusiasm this time and hands me his T. rex . "You can take him, if you want," he says. "His tail's broken, but—"

"I would *love* to, J." I kiss his cheek. "He's always been my favorite."

"I know." His eyes don't leave the toy in my hand. "I was going to give you the triceratops, but . . ." The fact that he would part with any of his toys at all nearly brings tears to my eyes.

"If you ever change your mind and want him back for a little while, you know where to find him. Okay?"

He nods slowly, thoughtfully. "Do you think Nick wants one?"

My eyes widen. "I think Nick would love one, if you want to part with another. You know how he feels about the classics. Dinosaurs are *very* classic."

That earns me a smile, and Jesse drops his hands to his sides. "If you each have one, you could keep them together."

"Yes, we could." I eye him quizzically. Jesse might never say it, but it's obvious he's grown attached to Nick already, which makes me so happy. "Why don't you go pick one out for him? You can give it to him when he comes back with more boxes."

Jesse turns without a word and shuffles into his bedroom. With a sigh and a happily aching heart, I turn back to my clothes scattered around and heave out a breath. I have a hundred things to do this week, including the GRE exam and finishing up Professor Murray's project. I have work and a calendar filled with things to do with Jesse, not to mention unpacking at Anna's. But, somehow it doesn't feel overwhelming like it usually does. Maybe it's the fact that I feel like, for the first time in my life, I'm not so alone. Maybe it's the fact that I have Nick, and life, despite its craziness, finally feels . . . right.

The floor creaks outside my bedroom, and I smile. "That was quick. Which one did you decide on?" I glance over my shoulder to find my dad, standing in the doorway this time. His hair is a little mussed, which I'm not sure I've ever seen, and his hands are in his pockets. There's a darkness under his eyes I've never noticed until now, either.

"You're home," I say. "I thought you didn't come back until tomorrow?" I can't remember the last time my dad was upstairs, let alone in my bedroom.

His mouth draws into a regretful smile I don't expect, and he nods. "Your mother and I spoke this morning about a few things, and I decided to come home early."

"Oh." It's surprising, but then again, so much about my dad is surprising the more I learn about him. I'm not sure if they talked about a divorce, my journal, Jesse, or all of the above.

"I figured I should be here if my daughter's moving out of my house."

I don't say anything because I can't think of anything worth saying. *Yes. It's true. It's better this way. I honestly didn't think you'd care.* Nothing feels adequate.

"Bethany," he says in a low rumble. It's beseeching in a way I've never heard from him. "I've had a lot of time to think, and I wanted you to know that I'm sorry."

Meeting his glassy gaze, I feel unwanted tears in the backs of my eyes. The fact that he's even up here talking to me is huge. Now, an apology?

"I shouldn't have pushed you so much. I should've realized something was wrong and gotten you help with your schoolwork. Dyslexia—"

"It's okay," I whisper. "You didn't know."

He shakes his head and peers down at his feet. "No. It's not." The weight of his regret constricts my chest and burns the back of my throat, forcing me to swallow.

Dropping my clothes on the bed, I turn to face him fully.

"I've made a lot of assumptions about a lot of things, when I shouldn't have. I should've been more curious and listened to you. I shouldn't have assumed you were like—"

"Mom?" I ask, understanding for the first time what a father's fear might be, knowing his wife betrayed him and fearing his daughter might be headed down the same path. Though the betrayal I felt with Mike is nothing compared to that of a husband and wife, I feel strangely closer to my dad, having had a glimpse of what he must've felt the day he found out and how it has haunted him every day since.

"Mom told me," I say without thought.

When his eyes meet mine again, he looks confused.

"About Jesse." I nod down the hall, and it takes him a minute to understand what I'm saying. Then, realization deepens the creases around his eyes.

When he can't seem to take the silence anymore, his eyes shift around the room, landing on my half-packed boxes. "I met Nick," he says. His gaze shifts to me. "He's got a good handshake."

"Does he?" I smile. Even if he doesn't say it, I know my dad will try to change, at least as much as he can.

He nods, like it's his way of approving of Nick, before the silence grows too heavy and he straightens. "I'll let you get back to packing."

He retreats from the doorway almost instantly, but I continue to stare at it. I hadn't expected him to come up here, let alone apologize, but apparently, I needed it. The heaviness that remained around my heart lifts a little bit more.

Peering around my bedroom, I think about how much time

we've all wasted, locked in a constant state of resentment. All it took was a couple difficult exchanges—a handful of words—and everything feels lighter. Better. Promising. When my eyes land on my journal again, I smile.

# FIFTY-THREE
# BETHANY'S JOURNAL

## APRIL 25TH

*Today is a good day. There's a hum in the house, instead of a heaviness. It's relief, I think. I can feel it all around me, and I'm grateful. While I don't know what's going to happen between my parents now that I know the truth, or with grad school, it feels like everything will be okay, like we might still have a chance to become an actual family. All the crap that's led to this moment suddenly seems worth it. - B*

## FIFTY-FOUR
# BETHANY

PEERING UP at the exposed beams, freshly stained cherrywood, I admire Nick's work. Having seen the before photos and watching him add in the final touches, I wonder if he doesn't still hold a small place in his heart for architecture and design, no matter how much his dad has tainted it for him.

The barn is beautiful, a perfect representation of all that's happened in the past month. Relationships, broken and ignored, that only needed a little elbow grease and attention. Now, Sam has this amazing place to call her own, and Nick and I have by far the best project in class. It only took tears and heartache to make it happen.

I unwrap the final indigo embroidered lampshade and screw it into place. It's all come together so nicely, I almost hate to call my work finished. Almost.

A shadow descends over me in the sunlight, and I peer down at the open slider.

"Oh my God, it's amazing!" Mac gasps in the doorway as she and Sam step inside, Sam's boots and Mac's wedges clomping in unison on the cement. "Sam told me it was almost finished, but I never imagined . . ." Mac glances from me to Sam. "This was *the barn*," she says, in complete amazement.

"Yeah, good job, Mac," Sam drawls and they walk further inside. Sam runs her fingers over the reclaimed wood surface of the counter. "I think my favorite part of all of this is the chalkboard wall. We've needed a central message board for so long."

"Now, if you could only reach it," Mac murmurs, and I stifle a laugh.

I haven't talked to Sam or Mac much since the beach, I've been too busy, and I think Sam, in particular, has been giving me my space.

Crumpling up my discarded packing materials, I head down the loft steps to my garbage pile on the floor. "You'll have a rolling ladder for the chalkboard soon," I say, glancing at Sam. "Nick put it together out back. He's going to finish installing it tomorrow, once he gets the rails in."

I survey the brushed metals and warm woods that fill the space —industrial and contemporary with a rustic flare, exactly the way I'd envisioned it when I first started the project. There's exposed shelving, soon to be filled with informational books and purchasable horse products, large, drop-down hanging fans to help with the summer heat, and the old barn doors that serve as a conference table.

Everything is functional. Everything is chic. Everything is perfect, and I can't remember a time in life that I've been so proud of myself. "Everything should be finished by tomorrow," I tell her. "A day ahead of schedule."

Sam laughs and plops down on one of the wood benches at the conference table. "You could've finished after graduation, for all I care."

"Well, I'm an overachiever," I admit. "And, mostly, I wanted to shove this project in my professor's face."

"That's what Nick said." She splays her hands out on the table-top. "So, this is where we'll be meeting with boarders now, huh?"

I shove a ball of plastic wrap and used zip ties into the trash-can. "If you want. Alison will be upstairs, I'm assuming, so you can do whatever you want down here."

"Oh my God!" Mac gasps from the photo wall. "I haven't seen this picture in years." She looks over at us, mouth parted and gaze set on Sam. "Have you seen these?"

My heart thumps a bit too wildly for my liking, and I hold my breath as Sam walks over to the photos. They both stare at the wall —at the old pictures of them as kids, Sam and Mac on horses, some with Sam's dad around the ranch.

Sam looks at me. "Where did you find these?" Her voice is barely a whisper, and I'm not sure if that's a good thing or a bad thing.

I swallow. "Um, in an old box of office stuff I was going through that Alison brought out last week. I had a few hundred dollars left in the budget, so I got them all matted and framed. I figured they were a part of this place and they should be displayed, not discarded in a box somewhere. I hope you don't mind."

Gaze fixed on the wall, Sam slowly shakes her head. "I love it," she breathes. Then she looks at me again, shoving her hands in her back pockets. "Thank you, Bethany."

I feel my cheeks burn a little. "You're welcome." Sam reaches out and touches the frame of the largest photo—the one of her dad —and my heart breaks for her a little bit.

With a subtle smile and what looks like gratitude in her eyes, Mac walks back to the conference table, leaving Sam to her thoughts. "You want to do my office next?" She looks at me, hopeful.

"Maybe after things calm down a little," I tell her. I still have graduation and grad school to worry about. "I can't really take on another project right now."

"Drats. Well"—she shrugs—"if you change your mind, let me know. I have to warn you though, Sam tells me I'm high mainte-nance, so you'll have *that* to deal with."

"Thanks for the warning," I say with a chuckle. I appreciate the pleasantries, but I'm still trying to figure out why they're both here, exactly.

"So," Sam starts, as she joins Mac at the table. "What are you doing tonight, Bethany?"

Her question surprises me. I brush my hands off on my jeans and glance between them. They look a tad uncertain and expectant. "Hopefully celebrating my GRE score. I get the results in about an hour." They look at each other, and I swallow. "Why do you ask?"

"Well, we wanted to invite you up to Mac's rooftop tonight," Sam says.

"Why, are you going to push me off," I say glibly, but they don't laugh at my joke.

Instead, they look at each other again, and Mac takes a few steps toward me. "Look, we're sorry about what happened at the beach. We were total assholes—Sam, specifically."

Sam rolls her eyes. "Thanks."

"Well, it's true."

"You guys, you don't have to apologize," I tell them, waving the impending awkwardness away. "It's fine." I don't want to go back and rehash the past, not when I feel like things are finally moving forward.

"No," Sam says, coming closer. "It's not fine. And, as a true apology, we wanted to invite you to our super-secret, girls only, rooftop drinking and stargazing night out. It's tradition when the weather starts getting warmer . . . We thought it would be nice to add another girl to our group, seeing how it's always been just the two of us."

Mac looks at Sam and puts her hands on her hips. "Two *is* pretty pathetic."

Sam nods and looks at me. "So, what do you think?"

In all my life, I never thought I would be invited into Sam and Mac's personal circle that's only ever consisted of them. It's touching and makes me happy, which is why I hate that I have to say no. "Can I take a rain check? I'm meeting Nick tonight when he gets off," I explain.

"Yeah, but that's at like, two," Mac says with a scoff. "We can get in plenty of girl time before then. Besides, I have a ton of questions I want to ask you."

"Well," I say, unable to resist a smile. A night of interrogation isn't on the top of my bucket list. "As awesome as *that* sounds, I'm working on a surprise for Nick, and I have a lot to do before he gets off." Then it hits me—between the two of them, they know everyone. "Actually . . ." I take a step toward them. "Maybe you guys can help me."

# FIFTY-FIVE
# NICK

I IGNORE my exhaustion as I hurry up the stairs to my apartment. I know Bethany's there, waiting for me. She's probably asleep, but other than working on the barn, I haven't seen her in a couple days, and I'm jonesing to feel her in my arms.

The living room light glows through the curtains, and selfishly I hope she's still awake, even though it's nearly 3AM. Better than that, when I open the door, I'm greeted with Bethany wearing a slinky baseball outfit that hugs her in all the right places and exposes her legs for days and a heart-stopping smile.

"Holy hell," I rasp and drop my jacket at the door. "What the hell did I do to deserve this?" I step inside, unable to contain my smile.

She walks over to me, cheeks flushed, like she's embarrassed, but it makes me want her all the more. "You did all this for me?"

"No," she says, "Chris Evans is on his way, I thought he might like it."

I frown. "What?"

"Captain America—never mind. It was a joke." She wraps her arms around me. "Chris already left." With a wink, she leans in for a kiss.

305

"Hey now." I growl against her mouth, making her laugh. "No teasing me." I pull her in for another kiss, inhaling her scent I've been deprived of.

"Wait," she says, pressing her hands to my chest. "Before you get too excited, I have something for you."

"I thought *you* were my surprise."

"Only part of it." She winks again and trots into the kitchen. She returns with a cocktail glass in each hand. "Please, Mr. Turner, have a seat."

She nods to the couch, and I sit down. I'm not sure what the hell is going on as I take my glass from her.

My eyes widen. "Is this the pickle martini?"

"Try it and see."

I bring it to my nose, knowing it doesn't smell right but then Bethany isn't a bartender, so I don't say anything. Tentatively, I take a sip. I cringe as the liquid goes down, and nearly spit out the contents.

"Say cheese," she says and snaps a picture of me with her phone. She's laughing uncontrollably, and I realize I've just been duped. "You sneaky sphynx. You gave me a Manhattan?" I shake my head, incredulous. She knows I don't like vermouth.

"I have proof your scrunchy-face was worse than mine. I think that means I just won the bet."

"The outfit is your apology, then?" I wipe the taste of it from my lips. "Trickery," I mumble.

Bethany leans in. "There's one more thing," she says and hands me the cocktail she had in her other hand. "*This* is the martini. I promise."

She climbs off the couch and hurries down the hall.

"This better be a legit drink or you're going to be sorry," I call. I take a sip and moan. "*Much* better."

"Here's your surprise," she says behind me, and I turn around to find her holding a metal placard the size of a baseball diamond that's etched with a black and red serif font – Shortstop.

"What the hell?" I breathe, and get up from the couch. I've been thinking a lot about the bar, but until tonight, I hadn't decided anything. I take the sign from her, the weight of it in my hands giving me chills. "You made a sign for me?"

She shrugs. "Mac, Sam, and I thought you might need a bit of motivation. So, they helped me pull some strings."

"They did, did they? And what, may I ask, makes you think I'm actually going to do this?"

"Because you want to and there's nothing stopping you now," she says so sure of herself.

My heart is hammering in my chest at the possibility, and I can't get a single word out before I pull her into my arms. I barely register the sound of the sign hitting the ground as I take her lips in mine and kiss her senseless.

That's when it hits me. "The outfit," I say. Bethany bats her eyelashes at me. "The drink . . ." It's my fantasy—well, a joke, anyway.

"I won't hold it against you that you didn't pick up on it sooner. You've had a long night."

I kiss her again, more gently this time and breathe her in. "Well, it looks like we have another project to work on after graduation." It's both a declaration and a warning—she better get out now, while she can.

"Good." Her stormy gray eyes search mine. I worry for a split second that I'll find a shred of doubt in them, but there is none. Her smile widens instead. "This is really going to work, isn't it?" she asks, like she's realizing for the first time what I've known all along.

"Of course it is. I told you so, didn't I?" I take a step back, ready to boast my victory, then remember the whole reason she was coming over tonight. "Wait, you haven't even mentioned your test . . . did you get your score?"

She shrugs and looks down at her feet. "I only got an eight hundred," she murmurs, but when she looks at me again, her smile is wide and she begins jumping up and down, like she suddenly can't contain herself, like she's been holding in her excitement for too long.

"And you were worried." I shake my head. "This is cause to celebrate." I lift her into my arms. "Bethany Fairchild," I tell her, licking my lips. She giggles and looks at me expectantly as I walk her down the hallway. "I'm going to immortalize your body right now. Do you have any objections?"

With a trill of laughter, she shakes her head, her ponytail tickling the backs of my arms. "No objections."

"Good," I say, triumphantly tossing her down onto my bed. "Because I am never letting you leave my room."

# EPILOGUE

## NICK

## 8 MONTHS LATER

"NICK," Bethany grunts from over by the unpacked inventory. "I need help with this one." She huffs, and the strain in her voice has me maneuvering around Anna Marie and Trent, my two staff for the night, and into the back room as quickly as I can.

"Babe," I chide, taking the case of beer from her. "I told you I got these ones. If you *really* want to help, make sure Anna doesn't drink all the bubbles before I get a chance to officially open the bar."

Bethany gives me "the look" but pecks me on the cheek. "Let's be honest, you're only stocking it for her anyway," she clarifies.

"Yeah, I know. How did I let her talk me into that, exactly?"

With an airy laugh, Bethany brushes her hair out of her face. "It seems I'm not the only one who can't tell her no."

I concede and shake my head. "Hey, I thought you were supposed to be at home studying? Your final is important. You don't have to help me get ready for tonight."

Bethany wraps her arms around my neck and tilts her head to the side, giving me another one of her looks. "Grad school is important, but this is *huge*, and I want to be here with you. Studying can wait for one night."

Slowly, I lean in and kiss her. Happy. Grateful. None of this would be happening if it wasn't for her. "I love you," I say, breathing her in. Everything about her is comforting and makes me feel whole.

"I love you, too, but you can show me later." She winks and turns to walk away. "We have an opening to prepare for—oh," she says, stopping short. "My dad said he'd be late—some meeting or something. But they're definitely coming."

"Good. I couldn't have done this without him."

Bethany's mouth quirks up and she studies me a moment.

"What's that look for?"

"I think it's good you two are partners," she finally says. "It's forced him to get to know you better."

"True, and I got my dream bar in the process. But, if everything works out accordingly, we won't have to be business partners for much longer."

Bethany shrugs. "He knows you're good for the money. My dad might have a big learning curve when it comes to fatherhood, but when it comes to this stuff he knows his shit. He wouldn't invest in a risk."

I follow behind Bethany and set the case of beer down on the counter beside Trent. "These can go in the fridge when you get a sec."

Trent nods.

"Like I told Bethany," Anna Marie says. "We got this." She finishes lighting the votive holders. "Go say hi to your early arrivals. I'll keep an eye on everything back here, don't you worry about a thing." She winks, her smile mischievous as always.

"I'm going to regret hiring you, aren't I?"

She tosses her brown hair back and lifts her shoulder. "I don't know, it's only one night a week. How much trouble can I get into?"

"Ha! Do I even need to answer that?" Taking a deep breath, I peer around the bar, making sure everything is in place. It's exactly how I'd always pictured it—Mac's photos of the crew over the years, of baseball and hockey games, camping and beach trips lining the brick walls, black and white photos of old Downtown Saratoga for that nostalgic flare I wish we could stay in forever.

"Yo, Nick!" Mac calls as she and the gang walk through the front door. She's dressed like it's a fashion show, not a bar opening, and I welcome her with a smile. They've seen the bar a hundred times already, the guys helping me gut the place and the ladies taking the lead on the finishing touches, but they look around in awe all the same.

Sam moves in for a hug first, and I have to bend down to fully appreciate it. "I'm so happy for you," she says, squeezing me. "Congratulations."

"Thanks, Sam. It only took eight months." I nod behind me. "Bethany's back there."

Sam kisses my cheek and heads over to the bar.

"Eight months is nothing for a lifetime of living your dream," Mac admonishes, and I pull her in for the next hug. "I have to say, my photos look great in this lighting."

Chuckling, I give her a final squeeze and let her go. "I'm glad you think so, Mac. Your happiness is all that matters to me."

I shake Colton's hand and glance around for the squirt. "You didn't bring mini you tonight, Mac? I thought she'd want to see her handy work." I point to the picture Casey colored for me, hanging front and center on the wall.

Colton laughs. "As much as I like you Nick, I would never let my six-year-old daughter come into your bar."

"All right," I say. "All right. We'll revisit this conversation when she's seven."

The front door opens again. Aunt Alison and Cal walk in, she looks like an angel next to a tatted-up biker.

She untwines her arm from his and walks over to give me a

hug. "I'm so proud of you, honey," she says. "I hope we're not late. This place looks amazing."

"No, you're right on time. And thanks. I couldn't have done it without the crew." I glance over at Bethany, admiring how hard she's working behind the counter, especially when I told her she didn't have to.

"Babe."

She looks at me, blinking.

"Come here and say hi." She's in hiding. Not because she doesn't know everyone and not because she doesn't get along with them, but because she wants to give me space to be with my friends and family. "You're a part of this too," I remind her.

With a sheepish smile and a nudge from Sam, Bethany sets the limes she's holding onto the counter, wipes off her hands, and finally steps out from behind the bar to join me.

The door flings open and Bobby comes in, arms out. "Let the festivities begin!" he shouts. Cal glares at him as he walks over and claps me on the shoulder. Bobby grins and beelines for Anna Marie without saying another word.

Shaking his head, Cal looks at me. "Nicholas . . ." He extends his hand, his eyes shift around the room. He's a big guy, imposing even, if I didn't know he was such a softy on the inside. "I'm proud of you, kid."

"Thanks, Cal."

Bethany stops beside me and twines her fingers in mine. "I'm not sure if you've met Bethany yet, but—"

"Mac's filled me in, I think," he says and dips his head in hello. "Nice to meet you, Bethany. You've got yourself a good man right here," he says. "Even if he does have questionable habits." He glares at me, and I have to laugh.

"Dad," Mac says, smacking his shoulder. "Nick's a grown-ass man, he can do whatever he wants. Plus, he quit smoking months ago. Leave him alone."

"Hmm." He mutters something and Aunt Alison smiles. "Come on, Cal, I'll get you a drink."

"Try the Russell's Reserve," I tell him, knowing he's a bourbon man. "It's my favorite."

"Oh, God," Mac grumbles. "Here we go."

I flash Mac a shit-eating grin. "I'm gonna get your dad faded tonight," I mouth.

She smacks my shoulder this time. "You better not."

Laughing, I glance around the room, taking it all in as my friends chat amongst themselves and order drinks at the bar. Trent and Anna look like they know what they're doing, which makes me breathe a little easier, and I let out a content sigh. The doors haven't even opened yet to what I hope will be the masses, and I take the silent moment to bask in the glory of it all.

I'm shaking, I realize. Standing here, in my own bar is the most surreal experience I've ever had. It's exhilarating and exhausting, and part of me can't believe Shortstop is an actual place.

"Oh, look at all the people!" my mom exclaims as she comes out of the bathroom. Her makeup is done and her clothes are changed after a day of helping us set up and prepare. "I was only gone for a blink and now look. How exciting!"

"Ma, you were hogging the bathroom for like, an hour. You could've gotten ready in the office. *Or* gone home to change."

She waves me away. "Hush. I'm finished now." She leans in to kiss Bethany's cheek. "I'm so proud of you two. Nick, your father's on his way. Oh—and before I forget, family dinner's at your father's house next week. I'm having my carpets redone."

"Okay. Fine. Remind me later, would you?" She nods and Aunt Alison calls her over to the bar.

Bethany rests her hand on my shoulder. "Are you happy?" she asks quietly.

I admire the smiling faces that fill the room and the laughter above the low music of the jukebox. "Yes. I am."

She looks up at me, her gray eyes smiling. "Good."

I kiss her forehead, appreciating a moment together before things get even more chaotic.

"So," Reilly says with a grin. He walks up beside Bethany and I, a beer in his hand. "How does it feel, big shot?"

All I can do is shake my head in awe. "Eight months ago, it was all a dream, not even a goal. Now I have a bar." I think about how much my life has changed this past year—how much all of our lives have changed. Sam and Reilly are finally together. Mac has Colton and Casey. And me, I have the only woman I've ever really wanted. "We've all had a crazy couple of years, haven't we?" I squeeze Bethany's hand in mine.

"Yeah," Reilly says. "You could say that. It's like we're adults or something."

"I know, dude. I have *a bar*," I repeat.

Reilly chuckles and tips his beer. "Life is good."

I pull Bethany closer. "Yes, it is."

## THE END

Be sure to snag the Saratoga Falls Memory Book exclusively from my shop. You'll get a look at what brought the crew together, and a few other familiar memories explored along the way. :)

# AUTHOR'S NOTE

Well, you made it through the Saratoga Falls series. While I'm not writing off the possibility of another book in the future, I hope Nick and Bethany's story was a satisfying conclusion to Nick, Mac, and Sam's shenanigans. It feels right to take a break here—with the crew's stories nicely wrapped up, leaving other Saratoga Falls characters' lives ripe for more curveballs and adventures (cough—Anna Marie and Bobby).

All in all, this book was a surprising story for me to write in many ways. First, I thought it would be difficult to do Nick's character justice, but it ended up feeling natural and being really fun in the end. Since the beginning, Bethany's character has been one I've wanted to shed light on and develop deeper, making her more of a gray, misunderstood character than the typical mean girl trope. I even put a little bit more of myself into her than I'd planned, specifically, my struggle with dyslexia. Each crossed out word in her journal entries were words I mangled while writing them, so I left them that way. And, as you can probably tell, I like to tackle some of the darker, less spoken about parts of real life, which I was able to do in this story as well. Autism, in particular, was something I wanted to learn more about. In fact, I want to thank Tracey

Ward for taking the time to ensure Jesse's character was true to that of a child his age on the spectrum, having raised her son who is also Autistic.

I also want to thank the real-life Nick, Anna Marie, and my crew for being so excited about these books and giving me so much material to build such fun-loving characters from. Nick, maybe someday we'll finally actually have a Lick's, and Anna, you can be our bubbles girl. While I doubt Nick will ever read the books he stars in, I know the girls will share it with him. So, Nick, know this: you've inspired a character that readers love, and one that will forever be with me.

Most of all, I want to thank you, reader, for buying my books, for caring enough to read them. Take it from someone who got red marks on all her English papers: you've made my dreams come true. I hope you enjoy my other series as much as I hope you enjoyed this one.

As always, happy reading adventures!

xox - Scarlet

(AKA Lindsey)

# CAN'T GET ENOUGH OF THE SARATOGA FALLS CREW?

You can purchase the **Saratoga Falls Memory Book** exclusively in my bookshop. The Memory Book is a collection of stories from Sam, Mac, Nick, and Reilly's childhood and young adult years, leading up to their swoon-worthy love stories.

You can sign up for my monthly newsletter here:

# OTHER BOOKS BY SCARLET
## (AKA LINDSEY POGUE)

SARATOGA FALLS LOVE STORIES

(Recommended reading order)

*Whatever It Takes*

*Nothing But Trouble*

*Told You So*

*Memory Book Story Collection*

**SURVIVAL FANTASY & ADVENTURE WITH ROMANCE**

**FORGOTTEN LANDS WORLD**

(Can be read as stand-alones)

FORGOTTEN LANDS

*Dust and Shadow*

*Borne of Sand and Scorn Prequel Novella*

*Earth and Ember*

*Tide and Tempest*

RUINED LANDS

*City of Ruin*

*Sea of Storms*

*Land of Fury*

**THE ENDING WORLD**

SAVAGE NORTH CHRONICLES

(Should be read in this order)

*The Darkest Winter*

*The Longest Night*

*Midnight Sun*

*Fading Shadows*

*Untamed*

*Unbroken*

*Day Zero: Beginnings*

THE ENDING SERIES

*After The Ending*

*Into The Fire*

*Out Of The Ashes*

*Before The Dawn*

*The Ending Beginnings*

*World Before*

THE ENDING LEGACY

*World After*

*The Raven Queen*

# ABOUT SCARLET ST. JAMES

**Scarlet St. James** is an avid romance reader with a master's in history and culture. She wrote her first book in the Saratoga Falls Love Stories when she was in high school then set it aside, thinking it would never see the light of day. She was wrong. Once Scarlet was published as a post-apocalyptic romance author under a different name, she revisited the Saratoga Falls crew and finished their series. Now, she's back to her romance roots! Her stories cross genres and push boundaries, weaving together facts, fantasy, and love stories of epic proportions. When she's not writing romance, Scarlet is plotting survival and fantasy adventures as her alter ego Lindsey Pogue. She lives in Northern California with her husband and their rescue cats, Beast and little Blue.

Made in United States
North Haven, CT
06 September 2023

41227703R00195